Take this ring and be my wife. Make me the happiest man on earth.

Patrice had accepted Jonah's proposal grudgingly, because she couldn't have Reeve. How ashamed she was of her shallow motives for promising herself to such a fine man. But just as she had failed him when he was alive, she vowed to honor him in his death.

Jonah had died a hero. She would act as his widow as surely as if they'd been wed. And so, Reeve Garrett could be nothing more than the object of her scorn and hatred. There would be no weakness where he was concerned. She owed her determined stand to the memory of all those who'd died defending their homeland.

Reeve Garrett had had his chance to hold her heart.

Now, he would know only her contempt.

Other Avon Books in
The Men of Pride County Series by
Rosalyn West

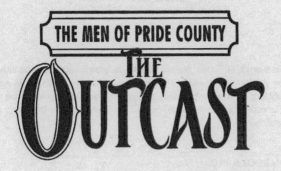

THE MEN OF PRIDE COUNTY
THE OUTCAST

ROSALYN WEST

AVON BOOKS ◆ NEW YORK

AVON BOOKS, INC.
1350 Avenue of the Americas
New York, New York 10019

Copyright © 1998 by Nancy Gideon
Inside cover author photo by McClain Studios
Published by arrangement with the author
Visit our website at http://www.AvonBooks.com
Library of Congress Catalog Card Number: 97-94307
ISBN: 0-380-79579-5

First Avon Books Printing: February 1998

AVON TRADEMARK REG. U.S. PAT. OFF. AND IN OTHER COUNTRIES, MARCA REGISTRADA, HECHO EN U.S.A.

Printed in the U.S.A.

WCD 10 9 8 7 6 5 4 3

For Diane and Tom Potwin,
and my friends at the *Literary Times*.

Thanks for pushing me out onto the
information highway.

The Outcast

Prologue

To men at war, the approach of dawn was a time filled with apprehension and anticipation. When heavy mists thinned over the country's middle states, one could be faced with breathtaking landscapes untouched by strife. Or one could discover an opposing army with bayonets affixed and cannons ready. Much needed rest, a long hard march or a bloody confrontation, there were no guarantees.

But for Reeve Garrett, the new day brought one certainty, death sure and swift, unless he could do something about it.

"Sergeant Garrett, I understand your position, but you must understand mine, as well. The man admitted to treasonous activity and was duly charged for his crime. The time for leniency is long past. If we don't make strong examples, we invite

1

this sort of thing over and over again, and I, for one, don't want this war to go on forever."

"I do understand, Cap'n, but putting that man before a firing squad will not serve justice. He's no traitor. He doesn't even believe in this war. If he confessed, it was to protect someone else. Hasn't enough innocent blood been shed by both sides, sir?" Reeve paused, drawing a slow measured breath before stating his final argument. "Cap'n, the man is my brother."

For an instant, sympathy softened his superior's gaze, but only for an instant. Then, once again, he became a soldier and not a family man who understood the pain of losing a loved one to the insanity surrounding them.

"I'm sorry, Sergeant, but I can't let that influence my decision. If I made an exception in your case—"

Reeve swallowed hard and squared up his rigid military stance. His voice was taut and emotionless. "I wouldn't expect you to, sir."

The war-weary officer leaned back against the center pole of his temporary command post. "You've about a half hour, Sergeant, before the order is carried out. If you can get him to name names, I'll reconsider. I'm not interested in having another Southern martyr on my hands."

Reeve didn't react outwardly, but relief weakened his reply. "Thank you, sir. I won't be forgetting this."

"You're a good soldier, Garrett. I need good men who aren't pulled in two directions, if such a thing is possible when we're called upon to take arms against our friends and families." He sighed. "See what you can do, Reeve."

"Yes, sir."

* * *

When the tent flap lifted, the prisoner inside turned with a look of contented resignation. That expression altered in surprise.

"Reeve, I didn't expect to see you." Then a more somber, "Have you come to get me."

For a long moment, Reeve couldn't force sound through the constriction in his throat. Finally, he managed a hoarse, "No."

Jonah Glendower nodded, neither relieved nor curious about his fate. "I'm glad for the company. I was hoping you'd come to say good-bye."

A sudden, swift anger cut through Reeve's thickening remorse. Anger at the situation, at the thought of losing his brother, at the other's willingness to meet his end. He let the flap drop behind him, shutting out the sight of the pair of guards just outside, and casting Jonah into shadow.

"I've come to shake some sense into that fool head of yours. There's no way I'm gonna let you go out to face those guns."

Jonah blinked. "You've come to help me escape?" His incredulous question shocked the both of them.

Reeve cast a quick glance back at the tent flap, gauging if the words might have been heard. "No."

Jonah smiled slightly and nodded as if he approved. That stoked the flames of Reeve's rarely vented temper.

"Not that I haven't thought about it," he growled in his own defense. "We wouldn't get more than ten feet, is all."

Again that accepting nod. "And someone has to go back home to help Daddy. You're better suited to it, Reeve. Always have been."

A strangled sound of exasperation wrenched

from the brother in Federal blue. "I don't want to take your place at the Glade. I never wanted that."

"I know." But somehow, that kindly absolution just made things worse.

"Dammit, Jonah, I'm not going to let you do this!"

"Yes, you are."

Reeve stared at him. What did that mean? That Jonah didn't think Reeve valued his life over the call of duty? He began to pace, emotions boiling deep down in his belly, tightening with every tick of his timepiece hurrying them toward dawn. "You're gonna talk to me, Jonah, and you're gonna tell me why you confessed to doing something I know you'd never do."

"How can you be so sure," came the cool challenge, so unlike his practical brother, it scared Reeve down to his boot soles.

"Because I know you," he argued, mainly to push back his own fear, his fear that Jonah had indeed done something to deserve his fate. "This isn't your war. You're not a part of that secession madness. Hell, you were the one who convinced me that keeping to the Union was the only way we could survive. It was your conviction that called me to put on this uniform when everyone else was reaching for Confederate gray. You were the only one thinking clear. I don't believe you'd go against those beliefs any more than I could."

Jonah simply stared up at him with a trace of a smile, goading Reeve to the point of violence.

"Don't just sit there smirking. You are gonna tell me who in Pride County has been spying for the Rebel cause."

"Why? So you can put them in here? Who'd you

rather have here waitin' on that firing squad, Reeve?"

"Damn near anyone but you," he blurted out harshly, voicing sentiments he'd always kept concealed.

"You don't mean that."

"Yes, I do."

But then something in Jonah's intense demeanor reached through the anger, through the despair to give him pause. Who could be behind the treachery? Who would matter so greatly that Jonah would face his death without blinking, sure of him condoning his reasoning?

Reeve sucked an abrupt breath. It hissed noisily between clenched teeth.

He knew. Without asking. Without hearing. And Jonah smiled, seeing his dawning awareness of the problem.

"It's better this way, don't you see?" Jonah continued calmly.

"No." Reeve shook his head, his vision skewed by the sudden welling in his eyes. A pull of loyalties that had nothing to do with the uniform he wore, rent his heart. He started to turn away when Jonah rose up to catch on to his shoulders, holding him still despite his struggle for release. "No," he repeated with a wrenching sorrow. Jonah embraced him easily, as if he'd always been the strong one instead of just the opposite.

"You know I'm right." Jonah's arms tightened to contain his brother's negating moves. "You do, Reeve. That's why you're not going to stop me. Because we both know it's better if I take the truth to the grave with me. That way it ends here, and no one else need suffer for it. No one we care about."

Reeve's hands fisted in the back of Jonah's shirt. "Damn Deacon—"

"Shhhh. Hush now. No good will come of it." He pushed Reeve away, but the other refused to look up at him. Reeve's shoulders slumped. His breath came in raw hitches, conveying the tortured state of his soul.

"Don't do this, Jonah. What'll I tell Daddy?" In his despair, Reeve forgot formality and spoke familiarly of their father for the first time.

Jonah's hand cupped the side of his head. "You tell him I've been trying all my life to be the kind of man he wanted me to be—the kind you are."

"You don't have to die to prove it!"

"You say that because you've never felt the need to prove anything to anyone."

Reeve's jaw worked fiercely, denial knotting up around truths he'd never shared. Until now. "You're the best man I know, the best friend I've ever had." Still, he wouldn't meet Jonah's eyes.

"Then walk out there with me, Reeve. My leg's stiffened up some, and I don't want them to think I'm lagging behind 'cause I'm scared."

The sheen of anguish turned Reeve's gaze to liquid gold. It spoke eloquently, passionately of things he couldn't voice as remorse twisted about his vocal cords.

"You know I'm right. You'd do the same."

The slightest of nods was Jonah's answer. It was enough to vindicate him.

"Tell Patrice I'd have been so proud to take her as my wife."

"I will." The faintest of whispers.

"And you tell her not to mourn me. Tell her it was my choice."

Reeve nodded, nearly suffocating on the wad of grief he couldn't swallow down. He was remembering a summer's day, the three of them lying back in a sweet-smelling meadow, chewing clover while Jonah and Patrice spoke of secrets and dreams, and then the two of them provoking, pleading, and finally tickling him into almost embarrassing himself when he wouldn't share any of his own. How he'd loved them both that day.

How he loved them still.

"Sergeant," came a respectful call from the other side of the flap. "It's time, sir."

No more late-night philosophizing. No more struggling through pages of the classics, faltering over words Jonah would patiently sound out for him. No more bond of camaraderie that was never so strong as in this final moment leading up to no more Jonah. Ever.

It was a finality Reeve couldn't face.

Crazy ideas reeled through his mind, panicked, desperate thoughts that were as far-fetched as they were suicidal. Overpowering the guards, risking the guns, stealing a horse, abandoning his duty . . .

"Reeve."

The quiet way Jonah said his name anchored him back to reality.

"Don't let me down. I plan on showing those Yanks the stuff we boys from Pride County are made of."

And emotions wailed mightily beneath Union blue cloth, never to be expressed aloud.

They stepped out into the dew-drenched morning. Daylight dazzled in prismed flashes, promising a glorious sunrise. The last one Jonah Glendower would ever see. As if oblivious to that fact, he strode across the wet ground to where his executioners already formed a rigid line. He held to Reeve's shoulder to offset his terrible limp. Despite his bold words, his hand shook when he lifted it away.

Reeve stood beside him for a long moment, his features immobile, cut from granite.

"Step back, Reeve," Jonah prompted at last. "I don't know if these boys can shoot, and I'd just as soon you not catch a stray. I don't need you to hold me up anymore."

"I never had to," he answered softly. Then he turned and marched briskly to the end of the firing line.

Jonah refused a blindfold after words of eternal comfort were spoken by the brigade's chaplain. Instead, he stared straight ahead, into the blaze of the sun, while the orders were called out in crisp, clear sequence.

"Ready arms . . . take aim . . . fire."

Reeve's body jerked with a violent recoil as a volley of rifle reports exploded through the clean morning air. His eyes squeezed shut of their own accord, sparing him from the instant of impact. When he looked at last, it was to assure himself that the end had been quick and merciful.

Nothing like his own would be.

Chapter 1

He'd seen thousands of graves over the past four years, some dug by his own hands, some just trenches or ravines where bodies lay frozen in death when there was no time to do right by them. But of all those final resting places, none touched more deeply to the heart of Reeve Garrett than the simple whitewashed cross with two words scratched into it: Abigail Garrett. No date, no cherished words of remembrance.

And no inclusion in the fancy Glendower plot up behind the main house.

His mother wouldn't have wanted that. For twenty-four years, she'd done her best not to create a breath of scandal for the Glendower family. With one exception. Him. Even then, she'd given him her name, not his father's, and continued to live in the discreet shadows, raising her son, asking for nothing but a decent wage in exchange for her skill with

9

a needle and a place for her child to grow up. It wasn't her way to demand her due. She'd loved Byron Glendower as much as her son came to hate him. A quiet, gentle, forgiving soul, accepting of her place in life, she'd tried her best to instill those virtues within her headstrong son. To no avail.

Reeve knelt and placed a hand upon the neatly tended earth. Someone had trimmed back encroaching grasses and had recently placed a bouquet of flowers beneath the cross. Someone had taken the time to care for her. Where had that conscientious soul been when his mother was alive?

He drew a quick breath, unable to fight down the sentiments his Abigail disapproved of: resentment, bitterness, anger. She'd always bid him to be grateful for what he had. Perhaps for her, it had been enough. But never for him. His mother hadn't understood what it meant for a man to control his destiny, to take pride in his possessions, to provide for his loved ones. Those things were denied him by the same man who gave them a place to live but not own, who allowed them things to care for but not to claim. The man who time and again extended a name but no dignity.

Home for Reeve wasn't the big plantation house set in the center of lush bluegrass acres. Unlike his half brother, Jonah, he'd passed his years in a modest clapboard cabin, sweltering under the eaves in the summer, huddled close to the main room's hearth in the winter. There was no ballroom, no parlor, no ladies' receiving room. Theirs held a pantry, a great room and his mother's bedroom down, and his own loft area up, framed by big windows to let in the breeze, and a narrow front porch to while away leisure hours they never seemed to have. A house, not a home, because it didn't belong to them. A token to remind them of who they belonged to.

The place was in sad repair, boards in need of paint, several windowpanes gone, porch rails missing. But those weren't the details that bothered Reeve. It was the sense of emptiness, of rooms devoid of life or love. For four years he'd dreamed of the scents of beeswax and brown gravy, for the sound of soft singing and the hum of thread pulled in endless repetition as his mother plied her trade as seamstress for the Glendower family, for the sight of his mother's head bent over sumptuous fabrics he could never afford to buy her, affixing lace and baubles for cotillions they could never attend. Instead he was greeted by silence and sorrow. A grim homecoming after a grim four years.

The sun-warmed earth clumped within his palm as his hand fisted. He'd never had the chance to do the things he'd promised that would better her life. He'd never taken her to Louisville to see a play with real actors and stage sets. He'd never seen her wear a gown made by someone else's hands. Though she smiled, he'd never heard her laugh. Contentment wasn't quite the same as happiness. But she never complained. And she never knew what she was missing.

"Oh, Mama, why couldn't you have waited. I wanted to see you again so bad. There were so many things I never told you."

Tears didn't come, though his anguish crested. He guessed he was all cried out by the end of the second year of war. After that, he'd stopped feeling things. After Jonah. He thought coming back to the Glade would wake those dormant emotions, the tender ones that had no place on the battlefield. But he was as empty inside as the cabin behind him, no life or love left in either of them.

He was wrong about that. He realized it the second he glanced up from his mother's grave.

Patrice stood, still and startled. With the aura of the sun framing her in hazy gossamer, for a moment, he doubted his vision. Then slowly, one by one, the blossoms she held clutched to her bosom began to fall.

And a whole flood of sensation surged through him, a tidal wave of emotion. The rip and ebb of them tore his control to pieces.

He'd imagined their meeting so many times, it was etched upon his heart and mind. But when confronted with the reality, each tiny discrepancy caused a confusing shock to his senses.

She'd aged. That surprised him. His memories were so sure, so strong; that picture of her clinging with a prideful disdain to Jonah's arm as he rode off to join the Federal army. She'd been furious with him, hadn't even told him good-bye. There were so many pleasant slices of the past he could have held to, but that was the moment he remembered right down to the detailing on her frothy blue day dress. Maybe because he feared he would never see her again.

Or that the next time he did, she'd be another man's wife.

He'd been wrong on both counts.

He'd seen her again at Jonah's burial.

She'd slapped him and vowed to hate him until the day she died. He believed her. But that didn't stop him from dreaming about her.

Patrice Sinclair was no flashy beauty. Her finest

qualities didn't dazzle or bewitch. Hers was a cool loveliness, classic lines, sleek, refined; a thoroughbred, not a show pony. He'd probably been in love with her ever since the day she'd sassed him when he told her she couldn't ride a frisky colt. Then she'd gone ahead and proved she could. She'd ripped her pretty party dress and caused her family no end of embarrassment, but as her brother dragged her away, she'd looked back over her shoulder to give him one last superior smile. *I told you I could!* And his heart was gone.

But thoroughbreds didn't mix with ordinary stock. Trust Patrice to go against that grain.

For all her sophisticated ways, Patrice had a temperament as fiery as her unmanageable hair. She was a rebel. No brush or net could control her mane of auburn curls, and no rules of etiquette or tradition could tame her independent spirit. He figured she kept company with him just to defy the tenets of society that said she shouldn't. He'd tried not to let that matter to him. He tried not to cling so desperately to the memory of her whispering close to his ear in adolescent fervor, "I will love you until the day I die."

She'd changed. He no longer saw the gleefully defiant child. Before him stood a symbol of the South; battle-scarred, weary, worn, and resentful. Instead of silks, she wore a gown of plain calico. Without hoops, its drape accentuated the lean line of her legs. Milk-soft skin that never felt the harsh effects of the sun was now tanned and showing creases at the corners of her eyes, one for every hardship she'd endured. Where before he'd seen spunk, now he sensed a certain toughness. It made her all the more appealing to his hungry eyes.

"Reeve . . ."

"Hello, Patrice."

Spoken with the neutrality of near strangers. They were anything but.

"You came back." Firmness conquered the tremulous disbelief of moments before.

"I told you I would."

Reeve stood, and he swore the way her stare swept over him from uncovered head to scuffed toes burnt with the same brushfire longing that streaked through his veins.

Then the heat was gone.

Her voice held frostbite in every word. "You're a fool if you thought you'd find a welcome here."

He saw it then, a bitterness as hard as the diamond set in Jonah's betrothal ring. She still wore it on one clenched hand, a symbol of all that stood between them.

He'd seen hurt in her eyes when he'd ridden away the first time, hate upon the second. Some small wounds healed and were quickly forgotten. Others filled with ugly poison. Patrice's had festered for quite some time.

And obviously, her feelings hadn't changed.

Without another word, she turned to stride away in a majestic indifference, not bothering to observe how it cut him to the bone.

After a long minute passed, Reeve bent to pick up the scatter of flowers she'd dropped in her dismay. They weren't the fragile hybrid roses once nurtured in the Sinclair gardens. But then, neither was Patrice. Not anymore. She'd brought an armful of wildflowers, the kind that grew plentifully without rhyme or reason across the countryside. Hardy, colorful blossoms that could weather just about anything and still thrive. Like the Patrice who walked away from him without a backward glance.

Carefully, he arranged the bouquet upon the gently mounded soil of his Kentucky homeland, then reached back for the reins to his mount. It was time to face the moment he'd dreaded for four years.

Time to go up to the main house to see what kind of welcome awaited.

"Patrice Sinclair, you take those stairs like a young lady."

The gentle reproof caught Patrice in mid-stride, her skirt hiked up nearly to her knees. Immediately, just as if she were once again a child of privilege struggling to learn social graces, Patrice paused, smoothed the calico the way she would finest sateen, then continued up the porch steps to where her mother sat in the shade.

"I'm sorry, Mama. I forgot myself."

Her modulated voice didn't fool Hannah Sinclair. She set aside her needlepoint to take a closer look at her daughter. Noting her high color and the frantic brightness of her quickly downcast gaze, panic settled within a heart attuned to personal sorrow.

"What is it, Patrice? Is it Deacon? Have you had news?" When no answer came at once, Hannah drew a tight breath. "You wouldn't think to keep such information from me, would you, thinking I'm too frail and foolish to accept it?"

Her mother's pain cut through Patrice's private agonies and she swiftly knelt at her mother's feet.

"Oh, Mama, no. It isn't Deacon. I wouldn't hide news, good or bad, from you. I'm so sorry I frightened you."

Air left Hannah's lungs in a tremulous whisper.

"Not a day passes when I'm not praying to hear something, but at the same time, dreading what that word might be."

Tears glistened as gazes met and the two women shared an empathetic embrace. Then Hannah pushed away, ending Patrice's hope that her mother had forgotten the cause of her concern.

"What's got you all upset, honey?" A gentle palm skimmed one flushed cheek, holding Patrice in place when she thought to rise up and escape the question. "Talk to me, Patrice. You used to confide in me. I know you carry more burdens than a young lady should, and I don't want you to think you can no longer come to me with your troubles. I'm not much good for anything but advice these days."

"Mama, that's not true."

"Of course it is."

Patrice wouldn't insult her by arguing. Both knew the fragile state of Hannah Sinclair's health. Though Patrice often longed to pour out her soul to a sympathetic ear, she couldn't risk the strain upon her mother's delicate nerves. What would the protected and pampered Southern flower who'd gone from the nurturing of one overbearing man as father to another as husband, know of the havoc in her heart? How could she advise on matters of disloyalty and forbidden love when she'd never made an independent suggestion on her own? Her finely bred mother would be distraught if she knew of the dark passions torturing her daughter's soul. So Patrice hoarded the hurts and the anger to herself, heaping them upon a spirit already bowed by more miseries than it was meant to hold. Just this one more wouldn't break her, not this atop all the others.

News of Avery Sinclair's death left Hannah a puppet whose strings had been cut. Without the master to manipulate her movements in the proper way, she couldn't function on her own. She fell into a listless despair, unable to make a decision as small as what to wear without Patrice to coax it from her. While she lay upon her couch, rereading old letters from courtship days until illegible from her weeping, Patrice was forced into the roll of mistress of Sinclair Manor. She'd had to push aside her own fear, her own pain to deal with the daily crises of finding food or selling off the silver to buy seed for vegetables. While Hannah drifted through the hazy afternoons upon daydreams of long ago, Patrice was on her knees in the dirt, using a sterling pie server as a spade to plant tiny seedlings that would feed them over the long winter months. She and Jericho Smith, their only remaining servant, sat together over the last of the coffee discussing their defense should marauders return to take what little they had left while Hannah asked again for two lumps of the sugar they'd run out of months ago. And as Hannah slept smiling in the thrall of her memories, Patrice wept into her pillow, afraid that every night sound bore a threat, terrified that the next day would bring the news that with her brother's death, all was lost. As matriarchal figurehead, Hannah was a symbol of poise and refinement, but for a source of strength and courage, Patrice learned to look inward.

"Go back to your needlework, Mama. Everything's fine."

And she smiled to offset the damning certainty that nothing would be the same again now that Reeve Garrett had returned.

The sound of approaching hoofbeats ended the need for further talk. Both women looked around. There was no mistaking the horseman. No one else melded into an animal to form one muscled unit. And few wearing Union blue traveled alone in Pride County.

Patrice stood slowly, forming an imposing column of support and defense at her mother's side, no less wary than she'd been of the nightriders come to burn her house around her. She held a frail hand in one of hers, mindful not to crush the slender fingers in her agitation.

The rider dismounted, a handsome figure, proud in bearing, determined in manner. He paused long enough to loop his reins through the brass tethering ring before striding to the stairs. Patrice stiffened a degree with each step he came nearer until she was as rigid as buckram stays. She pulled quick, insufficient breaths between the firm clench of her teeth. The sound whistled ominously beneath the modulated greeting her mother gave.

"Why, Mr. Garrett, what a surprise."

Hannah Sinclair was too well bred to reveal the nature of that surprise, whether good or bad. Instead, she smiled, showing no less welcome than she would to Breckinridge, himself, had he come to tell them the Confederacy had been saved. Her free hand extended in invitation.

Reeve took the frail hand and raised it gallantly to his lips. His gaze never strayed from the neighboring matriarch to the seething female at her side.

"Miz Sinclair, you're lookin' lovely, as always. After four years, a man gets hungry for such a sight to remind him that he's come home."

Ignoring Patrice's indignant snort, Hannah

blushed prettily. "Go on with you, Mr. Garrett. I don't remember you as given to such excessive flattery."

"I'm not one for speaking less than the truth, ma'am."

That pleased Hannah as much as it annoyed her daughter.

Only then did Reeve glance at Patrice for a perfunctory nod. "Miss Patrice."

Patrice's glare bored holes through him.

Hannah withdrew her hand but not her hospitable manner. Encouraged, Reeve lingered on the front steps, seeing an opportunity to learn things Patrice hadn't stayed long enough to tell him.

"Is your family visiting here at the Glade, Miz Hannah?" He glanced about, seeing no driver or carriage.

Hannah indulged him with a sad smile. "Alas, Mr. Garrett, the Glade has been our home for the past months. The squire was kind enough to offer his generosity."

"Seeing as how close we were to becoming family." Patrice added that like a rapier stab. Her stony expression gave nothing away but her stare was razor-stropped sharp.

Reeve remained unflinching as he turned his attention back to the elder Sinclair lady. His brows knit with apprehension.

"Has somethin' happened to the Manor?"

"We have more than just chimneys remaining, which is far luckier than most who've entertained Yankee vermin."

"Patrice," Hannah cautioned gently. "The Manor has been fortunately spared, but the squire didn't feel it was safe for us to stay there without our men-folk.''

"Too much dangerous riffraff roaming about," Patrice added with a venomous purr.

"Your husband and son?"

"Mr. Sinclair fell at Chickamauga." Hannah nodded at Reeve's quickly expressed regret. "We haven't received word of Deacon, yet. He was in the field on his own much of the time. No one can tell us . . . anything."

"I'm sure he's fine, Miz Hannah. Deacon's a clever man, a survivor." The way he said it wasn't exactly a compliment. Remembering that he spoke to the man's mother, Reeve took a moment before he could continue in a neutral tone. "There was a lot of confusion at the end and a lot of units broke apart and lost touch. It's nothing to worry over."

"We will surely rest so much better for your platitudes, sir."

"Patrice, Mr. Garrett is trying to be kind."

Patrice's patience fractured. "Mr. Garrett might well have shot Deacon, himself, for all we know. He's not above such things as he's proved in the past."

Reeve never twitched a muscle. His flat stare fixed with Patrice's, absorbing its rancor without response.

Hannah paled dramatically, shocked by her daughter's bad manners as well as by her words. "You will apologize—"

Patrice's head shot up like a fierce wild horse's.

"Not to him! Never to him!"

Her eyes glittering with furious tears, Patrice whirled away rather than recant before her mother's persuasion. As the door slammed behind her, she

heard her mother's stammered apologies to a man
who deserved none. Not from them!

Leaning back against the papered wall, Patrice
squeezed her eyes shut, forbidding the dampness to
escape while she hung on the husky timbre of his
speech, feeling it thrill along her senses with mad-
dening results, berating herself at the same time for
succumbing to that frailty of heart. It shouldn't have
been Reeve Garrett out there charming her mother
with his soft drawling manner and awkward charm.
It should have been Deacon, Jonah, any number of
loyal Southern patriots whose honor was blighted
by that traitor's very presence.

But Reeve returned, mocking their sacrifice, torturing her resolve.

And she could never forgive him for that. Never.

"Patrice? Is something wrong, child?"

Her gaze flashed up wildly, her upset and turmoil clearly displayed before she was able to mask
both with a genteel smile. "I thank you for your
worry, Squire. I've had a bit of a shock, is all."

Byron Glendower held most of the power in
Pride County in one well-manicured hand, but no
one would guess it by looking at him. He wasn't
big or blustery or surrounded by an air of self-
importance. With his wispy hair, rail-thin figure,
and myopic eyes, he appeared more a gangly egret
than an aggressive bird of prey. But that was outward appearance. Within roared a lion-strong ambition, an ambition to pull a man from his home in
Virginia to stake new territory in a raw lush land
where dreams were measured in horseflesh and
success by the legacy a man could pass on to his
heirs. A legacy not worth much in the war's after-

math. Not with one son dead and the other unwilling to accept his place.

"Shock? Your brother—"

"No."

How could she prepare him?

Then she didn't have to.

The sound of Reeve's voice brought a wash of shameless joy into the squire's eyes. Patrice glanced away, honoring his privacy, resentful of the welcome she saw in that flash of recognition. Because it echoed her own traitorous response. But when the squire spoke, his words were rough with caution.

"What does he want here?"

"You'll have to ask him."

Byron Glendower went out onto the porch to do just that.

Father and son exchanged long, stoic looks. Assessments were done with no flicker of warming. Glendower broke the silence with a restrained statement.

"You look well, boy."

"Not a scratch in four years."

His claim hung, almost a challenge in the way it was defiantly rendered. Finally, the squire nodded.

"Are you here to stay or just passing through?"

"Depends."

"On?"

"I'd like to stay on at the cabin. I'll work off the cost . . . like my mama did."

"Reeve—your mother—"

The lines of his face tightened into chiseled planes. "I know. I saw her grave. I'll want to know about it . . . later."

The squire nodded again, sorrow seeping into his tired gaze. Then, a slight edge of hope nudged in.

"The cabin is yours, of course, but you don't need to stay down there. The house—"

"The cabin's fine, sir." And that put an end to his invitation, the one extended time and again but similarly discarded with a prideful contempt. As if the offer was beneath consideration.

"Come in, Reeve. You must be hungry."

"No, thank you. I'd just as soon settle in."

The second, more obvious rejection, took a greater toll upon the elder's expression. It hardened to mask the pang of disappointment. "Whatever you want, Reeve. Come up to the house when you're ready. We'll talk then."

With a bow to Hannah Sinclair and a quick glance toward the door through which Patrice had disappeared, Reeve turned without a sound to remount his horse.

"I see you've taken good care of Zeus."

Reeve patted the stallion's finely arched neck. "I promised I would, didn't I? He's glad to be home."

Just as he, despite all his arguments, was glad to be back.

"Reeve, it's not going to be easy, you being here. Not for any of us."

"Nothing's ever been easy for me, sir."

He wheeled the animal away, leaving his father to stew on the complexities his arrival would cause as soon as word got out that a traitor was back in their midst.

Chapter 2

◦◦◦

"Kill 'em all!"
        Reeve shifted in the rocking chair as the fierce Rebel yell cut through his dream.

"No prisoners!"

His head rolled against the wooden back as wild war cries echoed in his mind, as memories caught on the sunlight glinting against the cold steel of brandished sabers. Memories not from any battle-field but from the smooth lawns of the Glade as pounding hooves churned up great clods of Kentucky bluegrass. It wasn't an engagement between North and South he looked back upon but a skirmish of young Pride County blades trying to impress two of its loveliest belles.

He could see Patrice Sinclair and her friend, Starla Fairfax, languishing in the shade like hothouse blossoms in bright petals of aqua and jonquil-colored silk. Over the fluttering of their fans, excited eyes followed the boys on horseback as they played at war with Mexico. His friends, though he was not their equal; Noble, Mede, Tyler, and Jonah, still at the age where social standing didn't matter when it came to roughhouse. Only Noble could sit a saddle half as well as Reeve, and all vied to have him on their side as they reenacted the stories Mede's father told them of his forays in the frontier of Texas. It was afterward, when they'd be called up to the house, that Reeve couldn't follow. To the illegitimate son of Byron Glendower, the county's tolerance extended only so far.

While good enough to rattle sabers with, he wasn't acceptable when it came to clattering fine silver over meals. As a young man just coming into his own awareness of self and place, he resented the hell out of it.

And the one he resented most, was Jonah Glendower.

It was impossible not to be jealous. Jonah had everything he wanted—a name, a fine home, the best horseflesh in Kentucky, the respect of the county. All just because of who he was, not because he'd done one damn thing to earn it.

And if whispers were believed, he'd have Patrice Sinclair, as well. It was common practice for sprawling families of wealth and stature to interbreed. Jonah and Patrice were considered a prime match . . . by everyone but Reeve and Patrice, herself.

Patrice was the best the county had to offer, though certainly not the most traditional. She was a rule breaker, a reined-in hellion, chomping at the bit. It would take special handling to gentle her, and a willingness to be thrown more than once. Not every man could appreciate that trace of wildness.

Few would be wise enough to recognize the value of that spirit and not break it. He wasn't sure Jonah was one of them, even though he knew his half brother had loved their neighbor just about forever. And it looked like he'd have her.

Something about that wedged up tight and hurtful beneath Reeve's ribs.

It was when Mede called for a horse race that the idea came, a shameful stab of envy overruling all else. Patrice, ever outrageous, named a kiss from the lady of choice as the winner's reward. He wanted that kiss more than anything—anything except the chance to humiliate his rival in front of all.

Jonah didn't ride. He had a deep abiding fear of horses, considering them unpredictable and a touch demonic with their high-strung manner, flashing eyes, and flaring nostrils. He looked stricken when Reeve jumped down from his huge stallion, Prometheus, to offer the reins and a silky, "Here, Jonah. You can take my horse."

Apprehension shadowed his half brother's gaze, but when he glanced back at the lovely Patrice Sinclair, all sunset-soft with her burnished hair, sky-blue eyes, and pastel gown, he took the reins with a tentative courage.

"Reeve, his daddy's gonna wear welts on you if you put his boy up on that black of yours," Tyler warned. "He's gonna git himself kilt."

His daddy. Not *your daddy.* Reeve's resentment simmered. He gave the reluctant Jonah a nudge. "Go on, Jonah. All you have to do is hang on."

And he'd smiled encouragingly, seeing his half brother's fear, knowing he wouldn't be able to control the big horse once it sensed its rider's lack of confidence. He watched Jonah square his shoulders, trying to be worthy of Reeve's pride, trying to win over Patrice's admiration. Then he'd climbed aboard.

Four horses broke from the line, surging forward as one. Three returned. They found Jonah lying bleeding and broken in the woods, where he'd been thrown, just as Reeve had known he would be. But he hadn't known that Jonah's leg would be so badly shattered, he'd suffer months of agony and be left with a permanent limp.

When Squire Glendower, in a rare and frightful fury, demanded to know who was to blame for his son's laming injury, he never expected Jonah to speak up weakly, insisting that his own foolishness was at fault. He defended Reeve against Tyler's rec-ollections. In his relief not to be named responsible, he thought Jonah a gullible fool. Until his half brother, on his bed of pain, met his gaze, and with one direct exchange, let Reeve know that he was aware of what had been done and why.

Reeve jerked from his dozing. Something awak-ened him. He felt a presence before actually hearing anything again, a skill developed in self-defense while on picket duty. Hairs bristled at the nape of his neck as intuition rustled by on the way to stiffen all his major muscles into a pose of readiness. He drew his pistol from the cartridge belt hanging over the back of his chair.

Alerted senses picked up tiny clues of identity even as he stepped out onto the narrow porch. The scent of warm bread and warm woman teased his nostrils into a welcoming flare. The sound of fabric playing loosely about a soft-footed stride told him it was a woman, but that didn't necessarily lessen his danger. Threat came in all sorts of guises. He squinted against the brightness, concealing the gun behind his back.

Patrice stood at the foot of his stairs. She held nothing more deadly than a basket and a stony stare. Feeling foolish about the pistol, he tucked it into the band of his trousers at the small of his back. His expression betrayed no sign of welcome.

When he didn't address her, Patrice scowled, unhappy with the burden of making the first gesture.

"My mama didn't like the thought of you down here starving."

"Bet it didn't bother you none, did it?"

Patrice ignored that and thrust the towel-draped basket toward him. When he didn't come forward to take it from her, her displeasure grew. She was forced to climb the steps and come close to him.

"It's not much, but then nobody around here has much these days."

"Keep it. I don't need charity."

The basket dangled between them in awkward offering, tension escalating with each second it remained unclaimed. To withdraw it would be accepting insult, to expend more words in persuasion was farther than Patrice was willing to go. Through gritted teeth, she said, "I wouldn't give you any. You know my mother. She has a soft spot for any stray. I won't have her fretting over your worthless hide. Take it."

"Well," he drawled out. "Since you put it like that."

He watched her starch up as his hand stretched out. He curled fingers around the woven handle, purposefully brushing hers. She let go so quickly the basket took a precarious tip.

"Smells good."

She smelled good. Like a summer day. Woman smells he hadn't enjoyed for a long time.

She started to turn away, and suddenly Reeve couldn't bear for her to go.

"I suppose offering to share this with you wouldn't be much of a temptation."

"I have already eaten." Her gaze said plain that his company would do little for her appetite even if she hadn't. Again, she started to leave. Reeve took a hurried step forward.

"Then how about sharin' a little news?"

She didn't turn. "I don't want to share anything with you, Reeve Garrett."

"Patrice . . . please. I've gone out of my mind these past years, not knowing. When I last saw Noble, he was in a skirmish with Morgan after Shiloh." Reeve closed his eyes against the memory of Noble Banning rushing fearlessly into the jaws of danger. There was an instant when their gazes met and held, exchanging an eternity of shock, gladness, and horror that they would meet again as enemies. Then their horses plunged past one another, getting lost in the confusion of battle. Reeve was shaken for days afterward. He'd haunted the site, checking the Confederate dead, questioning those taken prisoner. But none could tell him the fate of his friend.

Until now.

"He was shot at Barboursville."

Reeve's knees buckled, causing him to sway in a moment of weakening remorse. "Killed?" He locked his joints against the inevitable facts, as grief rattled along his bones.

"No. He was taken prisoner." Patrice revolved slowly, not in time to witness the stark stamp of relief upon his features. He was in control again by the time she looked up for a grim recital. "Last I heard he was at Point Lookout Prison in Maryland. The judge wrote everyone from Jeff Davis to Lincoln himself, begging for his release. But by then, they weren't doing any more prisoner exchanges. I don't know what happened to him."

Reeve was tormented by the remembered sight of Noble's hat plume bobbing above the dusty melee. He vowed he'd find out if he had to ride all the way to Maryland. It might take months, records being in an appalling disarray.

"Last we heard of Mede, he was in the Battle of Franklin."

Reeve flinched, consequence delivering the force of a gut punch. He'd seen the lists; pages and pages of the dead—of those they'd been able to recognize. Many would never have a name put to them. Over a fifth of the Army of Tennessee fell. Was that Mede's fate? He reeled, buffeted by ungovernable distress. "Tyler?" he managed in a tight-throated whisper.

"His father bought off his conscription. He never left the county. His idea of patriotism was joining the Home Guard with the Dermonts to harass the helpless instead of furthering the Cause."

The Cause. That stupid, damned Cause that tore families apart, forcing brother to face brother on a field of opposing honor. Madness. Jonah had been right about that. He only half listened as Patrice ran down the other familiar names that would be faces no more. Just ghosts of a past glory. Sacrifices to that bloody Cause. He numbed his mind to it. To the endless lists of tears he'd see forever in his nightmares. Looking back was too hard. Looking forward was where he had to focus if he was going to claw his way out of hell.

Patrice paused, noting his drifting attention.

Was he so disinterested in those who'd died standing on the other side of the barrel from him? Her mood chilled as she beheld him, standing there in his Union blue, looking fit and fine—not a scratch on him!—while the rest of the county staggered under the yoke of its losses. And he'd yet to speak a single word about the one life that wedged between him and everyone else in Pride—the life he'd taken in the line of his damnable duty.

He'd yet to say he was sorry about Jonah.

Finally hearing the silence, Reeve glanced up to find himself on the receiving end of Patrice's contempt. And it wounded as all the stray bullets and flailing bayonets had failed to.

"That's all the sharing you'll get from me," she spat out at him.

Then he completely disarmed her.

"Thanks for seeing to my mama. She'd have liked the flowers."

Patrice struggled for balance, her equilibrium upset by his unexpectedly intimate approach. Because she wavered and weakened, her words were harshly clipped.

"I liked your mother. It had nothing to do with you."

He didn't retract the thanks or add to it. There was nothing for Patrice to do but retreat before the situation worsened. She whirled away, but his voice followed.

"And thank your mama for worrying over me."

She ran the rest of the way back to the house.

* * *

Reeve ate alone. The meal he'd hoped to savor, his first back home, could well have been sawdust.

It was so quiet. He'd gotten used to the rustle of an army settling down for the night. He'd actually taken comfort in it. Here, stillness pressed in all around him, engulfing with a sense of isolation. And with the quiet, came the ghosts.

It wasn't going to be easy, the squire said. It was going to be hell, for all of them, and Reeve knew it. It would have made so much more sense just to ride on, to where he could start a new beginning, away from past prejudices and future complications. This wasn't his home, not really. Not so much as a hand-ful of dirt belonged to him. It was Squire Glen-dower's home. Home to the wealthy of Pride County, a county that had chosen pride over prac-ticality when casting its lot to the cause of the South. And he would find no welcome. Even before, when he wasn't quite up to their social standings, at least, he'd been one of them. Now, he was a complete outsider.

Was it worth the effort to win them over?

He'd lived his life not caring what anyone thought or said. He was Byron Glendower's bas-tard, and if the squire didn't care enough to change that, why should he make it matter to him? He'd worked at the Glade to provide for his mother. But if that was the only reason, what held him now?

He was too tired to consider his reasonings, too afraid of what he'd discover now that his defenses were down. Easier to accept the situation than to try to explain it. It always had been.

He bedded down in his mother's first-floor room, not just because it was clean and well aired, but because her spirit lingered there, allowing him one last chance to surround himself with her loving presence. He lay back and shut his eyes. He'd trained his body and mind not to waste the opportunity for rest when it came, so sleep engulfed him almost at once.

And he dreamed. Of a bobbing hat plume. Of the deafening report of rifles following the command of "Fire." He slept but he didn't rest. He would never rest again.

"Patrice, you're as restless as a cat tonight. Sit down. You're positively wearing me out just watching you."

"I'm sorry, Mama."

Patrice collapsed into the wicker chair beside her mother's chaise. Warm evening air stirred across the second-story veranda in a soothing caress, but nothing could calm her feverish state.

"It's Reeve Garrett, isn't it?"

Hannah didn't look up from her embroidery to catch her daughter's expression of dismay. Patrice was quick to recover.

"I refuse to give that Yankee trash a second thought."

"Then why haven't you been able to think of anything else since he got here?"

The gentle chiding goaded Patrice back up to her feet. She prowled the rail, denying in her mind that her gaze strayed to a darkened cabin, denying in her heart that it beat just a bit faster knowing he was there.

"How do you expect me to feel, Mama? He killed my fiancé. He ruined every chance I had at a future. He destroyed the county's hope of survival."

"That's a lot of burden for one man to bear."

"Oh, Mama, you know what I mean. If it wasn't his hand, it was his will. He made his choices. And he chose to stand against us. What are we going to do now? Everything was hanging on my marriage to Jonah. We needed the Glendower money to keep the Manor running. The county needed Jonah to keep the bank solvent. Now everything is going to fold. And if Reeve Garrett isn't to blame, I surely don't know who is."

"He followed his own beliefs, Patrice. You, of all people, should admire that instead of condemning him for it."

Patrice stared at her mother as though a stranger sat before her, a stranger who'd remained silently supportive of all the right views, who never voiced an opinion of her own unless it echoed that of her outspoken husband. Hannah Sinclair, the epitome of Southern womanhood: docile, quiet, unobtrusive. She'd never uttered a controversial word in her life, only to take such a shocking stand now.

"You sound as though you approve of what he did! He took arms against our family, against his own family and friends! How can you see that as anything but vile? That's traitorous talk to the memory of my father ... and maybe to Deacon." Hot tears welled up into her eyes, shimmering with righteous anger.

Hannah Sinclair set aside her needlework and rose with insurmountable dignity to meet her daughter's fiery glare. "My memories are my own, Patrice, and so are my opinions. I may not have expressed them openly, but I have a right to feel them, nonetheless. If that makes me a villain in your eyes, I suppose I will have to bear that along with all my other sorrows."

And before Patrice could gather her thoughts to utter a proper apology, the stately lady in her widow's black moved inside through the open veranda doors.

Patrice stalked to the edge of the balcony, hating herself for bring yet another source of pain to prick her mother's weary spirit. "Damn you, Reeve," she cried in frustration. "You varmint. You always manage to turn everythin' upside down."

How could her mother fail to see the tragedy Reeve Garrett forced upon them with his self-righteous honor? Why couldn't he have bent to take up Confederate gray? Though Kentucky was mostly Union in support and sentiment, pockets of it held to Confederate loyalties. Pride was such a county, fierce in its beliefs, quick to fight for the South. Jonah was of the same mind and spirit as Reeve, yet he hadn't jumped at the chance to betray home and family. Reeve was the one constantly to brook convention, always to turn against the current to battle his way upstream. Why couldn't he, for once, have done the proper thing instead of the—right thing.

Patrice paced, unhappy with thoughts that bordered on the treacherous, themselves. She was no great supporter of the war but when the call came, she didn't hesitate to do her part to aid the Confederate Cause. It wasn't for slavery, though the Manor owned its share. It wasn't for state's rights. She had no political leanings and considered the windy debates tiresome at best. It was a feeling that came over her slowly, steadily as she fought to keep the Manor going during the absence of its menfolk. A slow, growing attachment to the land, to tradition, to roots sunk deep into fertile soil. And, for the first time, she understood her father and Deacon's obsession.

"It's more than buildings, Patrice, more than property," her father had told her. "It's your heritage, a place of belonging. You don't own it; it possesses you."

Apparently, Reeve couldn't understand these things, or he wouldn't have chosen the path he did. He had no ties to the land or family. His disrespect for all his father stood for was well-known. Why else would he turn his back on continual pleas for him to take his place within the Glendower home? He allowed what should have been his to pass to Jonah; the land, the house, the responsibilities . . . her—without a fight, without regret. What did he know of loyalty, of love? Admire him? Hardly! Coward was what he was. A shameless, turncoat coward. She struck at the tears clinging to her lashes, refusing to let them fall.

Jonah had proved to be the better man. He'd done the correct things. He'd given his heart, his soul to the Glade and Pride County. He'd surrendered his own personal dreams to become the son his father desired—the one Reeve refused to be. He'd given himself over to the betterment of the county, devoting his intellect and his time to the formation of the Pride County Bank helping his neighbors, his friends reach for a promising future. And he'd wanted to share it all with her.

She closed her eyes, picturing Jonah Glendower. Handsome, reed-slender, awkwardly self-conscious, bright, always a kind word and quick smile on his lips, never a glower clouding the sincerity of his gaze. A scholar, not a scrapper like his older brother. Why hadn't she ever appreciated his goodness, his strength while blinded by Reeve's blatant appeal? She'd taken the quiet, gentle Jonah for granted, and, now, there was no way to make that up to him.

Take this ring and be my wife. Make me the happiest man on earth.

She accepted his proposal begrudgingly, spitefully, because she couldn't have Reeve. How ashamed she was of her shallow motives for promising herself to a fine man. He hadn't deserved the rebound of her affection.

Just as she failed him when he was alive, she vowed to honor him in his death.

Jonah Glendower died a hero, and she would be his living tribute for the rest of her days. She would act his widow as surely as if they'd been wed. She would mourn him and avenge him as was her duty, to make up for her frivolous disregard for such things when they would have meant something.

And as such, Reeve Garrett could be nothing more than the object of her scorn and hatred. There would be no weakness where he was concerned. She owed her determined stand to the memory of Jonah, to her father, to all those who'd died defending their homeland.

Reeve Garrett had had his chance to hold her heart.

Now, he would know only her contempt.

Chapter 3

⎯⎯⎯ ᏍᏍᎧ ⎯⎯⎯

Zeus stood alone in the renowned Glendower stables. Stalls once holding the finest thoroughbreds in the country were empty of all but soiled bedding. Harness tracings oiled with pride until the leather reflected mirror-bright, hung dry and cracked in disarray. Such neglect, even by him, would have earned a horsewhipping from the squire, who held as much pride in the state of his stables as in the prestige of his home ... perhaps more.

"Easy, boy," Reeve crooned as he slipped in beside the animal. Velvety lips plucked affectionately at his shirt buttons. With brush in hand, Reeve began soothing repetitions along the dark hide, coaxing a lustrous sheen. Aside from the occasional twitch, the animal stood quietly, enjoying the sense of camaraderie between man and mount. They had a long history, bound by a promise not always easily kept. Reeve promised to see to the animal's care if Zeus brought him safely home.

"Feels good being in for the night, don't it, boy?"

Ears pricked forward at the sound of his low tones.

"Yessir, was a time when I wondered if we'd ever be dry again, but here we are, roof over our heads, snug as bugs. What more could we be wantin'?"

Zeus tossed his great head, throwing it over the divider to the next stall as if pointing out its emptiness.

"Company, eh?" The big stallion wasn't alone in that wish. Unbidden, the image of Patrice Sinclair tantalized. He shook off the unlikely mirage. "Well, you got me through the thick of it, didn't you, boy? Least I can do is turn you out to the best grass this side of heaven, with your pick of the fillies."

"Think he understands you?"

Though startled by the intrusion of his father's voice, Reeve didn't look around. He stretched down to pick up a curry comb and went to work on the shaggy mane. "Why, sure. Me and Zeus have shared many a conversation over the last four years. He's a fine listener."

"Well, don't go promising him his pick of the mares just yet. I'm afraid he's the only blooded animal the Glade has."

He paused in his movement of the comb. "Zeus don't belong to the Glade. He's mine." A quiet statement of fact.

"And you don't belong to the Glade either, I suppose."

Reeve didn't answer his father's curt rejoinder. Instead, he squatted down to prop one of the stallion's hocks upon his knee to pick at the hoof. Zeus fidgeted, sensing his tension.

"It's good to have you back."

Again, Reeve said nothing, remembering their parting words after he'd brought Jonah home.

"I give you a home and this is how you repay me! My son is dead. You should have been there to protect him instead of helping the enemy pull the trigger. It wasn't enough to put a knife in my back with your betrayal. Now you've stabbed me through the heart. Do you hate me so much? You've not only murdered my son, you've killed the future of the Glade. You ungrateful bastard! You'll never have what was his. Never!"

Now that same man who'd ordered him off the Glade at gunpoint, refusing to hear what he would say in his own defense, was extending the olive branch in truce after using it to whip him.

"You haven't said how long you'll be staying."

"No, I haven't."

More silence, ragged around the edges with strain.

"The Glade could use you, Reeve."

"The Glade?" He glanced up then, intense gaze demanded a more personal concession. Getting it, after a long pause.

"I could use you."

Showing no sign that his father's admission pleased him, Reeve bent back over the hoof. "To do what?"

"Rebuild."

"What makes you think the Glade matters to me one way or another?"

For a moment, he sensed his father's panic, a cold, shaky thing, smelling of sweat and fear. It ran through the troops like a fever during the quiet before a charge, in that instant where losing all meant more than loyalty, more than pride. A hesitation when strong men faced the reality of having no future. And it either broke them or made them more determined.

Byron Glendower didn't break easily.

"Because you're my son," was the bulwark he threw up before him. "You can't pretend with me, Reeve. I've seen you hunger after these acres all your life."

Reeve flung the pick he was using across the stall, the noise startling both man and animal. With hands gripping the knees of his Union trousers, Reeve glared up with uncharacteristic ferocity.

"Your son? Really? Now that you've got nothing left, you want to embrace me with sudden fatherly love? Or are you jus' planning to use me like you did my mama, to get what you want?"

His father slapped him. Reeve didn't move to put a hand to his burning cheek. It flushed a damning red while Byron seethed down at him. Never had father put a harsh hand to either of his boys, and the mood lay raw as an exposed wound between them.

"Stay or go," Glendower spat out at last. "I don't give a damn what you do. I don't need you to survive."

Then Reeve laid the cold truth of it bare. "Yes, you do."

For all his unimposing stature, Byron Glendower puffed out like an adder, all bluff and impotent threat. Reeve saw through it, and for the first time, saw his father as someone vulnerable. It shook him, but only for a moment.

"I'll stay . . . because of Jonah, not you."

Byron's hands clenched in the front of Reeve's faded shirt, twisting, jerking him up with fierce authority even though the younger was now the bigger and more powerful man. And there wasn't the slightest sign of weakness in his narrowed eyes.

"Don't you ever—ever mention his name to me again. You hear me, boy? You don't deserve to."

Reeve never moved. His eyes were flinty, his expression cold and remote. He rocked back against the stall when released. The two men regarded one another over this newly drawn line, both breathing hard, both unwilling to budge. The squire's jaw worked on words best not said, and with difficulty, he kept it that way. Because he knew, as Reeve knew, that he couldn't keep the Glade going on his own.

It wasn't until the angry squire stormed out of the barn that Reeve sank slowly down onto his haunches, back flush to the wall, fists lashing back to thud loudly against that unyielding wood. Then with bruised knuckles pressed to his mouth, he expelled a heavy breath and, with it, his hostility.

It wasn't going to be easy at all.

She watched him move through the swatches of light, pitching soiled straw with an almost fevered urgency.

He was wearing the hated uniform trousers with just the tops of his worn long johns above them. Sleeves were pushed up over muscular forearms, buttons undone to display a sheen upon his firm, broad chest. He worked tirelessly, like one of her father's machines. He moved like nothing she'd ever seen—strength, grace, fury all wrapped together in a sinewy coil.

With a vengeance.

He was angry. She could see it in the tight set of his jaw, in the furrows plowed deep where frowning brows drew together. A similar mood surrounded Squire Glendower when he'd returned to the house. She wondered who or what had started the fight. She'd never known Reeve to push a confrontation with the squire before, but now, these were different times, different men.

The difference was what drew her to the barns. She wanted . . . no needed—to prove something to herself. That she could be near him and not desire him. That she could look upon temptation and not give in like the impulsive child she'd once been. Reeve Garrett was no longer just the object of forbidden lusting, a dangerous symbol of what was denied her, and therefore all the more appealing. He was a reminder of what they'd lost and why, of what she'd lost. He was an enemy to heart and soul, a demon that must be faced or run from.

Even now as she watched him covertly, covetously, her pulse raced faster, stirred into a frenzy as never before.

He looked up suddenly, features registering surprise, as if her motives were completely transparent and her desire plain to see. But then his face settled back to its unreadable mask once more as he leaned indolently upon the pitchfork handle, mocking her tension with his ease.

"Something you wanted, Miz Sinclair?"

Once there was, she could have replied. Once, there was something she'd wanted quite desperately.

Instead, her expression hardened with displeasure. "Mama wanted to know if you were coming up to the house for lunch."

"Are you your mama's errand girl now?"

She refused to be baited. "Are you coming or not?"

"Not. At least, not now. I don't care to be fed at saber point. But thank your mama kindly for the invite." He wiped one sweaty forearm across his brow, and, as her gaze followed the movement, her mouth went totally dry. Had she been crazy to think she could ever be unaffected by him?

"Trice, what happened to my mama?"

The last thing she wanted to do was discuss something so intimate with him. She balked. "You should ask the squire."

"He's not the one who tended my mama's grave. You are. Guess that makes you about the only one who gave a damn. How did she die?"

Patrice swallowed hard against a tide of sorrow, her tone husky with it when she spoke at last.

"I guess you could say she was a casualty of war. A band of soldiers came for the horses. They had the squire at gunpoint. I don't think they expected any other resistance. Abbie stood in the door of the stable with a pitchfork and told them they'd have to go through her. They did."

Reeve's eyes closed briefly, the muscles of his face spasming. "Union soldiers?"

"No. Our boys. It wasn't intentional. One of the men got behind her and knocked her down with the butt of his rifle. She never got up. They all felt real bad about it."

"But that didn't stop 'em from taking the horses, did it?"

She didn't back down from the crack of bitterness in his words. "No."

She watched his shoulders slump, just a fleeting

show of grief too overwhelming to contain. In that instant, she fought the need to go to him, the need to put her arms about his broad shoulders to share a common bond of mourning. But to do so would compromise her promise not to give him comfort—one didn't provide comfort to one's enemies.

To her relief, the weakness lasted only a second or two. Then Reeve straightened and his taut posture made it easier for her to control sympathies he would most likely reject.

"I've got work to do," he said gruffly, turning his back on her.

"I'm sorry, Reeve." It came out unintentionally, but she was glad she'd told him when he paused and looked back through a gaze stripped down to naked emotion. In a blink, the look was gone, and his reply was carefully phrased to reveal as little as possible.

"I'm sorry, too, Patrice. About your father, about a lot of things. But I can't change 'em."

She pleated and repleated the folds of her plain skirt within the clutch of her hands. She had to know.

"Would you, Reeve, if you could?"

"No."

That one word, two little letters, drove a wedge between them, hammering it deep with the strength of his contention, burying it with the sweeping force of her resentment.

What else was there to say?

She'd gotten as far as dragging out her big trunk and was stuffing her sensible gowns inside. Why had she thought he'd changed? That she could change the way she felt about him?

Once again, she'd given him every chance to win her over . . . and he hadn't. Purposefully or foolishly, did it matter? He wouldn't admit he'd been mistaken, not about the path he followed, not about the result of choice, not about letting her go.

And what made her mad, truly, lividly, hopping mad, was that she wasn't sure which failing bothered her the most.

She caught her ring in the lace cuff of one of her gowns. The setting snagged, tearing the delicate tracery, ruining the elaborate pattern. She stared at it in dismay, knowing there was no way to repair it, no money to replace it. Her carelessness cost her dearly. Then she forgot about the dress, and touched the ring, thinking about other careless losses. She swallowed down the burn of tears at the back of her throat and took a deep, cleansing breath.

What was she doing? Running away wasn't going to solve things. There was no sanctuary away from the Glade. Fright trembled within her breast. What *was* she going to do? Stay here where she'd be constantly reminded of her ruined hopes and traitorous dreams? Where her days would be filled with the probability of running into *him*? Where her nights would be flooded with remembrances of what might have been?

She should have been Mrs. Jonah Glendower, mistress of this house and heir to its fortune. She should have had no worries about a crop lying fallow, about a house crumbling in disrepair, about caring for her mother and assuming a man's role. She couldn't stand begging favors, especially from Reeve. Not when everything could have been . . . theirs together.

She tossed her crumpled gown to the floor as angry panic shivered along her slender form. Help-lessness scared her. She'd always had the strength and judgment of her father and brother. She was too practical for a female, too independent-minded to do things the easy way. How she wished for an easier way now, and for a less realistic view of how things were and would be. It was no blessing to have an insight into the future.

Sighing, she picked up the dress, brushed it out, and restored it to the clothes cupboard. She faced facts, unpleasant or no. Her mother couldn't go back to the Manor, where there were few comforts and no safety. She was too frail, and Patrice was not fool enough to think she could protect and provide for them. The Glade was their only haven. No way would she let Reeve Garrett chase them out of it. He'd taken everything else, he and his repressive Federal bullies. He owed her the small sense of security she found under this roof.

And she owed it to him to make the consequences of what he'd done a constant abrasion upon what little conscience he could claim. If he couldn't—wouldn't—change the past, she'd see he was ever reminded of it. Of the pain he'd caused. Of the ruination he'd allowed to fall upon them. She wouldn't let him wear his guilt so casually. God, help her, she'd see he strangled in it.

And there was only one place to sanction that promise. Not in any church, but rather in her own chapel. Her home. She'd feel better there, stronger, more certain of her choices. But getting there was a problem. The Manor was miles away, and the only transportation belonged to Reeve.

Patrice smiled tightly.

How fitting that he should provide for her travel after causing her distress.

But she knew Reeve, and she knew he wouldn't just saddle the animal for her and let her go on her way. Not alone. Not without explanation. Not without humbling herself to make the necessary request, which she was in no mood to do. So she watched and waited. And at last, Reeve left the barn area to return to his distant cabin.

She ran quickly, lightly, with a trace of her old impulsive recklessness down to the paddock where Reeve had replaced broken slats and rails so Zeus could trot about the enclosure. The animal paused, pawing cautiously at the ground when she approached, bridle in hand. But, a well-trained beast, it came at her soft whistle and allowed her to slip the straps into place. She'd ridden all her life, both with ladylike decorum and hoydenish disregard. She chose the later, vaulting up onto the horse's wide back in an awkward bunch of petticoats to sit astride.

The big stallion responded easily to the pressure of her knees and guiding movement of the reins, but when Reeve's shout—at first anxious, then angry—sounded behind them, the animal hesitated, drawn to its master's voice. A brisk thump of her heels sent them galloping down the road, leaving Reeve behind in whorls of dust.

The sight of fire-scorched brick brought back an unexpected rush of horror and helplessness. Patrice slid down off Zeus's back, her knees buckling weakly. Gripping the animal's mane, she pressed her face against the beast's warm flesh until the anguish ebbed, until the panic subsided and the nightmarish pictures stopped replaying in her head. Only then could she look up and see what could be, what once was, instead of the sad neglect that stood before her now.

Still, it hurt. It pained to see her beloved home abandoned in disrepair.

"Dat you, Miz Patrice?"

"It's me, Jericho."

The young black man emerged from the hedges near the house, lowering the ancient rifle in his hands when he saw for himself who it was. "You got any word on Mista Deacon yet?"

"Nothing yet. Have you had any more problems here?"

"Nothing I ain't been able to handle, ma'am."

She smiled at the note of pride in his voice, a possessive tone well earned over the past year with just the two of them struggling to keep the walls and their world from caving in.

Jericho's father had served her family as driver, an elevated position in the slave community commanding respect and requiring a degree of responsibility that fostered trust. His sister, Jassy, had grown up beside Patrice, sharing her dolls and later, her dreams until, in a sudden move of uncharacteristic cruelty, Patrice's father had sold her off to a family in Louisiana. Patrice's heart broke, and, though she wasn't privy to the particulars, she figured it played a major role in the change in her brother from an approachable companion to a closed-off duplicate of her father. She'd asked her mother once if Deacon and Jassy shared a love affair. The question scandalized the fragile woman into her bed for a week. Patrice never asked again and accepted the loss of Jassy's friendship the way she was forced to accept the other losses to come.

Jericho surprised her by becoming the one dependable presence at the Manor once things started to collapse under the weight of war. He'd stayed behind when the others slipped away in the night, oftentimes taking whatever they could carry. He'd stood beside her on the front porch to fend off marauders even as its support pillars flamed around them. They'd have starved, plain and simple, over the last winter if it hadn't been for his cleverness at foraging for food. And when word finally came of her father's death, and the two women were invited to stay at the Glade until Deacon's return, Jericho stayed behind to keep the home fires burning and to discourage those who would try to strip the bedraggled plantation to the very frame boards . . . not that there was much left to take.

She owed Jericho Smith everything.

He took the reins from her, giving the stallion an appraising sweep.

"This here looks like Mista Reeve's horse."

"It is."

"He come back then?"

"Yesterday."

Jericho and Reeve had spent many an hour in the Glade's stables discussing horseflesh and harnessing. They were as close to friends as men of different color could be. Patrice could tell there were more questions he wanted to ask, but trained as he was to hold his tongue, they remained unvoiced. Jericho patted the animal's damp neck.

"I give him a ration of feed, if we gots any."

"Thank you, Jericho."

"Was there something you be wanting here, Miss?"

Patrice shook her head. "Just wanted to . . . look around. To feel at home again."

Jericho nodded, needing no further explanation. Without another word, he led the horse toward what had once been the Manor's barns.

The front entrance of the majestic redbrick manor was gone, so Patrice made her way around to the side, purposefully not looking at the tangle of weeds that was once her mother's famed garden. One couldn't eat roses, and the time for beautiful objects that served no practical function was over. Nothing reminded her more graphically than stepping inside her once opulent home.

Sinclair Manor was built for grand entertaining, for displaying family wealth, taste, and power in every dripping crystal prism, in each framed Gainsborough, in every yard of Aubusson and imported strip of hand-painted wall covering. What the war left was big empty rooms, impractical for daily use, impossible to heat or clean. A roof that leaked, a larder filled with vacant shelves. A host of guest rooms inhabited by ghosts.

She walked lightly so her boots would make no sound in passing. The endless echoing disturbed her. She traced her hand along the graceful curve of the staircase, the sounds of her and Deacon's squeals as they slid down from the upper floor as faded as the soiled stair runner. The brass carpet rods were gone, she noted with a touch of sad dismay. Her mother had put so much pride in them.

The double parlor stood raped of its grand furnishings, but Patrice could yet see them. She could hear the sound of laughter, of music, the clink of champagne glasses carried about on large silver trays. She could picture the fine company, the best

Pride County had to offer, and feel the whisper of her best friend's excited words against her ear.

"Aren't they handsome?"

Patrice could see them through the parted draperies, following Starla Fairfax's hungry gaze to the gathering of young men sipping whiskey on the lawn. A sharp poke to the corset stays knocked her from her dreamy lethargy. Her friend chuckled knowingly.

"Which one?"

Patrice cast a guilty look at her smug neighbor, then tried to look indifferent. "Which one what?"

Starla laughed at her prim manner. "Which one of them pretty boys has you all hot and bothered?"

Hiding the flush of her cheeks behind a fluttering fan, Patrice's gaze was nonetheless drawn back to the boisterous group who pretended not to notice their fair audience. "I declare, Starla Fairfax, your talk is as bold as that neckline."

Starla was far from shamed. "My brother would love to think he's the one turning your head. Is he? Then we could be true sisters."

"Tyler?" Patrice frowned as she studied the lanky green-eyed devil with his sly smile and hundred-proof temper. He was a sweet eyeful, all dark, Creole beauty, sure enough, but Patrice knew him too well to be fooled by slick charm alone. "Your brother packs a kick more dangerous than that bourbon your daddy brews. A girl would be crazy to cast her hopes his way."

Not at all offended, Starla surveyed the others. "What about Noble?" She all but purred his name.

Patrice grinned, watching her friend's cat-eyed gaze scald over the magnificent picture Noble Banning presented in evening wear. He was the image of what every Southern gentleman should be; all straight, prideful bearing with the drawling manners of a natural leader and orator. She knew Starla harbored a secret fancy for him that was as unrequited as it was passionate within her girlish heart. She chuckled. "I wouldn't dare. You'd snatch me bald-headed if I so much as smiled in his direction."

"Oh, pooh, Trice. That's not true." But she seemed pleased despite her protest. She nodded then toward the impressive figure wearing his father's Mexican War saber on his hip. It made him look every inch the hero. "Mede? I declare, he makes hearts beat faster every time he flashes those dimples of his."

Patrice agreed. Lycomedes Wardell was built solid and square-jawed, as formidable in stature as he was shy in manner. A combination the county girls found devastating. But Patrice would never think of him as other than neighbor and friend.

And that narrowed the field of heartbreakers down to two.

"A smart girl would grab up Jonah Glendower. He's gonna be filthy rich, and he's been hanging around your front porch all summer hoping for a sign the feeling's mutual."

Patrice let her thoughts linger over the younger Glendower issue and she knew Starla was right. Jonah was bright as a newly minted eagle, with all his father's ambitions and influence. Conscientious, intellectual, well-bred and pedigreed to the envy of his farm's best stallions, he was her family's choice. But not hers.

"But safe don't excite a girl like you, Patrice. Not like ole Reeve Garrett does. I don't know what you see in that surly boy." She giggled. "Other than the obvious."

The obvious held Patrice's attention. Long legs meant to mold to saddle leather. Brawny arms and strong hands made to master the most rebellious mount. Dark tawny hair mussed by the whip of the breeze, straying into eyes as mysterious and deep as one of the Glade's peat bogs. And just as dangerous to one as careless of her own sure footing as Patrice tended to be.

Reeve Garrett, Byron Glendower's illegitimate son, a study of unapproachable angles—rugged, hard, without a trace of softness except when he extended one of his infrequent smiles.

The sight of him made Patrice breathless.

"What are you girls doing, peeking through the curtains like a couple of nosy housemaids?"

Starla groaned and stepped away from the window. "If it isn't Deacon Sinclair, come to preach what's right and proper. Is Deacon your name or your calling?"

That barbed quip faded from memory upon Patrice's sigh. She turned from the room full of ghosts, from the figures haunting her lawn a lifetime ago.

She couldn't quite make her self go upstairs where the memories were more personal, more difficult to manage. Instead, she crossed into her father's darkly paneled study. There, if she closed her eyes tight and inhaled, she could catch the hint of cigar and success lingering in the old wood and dusty volumes. His clipped voice resided in the tap of tree branches against the grimy panes.

"Patrice, you are a Sinclair. Never forget that and never let anyone else, either."

He'd made it a struggle to maintain that Sinclair

perfection. He'd almost lost Deacon, but at the end, his son had come around to be the brilliant protégé. She'd been the disappointment, always scoffing at tradition, always kicking up heels in the face of decorum. She hadn't understood back then the weight of responsibility that came along with the name Sinclair. It meant providing for those who depended upon you for strength. It meant being an example of what was right and good to those who were striving or uncertain. It meant wedding oneself to a lifestyle of privilege that became a prison of restraint. Such tremendous changes to make over the period of a few years. She needed to talk about them with someone who would understand the significance. She needed Deacon in a way she never had before. He'd gone through the same changes, and she wanted to ask how they'd felt, inside him. If he regretted the loss of his freedom to the shackles of duty.

She and her brother hadn't been close since childhood. She'd always sensed he was mildly disapproving of her, and, when younger, she'd enjoyed making his straitlaced sensibilities wince. Now, she yearned for the chance to feel his admiration, to hear him say he was proud of the woman she'd become.

The paint on the doorjamb scratched rough and cracked beneath her cheek. She leaned against its support the way she wished she could rely upon his presence, so stalwart, so sturdy. She wanted to weep, to wail, but in the end, constrained herself to a whisper.

"Deacon, please come home. I can't do it alone."

* * *

Dark clouds charcoaled the afternoon sky by the time she left the house. Approaching rain salted the air and cooled the breeze blowing against her skin, warning of a fast-brewing storm. Not wanting to get caught at the Manor in a deluge lest her absence frighten her mother, Patrice called to Jericho to bring her mount, anxious to be indoors when the heavens split in earnest.

But it wasn't Jericho who brought Zeus up to where she was impatiently waiting.

It was Reeve.

And he was mad as hell.

Chapter 4

❦❦❦

"**I** must not have heard you ask to borrow my horse," Reeve said casually enough. "Of course I'm sure it wasn't stealing, that being a hanging offense and all."

She had the nerve to look angry at him for demanding she make an accounting. It was, after all, his horse in her barn. He'd come all the way after them on foot, was tired, hot, and none too amused. And she stood there glaring bullets, furious with him because he dared question her right to what was his.

Her reply amazed him.

"I didn't think you'd mind."

He gave an incredulous laugh. "Not mind you running off with a purebred animal in a county crawling with thieves, cutthroats, and worse?"

Her delicate nostrils flared at his implication that the horse's and not her own safety had him so worried. Big blue eyes narrowed to ominous slits.

"I would have protected it with my life."

He snorted. "Then I'd have that on my conscience and no horse, either. No sensible female would parade herself around the countryside alone in times like these."

Her hands fisted at her sides. If she'd had a gun, Reeve figured he'd be sucking air through a new orifice. But better her angry than the other things he'd imagined while racing on foot to the Manor.

The horse never once crossed his mind.

"Jus' ask from now on, and I'll take you."

"You'll take me?"

He could see the clouds of her displeasure massing, piling darker and darker one atop the other, forming a magnificent thunderhead of rage. He waited stoically for the downpour.

"Ask you?"

Lightning strobed in her stare.

A smart man would take cover.

She drew a deep draft of air and let it blow.

"Who do you think you are, sir, to dictate when and where I go? *Ask you?* I'll do no such thing. Let you take me? I'd as soon walk as 'borrow' your horse or depend upon your charity. I want nothing from you, Reeve Garrett."

Though not the wisest thing to do, he crooked a cynical smile. "But my horse came in mighty handy, didn't it?"

Her teeth clenched tight. Her cheeks flamed as fiery as her hair. She started walking.

It was more stomp than stride.

Reeve watched with some appreciation, reminded of the impulsive girl who'd give way to tremendous—and foolhardy—tempers that made her act before thinking things through.

And foolhardy it was if she meant to march all the way back to the Glade wrapped only in her indignation.

Especially when it began to rain.

At first, the misty spray felt good upon her face, cooling her temper, restoring her reason. And it felt equally good to vent her temper for the first time since her pampered life was wrested from her. Then, the rain grew in intensity from gentle sprinkle to pummeling downpour.

Pride made a miserable umbrella.

Strands of wet hair plastered themselves to her face and clung coldly to the back of her stiffly held neck. She blinked rapidly to keep persistent drops from skewing her vision. Practical calico proved a poor shield against a steady rainfall. Her skin chilled. Her skirt sucked up more water than a thirsty sponge. Fabric dragged in the muddying drive, hampering bold steps, tangling about her legs like cold plasters.

By the time she reached the road, she seriously rethought her situation. Maybe she should turn around and seek shelter at the Manor rather than court pneumonia in the brutal weather. If the storm didn't settle in for the day, she'd have plenty of time to make it back to the Glade after the worst of it was over.

She squinted heavenward. A solid black mat hugged close to the shoulders of midday, offering no relief. She paused, feeling the ground seep up over the tops of her half boots. Time either to sink or surrender.

And then she heard the jingle of bridle tracings.

A quick glance confirmed the worst. Right behind her, Reeve slouched indolently in his saddle, looking not at all uncomfortable in the deluge.

"Like a ride, Miz Sinclair?"

Suddenly, she decided she'd surrendered quite enough to Reeve Garrett and those like him.

That determination kept her going for close to half a mile. By then, she was tripping on her sodden hem, blinded by the sluicing, endless stream of water runneling down her face. Lifting bags of bricks would be easier than wresting her feet, first one, then the other, out of the quicksand the road had become. Her muscles ached. Her knees wobbled. Breath clawed up her throat in ever more desperate struggles for escape. How she hated Reeve's mocking smugness, his patient stalking, as he waited for her to relent and beg his aid. How she despised him for forcing her to continue the ungainly floundering in muck nearly up to her knees. Let him watch, let him wait, let him laugh. She'd give him no satisfaction.

Then she spotted salvation at the bend of the road up ahead. A huge oak boasting a mammoth spread of branches waited, offering dry patches of ground between gnarled tunnels of overgrown roots. Focused upon those arid patches of grass, she started when Zeus suddenly moved up beside her. Stopping in the wallow of mud, she grimaced up into the flood of rain to see a broad, callused palm stretched down to her.

"Enough of this. Give me your hand."

Thinking of that dry nook only yards away, she glared at his hand. "I do not need your assistance, Mister Garrett."

"Patrice." Warning growled from him.

Then the air around them concussed with a sound so huge and light so blindingly bright, Patrice thought for a moment that they'd been hit by cannon fire. Zeus reared away in panic. Reeve fought to bring the animal under control as Patrice crouched with palms pressed over her ears. In a frantic daze, she looked about, stunned to see that giant oak had split asunder. Twin halves peeled back from a center core, smoking from the bolt that cleaved it in two. Sparks crackled through the air in a maddened dance, then all was still except the rain and the pounding of her heart.

She stared at the spot where she might have been crushed had Reeve not stopped her.

She didn't protest when Reeve leaned down from the saddle to draw her up in front of him. Numbed by her close brush with death and chilled to the bone, she lacked the strength to muster a rebellion. She wanted to get to the Glade, where warmth and welcome waited. And if that meant sharing the saddle with her enemy, it was now a necessary sacrifice.

Until he slipped off his Union jacket.

The instant it settled about her shoulders, a sensation of security seeped in along with the lingering heat from his body. Wool abraded her chafed skin the way its Federal blue color rubbed her pride raw. It occurred to her to shrug it off in a gesture of contempt, but he must have guessed her train of thought, for he pulled it tight, buttoning it to trap her inside its protective folds.

Patrice sat rigidly balanced atop his thighs, caught between the brace of powerful forearms. Awareness of him beat through her veins the way the rain peppered her unprotected face, icy hot and impossible to ignore.

Without the covering of his jacket, Reeve's shirt fit against him with an almost transparent wetness, delineating each muscular swell and intriguing hollow. The usual tousle of his untamed hair was slicked back with satin luster. A dappling of moisture highlighted the angles of his face and caught in the stubble at his chin. As close as she was, she could see whorls of desire darkening his irises despite his ruthlessly held control. Evidence of it squared along his jawline and thinned his lips into a narrow, negating slash. He didn't like the pull of intensity any more than she did.

His large hand opened at the back of her head, cupping it, compelling it to bow and seek shelter against his shoulder.

She should have turned away, denying what snapped between them in that unguarded moment to prove he had no power over her emotions.

Instead, she bent.

Her cheek nestled into the lea between shoulder and throat, finding a comfortable valley in which to rest. Immediately, she felt the bunch of his thighs as he nudged Zeus into a cautious lope as the steadying curl of his arms kept her close. But though safe in that coddled embrace, Patrice found no relaxation.

She'd always felt the basic attraction between them, something hot and animal and impossible to explain. It had nothing to do with the warmth and respect she felt for Jonah. It was somehow beyond the respectable and perhaps that was why, in her reckless youth, it was so alluring. No matter how earnestly she flirted with the rest of her Pride

County beaux, Reeve Garrett claimed her undivided notice. Escorted into the dazzling affairs the Glade hosted before the war, she was oblivious to the music, the finery, and the witty conversation of her current partner. She homed in like a bird dog on the scent to the scruffily handsome outcast as he stood outside with the drivers and grooms, sharing liquor out of cornhusk-bound jugs instead of champagne from crystal at Byron Glendower's side. By his choice. Always by his choice.

She'd catch him watching her as she swayed up the wide stone steps in her hoops and frills, bare shoulders gleaming in the candlelight, her gloved hands curled upon some gentleman's forearm. And he'd nod, that infuriatingly bland smile a mockery of everything she'd hoped to inspire in him after hours of tedious preparation. She always dressed for him, determined just once to wake the blind devotion she stirred with little effort in every other eligible male in the county. Only Reeve seemed impervious. And how that galled her. How that made her want him all the more.

She felt his heartbeats, hard and strong, where the weight of his arm pressed her to him, and she wondered now, as she'd wondered then, what it would take to make that heart pound like a racehorse's hooves in the final stretch. He was always so calm, so controlled it made her feel all the more foolish for her giddy lusting. For being unable to forget the thrill of being in his arms after she'd goaded him into teaching her about kissing. But that was before she made her official debut in society

There were times when she believed she'd imagined it all, that he'd never been the least bit interested in her. And then, she'd catch him staring at the oddest times with a look so hungry, so fierce, it scared as much as it excited. Again, by choice, he hadn't acted upon what she'd seen in his eyes.

And now, she could not allow him to.

She compromised her every angry word and vow by lingering against him, absorbing the heat, the power, the joy of his nearness. But on a private, selfish level, she didn't care. She'd wanted to be held like this forever. She'd underestimated his effect on her will. It melted like butter with that first inhalation of wet wool mixed with his own hot, musky scent. She'd berate herself later, but for now, she couldn't shun the opportunity to bask in pleasures long imagined.

Byron Glendower watched them come up the drive.

He'd been standing at the parlor window for some time, sipping whiskey, indulging in sorrow and uncertain sentiment. He didn't know what to do about Reeve. He never had.

His one great wish was to create a capable heir for the Glade. A selfish want, that desire of a man to immortalize his achievements by leaving a part of himself behind to attend them. Toward that end, he'd married young, to a delicate creature with whom he'd only a nodding acquaintance. She was of a fine pedigree, bringing the wealth and prestige he needed to carve out a monument to the name Glendower. But after three miscarriages, he began to fear he'd have no one to inherit his dream.

Then he met Abigail Garrett, an attractive widow whose needlework was renowned in Pride County. While arranging for her to outfit his wife for a new season, they began a passionate affair which culminated in the birth of a son. A fine, strapping son, the kind a man boasted of . . . or would if it were his legitimate issue. Foolishly, he tried to convince Abigail to relinquish the boy into his care, but the proud woman would have none of that. The best he could do was provide her a cabin upon the Glade's many acres, a place where he could watch over the boy at a judicious distance.

And then his wife gave birth to a legal heir. A boy. A small, spindly child of continued ill health. A child much like he had been.

The irony of it. The boy every man dreamed of just out of reach. A weak child of uncertain future holding all his hopes.

His wife knew of Abigail and the boy, but women accepted such things without comment. And he kept to his vow not to resume his affair once a legitimate heir was produced.

He hadn't meant to hurt either his wife or his son with his blatant favoritism, but Reeve, without trying to, far overshadowed his half brother. He was strong as an ox, courageous to a fault, honorable and dependable as the day was long. He understood the land, and the livestock loved him. The perfect son in all but name. And that, Reeve refused as stubbornly as his mother. Cautious, remote, and suspicious of his father's motives, he refused to give homage or love, only labor.

He'd tried to love both sons equally, but it was difficult when all he could see were Reeve's strengths and Jonah's weaknesses. He watched with unconcealed delight as Reeve developed a natural gift for dealing with horses. His disappointment was apparent when, despite his best efforts, Jonah couldn't overcome his fear of them. Then the accident happened. And Jonah was forever handicapped with a shortened leg and obvious limp.

He couldn't fault Jonah for not trying his hardest to please him. What the boy lacked in physical prowess, he made up for in mental acuity. He worked miracles with the Glade's books, then went on to establish the county's first bank. His charity and kindness earned the love of all, and Byron tried to be one of them. But he couldn't quite forgive the frail Jonah for not being Reeve. He tried to make up for that lack of affection by showering him with admiration. He hoped he succeeded.

Then, Byron saw a way around Jonah's shortcomings. If he couldn't be the sturdy heir Byron desired, than perhaps he could pass that wish down to the next generation. A fit, prime grandson. And he saw Patrice Sinclair as the perfect mate to bring about that accomplishment. Of blooded stock and sturdy lineage, she had more than enough vinegar and spirit to make up for what Jonah lacked. He couldn't have been happier to announce the engagement to friends and family. And for the first time, he embraced Jonah with genuine fondness.

Then Reeve brought Jonah home for burial.

Terrible words were exchanged at that grave site. Byron wasn't sure which spurred his fury, the fact that Reeve had taken an active part in the death of his heir, or that Reeve, his treasured son, his pride, had failed to stand by him and his beliefs, defying him openly to join the enemy cause. That choice stunned him and embarrassed him before his neighbors, leaving him in the awkward position of how to explain when he couldn't. It broke his heart.

Now Reeve was back, and a mixture of resentment and relief twisted though him. Here, he had another chance at a future for the Glade. To take it meant swallowing the humiliation of having his son turn against him, the insult of Reeve's refusal to apologize for his part in all their miseries.

But there was so much to gain in the balance.

At the moment, he had nothing but the roof over his head and a tax debt he couldn't meet. His labor force was gone, fleeing down Freedom Road. The only blooded animal on the farm belonged to Reeve, and therein lay all his hopes. Though they'd argued about everything for years, he knew Reeve loved the Glade with a fierceness to rival his own. And he knew he could count on the boy to do the impossible to bring things around again.

But he didn't know how to tie him both to family and farm until he saw him ride in with Patrice Sinclair across the saddle.

He hadn't believed anything could get them that close together. A fiery, willful girl, Patrice never shied away from speaking of her hatred for "that lousy, cowardly traitor." He granted her those forthright opinions. Since the engagement, she felt like family to him, prompting his invitation for her and her mother to stay at the Glade.

It came to him. A stroke of inspiration.

Patrice Sinclair. He liked her. He knew she would have been good for Jonah.

Would she be equally good for Reeve?

A future could yet be bred at the Glade, a future generation, strong and fit and proud.

All he had to do was convince Reeve and Patrice to fulfill their part by getting past the tremendous obstacle of Jonah's death. To give him the grandchildren he demanded.

Which would be about as easy as getting the county to accept Reeve back into their fold.

The fact that Reeve made no attempt at conversation made the ride easier for Patrice. She didn't want to make pleasant small talk with him. Nothing about their verbal exchanges was pleasant. The silence allowed her to lose herself in escape, to feel, to experience the strength of a man's arms, especially *this* man's arms. But the moment was over.

"You can let me down now."

The firm band about her waist didn't ease.

"I'll take you right up to the door."

Being delivered to the front steps on the lap of Reeve Garrett held no great appeal. A stalemate ensued, her twisting in irritation, him refusing to relent because he was suddenly enthralled with the feel of her damp curves rolling against him.

"Put me down now."

Her sharp tone held the authoritative snap one used to chastise a displeasing servant. For an instant, his arm tightened, mashing her to his hard chest, just to prove he was in control of her descent. Then abruptly he let her go. Without the support of his arm to position her, the moment he relaxed his knee, she slid forward into empty air like a clumsy flightless bird in sodden feathers. She landed on her feet with a jaw clacking impact, arms pinwheeling for purchase as damp skirt and petticoat mummified her legs together. She caught Reeve's boot as her heels slid out from under her. Then came the indignity of him grabbing on to the back of her jacket to lift her up and brusquely deposit her on her feet.

"It would have been a mite easier for me to let you off at the door, but suit yourself."

He gave a tug on the jacket collar, forcing her to lift her arms so he could strip it off her as if he were unmaking a rumpled bed.

Exposed to the cold rain once more, she stood shivering, glaring up at him. "Thank you kindly for the ride."

His lips gave a slight twist. "My pleasure, Miz Sinclair."

She was about to turn loose the tide of her temper when the sight of another soggy rider coming down the drive distracted her. Reeve followed her puzzled stare.

"Expectin' someone?" His hand drifted down toward the pistol on his hip. Just in case.

"No. Who'd be crazy enough to go out in this weather."

He was about to point out her own folly when she gasped, a strange little sound somewhere between a strangled sob and a glad cry. Then she was running, her heavy skirts hoisted up out of the muck, her feet flying.

Reeve squinted at the approaching figure, recognizing but not knowing quite who it was. A shabby soldier, like thousands he'd seen on the road, gaunt, whiskered, riding a broken-down excuse for a cart horse. Probably another beggar looking for a hot meal and a night out of the weather.

Something about the angle of his shoulders defied the term vagabond. Though his head ducked to let the rain roll forward off his hat brim, a prideful starch straightened his spine.

"Deacon!"

Even without her joyous shout, Reeve knew him,

for the instant he saw her racing toward him, the rider lifted his head. A heavy beard couldn't disguise the patrician features and ice-cold eyes of Deacon Sinclair, come home to claim his family.

Chapter 5

He stepped down off his winded mount just in time for Patrice to slam into him, all twining arms and salty tears. He rocked from the velocity, then, after a moment's pause, he lifted his arms wearily to enfold her in a circle tight enough to seal out the rain and the world. His head bent slowly, turning so his cheek found rest atop her wet hair. And a long, satisfied sigh escaped him.

"Deacon—"

Patrice tried to look up at him, but his embrace banded more securely, his palm controlling the cant of her head as he whispered a hoarse, "Not yet."

She relaxed against him, hands kneading the threadbare fabric of his coat, losing herself along his long-boned lines. Still not quite believing he was there. Alive. Finally, he angled to press a nearly nonexistent kiss upon her brow.

When he stepped back, Patrice felt instantly vulnerable once more. Her voice trembled.

"You look terrible."

"I smell worse. This is my first bath in months."

She touched his haggard face. It was wet. From the rain, he'd say. "I'm not sure I like the beard."

"It'll be the first to go, right after these clothes."

Did he mean the uniform he'd ridden away in with such pride? She frowned slightly, palms stroking over the gray wool with its fortuitous lack of bullet holes.

He glanced toward the house. "They told me in town that you and Mother were here." Then his gaze touched upon Reeve, who watched the two of them inscrutably from a distance, his Union coat draped over his shoulders. The muscles of Deacon's jaw flexed beneath the stubble. "That he was here, too."

Patrice rubbed his forearms to distract him. She wanted nothing to sully their reunion. And she wasn't ready to have her ride with Reeve examined, either by her shrewd brother or within the uncertainty of her own heart. Better to let the issue slip away. "Come up to the house. Mama will be so thrilled to see you."

They walked side by side, Patrice tucked in beneath the curl of his arm, her own snug about his middle. The used-up horse trailed behind them. Deacon spared Reeve another glance when they came nearer, the kind of look one gave an invisible servant.

"Take care of the horse."

Delivered with an offhand indifference, the command fell flat.

"Didn't you hear that Lincoln freed the slaves?"

Deacon stopped. A deceptive stillness came over

his face. His eyes glinted, ice over slate. Reeve didn't relent beneath that saber-sharp glare. He met it with a cool repartee of his own, and said, "Ask me. Don't tell me."

"*Please*."

Another beat of challenge passed. Afraid she'd have to throw herself between them, Patrice tugged at her brother. She didn't want his homecoming to dissolve into a fistfight in the mud. She cast an impatient look at Reeve. Only when her gaze took on an edge of entreaty, did he respond. Without a change of expression, he reached for the sorry creature's reins, his comment low, and to Patrice, a puzzle.

"I'd never walk away to let another suffer for my arrogance."

Deacon stood rigid as one of the plantation's pillars. It obviously meant something to him. But before the confrontation could develop, Patrice hauled on his arm.

"Deacon, I'm soaked clear through. Could we go up to the house now?"

He backed down incrementally, movements still stiff, like a bristled dog being pulled away from a rival. Patrice jerked hard to break the steady fix of the two men's stares. Then Deacon came obligingly to enter the dry confines of the Glade.

There, he surrendered to his mother's embrace, resting his head upon her shoulder like the needy boy he hadn't been for many years.

He ate to satisfy a long-starved need. Though clean-shaven and wearing a set of Jonah's clothes that he couldn't have squeezed into before the war began, though he was meticulous in manner, a dif-

ference in her brother bothered Patrice. She couldn't
name it. He'd always kept his emotions closed off
from those around him, even those he cared for, but
now she sensed a deeper remoteness, a void that
scared her.

He never said what part he played in the defense
of the South. Through the first years of the conflict,
he'd stayed in Pride County, sporting no uniform,
no rank, but a secretive silence that whispered of
important business. Business one didn't ask after.
Just glad to have him home when so many Southern
women were left to their own devices, Patrice never
questioned him. But she worried.

It wasn't until after Jonah's death that he appeared one day in officer's regalia to announce he
had things to take care of in the Confederate capital.
A subtle edge of danger hung upon that cool statement, warning them not to ask his reasons. Again,
they didn't . . . they were afraid to. Patrice wondered. Her brother had a gift, a certain blankness
that shut off the exchange between heart and mind.

And she hoped he wasn't an assassin.

She thought he'd be terrifyingly good at it.

They had letters, few and far between. His words
echoed vague sentiments. He mentioned the weather in whatever state he'd been in and promised their
mother he had plenty to eat. He wrote them about
his father's death, a letter so stark and stripped of
feeling it might well have been a telegram from the
government. Then, for the last year, nothing.

And it was clear that Deacon meant to go on as
if the past four years never happened.

"As soon as the weather breaks, I'm heading to
the Manor. I understand it's still standing."

"I've seen to it." Patrice straightened beneath his cool perusal, pride surging when he allowed her a thin smile.

"You're more than welcome to remain here."

"No disrespect, Squire, but I'd like to have my family at home as soon as possible."

"None taken. Whatever I have is at your disposal. We weren't as hard hit as some of our neighbors." He broke off in embarrassment. He didn't need to finish. They all knew it was because Reeve served the Union cause. That kept the scourge of Yankee scavengers from their door.

"What I'm going to need is man power. I heard tell all our darkies ran off at Abe Lincoln's call."

"All but Jericho," Patrice told him. "I don't think I could have held on without his help."

Deacon nodded. "He's a good man."

"I wish I could help you there, son," Byron continued, "but I'm no better set than you. Reeve's the only pair of capable hands I have, and you're welcome to use him . . . if he's agreeable."

Deacon never blinked. "I don't think it will come to that."

Byron Glendower sat unhappily at his table. With the reappearance of Deacon Sinclair, he saw his influence over Patrice about to end. Deacon would never allow a match between his sister and a man considered the county traitor. As long as Reeve was out of favor in the community, matrimony was inconceivable.

So he had to find a way to make Reeve more palatable to his neighbors.

It was going to be like forcing castor oil down their throats.

Might as well start now while taste buds were coated with a fine meal.

"We've had so little chance to celebrate anything. I'd like to throw open the doors of the Glade and invite all our friends and neighbors . . . a welcome home for Deacon and our other brave boys."

Deacon's features turned to granite. *Like Reeve?* was the question in his frost gray eyes.

Byron pretended not to read it there.

"Once everyone's here, if it gets out that you need help, I'm sure you'll get it. The boys of this county pull together. Always have."

"Those of us who are left."

Refusing to let the mood go sour, Patrice turned to her mother with a feigned excitement. "I think a party would be wonderful, don't you, Mama? And we could arrange everything, Squire, a sort of thank-you for all you've done for us these past months."

Byron smiled at her. "I'll leave everything in your capable hands then." Because she was playing right into his.

Patrice stepped out onto the broad front porch, letting the door close quietly behind her. Deacon stood at the stone steps, hands stuffed in his pockets, shoulders slightly rounded, a casual pose that on him struck her as vaguely alarming. He stared off into space, focusing on nothing in particular, looking a little lost.

"Deacon?"

When he turned, there was something in his expression she'd never seen before. A certain wistfulness, maybe even sadness. Surprisingly, he didn't conceal it behind the stoic mask he always wore.

Instead, he waited, more approachable than she could ever remember, for her to come to him. She touched his forearm in a hesitant overture. His hand slid out of hiding to engulf hers in an unexpected press. He didn't let go.

Warmed and mystified, Patrice said, "It still surprises me to see you here. I'd almost given up hope."

"So had I. More than once."

It must have been very, very bad for him to make such an admission. She gave him time to say more, but he didn't. She wasn't surprised by his silence. He would never share his weaknesses with her. He wouldn't know how.

"So you plan to rebuild the Manor?"

"Of course. Father would expect me to." At the mention of their father, the stiffness crept back into his joints, straightening him, steeling his features into confident angles of strength and purpose. His fingers loosened about hers but she wasn't ready to release him yet.

"Just for Father?"

"For us. It's our home. And it's mine, now." He said that carefully, testing the sound of it. *Mine*. Liking it. His posture squared up even more, and, with an abrupt revolution toward the distant location of their home, he managed to pull his hand free. "I'll start with the house and the necessities, then get the mill going again. The acres will have to wait because the tax collectors won't. I'm not going to lose it, not an acre, not an inch." And it could have been her father standing there, speaking with such cold ferocity.

As much as she regretted the loss of the openness of moments ago, Patrice took comfort in his authoritative stance. She no longer had to make the decisions. After all the years she spent chafing within the role of the pampered sex, she took refuge in it now, grateful for the strong male support and leadership her brother supplied. And equally determined to do nothing to make his task of rebuilding harder.

Suddenly, the topic of conversation shifted, startling Patrice.

"What were you doing with Garrett?"

Taken off guard, she had no time to construct a palatable lie. "He gave me a ride back from the Manor, that's all. I went over this morning to check on things and got caught up in the storm. Nothing for you to get all bothered about."

"And he just happened by."

"I don't know." Her tone sharpened defensively. Her cheeks heated. "Maybe."

"More like he was following you. What does he want from you? Forgiveness? Don't involve yourself with him, Patrice. Don't forget what he is, what he's done."

She skewered him with a bitter glare. "I don't need you to remind me, Deacon. I can't look at him without remembering how he's ruined my life."

Inexplicably, her brother's mood softened. "I'm sorry, 'Trice." His fingertips grazed her shoulder, their touch tentative, his manner awkward with both the gesture and the apology. "Has it been hard for you having him here?"

This time, she sidled away to block his clear view of her expression. "Not too bad. He doesn't come up to the house. I can almost pretend he doesn't exist." What a blatant lie that was. Absently, she rubbed the ring on her left hand and gave a slight jump when Deacon's clasp covered hers.

"Your life isn't ruined, Patrice. Another man will come along who can make you as happy as you deserve to be."

A soft sob choked up in her throat. With one swift move, she spun and hugged to him. That, he hadn't prepared for. He went rigid.

"I love you, Deacon. I'm so glad you're home."

Gradually, his own arms banded her within a loose circle, this one as reserved as the first had been impulsive. "We're not home, not yet. But we will be, I promise you. You and Mother will be taken care of. I'll see to it. I'll see to everything." And his vow sounded more like a vendetta than a goal.

Reeve sat in the semidarkness of the stable, pieces of harnessing strewn all around him. Meticulously, he cleaned and oiled each strip, polished each buckle before reassembling the unit and making it good as new. At least, he tried. Some were beyond repair, too cracked and neglected to take back the shine and suppleness of care.

Here in the moist warmth of the stalls, he could lose himself in the familiar. It was a world he took comfort in, one he could control. Not like the fancy goings-on up at the house.

It shouldn't have mattered that Deacon Sinclair was back. They had never been friends. Deacon was of a society unto himself, preferring to walk above the rest of humanity rather than among them. If there was any trace of humanity in him at all. Reeve had reason to doubt.

Yet Patrice welcomed him back as a hero, looking right past the stains of war bloodying her brother's hands. He and Deacon carried the same sins, yet the other's were forgiven. Such predictable irony.

He tried not to think of Jonah, but his shadow was always there, right behind his every feeling, his every move. Even after two years, the questions nagged at Reeve, insistent, like a wound refusing to heal. What prompted Jonah to step from his own neutrality into the face of war—on the wrong side?

He picked up a bridle and started to disassemble it. He couldn't get the headpiece free, the buckle frozen in a caking of rust. He worked at it, bending, tugging at the leather.

Damn Jonah, anyway. Why hadn't he stood by his beliefs and stayed alive to marry Patrice and become the next master of the Glade like he was supposed to? Anger surfaced in a scalding wave, an anger at Jonah for putting him back into an impossible position by choosing to die. Tempting him with what was always beyond his reach.

He threw the damaged harness to the ground. It was beyond repair. Just like his relationship with Patrice.

The heat was there, all right. Enough heat to burn the Glade down around them the way Sherman had Atlanta. He'd been scorched by the fit of her against him, the way her breasts flattened upon his chest, the curve of her hips notched in between his thighs, the tininess of her waist surrounded by the brawn of his arm. She made a man's passions ache like a bad tooth. But that was wanting, not loving. And for him, it was permanence or nothing.

So, he figured wryly, he might as well get used to the ache.

In dying, Jonah Glendower was as big—if not

bigger—obstacle than he had been when he was alive.

"Reeve?"

Caught up in his brooding, he hadn't heard anyone approach. He reared back, startled, wondering anxiously what had shown on his face in those few unguarded moments. Byron Glendower was the last one he wanted to allow any control over his weaknesses.

But the squire seemed preoccupied with whatever was on his own mind. "Reeve, we need to talk."

Recovered now, Reeve regarded him with a flat stare. "So talk."

"Not here. Up at the house."

Reeve tensed, suspicions alerted. "Here's fine." Here, he'd be on his own terms, not off-balance in his father's world.

But perhaps that's what the squire had in mind when he insisted, "What I have to say can't be said here. I'll be waiting in my study . . . You have time to clean up first."

And then he was gone, leaving Reeve unsettled.

What kind of interview required clean clothes and the main house?

He wasn't sure he wanted to know.

Chapter 6

⟡

Though he'd lived at the Glade all his life, Reeve's visits to the main house were rare and probably countable on one hand. Coming up from the barns, bringing the scents of horse and toil with him to spite the subtle order to make himself presentable, Reeve tromped across the pastel rugs, leaving a trail of muck, straw, and worse without a twinge of conscience. He wasn't a guest, so he didn't figure he had to dress like one. He was responding to a summons, not an invitation for tea.

Byron looked up from the paperwork strewn on his desk to give his son a thorough scrutiny. He couldn't fail to miss the significance of the dirty boots and well-worn clothing. Though his expression remained rigid with disapproval, inwardly he was pleased by the show of rebellion. He liked fight. He admired pride. And he'd never been so impressed with his son as he was right now as he stood squared off and ready for battle.

"Sit down, Reeve."

"I'll stand. I don't want soil your fine furniture, sir."

"It's going to be yours to soil, so sit."

Reeve was taken aback for a moment, just as Byron intended. Emotions flickered through his son's steady stare, foremost among them wariness, surprise, and, not missing, just a snap of anticipation. That was good. He gestured toward the chair opposite his huge walnut desk. Reeve came forward with a stiff reluctance to settle on the edge of the leather seat. Although his palms rested easily on his thighs, his posture remained spring-loaded.

"We've said some pretty harsh things to one another since you got home," the squire began. "Let's put that behind us."

Reeve studied him for a long moment, trying to read behind every nuance of his words. He came away unsatisfied. "Sounds simple."

"It could be. If you'd be willing."

"Why should I be, Squire?"

Byron frowned. "Would it be so hard for you to call me Father?"

"Yes."

The crack of Reeve's answer warned he was moving too fast. He backed up and began again at a more leisurely pace.

"We haven't agreed on much in the past, but I believe when it comes to the Glade, both of us have common ground. We've both put sweat and time and patience into this place, and we've both felt the pride of a job well-done. Will you give me that much?''

Reeve hesitated, then allowed a brusque, ''Yes.''

''Good. We've both done our parts, you from down there, me from up here. And we both deserve to reap a reward for our efforts.'' He watched Reeve's eyes narrow with caution. ''Only right now, there isn't much reward to be had, only more hard work and more commitment. That's what's ahead of us, boy.''

No facial response, but Byron could see Reeve's grip tighten on his pant legs as he leaned slightly forward. Listening.

''If you put in the work with me, I think you're entitled to share in the reward. Don't you?''

''What would that be?''

Byron spread his hands wide, offering the ultimate reward. ''All this. The Glade.''

He heard the breath hiss from between Reeve's teeth. But his gaze was still wolf-cautious with distrust and disbelief. ''You want to give me your farm?'' he restated softly.

''Our farm, Reeve. If you won't take it as my son, then earn it from me. I can't bear the thought of it falling into a stranger's hands.''

Reeve's expression twitched in equal distaste. Still, he was far from receptive. ''What would I have to do to earn it, providing I'm interested.''

Oh, he was interested, all right. His stare glittered. His hands worked restlessly against the rough fabric of his Federal-issue trousers. He'd done everything but snap at the offer like a hungry predator. But knowing Reeve as he did, it was too soon to relax. Coaxing wasn't the same as capturing. He might have tempted his wary son up onto the porch, but he was a long way from getting him inside. And that's where Byron wanted him.

He smiled. "Nothing you haven't been doing already."

It was too neat, too easy. Reeve circled the offer mentally, sniffing at it, nudging it, expecting a trap. He'd never had anything just handed to him free of charge before. There had to be a catch.

What if there wasn't?

His palms grew damp. He buffed them nervously against his pants. Something didn't feel right, and he refused to give in to hope until he found out what little sacrifice he was going to have to make.

"That's it?"

"That's it. What do think?"

He leaned back in the chair, giving himself time to assess the situation. The squire appeared easy with the terms, his expression open and without guile. Then why were his fingertips lightly tapping the surface of his desk. Tapping. Tapping. Anxious. Like the quivering jaws of a bear trap about to be sprung.

Not on his neck.

"I'll think about it."

Glendower's features clenched in impatience but, ever the negotiator, he managed to nod. "You do that, Reeve."

Reeve waited, but nothing followed. His father sat regarding him with a bland smile, business concluded and content with the postponement. A prickle of uneasiness shivered along his skin, a feeling of being fixed in a sniper's sites while he watched for a clean killing shot.

"I'll let you know." Reeve stood slowly, not daring to consider the proposal while yet in the squire's office. He knew there was something else crouched just out of sight, some little something that would spoil the whole deal. His father had been so careful not to bring up Jonah or loyalty or even shared blood. He approached it like a straightforward arrangement of services for pay. And that's what Reeve wanted, wasn't it? No complications, no surrendering of personal honor? Why the reluctance then? Why didn't he just say yes?

Perhaps because he knew his father too well.

He was halfway to the door when the other shoe dropped.

"Reeve, there's a condition I should mention."

Reining in his wry smile, Reeve turned back to face the elder schemer. "And it is?"

"It's not just the Glade I've been working my whole life to build, it's the name Glendower, as well."

Reeve's mood hardened like concrete.

The squire hurried on. "I don't expect you to make any changes now. You've made your opinion on that very clear. But when I'm in the ground, I want a Glendower living in this house. If not a son, then a grandson bearing my name."

Reeve's snort of amazement became a harsh laugh. "So it's the bloodline that has you worried." He shook his head. "Your vanity is unbelievable. No, I take that back. I believe it. And knowing you, you probably have the perfect broodmare already picked out to beget you that heir."

"Patrice Sinclair."

The blunt reply rocked him harder than a blow to the midsection. He could do no more for several seconds than gape in shock. Jonah's fiancée. Then he laughed again, a bitter sound this time.

"Did it occur to you that she hates my guts? What did you plan on doing? Cross-tying her in a stall while I mount her like one of your servicing studs?"

"There's no need for such crudity."

"You'd better believe there's a need, 'cause there's no other way she'd ever let me within spitting range, let alone close enough to sow the seeds of your immortality."

"Don't underestimate the situation, boy. Miss Sinclair has plenty of reasons to be agreeable." The squire actually smiled then, and that scared Reeve to death.

And it shot a thrill of expectation clear through him.

Glendower's confident smile widened. "You chew on it for a while, Reeve. Then we'll talk again."

Reeve found himself standing in the hall, stunned lightning-struck stupid by what had transpired.

He could have everything! The Glade, Patrice, the Glendower name.

Everything.

Except the respect that went with those things.

His elation withered like bluestem in the first hard freeze.

He didn't mind the hard work. No one worked harder than he could toward a goal. He knew the land, he knew horses . . . and he knew the people of Pride County.

The squire looked up in surprise as Reeve strode into his study, walking straight up to plant his palms firm on the big desk.

"I musta been crazy to even consider what you

had in mind. Nobody buys me off like breeding stock."

"Reeve," Byron said reasonably, "that's not what I intended."

"No? Then why does it feel like you've just made me your new whore?"

He watched the color ebb from his father's face, that dead white replaced by a slow-rising red. Behind thick spectacles, his eyes slitted in fury. Remarkably, he held to his temper as he spoke slowly, forcefully.

"If you feel that way, don't place the blame on me. I made an honorable offer to you. If you want to make it into something ugly, I can't stop you. But you consider this, Reeve. How else can a man like you even think to hold what I'm prepared to give you? You think chances like this come along like the crocuses every spring? This is it. This is your only way out of that cabin and into a decent life. You've made it impossible for me to give it to you any other way. There it is. Take it, if you're man enough to hold it, or leave it if you're the coward the people of this county are going to say you are."

"They won't accept me."

"Make them."

"I'm not one of them."

"Don't underestimate the power of my name. You're my son, and no one refuses me."

"They'll say I had Jonah killed, so I could have his inheritance."

Glendower went very still. "Did you?"

"No."

"Then prove it to them."

"How?"

"One at a time. One at a time. You told me you

were staying because of obligation to Jonah. What better way to honor Jonah's memory than by taking care of the woman he loved? You can give her the things he meant to give her, things she has no chance of getting now, the way things stand."

He could hear his own words, spoken thickly in earnest. *I don't want to take your place at the Glade. I never wanted that.* Breathing hard, mind spinning frantically, Reeve made tight circles like an animal with its leg caught in jaws of steel. The pressure ground down on him, cutting, tearing painfully. Part of him screamed for him to chew it off and gain his freedom while he could. Another whispered that the pain would ease if he'd relax and accept. He stopped his pacing and faced his father.

"I have a condition, too."

"Thought you might. Let's hear it."

"Patrice can't know anything about this. She's got to want me for myself, not because I've got the Glade and the money to save her family. I won't have her making that sacrifice. I won't go through the rest of my life . . . not knowing."

Byron didn't say anything. Frown lines gathered between his brows.

"That's it. Take it or leave it. If she can't forgive me, there's no point in me having all this, 'cause you won't get your grandchild."

Panic stirred in the squire's expression. "There are other women . . ."

"No. Just Patrice. It's her or the deal's off. You get to buy me, not her. She has to want this for herself. That's my condition."

A long minute passed, then another. Then Byron Glendower extended his hand.

"Done."

Reeve looked at that outstretched hand, seeing his future there within that uncallused palm. And once those fingers closed about his hand, he would be imprisoned there forever, never able to free himself from the grasp of this greedy, ambitious man.

Everything he ever wanted. All he had to do was take it.

His father's grip was surprisingly strong. One press of flesh to flesh, then the contact ended.

And Reeve had the awful suspicion that he'd just shaken hands with the devil in exchange for his soul.

"I want you to move up to the house."

Reeve recoiled from that suggestion. "Why?"

"It would look better. How do you expect to mingle with the cream of the county while living down in the woods like spoiled milk?"

He bristled in offense at the words while realizing their truth. "All right." And with that, he was committing himself to change, to a loss of self. And to the pursuit of Patrice Sinclair.

The magnitude of what he'd done didn't settle in until he was closing up the cabin. It had happened so fast. Once the momentum got ahold of him he'd been sucked under quicker than a sand bog. The crafty old man knew just what strings to pull to make him dance. And he'd been stepping to a lively jig.

"Mama, what have I done? Did I do the wrong thing? Did I do it for the wrong reasons?"

He sank into his mother's chair, closing his eyes as his head rested against the high, carved, wood back. The movement of the chair continued to and fro, a soothing repetition that worked its calming magic upon the frantic beats of his heart, quieting his fretfulness just as it had when he was a child.

Wasn't he doing what Abigail Garrett had always wanted? Hadn't her most ardent wish been for him to be one of the Glendower family? She'd urged him since the time he was old enough to understand what the word illegitimate meant to talk to his father to get a piece of his future guaranteed. His flat refusal broke her heart.

How could he accept a name that was too good for his own mother to claim? By moving up to the big house and becoming Byron Glendower's child, he was distancing himself from the woman who bore him. And though Byron's legal wife was never rude to him, he always saw a terrible fear lingering in her manner, a fear that he would usurp her son's place in his father's heart and will. He couldn't blame the woman for her resentment. The entire situation created strife . . . with Byron manipulating them all from its center.

But his mother was gone, and his actions couldn't hurt her. There was no Mrs. Glendower to shame with his presence, no Jonah to compromise with the competition for their father's love. There was just the Glade and an old man looking to go on forever by continuing his line. And if he could benefit from that, why shouldn't he?

And then as he was carrying his meager belongings up the central staircase toward the room the squire had assigned him, he happened to glance up and see Patrice standing there on the second-floor landing.

It was as if that picture had been waiting there in his heart for the right time for him to step into it. Patrice Sinclair Garrett Glendower, hostess of his home, love of his life, mother of his children. And the notion that soon she could be waiting there for him, escorting him to a room they shared, to a bed they christened with love and the seeds of eternity sent a chilling dizziness through him. He paused there on the steps, breathing deeply to control his careening expectations.

Slowly, as she took in the significance of his presence and his belongings, the expression on Patrice's lovely face altered from surprise to one of contemptuous loathing. And she turned from him without a word.

From somewhere down the lengthy hall, he heard a door slam upon all his hopes.

Chapter 7

——❦——

Deacon Sinclair stopped in his tracks at the sight of Reeve Garrett, reins in hand, planted on the wagon's seat. Scowling fiercely, he stalked to the horse's head to grip the leads.

"The squire told me I could have the wagon to head over to the Manor this morning."

"That's where I'm headed. Ain't got all day. Climb aboard."

"What?"

"How many times you actually lift an axe, Deacon? A hammer? Pounded a nail for yourself?" Reeve smirked. "That's what I thought. Squire asked me to go along to see you didn't hurt yourself."

"I don't need you." Though still calm, Deacon's voice was edged with an icy sharpness.

"Yes, you do," Reeve drawled out, unconcerned with the other's objections. "If you want to move

your family home anytime soon, you need me.
Sooner it gets fixed up, sooner you're out of here.
You're a smart man, Deke. That should make sense
to you."

Deacon's frown deepened because it did make
perfect sense. And better Garrett stay where he
could keep an eye on him instead of remaining here
where unchaperoned meetings with his sister were
more than likely.

"Move over," he growled. Without a word, Reeve
complied, snapping down the reins on Zeus's back
before Deacon got settled, nearly tossing him over
the seat back onto the stack of lumber in the bed.

Their partnership was off to a good start.

Reeve kept his opinions on the future of Sinclair
Manor to himself. There was no way Deacon, with
his lack of practical skills, could ever make it livable
again. Not with the equipment at hand and the lack
of pure grunt labor. Deacon was a soft aristocrat
used to wielding his authority, not his muscle. He
didn't know the first thing about building or actual
physical endeavor. Reeve shook his head to himself
as he pulled on his heavy gloves. Patrice was going
to need a place for her and her delicate mother to
live. It wouldn't be here at the Manor, it would be
with him at the Glade.

Deacon could fend for himself.

He watched the stiff and proper owner of all the
disrepair circle around from the back, scanning the
eaves as if he had a notion of what he was looking
for. Reeve waited for him to pronounce his findings,
ready to pounce upon them as statements of ignorance.

Deacon stopped just short of standing next to him and cut right to it.

"Looks like the soffits are gone. There's dry rot all over the west wing and the brick is in bad shape there by the south corner. Both will need to be replaced. Roof probably leaks, but I haven't gone up under the eaves yet. That burned entryway needs to come down. And that's just the outside. If I can get it buttoned up tight, I can worry about the interior rooms another time."

Reeve gawked at him.

Deacon spared him a wry glance. "Did you think I spent all that time at school learning to taste wine? Man's got to know what he's dealing with, and right now, I'm dealing with a house that going to fall down around our ears unless some quick work is done."

"I'd say you're right."

Without asking for suggestions, Deacon walked to the wagon to grab out several long coils of rope.

Hearing a soft tread come up behind him, Reeve turned to Jericho. He jerked his head toward Deacon. "He know what he's doing?"

Jericho nodded. "My guess would be he does. Mista Deacon, he don' start nothin' lessen he looks at every angle first. Either jump in, Mista Reeve, or gets outta the way."

Deacon strode by them on his way to the front of the house. He carried a three-pronged hook and was threading the heavy rope through a large eye in its handle. "Jericho, I'm going to need some pry bars. Have we got anything like that left around here?"

"Yessir, I believes we do."

Taking a firm stance, he played out a length of

hemp, then balanced the hook in his right hand. With a powerful sidearm throw, he let it fly. Reeve watched in amazement as the hook swung around one of the ruined pillars to affix itself to its own tail. Deacon gave a sharp tug to make sure it was secured before looking to Reeve.

"Will that horse of yours pull on command?"

Catching his direction, Reeve nodded, and soon Zeus was tethered to the rope with Reeve at its lead while Deacon and Jericho worked levers under the base of the scorched column. At a signal from Deacon, Reeve guided the horse forward until the rope yanked taut and the animal began to strain.

"C'mon, Zeus. Dig in."

Slowly, the timbers creaked, and plastering fell in huge chunks. With a great groan, half the front porch came down in a dusty heap. Ruefully admitting to the logical genius, Reeve backed Zeus to slacken the rope so Deacon could lasso the other support pillar. The second portion didn't come down cleanly, the column breaking apart in the center with the heavy triangular entablature still attached to the upper story upon dangerously damaged supports.

Muttering an impatient oath, Deacon waved Reeve to the far side of the tottering structure, then arced the rope over the top to him. And they both began to pull. Nails screeched loose from brick. Weakened boards snapped. The whole thing groaned, hanging precariously, as if by some denying force of gravity.

"Jericho, get that bar between the brick and those timbers," Reeve called out. "We go on three."

Deacon set his feet, spat in his palms, then grabbed hold of the rope, nodding.

"One . . . two . . ."

Another voice cut in sharply. A woman's voice. "Deacon, move on back from there. You're too close."

". . . three."

And as Patrice watched in horror from the back of her brother's scruffy mount, she saw the entablature collapse almost in slow motion, parts of it dropping straight, other pieces breaking off before plummeting downward—right at Deacon. As she screamed his name, he threw up his arms to protect his head just an instant before the debris knocked him to the ground.

Reeve and Jericho were already pitching boards off him when Patrice knelt at her brother's side.

"Deacon? Deacon? Is he all right?"

A moan answered her, then a curt, "Get off me. I'm fine. We're wasting time here."

"He's all right," Reeve said with a touch of dry amusement as he levered off the last of the wood. Then he wasn't smiling. "Deke, don't move."

"I'm fine. Let me up so we can get back to—"

The heel of Reeve's hand struck his shoulder with a stay-put force, pinning him to the ground.

"What do you think you're—"

Deacon's angry sputter died off at the sound of Patrice's gasp.

"Oh, Lord . . . Deacon, do what he says!"

Deacon followed her wild-eyed stare and paled dramatically.

A long, jagged splinter pierced the meat of his forearm just below the wrist, exiting near his elbow, where the rest of it was buried deep in the dirt, holding his left arm erect like a flagpole. If not for his instinctive cover-up, the lethal spear would have gone straight into his chest. Fatally. Deacon stared at it, shock numbing him from the full brunt of pain . . . for the moment.

"Jericho, hold him down."

Deacon turned toward Reeve. "What are you—?" The rest was lost as Reeve cuffed his wrist, braced his upper arm with his other hand and pulled up firmly. Surprise and a sudden flame of agony tore a raw cry from him.

Reeve had his big knife out to cut away coat and shirtsleeves. Patrice gave a low moan and looked away.

"We've got to get him to town. He needs a doctor."

Recovering himself, Deacon said, "I don't have time to go to town. It's not deep. Just pull it out."

Reeve was examining it more closely. "An' leave hundreds of little splinters you'll have to dig out later? It's your arm, Deke. You want to lose it?"

"Have you got a better suggestion, Garrett?" Deacon hissed between clenched teeth. He was hurting now, in great throbbing waves from shoulder to fingertips. The later were trembling uncontrollably.

"It's just below the skin. If I cut a groove above it, I should be able just to lift it out."

"Reeve, you can't."

Deacon's head tossed restlessly side to side. "Do it."

"But Deacon—"

Deacon held up his good hand for his sister's frantic grasp. "It's all right, Patrice. He knows what he's doing. Don't you?"

Reeve looked to Jericho. "You got any alcohol, any whiskey around here? A needle and some thread?'' When Jericho nodded and ran to get what was needed, Reeve positioned Patrice so that she was kneeling with her brother's head on her lap, her knees bearing down on his shoulders. Reeve lifted the injured arm, placing it atop Deacon's rapidly moving chest, then looked into the sweat-slicked face.

"You gonna hold together for this?"

Deacon drew a single deep breath, and his entire system steadied. He regarded Reeve with a cool, flat gaze.

"Do it."

"Patrice, you hang on to his hand and elbow. Don't let him move."

"I won't move," came Deacon's cold assurance.

No, Reeve thought, *he probably won't*. And he started to cut. Deacon never made a sound, his arm never twitched as the blade opened skin and muscle to expose the wicked shard of wood. Reeve picked it out carefully, then took the bottle of rye Jericho handed him.

"This is going to—"

Deacon cut through his quiet warning. "Just do it."

As harsh liquor washed over the open wound, Deacon's breath sucked in and held, his body going rigid until it was done. Then, slowly, he relaxed, never making a noise even while suffering the fires of hell. Reeve stared at him, impressed by the show of control.

No wonder he'd made such a damn good spy for the Confederacy.

He turned his attention back to the wound. "Looks clean. It'll need stitching."

"Patrice can do it."

Seeing her sudden pallor, Reeve took the needle and thread. "I will."

"No." Patrice took the sewing materials from him, her voice surprisingly level. "I'll do it. I'm sure my talents with the needle are superior to yours."

And while her brother lay motionless on the ground, his eyes closed, his breathing regular, she stitched up his arm as if attaching lace to a cotillion gown. Her hands were steady, her stitches small and even, as good as his mother's, Reeve thought with approval. And when it was done, she made a good knot and bit off the remaining thread.

Deacon sat up gradually and flexed his arm. "Nice work. You'd have made a good field surgeon." His praise won a faint smile. He glanced over at the mess they'd made of the front entrance to his home. "Start clearing that away while Patrice binds me up."

Reeve stared at him, incredulously, but Jericho went right to work.

"You don't mean to stay?"

Deacon returned his look with one of mild irritation. "Of course, I do. I want to check that roof and patch what I can before nightfall."

Reeve wondered if it was brutal Reb training or his own background that made Deacon Sinclair such a hard piece of work.

In a matter of five minutes, his arm bandaged in strips torn from his own shirt, Deacon was up in the attic looking for leaks. And his sister was tying up her hair under a broad-brimmed hat. For the first time, Reeve got a good look at her. And he couldn't look away.

She wore pants. He was so startled by the surprising sensuality of those britches on her curves that his tone came out sounding angry.

"Does your mama know you left the house lookin' like that?"

"I am not a little girl under her mama's thumb anymore, if you hadn't noticed."

If he hadn't noticed before, he was noticing now. No, there was nothing childish about Patrice Sinclair. Just as hardship had weathered her soft skin, years had matured her softly feminine figure. Gentle swells were toned by physical efforts. No sign of the coquette showed in her confident stance. And there was no question of the effect those trousers had on his celibate state. It was turn away or disgrace himself.

"You'd best head back to the Glade. We got no tea parties to give here today."

She surprised him by gripping his arm and jerking him back around to face her. Her expression was fierce.

"This is my home, Reeve Garrett. No one tells me to leave." She tugged on heavy work gloves, the kind field hands used while cutting crops. "I have things to do. If you want tea, you'll just have to make your own."

She made it all the way around the back of the house before the chills started in. Knowing she was out of sight, Patrice allowed her knees to give way, going down on them in the overgrown grasses. Leaning forward onto the brace of her palms, her head hanging low while blood pounded between her temples, she let the shivers of sickness have their way. All the horror she'd pushed aside quivered up through her. Her stomach roiled. Her vision filled with a swelling sea of red.

Then, gentle hands cupped her elbows, lifting her into a swallowing embrace. She leaned gratefully into it, recognizing the hard planes on a purely sensory level even as her mind whirled in weak spirals.

"Close your eyes," came a quiet crooning. "It'll pass in a minute."

She surrendered herself to that suggestion. And eventually, the seesaw of sickness slowed and steadied, so she could take a calming breath. Her palms raised, resting upon the smooth bunch of his muscular arms. Holding on while her world righted itself. And she heard herself speak a raspy confession.

"I didn't go to war. I've never seen such sights. Reeve, what happened to my brother to make him so . . . so . . ." She couldn't find the word to describe the frightening lack of humanity in Deacon Sinclair.

"Don't know about Deacon, Patrice. But war changes men. It changed all of us."

Patrice couldn't take comfort in Reeve's explanation because the war hadn't changed her brother, it only accentuated the disturbing qualities of aloofness he'd already possessed. She pushed away, and Reeve let her go.

"I don't want him to see me like this," she murmured, wiping at her reddened eyes with a sleeve.

"Why?" Reeve's hand grazed the curve of her cheek. She went still as his rough thumb rubbed away the remaining wetness. "You look beautiful."

Patrice's gaze widened in sudden panic . . . and pleasure. She wanted nothing more desperately than to press into that big open palm, to allow them both this intimate moment. Her hand covered his. And drew it firmly down. Bowing her head slightly to break from his intense stare, she said, "Thank you for helping my brother. It was very kind of you."

A pause. She wondered if he was annoyed by her change of topic to one of an impersonal tone. Then he answered expressionlessly.

"He would have done the same for me."

Patrice didn't reply. Because she wasn't sure Deacon would have lifted a finger. She started to stand, and Reeve was quick to provide a strong bolster beneath her elbows. His touch didn't remain once she was on her feet, but she could feel the warmth, the power of his hands lingering against vulnerable flesh and vulnerable heart. Knowing both must harden to get her through the rest of the day, Patrice turned from him without further words, going back to the business that brought her to the Manor. Part of that business was pretending her foolish pulse wasn't racing with feverish excitement as she rubbed her palms over the places his hands rested. Pretending she didn't ache to feel them elsewhere, everywhere.

Scowling at her own misguided passions, she applied the pry bar to rotted wood with a destructive relish.

Reeve watched them work, stubborn and determined brother and sister. He admired their vigor even as he recognized the futility. A few replaced boards and a slathering of tar weren't going to return Sinclair Manor to its glory days. The whole world had changed, at least in the South. He didn't think they understood that yet.

"I'm gonna have to be leavin' soon, Mista Reeve."

He glanced up at Jericho, surprise evident. "Guess that'd be your choice now, Jericho, but you know how much these folks need you."

"I knows that. Miz Patrice and I, we had ourselves an arrangement. I stays on and helps her hold the place for Mista Deacon. Well, he be back, and I be thinkin' it's time for me to get on to my own work."

"You got a job waiting somewhere?"

Jericho's dark features firmed, and a fierce light gleamed in his eyes. "I surely do. One I been waiting to tend to for a lot of years."

A man didn't ask another man his business, so Reeve said nothing more except, "We'll all miss you, Jericho."

"This been like a home to me, Mista Reeve. It ain't easy to walk away. I reckon you understands that."

Reeve nodded grimly. Though they weren't the same color, they'd suffered along the same line of prejudice keeping them on the outside looking in.

"But home be family, Mista Reeve, and I gots family out there awaiting for me to find 'em."

"Your sister?"

"I ain't seen her for nigh on ten years."

"You know where to look?"

"I heard tell them folks that—bought her moved down Texas way. Guess that's where I'll be going. There ain't nothing for me here."

Reeve nodded. "I'll be hoping good things for you, Jericho." He knew the cost the other man was about to pay, that severing of soul it took to walk away. "Before you go, stop on by the Glade, and I'll see you get supplies. You got a horse?"

"I got two feet, and they's free to come and go. I thank you for the offer. I be hanging on here, just for a little bit, just to see Miz Patrice gets settled."

He cast a knowing glance at Reeve. "You gonna be seeing to that?"

Reeve allowed a small smile. "That's my plan."

The dark head nodded toward the roof, where Deacon was spreading on hot sealant to the weak spots. "He ain't gonna like it no more than his daddy liked the idea of him and Jassy."

"He's not the one who has me worried."

Chapter 8

For the second day, Patrice pried loose rotted boards until her shoulders ached and blisters formed atop blisters on her once satin-soft hands. Surprisingly, she enjoyed the work, the sense of participation in the rebuilding of their home. At the same time, she had to wonder what kind of life they'd have once they were back in the Manor.

As much as she wanted to believe that Deacon could save their family from debt and decline, she knew the hard facts. The pampered daughter of Avery Sinclair wouldn't have lost a second of sleep to worry. She was no longer that sheltered girl. She'd spent the past years grubbing for just the basics of survival, not the extravagances they used to take for granted. Wearing a gown to more than one occasion she'd once considered a tragedy. Now tragedy was what she glimpsed in her brother's eyes when she caught him unawares. Tragedy was choosing between buying food for the next meal or fixing shoes which had long since worn through on the bottom. But she had nothing to replace them with. And now Deacon talked about restoring luxuries. What were luxuries compared to shoes without holes?

She straightened and stretched in hopes of relieving the soreness plaguing her every move. So much left to do. She gave a soft laugh. Patrice Sinclair, belle of Pride County, battling wood rot with her bare hands.

"What's so funny?"

She smiled at her brother and shook her head, gesturing at her mannish clothes and tanned skin. "All this. It's either laugh or cry, and I've shed too many tears already."

His sweat-dappled brow furrowed in frustration and concern. "Why don't you go back to the Glade and help Mother plan her party." Obviously that's where he felt she belonged, embroiled in the frivolous while he shouldered the world alone. His sentiments touched her but were quickly dismissed.

"Mama doesn't need me to help her pick a color scheme, but this wall isn't going to repair itself."

"I can do it."

"Deacon, you can't do it all by yourself. No one can. I'm fit and I'm strong and I'm willing to work. Don't treat me like some fragile flower. This is my home, too. I love every board, every shingle just as much as you do. I've stood off marauders; I've dug potatoes with my bare hands, I've watched our people leave us, families I helped Mama bring into the world and cared for like they were our own. That was hard. This isn't hard."

His lean features flexed. Angry words were directed at himself for his own failure to provide.

"You shouldn't have to do any of those things. It's my place to see you don't have to."

"Not anymore, Deacon. We need each other now, don't you see that? Those days are gone and are never coming back."

He spun away from her. She could see the denying tension in his shoulders, his inner struggle in the clenching of his hands. "Yes, they will. I promised our father I'd carry on just as he would have. He wouldn't allow you to dig potatoes or pull down rotten boards."

"Then who's going to, Deacon? Look around. Do you see anyone else waiting to take my place so I can go have my hair rinsed with rainwater and set in paper curls while I'm bleaching my skin with buttermilk? Do you see a dozen men hanging on your every order, your every whim? Not anymore. There's just me, Deacon, and you and all this work to be done however best we can handle it."

He took a gulping breath. "I don't like it. I don't like watching you work like a field hand. I don't like seeing my home falling apart while I don't have so much as a penny to put it back together. I don't like knowing that I went off to war and came home to nothing."

"I don't like it either, Deacon. But I'm not going to let it stop me from doing what needs to be done."

He circled around and dropped down heavily upon the top step of the rear porch. Patrice sat between the spraddle of his knees, pulling his arms about her until he was leaning against her back. After a moment, he laid his cheek upon her shoulder and she felt a monumental sigh leave him.

"Oh, Deacon, we can't go back to what was, but we can go on to something new."

"I don't know anything else, Patrice. I was raised to control a plantation, not lay bricks. I'm so tired. I just wanted to come home to things they way they used to be."

"I know." She reached back to stroke his hair, to caress his cheek, pausing when she felt his fevered skin. "Deacon, are you all right?"

Not catching her concern, he rambled on in a disjointed tone. "I've done things, Patrice, things you could never forgive or come close to understanding. I thought they were the right things but now . . . Maybe this is my punishment, the punishment for my pride."

Not listening, Patrice swiveled on the step to place her palm to his damp brow. "How long have you had this fever?"

He blinked at her incomprehensibly.

"Deacon, you're burning up. How long have you been sick?"

"I'm all right." To prove it, he started to push away, gathering his feet beneath him, only to topple back in an uncoordinated sprawl. When he made no attempt to lift up again, Patrice did the only thing she could think of.

"Reeve!"

Deacon's eyes opened, their focus gone, their color flaming brightly. "I don't need him. I'm fine. Patrice, I'm—" His gaze did a slow loop and rolled up white.

Then Reeve was kneeling beside her. One look at the sweat-slicked face had him pushing up Deacon's shirtsleeve.

"What is it? Reeve?"

By then he'd bared the wound with its hot, reddened edges. The slightest pressure brought a noxious oozing from the stitched seam and an anxious moan from Deacon. Reeve had seen the signs a thousand times, and they weren't good.

"The wound's gone bad. It's poisoned his blood."

"But he'll be all right. Reeve? He'll be all right."

He glanced up, expression somber. A ragged wail tore from Patrice.

"No! I won't lose him. You tell me he'll be all right. Reeve, tell me!"

He couldn't lie to her. "I'll do what I can."

"That's not good enough! You tell me he won't die!"

"I can't."

She looked down upon her brother's flushed face. He was close to insensible now, as chills started working up through him. Wild with despair, she begged, "Then do what you can. Please, Reeve. Do what you can."

He called for Jericho, and the two of them carried Deacon inside, stretching him out on a chaise that had been brought into the front parlor. There was no time to take him back to the comforts of the Glade when his life balanced upon each passing minute.

"Jericho, your mama had a poultice she used to use for drawing out poisons. Do you remember how it was made?"

"Sure do."

"Show Miz Patrice how to make it." When Patrice balked, he pushed her toward Jericho. "Show her now."

"C'mon, Missy Patrice. I'll show you where to find the right herbs."

Reluctantly, she went with him, leaving her brother in Reeve's care. Grateful for her absence, considering what he had to do next, Reeve lit a candle then drew his knife, holding the blade in the flame until the metal glowed white-hot. When he turned back to the chaise, Deacon's stare was on him with a fixed intensity.

"Gotta reopen the wound so it can drain proper," he said with a calming firmness, then carefully moved Deacon's arm into position. He never expected Deacon's cool reply.

"No, you aren't."

Reeve never saw it coming. He was bending over, concentrating on the exposed injury. The blow struck like lightning, knocking him to hands and knees, his head ringing. He grunted as Deacon's boot smashed into his ribs but retained enough control to grab onto his foot. When Deacon tried to lunge over him, he yanked hard, and Deacon met the ground with a crashing thud. Then, despite his fever, or because of it, Deacon began scrambling toward the door, toward the rifle Jericho left leaning there.

"Son of a—"

Reeve shook off the effects of the first punch and dived to intercept. He landed across Deacon's legs, hanging on when he began to writhe and kick. Then Deacon rolled, and, looking into the bared saber steel of his glare, Reeve realized what a coldly efficient killing machine they'd made him. Without a sound, Deacon drove his palm up beneath Reeve's chin, clacking his teeth together with jarring force and momentarily putting out the lights. He followed with a vicious backhanded blow, but Reeve wouldn't be shaken. If Deacon got his hands on the rifle, he wouldn't hesitate a heartbeat before blowing him to hell. He had to be stopped, and there was no easy way to do it.

As Deacon's thumbs gouged for his eyes, Reeve slammed his head once, twice, upon the floorboards but the other wouldn't relent. He was unbelievably strong and fast, the mannered Southern gentleman swallowed up in dark, lethal purpose and momentarily fueled by fever madness. Reeve had his wrists, pinning them down, but Deacon butted him in the face, skewing his vision. As he tried to lever back on his elbows to reach the door, Reeve hit him, once to get his attention, twice to stop him. But he kept fighting with a tigerish tenacity.

"Deacon, stop! It's over! It's over!"

"No!" The word snarled from Deacon as he twisted onto his belly, then abruptly went still. " 'Trice, get the gun!"

Startled by the violence she'd come upon, Patrice dropped the basket of herbs she carried to snatch up the ancient rifle in response to the urgency in her brother's voice.

"Shoot him, 'Trice! He's trying to kill me. Like he did Jonah. Shoot him!"

Unaware of doing so, Patrice threw the rifle butt up to her shoulder, her finger taut on the trigger. She sighted down the barrel . . . right into Reeve's uplifted face. And hesitated.

"Shoot him!" Deacon screamed at her, his face a mass of bruising and blood. Deacon, her brother. She took aim again.

"Put it down, Patrice," came Reeve's steady command. "He's out of his head. Help me with him."

The rifle wavered.

"Patrice, for God's sake, don't let him fool you! You know what he is. He's the enemy. He's our enemy. Don't let him stop me. I have to get through."

Through? What was he talking about? She lowered the gun. Seeing her surrender, Deacon gave up his fight, closing his eyes with a wretched moan. Reeve said a brief prayer of thanksgiving and motioned to Jericho, who'd just come up behind Patrice.

"Help me get him back to the couch."

They got no protest as they settled him once more. His eyes opened fleetingly, gaze touching upon his sister as he whispered hoarsely, "How could you betray me? I'll never forgive you. I have to get through. I have to get through."

Seeing he was clearly delirious, Patrice set the rifle aside, the rush of fright still tingling through her. Then she knew a moment of doubt as Reeve drew his knife once more. He met her anxious gaze, his chiding her.

"Jericho, hold his arm. We've got to let the poisons out before the sickness gets any worse."

It was done quickly, with only a rattly groan from Deacon as his awareness slipped beyond the capacity for pain. She jumped to comply with Reeve's order to prepare the poultices. After she wrapped the steaming cloth about her brother's arm, she felt the probe of Reeve's gaze and glanced up in answer.

"Glad you decided I wasn't the enemy. Took long enough."

Patrice didn't smile. "I decided you weren't trying to kill my brother. That doesn't make you any less the enemy."

* * *

While Patrice sat with Deacon, keeping close watch on his soaring fever and replacing the poultices as they cooled, Reeve went back to work on the house. The physical release helped loosen the knots in his gut.

She'd almost shot him. For an infinitesimal instant he'd seen it in her eyes; enough hate, enough fury, enough courage to pull the trigger.

Not a real encouraging way to start a courtship.

He hammered fiercely, stopping only to suck at his thumb after it interfered with a downward swing. The pulse of pain helped him focus beyond the coil of his emotions.

What was he thinking? How could he hope to win the favor of these people when he couldn't earn their trust?

It was Deacon mucking up his hopes of romance. Deacon with his shadowy government past and murderous intentions. Such a prideful man despised losing. And he, with his Union blues and less than humble manner, was salt in those arrogant wounds.

Patrice loved her ice-cold brother, despite the lack of returned warmth. She saw him as her salvation.

So what was the point?

He was slaving over the home of a man who wanted him dead, to earn the love of a woman who resented all that he stood for.

What a fool he was.

Best he get the damned house habitable and move them on in and out of his life. Then he could get on with it.

But there was no appeal to getting on with life without Patrice.

She was the reason he'd come home.

Having her glare down the barrel of that gun scared the bejesus out of him. But it also quickened a pride and passion inside him that wouldn't be ignored. Here, he thought, in those moments he feared might be his last, is a woman worth loving, a woman worth risking everything to have. Her tremendous fire, her compassion, her common sense, her unwavering loyalty. To possess those things, to possess her . . .

But Deacon wasn't the only obstacle in his way.

There was Jonah, too. And that was something the two of them had to confront if time was ever going to bleed the poisons from her heart. Or the guilt from his.

Patrice laid another hot compress on her brother's arm, then sank down upon the floorboards next to his inert form. She touched his damp cheek and hoped she didn't just imagine a lessening in his temperature.

He was going to get better. She refused to consider the alternatives. Death. Amputation. Reeve didn't mention it, but she'd seen enough empty sleeves in Pride County to know the threat was real.

Tears wobbled upon the edge of her lashes, but she blinked them determinedly away. She wouldn't cry for what might be when what already was had taken such a toll of sorrow. Her brother was here with her, he was strong, a fighter.

"Oh, Deacon don't give up. I'll stand by you. We'll get through this." She didn't say how. She didn't know how.

Resting her head upon the rolled edge of the chaise, Patrice closed weary eyes to allow a moment of reflection. For so long, she had only had time to act. Now was the time to think, to plan. So much hinged upon Deacon, and she was afraid for him. He and all those who'd fought a losing war had to do battle again, this time against wildly inflated prices, smothering taxation, the destruction of their livelihoods, and—most damaging—the loss of their pride. To a Southern man, pride was all. Such men had no experience in humility and loss. She'd never known her brother to admit a mistake or apologize for a wrongdoing.

How, then, were they to survive?

"Is he better?"

The sound of Reeve's voice brought back the magnitude of what she'd been ready to do at Deacon's command. For a moment, she didn't respond, unsure of how she could and still save face. She'd been ready to kill him. In her panicked need to protect Deacon and her instinctive obedience to her brother's will, she'd been prepared to take a life. She glanced up slowly, knowing the right thing to do was apologize, to beg his forgiveness for her misrepresentation of the circumstance.

But the instant she beheld him, the words dammed up tight in her throat, caught behind a wedge of Sinclair pride. And at that moment, she understood completely how conflicted her brother must be between heart and mind.

She said nothing about what had almost happened.

"He seems to be."

Reeve waited, expectation bringing a lift to one brow. Obviously, this was where she was to throw herself at his feet in humility, pleading excuses for her brother's behavior.

Her shoulders squared, supporting the haughty

hoist of her chin. She wouldn't beg for what was well deserved. How dare Reeve Garrett demand sympathy after his part in their misery? Union soldiers had ravaged their home. Union arrogance had turned her brother into the dark, nearly soulless man who'd come home to her. Reeve's allegiance to the Union cause had cost her the man she was to marry. He *was* their enemy and not worthy of their trust.

But he had saved her brother's life.

"Thank you for what you did for Deacon."

The terse concession coaxed a faint curl of amusement. "For what? Tending to him, or seeing that he don't hang for murder?"

A bolt of outrage shot up Patrice's spine as Reeve bowed slightly and left the room. She glared after him, her chest heaving with indignation. The nerve! The gall!

The truth! She took a quick breath.

If either she or Deacon managed to pull the trigger, killing a former Federal soldier, martial law would place a noose around their necks without asking if they had reason for what was done.

In saving his own life, Reeve had spared theirs.

The starch went out of her proud righteousness. She was no better than any of the stiff-necked Rebs sulking over their defeat. She'd let pride dictate her reactions.

What hope did any of them have when dying with conceit was preferable to surviving in humility?

Chapter 9

~~~⌒◯⌒~~~

They came from all across Pride County, arriving in wagons, on foot, some even in the carriages that used to bring them there before the war. They came wearing taffetas shaken out for the first time in years, frock coats shiny with wear, and Kentucky or Tennessee regiment gray, ill fitting, patched, but proudly borne. They came out of the need of a social people to group together, pretending nothing had changed, to grumble and exchange stories.

And they came to get a look at the Yankee murderer living under the Glendower roof.

Acting hostess at her mother's side, Patrice silently thanked her mother for talking her out of wearing a widow's black in Jonah's memory. Hannah insisted the occasion be one for rebirth, not a funeral dirge, and produced lengths of treasured dove gray silk with silver lace for trim. In its off-

the-shoulder elegance, Patrice attended her first
party as a woman matured instead of a giddy
young girl full of dreams. As she greeted old friends
with a smile and extended hand, directing the ladies
to the receiving room and the gentleman to Byron's
study, where cigar smoke and laughter rolled out
in an ever-growing cloud, she caught herself sweeping the front steps and the shadows for a figure con-
spicuously absent. And gauging from the tension in
each guest, they were all wondering the same thing;
where was Reeve Garrett and would he dare put in
an appearance?

Squire Glendower spared no expense in re-
creating the former glory of their county. He hired
a string ensemble down from Louisville, and lilting
strains of "Shenandoah" danced upon air redolent
with the sweetness of spring blossoms. Though no
liveried house servants circulated through the
crowd, well-placed tables offered a dry Madeira
and lemonade punch, discreetly laced with Fairfax
Bourbon. The finger food wasn't elaborate but plen-
tiful, providing the best meal some of their neighbors had had for years. Conversation sparkled with
an atmosphere of family reunion, a mood Patrice
feared would spoil soon enough if Reeve showed
up in Federal blue.

"Might I say you ladies look lovely."

Both Sinclair women turned, smiling, toward
Deacon. He cut a suave figure in his officer's uniform, which Hannah had painstakingly cleaned and
formally creased. He surrounded himself with an
air of old-world elegance and precise manner. Patrice noted with some surprise how handsome her
brother was, with his long lines, lean muscle, and
self-enclosed stance. Pleasantly average looks honed

to a striking intensity of rapier intelligence and brooding purpose held the romantically inclined females of Pride County at bay. He intimidated without trying, lorded his superiority without conscious effort. And she wondered if any woman could garner the gumption to shake him out of his emotional exile. That was a woman she'd like to meet.

He offered mother and sister each an elbow to escort them inside the Glendower ballroom. Patrice took his left carefully, mindful of the sling he yet wore. He'd recovered quickly, casting off the infection faster than the distasteful obligation he had to the man who'd saved his life. He had nothing to say to Reeve, and Reeve made it easier by staying away.

Couples paired up for the first Virginia reel. Hannah blushed like a schoolgirl at Byron Glendower's invitation to join him in the promenade. She hung back, thinking perhaps it wasn't proper so soon after her husband's death.

"Go on, Mama," Patrice urged. "Remember what you told me. We're here to celebrate the future, not look back upon the past."

At that encouragement, Hannah shyly took their host's arm and was led away. Patrice sighed happily, not at all aggrieved to have only her brother's company.

"She looks better, don't you think?" At Deacon's noncommittal mutter, she said, "This is good for her, getting out with people, getting on with things."

Deacon's gaze followed the whirling couples. His expression remained remote. "They make it look easy."

She rubbed the rigidly upright column of his

back. "It could be. If you'd let it. Don't we all deserve a little reprieve from the sorrow and suffering?"

When he didn't reply, she decided a little teasing was in order to route his melancholy.

"You don't need to stand guard over me, Deacon. I declare, one look at your scowling face would scare away any chance I have of finding a suitor."

He blinked down at her, startled, missing the jest until her devilish grin betrayed her. She gave him a slight push.

"Go away. Go find some sweet lonely thing and charm her into taking a walk in the gardens with you."

"My, my, that sounds like right fine advice to me, darlin'."

Warm hands caressed the caps of her bare shoulders as intimately as the sultry agreement. Patrice turned to find herself within the coil of Tyler Fairfax's arms. Though his green eyes glittered from more than a prudent share of his daddy's whiskey, his smile was all honey-sweet irreverence. A powder keg of trouble, with his mama's swarthy Creole heritage, he could always charm his away around her irritation, just like his sister. She looked behind him, hopefully.

"Where's Starla? Is she with you?"

"*Mais non, chère.* Baby sister is still over in Chattanooga with some of Daddy's family. But she did tell me to see you was thoroughly entertained this evening."

Deacon closed his hand over one of Tyler's, drawing it off Patrice's shoulder. Ice tinged his casually spoken words. "I doubt she'd find a walk in the garden with you all that entertaining."

Tyler grinned wide. "Why, Reverend Sinclair, how would you know unless you tried it yourself? I pity a man who takes himself so seriously."

"Better than being a man whom everyone takes as a joke."

Tyler's jovial expression didn't alter, but a hard brilliance turned his eyes to emerald jewels. "Perhaps you'd like to share that joke with me, Deacon."

Patrice angled between them and snatched up Tyler's hands. "What we're going to share is this next dance." She pulled a practiced pout. "Unless you don't want to dance with me."

Tyler responded gallantly, twining her arm around his. "Why, darlin', I'd have to be a dead man not to want you. For a dance, that is."

She laughed, then shot her glowering brother a "behave yourself" glare as Tyler led her out onto the floor.

As they waltzed, Tyler managed both to annoy with his too tight embrace and delight with his sassy humor. She knew what he was—a sly, unreliable drunkard with dangerous colleagues and a badly scarred past, a man with no allegiance except to himself and his sister, and no compunctions about smiling as he fed a friend poison. But she couldn't help liking him. She'd seen a deep-seated sweetness he allowed to escape on rare occasions, such as playing sensitive confidant to both her and Starla as they struggled with youthful fancies. However, the dark streak of his temper struck without warning, making his mood unpredictable and those who knew him wary.

But now, as he moved her about the floor pressing as close as he dared, he was all charm and dimples, and Patrice let herself enjoy his company.

"Tyler Fairfax, please step back, sir. There is not room inside this dress for the both of us."

"Ummm. There could be."

She shimmied to discourage his fingers from playing about the back fastenings to her gown.

"Is there a woman over the age of twelve and under ninety who hasn't slapped your face?"

"There are a few, darlin'. A few," came his cocky boast.

"I am not plannin' to be one of them. And if you don't let some air pass between us, my brother is going to give you more than a polite little love tap on the cheek."

"I ain't afraid of your brother." Still, he backed up an inch or two. "Besides, lookin' the way you do tonight, it just might be worth it."

"If I for one minute took you seriously, you'd run like a rabbit in the other direction."

His smile flashed white and wide. "Try me."

He spun them through a breathless sequence of turns, leaving her clinging to him dizzily when the music abruptly stopped.

All eyes focused on Byron Glendower as he stepped up onto the raised musicians' platform with a glass in hand.

"Friends, this is a special night for us," he called out loudly to quiet the murmur of conversation. "A night we can get together and thank God and the Union Army of the Tennessee's poor marksmanship for letting our fathers, husbands, sons, and brothers come home safe and sound. Tomorrow, we've got a special memorial service for those we won't see again, but tonight, tonight is for those who are still with us. Raise your glasses with me in a toast to our brave Kentucky sons, the best of Pride County,

those here with us and those we hope will be joining us again soon. A toast to Deacon Sinclair, to
Ray, Poteet, and Virg Dermont, Fowler Jennings."
He went on and on, hoisting his glass to each man
whose name he called, inviting the others to do likewise. "To Tyler Fairfax who stayed home to protect
the county."

Tyler beamed at the praise while his hand slid
lower and lower down the back of Patrice's gown.
He leaned close, his breath whiskey-warm, to whisper, "I told you I was a hero."

"And to my son, to whom we all owe so much."

Patrice waited, her glass aloft, wondering why
he'd mention Jonah in this toast to the returned.

Byron swiveled slightly, tipping his goblet.
"Reeve Garrett."

Silence. Not a glass moved. For the longest moment, not a breath exhaled as Reeve, clad in dark
formal attire, came up to stand beside his father,
bold as brass.

And from the back of the room, glass shattered
at the feet of Deacon Sinclair before he turned and
left the room.

Beside Patrice, Tyler made a soft sound trapped
between a chuckle and a snarl. His smile took a wry
twist as he upended his goblet, pouring its contents
onto the floor.

The remaining guests were more polite. Glasses
were returned untouched to the tables and backs
presented to the father and son on the riser. The
music started up again, and the party continued in
a unified snub.

Reeve laughed softly. "Told you how they'd welcome your subtle overture." He moved off the stage

and back into the shadows, where he wasn't the cutting target of every covert glare.

Byron refused discouragement. "It served its purpose. They've seen you, and they know I'm not ashamed to call you son."

Reeve bit back his response to that. He watched Tyler Fairfax lead Patrice out through the French doors to the darkened gardens beyond. "Am I excused from this little horse show now?"

The squire had seen the object of his attention but withheld his smile. "Absolutely not. You're here to take advantage of this gathering. Mingle. Hold your head up. Act like you don't care what they think."

"I don't," Reeve snapped. "It's just that these are good people, for the most part, and I dislike pushing myself into their sorrow."

Byron sighed angrily. "Fine. Do what you will, Reeve. But remember, these are our neighbors, and it's better to have them as friends than enemies. One at a time, boy. One at a time."

Reeve tried to do things his father's way. He walked through the gathering, finding himself confronted with a wall of shunning backs as those he approached turned pointedly away. No one said anything. The slash of their stares said it all. The pulse of their hate was a palpable force. He could ignore it without problem but it wasn't going to further his cause of finding acceptance among them. One at a time.

"Judge Banning, you remember me, don't you, sir?"

Noble Banning's father was a judge in name only, an honorary title and as close as the scalawag ever got to the letter of the law. He immersed himself in politics now, and from what Reeve knew of that unscrupulous group of liars, Judge Banning was well suited as their peer.

Banning squinted at him. "Yes, I remember you. You were once my son's friend."

"I'm still his friend. I was wondering if you'd heard any more about where he is. If he's in a Federal prison, perhaps I could pull some strings and—"

The judge cut him off cold. "We don't need your help, sir. Noble is out fighting on the Western frontier. He was able to secure his own release . . . no thanks to you or your kind. And were I you, I would not be so free in bandying about the word 'friend.' Noble might think different about it now."

Without an excuse me or an end of conversation, the judge walked away from Reeve as if he'd become suddenly invisible. Reeve didn't mind the snub. He'd learned his best friend was still alive. But was Noble still his friend?

He moved on, coming to the next likely stop.

"Cap'n Wardell?"

Daniel Wardell once rode with the Texas Rangers, as tough and ready a group of men ever assembled. He'd won honors in the Mexican War along with a head wound that left him partially blind. Built thick and strong, like his son, his infirmity cost him none of his tenacity. He angled his head to one side to get a look at Reeve through his good eye. His features tightened.

"Garrett."

"Have you any news of Mede?"

Granite expression crumbled slightly with his low admission. "Nothing. Not a word. The missus, she checks every day, but his name hasn't come up on any of the lists. That's good, I guess."

Reeve nodded, the heaviness around his heart dragging upon him. "Be much obliged if you'd let me know if you get any word."

Wardell studied him through his one unwavering eye. He knew people. He was alive because of his ability to make snap judgments about the good or bad in a man. While he wasn't ready to forgive, he answered with a crisp, "I'll do that."

Reeve's gratitude was unmistakable even to a broken-down old lawman with one filmy eye and another short of sight. But considering the company, he offered no further sympathy. His nod curt, he dismissed Reeve and went back to his watered-down drink.

Well, one shot to the head and one stay of execution. Reeve couldn't expect any better than that. At least no one had thrown stones at him . . . yet.

His crosscutting through the hostile crowd brought him to the bank of French doors. He studied the one Tyler and Patrice had disappeared through. He had no right or invitation to follow them. Patrice's honor was her brother's business. But Deacon was nowhere in sight. No, he couldn't go charging out to interrupt a moonlight tryst. But on a balmy evening there was no reason he couldn't take in the night air, especially after suffering frostbite from his neighbors's glares.

Casually, he slipped outside and began strolling along the terraced bricks, trying not to be obvious in his scouring of the bushes. He knew Tyler Fairfax too well to think he'd invite a pretty lady out into the darkness just to breathe in the fresh scent of spring. He started to walk a little faster, stride brisk, tense.

Then, from down by the formal herb garden, he

heard a woman's cry of distress. Patrice. And that's all it took for him to plow through the shrubberies with bloodshed on his mind.

"Quite the entrance our friend Garrett made tonight."

It was hard to decipher Tyler's feelings on the matter as he guided her from the terrace into heavier darkness. Patrice went unprotestingly. She had no fear of being alone with him. They had come down to a quiet formal garden where the sounds from the party were whispers and night music played.

Then Tyler stopped her, coaxing her to look up at him. He wasn't much taller, so there was no sense of intimidation or threat, just an old friend and confidant curious over the state of her heart.

"You were in love with him once. Are you still?"

His bluntness set her stammering. "N-no, of course not. What gave you the idea that I ever cared two hoots for him."

His fingertip traced along the ridge of her collarbone, eliciting an unintentional shiver. "I'm not the fool your brother takes me for, darlin'. An' my sister's got a big mouth."

"Starla told you?" Shock and a sense of betrayal overwhelmed her.

"Now don't get mad. She was just tryin' to keep me from making that big a fool of myself. I've always liked you, Patrice, you know that. I just asked her if she thought it could be more than liking."

"And she told you I was in love with Reeve?"

"Not straight out. She put it fancy so it wouldn't hurt my feelin's, something like your affections were otherwise engaged or you would most certainly fall captive to my charms."

Patrice relaxed and chuckled. "And were they hurt, your feelings?" She phrased it lightly, but he didn't miss the tenderness beneath it, her wish that it not be so.

"*Non*. You know me, darlin'. I'm as shallow as a puddle when it comes to things of a romantic nature. Always regretted not getting to kiss you though. Bet you'd have delivered up one hellacious slap."

She smiled, toying with the collar of his frock coat. "Maybe not."

Knowing Tyler's reputation, it probably wasn't the wisest thing to go off into the shadows with him and make flirtatious remarks about kissing. But Patrice felt as close to him as she was with his sister. And she knew that behind all the bluff and bullying lurked a fragile heart that could easily be broken.

He looked at her, half-smiling, mystified by what he heard until her hand strayed up to his chiseled features, palming his cheek, drawing him toward her. He gave a quick inhalation of surprise then bent unhurriedly to claim her soft mouth.

Patrice wasn't sure what she'd expected any more than she knew why she allowed him to kiss her. Perhaps it was a need to connect with another, to share an uncomplicated moment of closeness. Or simply to relieve some of the stresses Reeve Garrett's arrival had placed upon her emotions. It was unfair to Tyler, but he could be trusted to handle her heart with care.

His kiss was warm, pliant, surprisingly pleasant. His tongue slipped past her responsive lips for a leisurely exploration. The smooth tang of bourbon he brought with him was far from disturbing. No one had ever taken such intimate liberties with her before. She could blame the champagne, but instead of being outraged or horrified, she enjoyed the experience for what it was. Nice, but not arousing.

Tyler leaned back with a ragged laugh. "Oh, darlin', enough. Any more of that, and I'll be tempted to ravage you."

She responded to his husky innuendo with a hug. Tyler stood still and stiff, not daring to do more than place his hands lightly on the sides of her waist.

"Patrice, you stop teasin' this poor fool. I know this was all just to distract me from gettin' an answer to my question."

She batted her eyes up at him. "What question, sugar?"

He chucked her under the chin. "You an' my sister, two of a kind. Always playing with fire thinking you won't get burnt."

"You're a good man, Tyler Fairfax."

Her statement startled him, sobering his mood. He stepped back so his features were redrawn by shadow. "You're wrong there, darlin'. An' that's a dangerous mistake to be makin'."

Chapter 10

"Patrice?"

Reeve scanned the circle of meticulously laid bricks awash in moonlight. He saw cozy benches and neatly edged triangular herb beds divided by the narrow path. Crushed thyme and bay leaf scented the air. But no sign of either Patrice or Tyler. Breath chugged up from his chest in a tempo borne of panic and rage. If Tyler dared—*dared*!—hurt her . . . He couldn't finish the thought. His and Tyler's friendship dated back to their first steps, but friendship wouldn't still his dark passions if one uninvited hand was laid.

Just when Reeve decided to try another path, Patrice staggered out of the bushes. She wobbled to a halt when she saw him, and stood staring like a startled doe, her eyes huge glittering pools of dismay. Tears streaked her ghostly pale cheeks. Kiss-swollen lips trembled.

131

His gaze lowered, taking in the evidence of his worst fears.

Grass and mud stained the bell of her gown, its silvery lace torn loose and hanging like beards of moss on a live oak. A damning rent separated bodice from skirt at the side of her waist and below, a deep slash scored through silk and cotton petticoat displaying hints of bare thigh.

A stark possessive instinct overcame him in an instant. In two long strides, he'd reached her and snagged her up tight against his chest, folding her close where nothing, no one would ever harm her again. His face mashed against her lopsided hair knot, his lips moving upon that russet satin, mouthing the sentiments spilling forth from his soul.

"Oh, God, God, 'Trice, I never should have let you come out here with him. I'll kill him. I swear, I'll kill him!" That last issued through clenched teeth.

She struggled wildly. At first he could hear only frantic noises from where her face pressed into his shoulder. Anxious, awful sounds. That finally became words.

"Are you mad?! Let me go, Reeve! What's gotten into you?"

"Patrice." He made his tone gentle, full of empathy. "I won't speak a word about what's happened here. I would never see you hurt by scandal. Just tell me one thing. Did he hurt you?"

She pushed back and stared at him, the glassy brightness of distress fading to a fog of annoyed bewilderment. "What are you talking about? Reeve Garrett, have you lost your mind?"

He cupped her elbows within his palms, preventing her from backing away from him. "I saw

Tyler bring you outside. You don't need to pretend. I can guess what happened. He can be persuasive, and he can be thoughtless when it comes to getting what he wants. You don't need to feel ashamed.''

He'd expected her to go all weepy and grateful at his vow to protect her virtue. Or at least, all prim and prickly in continued denial.

He never expected her to laugh.

The sound burbled up from deep inside her. At first he thought it was approaching hysteria.

Then an ugly sense of being the fool came over him. Patrice's fool. He set his teeth and growled from between them, ''What's so damned funny?''

Her voice was as sweetly tender as her amusement. ''Tyler? You thought he and I—that we . . . ?''

''Your gown . . .''

She glanced at the mussed state of her clothing. ''I stumbled off the path and fell.'' Her gaze softened as it lifted to his once more. Her fingertips touched his cheek, stilling his anger in an instant. ''For heaven's sake, Reeve, you've more sense than to draw such conclusions. I've known Tyler since we were children.''

''Men change, Patrice,'' he murmured, recovering from his fright with gruff defensiveness, ''and not always for the better.''

The touching flattery of Reeve rushing to her rescue, the heart-rending fact of his anger, his willingness to save her honor took a bittersweet turn. Where was that offer when it would have meant something? Patrice withdrew her hand regretfully.

''How well I know that. I've watched them change right before my eyes.'' She closed her eyes. ''Go back to your party, Reeve. As you can see, I'm fine.''

But she wasn't fine. As she readied to turn away, Reeve caught sight of a bright red stain seeping onto the ripped edges of her gown. Concern warred against the fact of her purposeful lie. Catching her wrist, he drew her close, his nose wrinkling.

"Don't play games, Patrice. You needn't lie to me. What you and Tyler do together is none of my business."

She slapped at his hand, wounded by his cool disdain. "I told you, nothing happened between us."

"The truth would smell sweeter if you rinsed out your mouth. Unless you've taken to the bottle, his bourbon is still on your breath."

"So I kissed him," she railed in anxious indignation. "So what? We're friends. You didn't make so much of the kisses you once gave me."

His glare stabbed through her haughtiness with a bayonet thrust. "We were children then and not responsible for our foolish curiosities. You no longer have that excuse. You were engaged to my brother. I don't want you sullying his memory."

She gaped at him, so shocked, so *amazed* that he, of all people, would choose such an argument. She couldn't think of what to say to express her outrage adequately.

Reeve watched her face go milk white. Her angry glare grew shiny with welling tears. He knew he'd gone too far, said too much. He took a breath, ready to apologize, but she spun away from him. With her first step, came a cry of surprise and injury as she clasped her thigh as it threatened to buckle. He was quick with his support, and Patrice, just as quick to shrug it off.

"Leave me alone! Go away!"

But even as she said those forceful words, she rounded over the favored leg, swaying to catch her balance. Reeve's arm scooped around her middle, cinching up to still her struggles as he towed her over to one of the whitewashed benches.

"Sit."

She obeyed, not because he told her to, but because she couldn't stand on her own. In her pain and confusion, she never thought to protest as Reeve knelt beside her to part the torn edges of her gown. He bared a long pale line of naked thigh . . . and the five-inch gash cut into it. Patrice leaned back, woozy with shock at the sight of all the blood.

"Did he have a knife?" Reeve's tone was so calm and quiet, it scared her.

"W-who?"

"Tyler. Did he cut you?" Again, the flat, dangerous control. Tyler wasn't much for pistols, but he had an unholy fondness for a wicked length of steel.

"No. Tyler—Tyler had already gone back to the house." She closed her eyes against the surge of sickness. "I—I fell. I caught my heel between the bricks and stumbled into the bushes. I snagged my dress on the sundial. I heard it tear, but I never felt anything . . . except embarrassment. And—and then you came along with your crazy conclusions. Oww!"

She jerked away from the press of his neckcloth.

"Sit still. Hold that there. Keep the pressure on. I'll be right back."

Numbly, she did as she was told this time.

Reeve stood, shrugging out of his frock coat. Without comment, he wrapped it about her trembling shoulders. Then he left her, huddled and shivering, bleeding all over his ascot, while he jogged down to the stables. On his return trip, he took a covert second to check the sundial, finding a red-stained scrap of gray silk hanging from its metal point. Chiding his clumsy handling of the situation, he went back to Patrice. He managed a smile as he went down on one knee. Hers was a faint echo.

"This is going to sting a mite," he warned as he blotted the area clean.

Patrice recalled her brother's stoic endurance and sucked a deep breath, vowing to be equally brave. Until Reeve dipped his fingers into a pungent salve and rubbed it into the raw furrow.

It burnt like grain alcohol.

Patrice bit back her wail of distress, clamping her lips together until they bleached white. Her hands latched onto Reeve's broad shoulders, her fingers sinking into hard muscle as her leg jumped and spasmed. He bent, blowing gently to cool the flame. As it gradually subsided, only then did Patrice consider their position; in the secluded darkness, her skin bared to his warm touch, his tawny head bowed and nearly brushing her bosom. An unsettling awareness began to burn hotter than whatever he'd smeared over her wound. Awareness of the way his hair curled over the back of his starched collar. Of the way his hands seemed so big and browned against the pale flesh of her thigh. Of his gentleness. Of the arousal simmering inside her ever since she'd caught sight of him in elegant evening wear.

His voice rumbled, a low vibration. "Forgive my words, Patrice. I shouldn't have said them."

"Words are easily forgiven."

His gaze shot up at the feel of her fingertips grazing his temple, hooking his hair back behind his ear.

Just that faint brush of familiarity galvanized his emotions. Heat pooled to his groin. His gut tightened as if bracing unconsciously for a blow. Memories of the last time she'd touched him with such feeling brought confused desire to spin in his brain.

I will love you until the day I die, Reeve Garrett.

She'd kissed him then with all a young girl's urgent passion, sealing her vow with the press of her eager lips. Did she remember the words as clearly as she recalled the kisses? If only she'd meant them.

Her expression was too complex for the strength of shadows slanting across her face. Her mouth pursed slightly with all the allure of one of those wet kisses. Her eyes became fathomless mists, deep, cool, and gray-blue, but something stirred there, something that caressed with a sultry whisper, that sparked, flint on steel. A question formed in tiny puckers between her finely arched brows. *Why? Why the distance, why the anger, why deny what we both are feeling?*

And because he could answer in one word, one name, he rocked back on his heels, letting the tenuous moment escape them.

He began making a snug wrap around her thigh, using his discarded waistcoat, securing it with one of the ruined ribbon bows now dangling from her sleeve. His movements were crisp, efficient, the way they would be if binding a thoroughbred's tendon while her hand continued to rest upon his shoulder. "You should see a doctor," he advised. His bland matter-of-factness couldn't quite offset the way his tone rasped in a low register.

"Doc Anderson fell at Nashville with a minié ball through his shoulder. We haven't been able to find a replacement yet." Her voice, too, was strangely pitched, higher, airier than he remembered ever hearing it.

"Then apply this twice a day and keep it wrapped until it begins to heal pink and free of poisons."

She made a face. "What is it, exactly? Some potion of your mother's?"

He ducked his head, not in time to disguise his smile. "It's horse liniment."

"That's what you use on the horses?" She pushed her palms against his shoulders, nearly bowling him over.

He laughed. The sound rippled, a fast-moving stream over a pebbled bottom, churning up dangerous emotions in its wake.

"Overlook its smell and sting, and it's the best healing medicine I know." He glanced behind him, toward the house. Dots of light shone through the bushes, fireflies on the dark night. "We'd better get back. Can you stand?"

"Of course." But when she tried, her legs jellied unsteadily. Reeve's bracing arm provided rescue. She leaned against him, tempting fate. To distract herself, Patrice looked down at her attire, horrified by what she saw.

"I can't go back in like this. I'll have to sneak in the back so no one will see me."

Reeve's interpretation was a dry drawl. "You mean so no one will see us together."

She didn't answer, which was his answer.

"Come on then."

Her first step wobbled. The second buckled. Before she guessed at his intention, Reeve dipped down, slipping his other arm behind her knees to scoop her up against his chest. As she drew an indignant breath, he anticipated her objections.

"Start wiggling around, I'll drop you flat."

Patrice shut her mouth, considering silence the better part of valor. Her arms circled his neck demurely as she pointedly ignored the quirk of his smile. Then she felt him stiffen as she snuggled in contentedly, her head upon his shoulder. And she heard him exhale in a long, shaky gust. The evidence of his distress made hers fade. She'd shaken up the staid and distant Reeve Garrett. There for just a moment, she'd seen an answering desire in his eyes, naked, vulnerable, excitingly raw. But he'd withdrawn behind the stoic facade he wore so well before she could pursue it. But it was there. She knew it now. He wanted her. That fact warmed through her like a smooth sip of bourbon.

Then came the bittersweet chaser; there was nothing either of them could do about it.

But for the moment, she could enjoy it.

As they neared the house, with its noisy revelry still going strong, Patrice was pulled from the dreamy delight of being held and coddled by a harsh, intruding voice.

"What the hell do you think you're doing with my sister?"

Reeve came to a stop, making no attempt to avoid Deacon's swift approach. Nor did he release Patrice in guilty haste.

Seeing that her brother was about to make the same ill-conceived leap to judgment that Reeve had earlier, Patrice hissed, "Reeve, put me down. Let me handle this."

He hesitated just long enough to let her know he was doing it because she asked, not because he felt he had to. Then, carefully, he eased her down, not relinquishing his support.

Deacon jerked to a halt, his gaze doing a quick assessment of his sister's appearance. His stare lifted slowly, dark, violent consequences glittering in his steely eyes.

To forestall the blow up to come, Patrice reached out her arms to her brother, and suspiciously, he took a step forward to intercept her.

"Oh, Deacon," she gushed. "I declare, I did the silliest thing. Tyler and I went walking down in the garden sharing news of Starla. I told him I wanted to take in more air so he went back to the house. Somehow, I managed to trip on the bricks and I fell and tore this beautiful dress Mama made for me. She's going to be so upset with me."

Deacon listened with no visible change of expression. Then his skewering stare went to Reeve. "Where does Garrett come in?"

"I hurt my leg. Thank goodness he heard me cry out. I made him carry me up here so I could find you. Could you help me upstairs before anyone sees me? I look such a fright, I'd just up and die if anyone noticed."

Deacon scowled. She sounded calm, though a bit scattered in her emphasis on female vanity. Perhaps she told the truth. Garrett gave nothing away. Still, the two of them, alone in the night, Patrice returning in a tattered gown, wearing Garrett's coat, clutched in the arms of their enemy. Perhaps she wasn't telling him everything.

Patrice chose that moment to utter a fragile moan, her body going limp enough to alarm him. Deacon secured her in the circle of his embrace as she lolled against him, seemingly dizzy and disoriented.

"Deacon, I simply must lie down," she murmured weakly.

"Do you want me to get Mother?"

"No. No, don't spoil her evening. I just feel a little faint, is all. Could you take me up to my room?"

Bred to be a gentleman, Deacon wouldn't think to deny the request. For the time being, the threat of Reeve Garrett was forgotten as he lifted her into his arms.

Patrice twisted to give Reeve a small smile before nestling her head trustingly upon her brother's shoulder.

I told you I could do it.

The receptive comfort of her tester bed was heaven. Deacon had no bedside manner. He didn't fluff her pillows or turn down the counterpane. He stood, eyes narrowed, waiting for her to ask for anything she needed.

Patrice needed to be alone.

"How bad is it?" He nodded to the crude wrap peeping through the rent in her skirt.

"Just a scrape." The understatement insured Deacon wouldn't linger. Or call their mother up to fuss over her. "It aches. A reminder to watch where I'm going." She smiled in chagrin. He didn't respond to it.

"Garrett—"

"Brought me up to the house. Nothing else. Can you interrogate me later? I'm suddenly very weary."

He didn't say anything for several seconds, nor did his suspicions ease. Finally, he said, "I worry about you, Patrice."

She smiled, attempting to lighten his somber expression. "That's nice to hear. You used to consider me a nuisance and pretended I didn't exist."

"You were a nuisance. I'm not sure what you are now, but I don't want to see you get hurt. Or disgrace the family."

"I'm sorry if being clumsy has disgraced me in your eyes."

He ignored her wry retort to say, "You know what I mean, Patrice. And you know who I'm talking about."

With a dismissing harrumph, she tossed onto her side, presenting her brother with her back. "Your faith in my good judgment is heartwarming."

Deacon loitered a moment longer, feeling he should say more to soothe her pique, not knowing what words would perform that miracle. In the end, he slipped out quietly, closing the door.

And Patrice drew Reeve's coat more tightly around her, staring into the dim shadows of the room, trying to deny that her brother had reason to worry.

Chapter 11

⌒◞◟⌒

The memorial service for Pride County's missing and dead drew in the sorrowful, filling the whitewashed church's pews and aisles to overflowing. It was the first step in moving on with lives gone stagnant during the war years. But attitudes were no easier to set aside than heartbreak, and when Reeve Garrett walked up the aisle the mood shifted in a furious tide from solemn reverence to a dangerous undercurrent of hostility.

As if oblivious to the stir he caused, Reeve slid into the pew next to the squire. The Sinclairs followed, Hannah stopping to usher Patrice in first despite Deacon's frown of objection to his sister settling in beside the subject of everyone's ire.

With hands folded primly on her lap, Patrice exuded an air of quiet reflection. Her head bowed, eyes lowered, she seemed immune to the stares and whispers around her. But she heard them, and those properly knotted fingers began to clench.

"How can she sit there next to the man who murdered her fiancé?"

"Why doesn't she swoon or demand he leave?"

"I heard tell they were living under the same roof together! Imagine that! Avery Sinclair must be rolling in his grave. He'd never allow such a thing."

"How dare he show his face in here! We should take a horsewhip to him!"

Then, a soft, sinister suggestion: *"We should hang him."*

A chill of outrage coursed through Patrice. Such sentiments didn't belong in church. Hate had no place beneath God's roof.

She canted a quick look up at him, but his immobile features gave nothing away as he sat straight and tall, staring over the heads of their murmuring neighbors. He didn't appear bothered by the threats, by the grumbles. So, why was she? They were feelings she should echo if she were a true Southerner and loyal to the ones she'd lost. Didn't she despise him for what he'd done, for taking part in the destruction of their way of life? Didn't she believe he should be punished for standing against his neighbors, his friends . . . his family? Wasn't she equally irate at the thought of him trying to insinuated himself back into their good graces? It was too late to say he was sorry . . . but then, he'd never done that, had he? He'd never made a statement of apology or remorse.

So, then, weren't these people rightful in their anger, in their sense of insult that he should intrude upon their sorrow, his very presence at this memorial a mockery of their pain? And hers? Those around her had lost fathers, sons, husbands, and brothers. She'd lost her father and fiancé. Thinking of them brought a huge hollow of hurt and longing; to see them again, to hear their voices, to feel the comfort of them close by. The same ache of separation weighed heavily in each expression of those gathered around her today, in all but Reeve's. Resentment simmered as she studied his emotionless facade.

Marriage to Jonah would have given her stability and the joy of a lifelong companion and friend who was completely devoted to her. And now ... now she had nothing, no prospects, no provider; she was a burden upon her brother and a symbol of pity to her friends. She was a widow to the South, ever draped in emotional sackcloth, held up to the scrutiny of those around her who would forever gauge the strength and sincerity of her mourning. A frivolous belle with milky skin and crowded social calendar now reduced to somber sighs and lonely nights. How much more isolated could the grave be when compared to her rigid role of self-denial. Her father and Jonah Glendower had lost their lives, but she had lost her right to happiness, her right to love.

Because the only man who could bring her both things was the same man responsible for her solitude.

Horsewhipping Reeve Garrett wouldn't bring back those they'd lost, wouldn't restore the glory of the South. But it would give them all a chance to strike back against the unfair burden of defeat, a means to vent their frustration and pain. And in the darkness of her heart, she blamed him, just as they did, and because of that darkness, she, too, could relish the thought of that lash falling upon the source of their misery.

She sat up straight and proud, placing an invisible wall between her and the target of all their scorn. Her eyes glimmered with anguish and determination. The unexpected weight of her brother's hand between her squared shoulder blades startled at first, then strengthened her pose of righteous anger. Someone should pay for Jonah, for her father, for all the rest.

Wasn't Reeve responsible for Jonah by his choice of uniform, by his presence at his execution, by his failure to repent?

Then, came a penetrating whisper from the shadows of her being: Wasn't she as much to blame for sending him to his death?

The magnitude of that secret shame multiplied as the reverend began his moving eulogy. As he listed the names of those soldiers who'd paid the ultimate price for Southern pride, a wail rose from Madeline Gurney, whose sons, twenty-year-old Titus, seventeen-year-old Jeffries, and fifteen-year-old Matthew, who'd yet to shave his first whisker, were among the fallen in Atlanta. Mary Malone and her young daughter-in-law sobbed for the sake of three-year-old Justin, who would never know his father. Captain Tom Drury gulped back his grief and dried his eyes with his one good arm as his son's name was mentioned as a hero under Chalmers. Then came a heartfelt prayer for twins Carey and Connor Wellington, who'd never seen battle. They'd both wasted away with dysentery before ever hearing a shot fired.

By the time the reverend came to Avery Sinclair, the church walls rang with lamentations for those names called before his. While Hannah had the comfort of Deacon's embrace, Patrice sat in stony silence, alone and lost upon the sorrowful sea.

Closing her eyes, she could visualize her father's face, the lean, hard angles so like her brother's. The authoritative sound of his voice as he directed the workers in the field pealed through her memory like distant thunder. Then there were the rare times, the treasured times, of them holding hands as a family while grace was said at the table, of catching her mother and father in a tender tangle of arms and lips, of Avery teaching young Deacon to wield a saber with agile aggression, his lessons firm yet patient. Of him taking her up on his great white gelding to ride in the safe circle of his arms as he surveyed the new hemp crop. Then, she could hear once again, the distraught sobs her mother tried to muffle in her bed at night after news came of his death. A huge wad of emotion lodged beneath her breastbone, an ever-tightening fist about her heart. Oh, Lord, how were they going to go on without his strong hand upon them all? Tears she was unaware of shedding dotted the front of her charcoal-colored gown, but no sound escaped her.

She should have pulled away from the warm clasp of Reeve's hand over hers. She should have refused to take comfort from such a source. Yet, when she stuck her fingers between his, twisting them together, the sense of isolation left her, replaced by the intimate pang of kindred spirits caught up in the same sorrow. She shifted their entwined hands to the pew seat between them, covering their intermingling with the fabric of her skirt. Perhaps her caution lessened the sweetness of the gesture, but Reeve didn't withdraw it. For the next name mentioned was Jonah Glendower and his big hand convulsed with near bone-crushing power even as his features betrayed no sign of his internal distress. A privately shared regret, just between the two of them who loved Jonah most. Then, when the next name was read, Reeve relaxed his hand, his fingers slipping free of her grasp. And Patrice mourned the loss.

In the end, the farewell service helped no one relieve the frustration and grief. It only bound the community closer together in its loss and strengthened its animosity toward the target of their anger. Reeve Garrett had come home, their loved ones hadn't. And there should be some way to rectify that irony.

After the final prayer, when reddened eyes were dried and comforting arms supported family, friends, and neighbors, the congregation rose. And to a one, they stood, glaring, silent, waiting for Reeve to precede them out of the church.

He strode down the center aisle as if unmindful of their piercing stares. His step was confident, his head held high, his shoulders remained unbent beneath the burden of their blame. And hatred smoldered at his indifference to their grief. Perhaps if he'd slunk out repentantly, if he'd wept and wailed unashamedly for the loss of his half brother and friends, if he'd had the decency to look to them for forgiveness, he might have found it. But his arrogance, his remoteness was a slap at them, and they wanted to strike back . . . hard.

And even as he passed between their staunch pillars of disdain, there were those already plotting their revenge.

"It wasn't supposed to be this way. You were the one who was going to stay safe at home. All this

was supposed to be yours, not mine. I told you I
didn't want it. I told you, but. you never believed
me, did you? Probably because you knew I was lying to myself."

Reeve Garrett's low tones blended with the whispering harmony of tree branches bobbing in the
wind under the heavy burden of new foliage. It was
a peaceful place, the Glendower family cemetery,
set in a quiet glade sheltered from signs of civili-
zation. The idyllic spot fostered a sense of direct
communication with nature and the souls long buried beneath the rich Kentucky soil. Only a few were
in residence, the rest of them lying across the moun-
tains in Virginia. Byron's father had an ornate plot
with a huge marble headstone. The delicate and
lovely Phoebe Glendower rested next to him, with
her son's relatively new space off to her right. Someday, Byron would take his place between them, a
family together for eternity. As to where he'd rest,
Reeve hadn't given much thought. His emotions
pulled him toward the whitewashed cross bearing
his mother's name, but his pride demanded he take
a rightful place here without apology or shame.

Jonah's headstone was firm against the back of
his shirt, and warm from absorbing the sun. Reeve
felt comfortable there, speaking to him as if he were
actually there instead of in a box six feet below. In
the soft caress of the westerly breeze, in the sighing
rustle of the trees, in the calming spring songs of
the birds above, Reeve felt his brother near and listening. He hadn't felt his presence at the church.
There, he'd sensed only the pain of those left behind, not the forgiveness of those who'd gone on
ahead. That's why he'd come to visit the well-
tended grave. To let Jonah know what was on his

heart and mind. And to, just maybe, receive absolution for what he was about to do.

He plucked at spears of bluegrass and tossed them down at his dusty knee-high boots, the gesture automatic as his thoughts fought for expression.

"I miss you, Jonah. You always understood without me having to say things out loud. Maybe I should have said them. Maybe that's why it's so hard to let you go. You knew me so well, and I'm beginning to think I didn't have the slightest clue about you. I never, in my wildest dreams, would have pictured you doing something so damn fool stupid. What were you thinking, jumping into a fight you didn't believe in. You knew the South didn't stand a chance of winning. You knew our survival depended on the North. Yet you went and threw everything away, for what? Deacon Sinclair? That sonuvabitch wouldn't have done the same for you. Or was it for Patrice? Was she involved? Was she the reason you gave up your life? I wish I knew. I wish you'd told me, then maybe I wouldn't feel so . . . bad."

The war was over. Why did the battle have to go on and on? He was so tired of the fighting, the justifying, the confusion. He wanted things to be simple again. Then he'd know what to do.

Jonah would have known. He'd always had such crystal-clear vision. Which was why he'd taken all the Glendower assets from his bank and, with Reeve's help, invested them in the North during the early years of the war to keep them safe under Reeve's name so as not to be taken as contraband.

Reeve closed his eyes against the glare of the sun, against the remembered glare of his neighbors' hatred. How was he going to make things up to those tight-fisted, close-minded people? Jonah would have known how to charm them with a humbling smile. But he'd never learned the act of humility. It would have been harder for him to swallow burning coals than to say he was sorry when he wasn't. He wasn't sorry he'd joined the Northern army. He would have been a hypocrite to do differently. He wasn't sorry he'd done his best to bring the tattered country back together, even if the wounds were raw and slow to heal. They would, eventually. But he couldn't be as sure about the feelings of those in Pride County.

He'd only to look at the glass panes broken out in his mother's cabin by vandals who'd done the damage and fled in anonymity. To see the smears of horse dung across the walls his mother had lived within, slept within, and taken such great pride in watching him grow within—to know the depth of their hatred.

They believed he coveted what belonged to his half brother. They believed he'd mercilessly had Jonah slain in order to inherit what was his. And in taking over the Glade, in courting Patrice Sinclair, he'd be proving it as clearly as if he'd stood up from his church pew to declare he was glad Jonah Glendower was dead.

How that tortured him. Because it wasn't completely untrue. There were times he'd cheerfully wished Jonah out of the way, times when resentment made a vile taste in his mouth he couldn't rinse away. Their father's poor judgment had made him a servant and Jonah a prince. And it wasn't fair. None of it was fair.

Then why did he feel so guilty claiming that which should have been his all along?

Because he loved Jonah as his brother, as his friend. Despite the fact that he had all that Reeve wanted. Jonah hadn't asked for it, he hadn't purposefully stolen it away. And the fact that Jonah always regretted that his good fortune was Reeve's bad luck made Reeve admire him all the more. And it made stepping into his shoes an awkward and difficult move.

Reeve sighed heavily. "If only you hadn't spoke up to spare me after that fall broke your leg. I could have gone on hating you, and none of this would bother me at all. Why did you have to make me beholden to you, then go and treat me like a friend instead of a rival? Why didn't you hate me for threatening what was yours? You should have. Why did you have to make it so damn hard to begrudge you anything? I'd have given my life for you, but I never expected you to do the same. I wanted the Glade, I wanted all of it, but I didn't want to step over your corpse to get them. You sonuvabitch, how could you do this to me?"

"He loved you, Reeve."

He didn't know which surprised him more, the feel of her consoling hand on his shoulder or the sudden intrusion of Patrice's voice upon his remorse. He hadn't known she was there, kneeling beside him, or how much she'd heard. He only knew how good it felt to know someone recognized his pain. For the moment, it etched starkly into every angle of his face, into the shiny brilliance of his gaze, in the very hitch of his breathing. Patrice was its witness. No way to deny it, no way to cover it up, so he didn't try. Instead, he let go, leaning upon her as he'd lean upon no other.

Because he'd eased her sorrow in the church, Patrice held his tawny head to her bosom now, letting him vent his emotions in great, gulping breaths. She stroked his hair and rocked them both in a soothing repetition. And she spoke the words she'd denied him for so long.

"He loved you, Reeve. He worshiped the ground you walked on. He was always saying, 'If only I could be more like him.' He thought if he could be, your father would have loved him."

Reeve quieted, shaking his head. "Why would he think that? He was heir to the Glade. He had everything."

"Everything but your father's pride. You had that, Reeve, and for that, he would have gladly traded all he had."

"I didn't want him to die, Patrice. Honest to God." The words tore from his wounded soul, so angry and raw, it hurt her to hear them. "I'd have traded my life for his if I could have. I don't know what got into him, some crazy fool idea that he could save others with his sacrifice. I let him do it. I couldn't stop him. He did what I would have done. Damn him! Why did he pick such a dangerous time to prove himself?"

Patrice knew, but she said nothing. The truth swelled to form a knot in her throat through which no words could pass. Because she couldn't tell him what he needed to hear, she felt driven to ease his guilt in another way. Her hand slipped beneath his chin, angling his head back so she could see his tormented features. Her own eyes glistened as she brushed the wetness from his cheeks with a touch so light it was like the intimate warmth of her breath upon his skin. He'd gone totally still, waiting, probing for her reasons with the intensity of his gaze. Because she feared what he might find if he looked too long, too deep, she closed her eyes. And she kissed him.

The first shy sweep became a lengthy savoring. She could taste the salt of both their tears. They didn't touch except for their lips. All senses sharpened, focusing upon that kiss, upon the soft receiving textures, the sweetness, the shock of forbidden excitement. An answer to all their wondering.

It was good between them.

She couldn't resist the need to explore. Her fingertips traced the contours of his face, learning its authoritative ridges and tempting hollows. She followed the strength of his rough jaw, down his throat, along his collarbone until, with hands and heart quivering, she flattened her palms against the unyielding wall of his chest to test the urgent passion pounding there. Her own pulse hammered in an uncontrollable response.

Lifting her face, her eyes closing, she welcomed the hunger of his mouth as it charted cheek, brow, and the tender curve of her eyelids before returning to her now-trembling lips for a thorough plundering.

"Again," she gasped breathlessly when they separated.

Because one more or a thousand more wouldn't be enough, Reeve hesitated.

"What do you want from me, Patrice?"

Her gaze flickered open, at first displeased by the interruption, then soft with sincerity.

"I want to feel alive again, Reeve. I don't want to

be buried here in this grave. I know it's awful to say so, but—"

His forefinger pressed to her lips, sealing in whatever else she'd say. "Don't apologize. Not to me."

She kissed the rough pad of his finger, then rubbed her cheek into his broad palm. She looked back up at him, her eyes luminous, vulnerable. "And what is it you want, Reeve?"

"I need you to forgive me, Patrice."

It would have been such a simple thing to say "I do" and let all the anguish of the past four years dissolve. She could say it, and they could go on from there. But she couldn't speak the words, knowing they'd be insincere. Not at the risk that the lie would someday haunt them.

She touched his cheek. Her tone quavered with emotion.

"I—I don't know that I can."

The disappointment, the crushing defeat of his expression made her wish with all her heart she could have given him the answer he wanted. Instead, she stood and left him there at her fiancé's grave to make her way in an awkward, slightly hobbling hurry back to the safety of the house.

Because it wasn't Reeve she couldn't forgive for the tragedy of Jonah's death.

It was herself.

Chapter 12

⟨ ◦◦◦ ⟩

Deacon Sinclair walked out of Pride's lumber mill and let all his pent-up frustration go in a savage breath. The name Sinclair had always been good for anything they needed. Right now, he needed lumber, badly, to continue his work at the Manor, to get his family tucked safely under their own roof. Dangerous currents stirred at the Glade, and he didn't like it. He needed beams for reinforcement, boards for new stairs, milled pieces to refit windows and doors, too damn much to be told he couldn't buy on name only anymore.

The mill's owner, Harve Barlow, was sincere in his apologies. It was business, and business can't be run on endless promises. How much business had his family brought to Barlow Brothers over the years? Enough to deserve this one favor, this one exception. But he couldn't get it. He had no credit when it came to trust, either. Barlow didn't believe he could rebuild and recover from his losses. It showed clearly in his sad eyes, in the regretful shake of his head when he said he was sorry.

Sorry. Sorry didn't keep out the rain! He forked his hands back through his hair and tried to get on top of his anger and fear . . . anger at his helplessness, fear that Barlow was right. He hated not being in control, and everything was sifting through his fingers—their home, the vast acres, his sister, his future. He needed to grab on tight before it was too late but didn't know how.

He needed money.

He needed a chance to prove what he could do on his own. And one depended upon the other.

He knuckled his eyes to rid them of the dust and weariness. When he opened them again, he faced the grinning visage of Tyler Fairfax, already well into his cups at quarter past noon.

"Heya, Deke. You're lookin' a little down in the jowls. Anythin' I can do for you?"

"Yes. Go away." The last thing he needed was the added annoyance of a sodden little mealy worm like Fairfax gloating over his miseries.

Not at all discouraged by his brusque remark, Tyler fell in step beside him as he started aimlessly down the walk. "No luck at the lumber mill, eh? Heard you was riding low on pocket change. Bad luck these days."

Deacon shot him a venomous glare. "What business is it of yours, Fairfax, whether I have a pot to piss in or not?"

Tyler kept grinning. "You can pee off the side of the road for all I care. It's Patrice I'm thinking about. I'm—my sister's right fond of her. Hate to see her living in a tent, collecting government meals, if you know what I mean."

Not liking his face rubbed into his inability to provide, Deacon snapped, "Have you got a point? Then make it!"

"Sometimes it's easy to forget who your true friends are."

"Are you saying we have some long-lost bond of friendship between us? If there is, I certainly don't recall it."

Tyler laughed. "Oh, no, Reverend. I know you got as much use for me as spit on your shoes. But we're on the same side, of the same brotherhood. And folks like us should stick together, especially now when we all need someone to depend on. Someone to take care of our interests and our families while them Feds is lookin' to grind us under their heels."

Deacon drew up, his impatience plain. "Are you talking about those cowards who ride around in the night scaring poor people to death with their torches and their threats? Where's your hood, Tyler?"

His smile lost none of its brilliance. "Why, I don't wear it when I'm out socializing."

"Only when you're terrorizing. I'm not interested in getting help from you or your friends."

"They're more than friends, Deke. They're family. They see to their own. If you was to ask, I'd have two dozen men with lumber and strong backs over at your place in an hour. You'd be tucked in snug by the end of the week. What do you say to that?"

Deacon started walking again, his stride brisk and purposeful. "I'd say you're wasting your breath and my time."

Tyler lagged back, slowing his pace so that Deacon outdistanced him. Then he called cheerfully, "You need help—with anything, Rev, jus' give me a holler. I'll be nearby."

"Just stay out of my sight, you little weasel," Deacon muttered to himself as he stepped up onto his ragged mount. He kicked it into a jarring canter, eager to escape all the frustrations he'd found in town.

But later, as he pounded in another board from his fast-dwindling pile, he mulled over the conversation. Sweat blinded his eyes, and the ache in his arm seemed to expand all the way to the roots of his hair. Finally, he leaned his forehead against the interior wall he was replacing. Water from the roof leak had rotted it from inside out, leaving an irreparable mess. He'd had to rip the whole section down, and now he hadn't the material to finish. That black gaping hole mirrored his prospects as the hammer clunked to the floor from his slackened fingers.

He wasn't a carpenter. He wasn't a mason. He was a man with a superior mind and shrewd instincts lost in a maze of drudgery. He'd been clever and quick enough to evade detection and capture by the Union's best spy hunters. He'd lived off his cunning for four long years, and now he was totally stymied by the lack of 120 board feet. Shoulders slumping, he closed his eyes and considered the unthinkable.

Ignorant bullies like Tyler Fairfax were a plague. Everything they stood for went against the grain of honor. Yet, when he looked back on all the things he'd done to survive, he was surprised that he'd balk at this one small point of dignity.

He knew why Tyler approached him. His skulking Home Guard was seeking a way to earn respectability now that they no longer had the sentiments of a war-torn county behind them. If a Sinclair backed their cause, their prestige and power would grow at a frightening rate. Giving in to terrorists was one thing, siding with a mighty Sinclair was quite another. If he bent to ask assistance, he'd never break free of their association, and that crafty schemer Fairfax knew it, too.

He hated it. The whole thing. The helplessness. The feel of strangling debt. The uncertainty in the eyes of his mother and sister when he made them vows he knew he couldn't keep.

With brow pressed to the hallowed wall of his father's empire, he felt himself sinking in a quagmire of desperation.

"Show me another way. Please, give me another way."

"You talkin' to me, sir?"

Deacon drew a labored breath and turned to meet Jericho's questioning stare. "No. Just talking to myself."

"You look all in, Mista Deacon. Why doan you go on back to the Glade and lets me finish up here? Gets some sleep. All this can wait 'til morning."

Deacon sighed heavily. It could wait. That was the problem. It would have to wait a damned eternity unless greenbacks started falling from the skies.

Or until he made a deal with the devil—Tyler Fairfax.

At first, Reeve thought he was alone in the Glade's big library. The lamps were unlit, and shadows stretched long and solemnly along its wall to ceiling volumes. However, as he took a step in from the hall, a sharp odor reached him, the unmistakable grain scent of rye whiskey.

When he recognized the figure hunched down in an engulfing wing chair as that of Deacon Sinclair, he started to withdraw, unwilling to disturb his privacy or initiate a strained conversation. Then, oddly moved by the other's crumpled state, and alarmed by the tumbler full of whiskey about to be upended on his father's expensive woven rug, Reeve crossed the room quietly, reaching down to relieve Deacon's dangling hand of the glass. He paused at the sight of the other man's palm, at the ugly rawness of burst blisters searing across it. Deacon Sinclair, who'd never done any task more strenuous than jotting numbers in a ledger.

Deacon muttered, his long fingers curling over the sores. Then, with a jerk, he came to a defensive awareness, focus sharpening at the possibility of danger. Seeing no threat in Reeve's presence, he relaxed back into the curve of the chair.

"Musta drifted off," he mumbled, rubbing at his eyes, then wincing as the skin pulled at the open wounds on his hand. He squinted down at them, his expression one of wry humor.

Without comment, Reeve left the room, returning moments later. Deacon glanced up in question when a pan of cool water was settled on his knees.

"Stick your hands in there," Reeve instructed with a gruff indifference. Deacon eased in, fingertips first, tensing as the medicinal soak met raw flesh. But he didn't withdraw his hands. He was stubborn, not stupid.

"That'll keep 'em soft so the edges won't tear.

You can put some salve on when they dry. What happened to your gloves?''

"Wore them out." He wouldn't share the fact that he didn't have the funds to replace them.

"I'll be stopping over at the Manor after I finish up the west paddock." Reeve made it a statement, so it couldn't be refused on the basis of pride.

"No need."

"I already planned on it," Reeve said, giving no weight to the remark that might imply he cared one way or the other.

"I've got nothing that needs doing."

Reeve gave a contradicting snort. "Just years of work."

Deacon leaned back, eyes closing, his voice a hollow deadpan. "But no materials to see it done. I've got taxes to scrape up from somewhere. That's going to take everything."

Reeve read between the lines of what wasn't said, deducing that Patrice and her family were very close to being destitute as well as homeless. "The mill won't give you credit?"

Deacon didn't open his eyes. "The mill won't give me sawdust without having money up front." He didn't bemoan the fact or display an indignant temper. And against his better judgment, Reeve allowed a growing admiration for the man, for his toughness and resolve to do right for his family.

"Have you gone to the bank?"

Deacon looked up then. His eyes took on a hard metallic gleam in the dim light. His reply was toneless. "Jonah was the bank. It died with him. I suspect as soon as some speculator snaps it up, all the loans will be called and what I'm doing now won't matter a tinker's damn anyway. There won't be a one of us who has a field, let alone a field hand to work it. We're beaten. We just don't know when to lie down and die."

He pulled his hands out of the water and began to blot them on his dirty trousers. Reeve grasped one of his wrists, halting the careless movements.

"I'll bind these up for you." He left no room for argument. Deacon didn't relax, nor did he resist. Then Reeve added, "Unless you plan to try an' shoot me again."

Not a muscle in the savagely lean features flickered. Then Deacon said, "Why should I pull the trigger when half the county is lined up to do it for me?"

Reeve wrapped layers of gauze into a snug protective cushion, then ripped the edges to tie them off. Only then did he answer.

"Thought you did your own dirty work, Deacon, then left others to take the blame." He gathered up the supplies with brisk efficiency, then stood to regard the other man with blatant contempt. "Or aren't you so willing to flash your true colors now that you've had to suffer the consequence of your own deeds?"

"Go to hell," Deacon told him. "Soon."

Figuring he'd done quite enough to warm Deacon up to the idea of accepting him into the family, Reeve left him to his preferred solitude, not at all surprised to hear the empty tumbler smashing against the door he'd closed behind him.

Chapter 13

For all the rebelliousness of her growing-up years, Patrice loved fine things. While right at home astraddle a half-wild horse or fishing with her bared legs planted in the shallows, she also found a soothing satisfaction tending the household larder. Her favorite time of the year was springtime, when her mother conducted a thorough cleaning and inventory of the Manor. All the exquisite laces and rich brocades came down from the tall windows, letting in streams of vigorous sunlight. The beds were stripped and linens hung out to absorb the fresh clean breeze. The heavy, closed-in sense of the cooler winter months was cast off with the opening of casements and doors, airing out the stagnant dormancy. Silver, china, crystal, and place linens lined up for counting and polishing, gleaming down the long cherry length of their formal dining table. As a child, she'd delighted in the rainbow prisms darting about the room as light sparked off etched glassware. As a woman, she lost herself in a dreamy languor while coaxing a mirrored shine in the sterling, imagining her own bridal treasury as she passed each lazy hour wrapped up in the sensory balm of beeswax and lemon oil.

She'd never felt a superior pride in the wealth of their possessions, but rather a serene contentment that went with handling, piece by piece, the history of her family. The sterling her great-grandmother brought from England. Delicate tatting done by an Irish second cousin three times removed, the one who'd passed along the red of her hair. Crystal purchased in Europe when her father took her mother for a leisurely tour the year Deacon was conceived. Fragile bone china, a reward for presenting a healthy daughter. Hers someday, with all the romantic memories gathered over decades and centuries past.

Years had passed since she and her mother conducted the springtime ritual. During the war, there hadn't been time.

Now, there was nothing left to count.

The airy lace of the parlor curtains was sacrificed for the overskirt of her mother's new gown to celebrate her husband's first visit home after eight months of a war they'd thought would only last weeks. She hadn't wanted him to take back the memory of her in faded cotton, but rather the elegant serenity of the world he loved. Crystal was sold to stave off creditors eager to claim their livestock. Most of it was stolen or eaten by the end of the year, anyway. Table linens and crisp batiste sheets were scraped, torn, and wound in balls to provide much needed dressings at battlefront hos-

pitals. Their sterling was looted by the first plague
of Yankees to swarm their property, the ones who
also made off with the contents of their smoke-
house. She'd cried over the china while boxing it up
to sell for basic staples of survival: salt, sugar, ba-
con, flour, all at outrageous prices. The fluted silver
serving trays and dishes disappeared one by one
into the knapsacks of fleeing slaves. All she had left
of her memories were a pair of simple candlesticks
and twin goblets edged in gold that she'd carefully
wrapped in the handmade front table shawl to hide
in an abandoned well in the woods.

A fine legacy. If she could ever find someone willing to accept her with her burden of guilt and debt.

All these things wove through her mind as she
slowly repacked the Glendower glassware used for
the party nights ago.

She held one of the graceful stemmed flutes to
watch the light fracture through it in dazzling
strobes. Beautiful. She sighed to think that it might
have been hers. All the treasures at the Glade
should have been hers as its intended mistress. Why
hadn't she wed Jonah in a small civil ceremony the
first time he'd asked her? Then she'd be lingering
over her own delicate crystal instead of storing it
away for another.

She'd always loved the stately elegance of the
Glade with its cool white-and-gray brick and terra-
cotta roof tiles. It had none of the aggressive arrogance of Sinclair Manor. It needed none. Opulent,
tasteful, inviting. She'd dreamed of living within its
spacious rooms since the first time she'd worn her
hair up. In her secret twilight imaginings, she pictured being swept up the wide curve of the staircase
in her husband's arms. Though she'd come close to

winning that Glendower mate, to her eternal shame, it was Reeve, not Jonah, who carried her toward the marriage bower during those restless fancies.

It was Reeve, not Jonah, she'd wanted to wed.

And since their kiss, she'd been able to think of nothing else. Forbidden kisses stolen between two youngsters couldn't match the consequence of those shared between adults. She'd wanted Reeve Garrett when she was a child. And she wanted him still.

A quiet step behind her caused her to jerk around, face afire, as if her thoughts were obvious for the intruder to see. The tip of her elbow caught one of the precious goblets, sending it toppling to the floor. Her gasp of horror wasn't loud enough to drown out the sickening sound of glass breaking.

Reeve bent to retrieve the pieces and studied the clean separation of bowl from stem before straightening. Wide-eyed with shock and dismay, it took Patrice a moment before she could lower her hands from her mouth to speak in shaky anguish.

"I'm so sorry. I was trying to be so careful."

"It's all right."

"But I know how valuable these pieces are and how your family cherishes them. I can't believe I was so clumsy."

He examined the glass dispassionately. "Don't mean anything to me."

Patrice felt a hot tide of embarrassment. Of course they wouldn't. They'd belonged to Jonah's mother. They were tokens of a past he didn't share.

"I'm sorry," she muttered again, not knowing how else to extricate herself from the awkwardness of the incident.

"It's nothing." He fit the pieces together. "See. It can be mended. A lot of broken things can be repaired . . . if the damage isn't too severe and you don't mind a few flaws. Sometimes, it makes the original stronger.''

His words stirred up a confusion within her breast. He was talking about the crystal, wasn't he? Not about them. They'd had no time alone together since the memorial service—since their kiss. Had he been as restless, as sleepless as she, wondering over the possibilities? Her hands developed a sudden tremor. She hid them in the folds of her skirt. She answered her agitation with a snap of temper.

"I wouldn't have dropped it if you hadn't sneaked up on me."

Unphased by the accusation, Reeve set the broken goblet on the table next to the rest of the half-packed set. The movement brought him close enough for her to feel his body heat. For her own to warm in response. He paused to look down into her eyes with a disconcerting directness. "I wasn't sneaking. I stopped in to tell you I was going into town."

"So? You don't have to clear your schedule with me." She turned back to the glassware but was afraid to continue with the task while her hands remained unsteady. She could almost feel him smile.

"I wanted to ask if you needed anything. Or if you wanted to ride along."

Town. It had been ages since she'd gone into Pride for reasons other than begging for charity to survive. How different to go with head high and heart empty of the shame of dire circumstance. She could bring home some small trinket to make her mother smile. A ribbon, a handkerchief. Nothing too grand. Those items were out of her financial reach.

She was about to respond with a yes. Then she caught a glimpse of Reeve's face, long and distorted in the line of glassware.

She couldn't show up in town with Reeve Garrett. What would her family's friends say? How could she force Deacon into making apologies for her thoughtlessness?

"Thank you," she mouthed stiffly. "But I have much to do here today. If I need something, my brother will get it for me."

Silence. She didn't turn around. Did Reeve guess the reason behind her refusal? She dared a quick peek up at him from under her lashes, but his features were impassive. Perhaps not. She'd just begun to relax when he drawled, "How thoughtless of me not to consider your reputation. I didn't remember you as worrying so much over what other people thought."

Confused by her willingness to hurt him for the sake of public opinion, she felt she should justify her uncomfortable stand, to both of them. Adopting his mother's diplomacy, she said, "That was when I was a child. I didn't care about family responsibilities then. I grew up, Reeve."

Reeve tipped his head toward her in a mocking salute. "Guess that says it all. Miz Sinclair."

Unwilling to let him walk away thinking so poorly of her motives, Patrice called, "It would only stir up trouble."

He looked back at her, eyes unwavering, intense. "I don't mind trouble . . . if the cause is worth it, ma'am."

She fidgeted, listening to the echo of his boots in

the hall. Dang him and his irritating way of making her feel mean and childish. She had good reason for not wanting to compromise either of them. Didn't he realize the county was a simmering pot of hostility just waiting for an excuse to blow off steam? She wasn't going to supply that reason if she could help it. And she wouldn't shame her brother, not for anything. Not even for the sake of Reeve's feelings.

"Oh bother," she grumbled, then went dashing after him.

Reeve was just starting down the porch steps when she reached the door.

"Reeve?"

He paused, glancing around.

"You could get me something while you're in town."

He waited, letting her come to him with the request. Digging through her pin money, she produced a coin.

"Could you pick up a good pair of gloves for my brother? He wouldn't ask for himself, and I hate to see . . ." Her voice trailed off. What could she say? That he wouldn't humble himself to plead for necessities, and her love for him couldn't allow him to abuse himself over a point of pride.

Reeve waved off the coin. "I was planning to anyway. A man of importance shouldn't carry calluses on his palms. Wouldn't want him mistaken for someone . . . like me."

The lack of rancor in his tone made her search for their meaning. Just a sketch of a smile touched his lips, enough to make her emotions buckle.

"Thank you, Reeve."

For a moment, a glimmer of genuine tenderness

shone from behind his studied calm. "I would do anything for you, Patrice. All you have to do is ask."

She watched him stride down to the barn, admiring his quick, light-footed movements as much as she was annoyed by the cocky angling of his shoulders. The man had a knack for turning her world upside down. *Anything?* She wondered.

War changed the county seat of Pride County. Some changes were as subtle as the sullen defeat on the faces of those he passed by. Others more blatant; spears of charred posts and a square pile of ash where a building once stood, the "Out of Business" signs propped up in too many windows. One of them was the bank.

Reeve stared at that notice with an ache of remorse. Jonah's prized accomplishment, born of a conversation between them on a sultry September night. Reeve, all sweaty from saddle-breaking a trio of two-year-olds ready for sale, had sat cooling himself with the fan of his hat, bared feet dangling in the reflecting pond. Jonah was pitching pebbles into the serene waters, brooding over the ripples that spread from the site of the interruption. Reeve asked what was on his mind, unprepared for the depth of his half brother's turmoil.

"I've got nothing to offer the Glade, Reeve. You, you've put heart and soul into it. Me, I fritter away the days improving on a worthless education because it pleases the squire to flaunt my intelligence. I'd rather he praise me for my value, but there's damned little I can do."

He rubbed at his bum leg. The gesture pierced Reeve's conscience, even knowing it was unintentional on Jonah's part. A reminder of how his jealousy had ruined another's life. A reminder of how Jonah as the bigger man had forgiven him.

"Any fool can sit a saddle and control a dumb animal." Too late, he realized what he'd said and quick to remove its sting.

"Hell, if I had a brain like yours, I'd be making the most of it instead of moping around, crying over what any other man who walks upright can do."

Jonah winced. He hated being accused of feeling sorry for himself. He glared at Reeve, with his long, strong body and enviable confidence, and demanded, "And just what would you do?"

"Do what you know. Do what you're best at. I've seen you make numbers get up and dance to any tune of your choosing."

He shrugged. "Daddy does the books for the Glade."

"Think bigger. There's more to this world than the Glade, even though the squire doesn't believe it."

Think bigger.

Reeve smiled at the now vacant and boarded-over building. Proof of just how big a man's ambitions could be. Without a word to the squire, Jonah built Pride County's savings and loan, using monies left him by his mother's wealth. His natural brilliance with numbers and generosity of spirit was behind the widespread expansion throughout the county. But that ended with the war.

It ended with Jonah.

Until his brother's vision had new light, no one would ever let Reeve forget that. And Patrice would have no opportunity to put aside her shame.

* * *

"I'd like to send a telegram."

Reeve had known Gates Hargrove, the telegraph operator all his life, as one of the county's middle class—not poor, not rich, but always envious. He lapped up to his betters like a hound dog and snapped at those who weren't in a position to benefit him. He squinted across the high counter, and snarled, "You got money?"

Reeve laid coins on the worn wood, mesmerizing Gates with the rich sheen of gold. Reeve arched a brow, waiting.

Tasting greed, Gates grumbled, "Where's it going?"

"To a Lieutenant Hamilton Dodge, Grand Rapids, Michigan."

Gates's features puckered tighter. "A Yankee friend?"

Reeve didn't answer. Instead, he took the lined sheet from Gates and wrote down in the neat lettering Jonah taught him the exact message he wanted sent. Then he pushed the paper under the gold coins and both toward the glaring operator.

"Send that, word for word."

Gates scanned the sheet, sucking his hollow cheeks in like bellows as his agitation grew. He glanced up at Reeve through eyes hard as scrap iron. "I ain't sending this."

"Times are hard, Gates. Be a bad time to have to find another occupation."

Cheeks still puffing like an adder's, Gates bent over his equipment. Reeve waited, expression stony. After the tapping stopped, Gates looked up with a narrow smile. "Something must be wrong with the wires. Takes days to trace it down to the source." His hand slipped stealthily over the coins.

"I can keep trying for you. Let you know when it gets through."

Reeve's hand slapped down over the pale, veiny one. "Try now. Only this time, use the key instead of the tabletop. Might make all the difference."

Gates attempted to twist his hand free. Reeve hung on for a minute, giving the gulping fellow something to wheeze about, then he let go. Gates pulled back as if snakebit.

"Heya, Gates, some problem here?"

"This fella won't believe that the lines are down. He wants to send a message up North." That last was heavily emphasized.

Reeve turned. "Hello, Tyler."

Tyler Fairfax hadn't changed since the days they'd played at war. He'd enjoyed the game then. Reeve figured he still enjoyed it now. They'd been friends because they understood each other. Tyler, the son of a wealthy distiller, used to idle hours and free sampling from his daddy's casks, made an amusing, clever companion, always with a mischievous scheme in mind falling just shy of doing real harm. Reeve guessed he'd crossed that line some time ago. His pranks were now tools of intimidation, if what Reeve heard was correct. Tyler's idea of loyalty always ran toward who he was with at the moment and how it would benefit him. He had the makings of a dangerous enemy.

"Heya, Reeve." He smiled wide, showing more teeth than a possum while his eyes remained emerald-bright and hard. "Didn't get a chance to say howdy over at the Glade the other night. Quite some party." Never once did he betray his actual sentiments, managing to say just enough to convey a suspicious ambiguity without giving anything of himself away.

Reeve could play the same game. "Heard you've been busy championing the folks of Pride."

"Yessir, found my true calling, you might say. If there's anything my friends and I can do for you, you jus' let me know."

"I'll do that."

Tyler kept smiling with a dazzling insincerity that had Reeve wondering how long it would be before the two of them tangled. It wasn't something he looked forward to.

"What brings you into town? An errand for the squire?"

"No, for myself. If I can get some cooperation."

Gates shrank under Reeve's withering glare, but his belligerent attitude didn't lessen. Instead, he looked anxiously to Tyler. And Tyler Fairfax reveled in that position of power.

Tyler's grin eased just a tad, just enough to light a cold fire in his eyes. "Be a good boy, an' send my friend's telegram." When Gates hesitated a beat longer, he nodded, urging, "Go on now. It's all right."

With a scowl for Reeve, Gates began tapping the key in earnest. Tyler placed a firm hand on his friend's shoulder.

"See there. You jus' got to know how to talk nice to folks."

Reeve didn't back down an increment, returning the fixed stare with like intensity. Finally, Tyler blinked, laughed, and patted his back with what might have been fondness. But wasn't.

"I won't keep you if you got places to go. Good

to see you, Reeve. I'm sure we'll be runnin' into each other again, soon."

Reeve smiled at that veiled promise. "I look forward to it."

After Reeve was safely down the walk, Tyler stretched over the counter top to snatch up the telegram. "Lemme see that." He settled back on his heels, his mouth curving as he read the contents. Tapping his chin with the edge of the paper, he mused, "What you up to, Reeve? You can bet I'll be findin' out."

Chapter 14

News of the bank in Pride reopening swept through the county on a tide of emotion. Hope didn't power the talk. For in the next breath, they identified the bank's new owner, Hamilton Dodge, as their worst nightmare; a Northerner and former Union officer, to boot. And when that Yankee carpetbagger headed out to the Glade his first evening in town, the rumor burnt with a new ferocity—Reeve Garrett had brought the Federal plague upon them.

A Southern home received guests as if they were long-lost family. But when the new banker settled next to his army friend at the Glendower table, he faced a trio of icy stares and one look of bewilderment from Hannah Sinclair, who at least remembered enough of her graciousness to ask about his trip.

"It was hellacious, ma'am. Damned Rebs tore up

so much of the track, I spent more time toting my own bags than enjoying the scenery." He gave a quick nod toward Deacon and Byron, who'd frozen in their seats at his choice of words. "Pardon my bluntness, gents, but I'm not much for traveling. Makes me tired, and if I don't get my rest, I tend to get cranky." He smiled up at Patrice as she stretched around him to fill his wineglass. Appreciation sparkled in his eyes. "Thank you, ma'am. If there's one thing you Southerners know how to do, it's serve your liquor with style."

The answering smile stiffened upon Patrice's lips. It took supreme effort not to upend the rest of the decanter into his lap. But the vintage was too good to waste on their abrasive guest, and such behavior would dismay her mother. So, with a killing glance at Reeve, she returned to her seat and fixed their company with a direct stare.

"So Mr. Dodge, when do you plan to open the bank's doors?"

"I've got one helluva mess to sort through, first, and I've got to find myself someplace to stay." His smile took a wry turn. "Seems every room in town is suddenly full-up. So much for you folks' reputation for hospitality."

"You'll grow on 'em, Dodge," Reeve murmured, grinning into his wineglass. It was his first dinner at the Glendower table where he was the only one comfortable, and he meant to enjoy it.

"Guess I'll be bunking in the back room of the bank. I was hoping I'd seen the last of nights spent on a sagging cot." He shrugged philosophically and focused on his soup.

The entrée was served in silence and consumed in haste as the air of tension increased by the moment. After clearing the dishes away and seating herself once again, Patrice glanced at the stony-faced men on either side of her, then chose to ignore the beseeching lift of her mother's brows pleading, *Don't make any trouble.* If no one had the gumption to ask what they all wanted—needed!—to know, she would.

"And once you get things organized, Mr. Dodge, how long will it be before you start calling in all our loans?" She canted another glare at Reeve, that look saying in effect, *You are responsible for this!* Then she waited to hear what their new banker had to say. Would he lie or tell them straight out?

Dodge chuckled. "I thought you bluegrass belles were supposed to be all blushes and no brain." Then he winced at Reeve's well-placed kick to his shin.

Patrice showed her teeth. Her honied voice purred, "Apparently you were misinformed, Mr. Dodge."

He nudged Reeve with his elbow, failing to provoke a reaction. Pushing his empty wineglass away and dabbing his napkin at his mouth with a sigh of satisfaction, he leaned back in his chair to regard the combative beauty with a level gaze.

"I don't know what notions you have about us monsters up in the North, but I wouldn't be much of a businessman if I bankrupted all my customers, now would I?"

Patrice cast a hopeful eye toward Deacon, but his expression remained still, and his brow, knit with suspicion. "Were you a successful businessman in—where is it?"

"Michigan," Reeve supplied, keeping a cautious

watch on the two of them in case they should go at it with the table knives.

Dodge grinned. "Born and bred and proud of it. And yes, ma'am, I'm a helluva businessman."

"Then you are obviously an exception compared to your other countrymen, for they have descended upon us like a swarm of locusts, determined to get fat off bleeding us dry."

"Patrice!"

"I'm sorry, Mama. But I'm sure Mr. Dodge would want me to speak the truth. I'd heard Northern men liked women of opinion."

Dodge smiled at Reeve, and murmured, "I see what you mean about her." Then to the flashing-eyed female, replied, "Yes, ma'am, I enjoy a woman who speaks her own mind, but not one who claims to be able to read what's on mine." With a nod to his uncommunicative hosts, he rose. "I'd best be on my way. I thank you for the meal and the conversation."

Once out on the broad porch, Dodge drew out a favorite cigar, clipped and lit it, taking a long inhalation before muttering, "Garrett, what the hell have you gotten me into?" He turned at the sound of his friend's footsteps. "Cheerful group. If they had a rope fastened in a loop, we could have had a party."

Reeve didn't smile. It wasn't funny. "They're scared. They're afraid you came down to pull their lives out from under them. It's going to take some doing to convince them otherwise."

"That why you picked me, for my naturally charming ways?"

Reeve snorted. "You're about as subtle as a cannonball. I asked you to come down because you're smart and tough . . . and you owe me the air you're breathing."

Dodge grinned. "Couldn't get anyone else, huh? You should have tried to save more lives, then you'd have had a larger group to choose from."

"After taking a bullet to save the likes of you, I gave up on heroics."

Dodge laughed at the cynical drawl. "Damn, I almost forgot how much I liked you. Can't say the same for the rest of your friends here in Pride."

"They'll warm up to you. How can they resist someone with your tact and diplomacy?"

"In other words, watch my back or I'll find a knife in it."

Reeve's somber nod took the humor out of the situation.

Grinding the cigar butt under his heel, the banker asked, "Are you sure you want me to use all of the money? There isn't a chance in hell that you'll get it all back in this century. Even with my genius."

"I'm not looking for repayment."

Dodge shot him a shrewd glance. "You're looking for forgiveness, and, if you don't mind me saying so, there's not much of a chance of that happening, either."

Reeve shrugged. "Stick to banking instead of fortune-telling, Dodge."

"I don't need a crystal ball to read these people loud and clear. But I'm starting to wonder if you didn't save me from that sniper so you could sacrifice me later." He shoved at Reeve's shoulder. "See you tomorrow, Sergeant. We'll have coffee, if I'm not too full of bullet holes to hold it in."

He untied his reins, then looked back up at Reeve. "I like your little lady. I imagine she'll keep your life . . . and your bed, interesting if she doesn't fillet you out with that sharp tongue of hers first." His bawdy wink was followed by an even cruder suggestion. "Get her between the sheets fast before she cuts off anything important."

"You've got a nasty mind, Dodge."

"It's the only thing that gives me comfort during my nights alone. I'll have to do something about that sad state of affairs soon." Grinning wide, he swung up on his piebald stallion and gave a negligent wave. "Hope these folks are more liberal with their daughters than they are with their trust."

Reeve lifted a hand. "Don't count on it."

"If you brought me down here to die, the least you could do is see I die a happy man."

Reeve watched him ride away. Hamilton Dodge was brusque and aggressive in manner. But he was one hell of a friend. Reeve just hoped he wasn't making the price of that friendship the other man's life.

"Are you crazy bringing him down here?"

Reeve didn't turn at his father's harsh question. "I don't think so."

"When word gets out that you brought a *Yankee* officer to handle our debts, what do you think is going to happen?"

"Reckon we'll find out fairly soon. Even if Gates kept to his oath of confidentiality, Tyler was there when I sent the telegram. I don't imagine it's much of a secret anymore."

"And this is how you intend to win folks over?"

Reeve looked at him then. His features were composed, revealing none of his angry impatience with the other's lack of trust. "It won't matter what they think of me if they don't have homes to live in or businesses to run. Dodge is a good man. He won't extend charity, but he will treat them with respect and fairness. He won't put any families out in the cold."

"And just where did you find such a saint who's willing to invest his money to save our necks?"

Reeve didn't answer with the entire truth. What he said was, "On the battlefield, where you learn real quick who you can depend on." What he didn't say was Hamilton Dodge wasn't putting up any of his own money. The funds to bail out Pride County came from the Glendower account Jonah had sitting safe in a Michigan bank earning a tremendous wartime return from investments Byron Glendower would likely prefer not to know about. Dodge wasn't taking the risk for the sake of their neighbors—he was. And if their plan to revitalize Pride County failed, the Glade, and all his dreams, would be ruined right alongside them.

Patrice frowned as her brother poured another ample glass of whiskey. She'd never known him to be more than a casual imbiber, usually just a taste to be polite. Deacon liked to have his senses about him. But lately, his intentions were far from social. They seemed more directed toward an isolating oblivion. And both she and their mother worried.

She waited until Hannah went up to bed before broaching her concern with the utmost caution. She made her tone light.

"Deacon, I'm going to have to carry you upstairs if you don't pace yourself a little more prudently."

He didn't look at her as he tipped up the glass for a long swallow. "Just leave me down here."

Not exactly the opening she hoped for. She had

to find a way through her brother's impenetrable shell to be any good to him at all. She'd watched the weight of his worries press upon his shoulders, and they were beginning to bow under the unrelenting burden. She needed to let him know she understood, that she wanted to help him. If she could make him listen.

He twitched away from the light touch of her hand upon his arm. Keeping his back to her, he moved to the bank of dark windows overlooking the night. His lean features reflected there in the pane—his moody frown, his troubled brow, the dulled opaque of his eyes.

"I'd rather do my drinking alone."

She refused to heed the dismissal in his flat tone. "I'm sure you would. It can't be pleasant having your sister watch you falling into ruin."

The line of his jaw flexed, but he said nothing.

"Deacon, talk to me. Please."

"There's nothing to say."

"Nothing? Or nothing you care to share with me?"

His silence told her to pick her own answer. She wasn't willing to settle for that.

"We're out of money, aren't we?" She was learning to read his silences. There was an affirmative in his momentary pause of breath, in the stillness that took hold of him. "How bad is it?"

"I'll take care of it." He gulped down the remaining liquor and reached for the nearly empty decanter. She gripped his wrist to halt the gesture. Tendons tensed beneath the cuff of her fingers, but he didn't try to pull away.

"How bad, Deacon?"

The snap of her demand broke through his silence. His eyes went narrow and flinty, regarding her as a threat. "I said I'll take care of it. Or don't you believe me?"

Patrice sighed her frustration and picked her words carefully. "Of course, I believe you'd do anything possible to secure our future and that of the Manor. I'm not questioning that, Deacon. I know how hard you've worked. And I also know what it's like to try to carry on, pretending you can make things as they were. While you were gone, I had that burden, and I know how difficult it is. No one expects miracles from you. Mama and I aren't fools. We can see how bad things are. We're not blaming you for them, and we're not going to be disappointed if you have to ask for help."

"Help? What kind of help?"

She could see by the tightening of his mouth and jawline he thought she was accusing him of failure, that she questioned his ability to take care of them. His defenses slammed up, making a prideful fortress to keep out reason. Whether to the drink or to the sense of defeat, she was losing him. She took a frantic gamble to keep him from slipping away.

"Go to the bank, Deacon."

"To that Yankee?" He stared at her, amazed, disbelieving.

"I don't like him either, but he's our only choice. We can't rebuild on dreams of the past. We need money. We need materials. Pride isn't going to supply them. The bank is where the money is. If you go to this man and explain our situation—"

"He'll strip us of everything we have without blinking an eye. You don't bare your throat to an enemy."

"He's said he won't foreclose—"

"Patrice, don't be a fool! What did you expect him to say? He's already got the power to take our lands. Now you want to just hand him our souls? What's come over you? You think Garrett brought him here to save us? You want to place our future blindly in that murdering bastard's hands?"

Patrice paled. A weakening panic shook through her. She scrambled for an argument, some way around her brother's distrust. She had to make him see it wasn't about "them and us." It was about people working together to rebuild their county.

"Deacon, please. The trust has got to start somewhere if we're to—"

"What? Survive? You don't survive by trusting. Trusting makes you vulnerable and gets you dead. You trust yourself, your own kind, your family. That's all. You don't give strangers power over you. You don't invite them to dinner and smile while they insult you and your ways. What's wrong with you, Patrice? Your feelings for Garrett making you soft in the head?"

Color flamed to her face. "At least I have feelings, and I've learned to believe in them. You've never cared for anyone or anything your whole life unless Father told you to."

Her accusation struck home. He winced, taking a step back. A host of emotions skirted the hard edge of his control but couldn't escape it. He spoke with a chilling tonelessness.

"You don't have any idea what I do or do not care about. I don't let my feelings rule my judgment."

"Then I feel sorry for you. You may call me foolish, but at least I'm not some frigid autocrat shut off from the world and those who care about me.

Not like you and Father. You're wrong, Deacon. You're wrong in this. We can't survive alone."

If her words reached him at all, his outward expression gave no sign of it. Fury and fear roiled beneath that blank facade as he said, "We're already living off charity. Something our father would never have allowed if he were still alive."

"No. He'd have us huddling in the shell of the Manor using our arrogance to keep us dry and warm."

The sting of his palm came so fast, she had no time to brace for it. Patrice clasped her burning cheek in surprise. Horror at what he'd done took momentary control of her brother's face. She could see the desperate apology working in those stricken features. Then he blinked and the chill was back, separating deed from consequence, making excuses when none were acceptable.

"I won't have that kind of talk. Not ever." His tone was as slick and cold as black ice. "We are Sinclairs. That name has always meant something in Pride and always will. I'll see to it just like Father did. I make the decisions now, and you will not go against them. Do you hear me? Do you hear me, Patrice?"

She heard and was sick at heart. It was her father standing there, giving one of his unbending lectures. Shutting out advice, closing out logic. Refusing to consider she had a mind and a right to speak it. Clinging to what once was instead of looking to what could be. And those age-old attitudes would be the death of them, just as the glorious South was dying from the same lack of vision. Her answer was quiet, toneless, as empty of life as her brother's expression.

"You've made yourself very clear."

As she exited the room, Deacon resisted the urge to call her back, to plead insanity, to beg her forgiveness. He suppressed those anxious cries of the heart by refilling his glass and taking another determined swallow.

It started as an aimless walk to work the shaking from her limbs and the numbing anguish from her mind. She moved through the thickening darkness aware of nothing but her misery. Though her cheek ached dully, that pain was mild compared to the shock scoring her soul.

He'd hit her. Her brother had struck her and turned upon her as if she were guilty of betraying him and all he stood for. That had never—ever—been her intent. Even through the glaze of her tears, she could see her mistake now. In confronting him with her opposing views, she'd backed him into a corner, forcing him to strike out or break down. How scared and desperate he must be feeling to resort to such drastic action. In trying to offer her assistance, she'd managed to close the door between them, perhaps locking it forever. For him to make any move in her direction now would mean confessing he was wrong, that their father had been wrong, that the war was wrong and their very standard of life was in error. He couldn't do that. Why had she thought he'd behave any differently than any man of the South raised to value respect over love, and pride over common sense?

She'd reached the stables. There, she leaned her forearms on the whitewashed rail of the empty breeding paddock, allowing the melancholy mood to possess her. Only the startling warmth of strong fingers upon her jaw shook her out of it.

"Who hit you?"

Patrice stared up into Reeve's thunderous features in alarm. Trapped by the obvious, she found herself stammering, "H-hit me?"

Reeve angled her cheek toward the pale moonlight, outlining it with a surprisingly light touch. "This looks about the size of your brother's hand."

His fierce tone dared her to disagree, so she didn't. Her chin notched up in a demand to know what made it his concern.

"You'd best tell me why before I march inside and beat the hell out of him. Not that any reason will be good enough to stop me from doing it anyway."

"Leave him alone." The defensive anger in her voice surprised the both of them. "This has nothing to do with you."

But of course it did. It had everything to do with him and the way her feelings for him were pulling her between lust and loyalty. How could she go against her own family, her own flesh and blood? How frivolous to let desire dictate to her.

"No man has a right to lay a hand upon a woman," Reeve growled. "I don't care if he is family."

Patrice jerked her head back, freeing herself of his bewitching heat. He was the one confusing her, making her doubt tradition. She'd let her misguided infatuation in him draw her away from propriety. She'd disregarded her duties in making an appropriate match, too caught up in his brooding mystery. She'd been helpless to resist. He'd kissed her when they were little more than children and had listened to her words of love, but never once had he returned them. Never once.

She was Patrice Sinclair of Sinclair Manor, not some fancy-free girl who could flirt and cast her affection frivolously. It was time she grew up and took her responsibilities seriously.

"My brother has every right," she told Reeve with a touch of indignation coloring her words. "He woke me up to my true place in life. I've indulged myself without caring who it hurt. I've obligations to my family that I can't ignore. Don't ask me to."

She walked back to the house, leaving him with a gnawing anxiety that somehow he'd just lost his hope of ever having her.

Patrice went directly to the library. With a wary caution, Deacon watched her approach. When her arms went around him, he went as rigid as one of the Manor's pillars. He didn't touch her. He was barely even breathing. It didn't matter to Patrice if he wasn't completely certain of her motives. What mattered was her conviction that she was doing the right thing.

Just as Deacon was sure he was doing the right thing when he found Tyler Fairfax seated on his half-completed front steps, grinning like a dog over a meaty bone.

"Heard you wanted to see me, Rev. 'Bout time."

Chapter 15

Patrice's sudden turnabout in mood and manner had everyone mystified over dinner. The abruptly meek and soft-spoken woman fell under close scrutiny as she sat beside her brother, nodding at his every word.

"We're going to have it all back," he announced in a broad stroke of optimism. Patrice smiled up at him, her gaze warm with belief. It made him pause, off-balance, then go on with renewed certainty. "I've got materials coming in tomorrow and enough workers to see us back in the Manor by the end of next week."

Hannah smiled her bewilderment. "Did you talk to that young man at the bank?"

"No, of course not. He's not getting his hands any tighter around our throats. Once we get crops in, we can shake him off our backs and we won't be beholden to anyone."

It sounded simple. Nothing was that easy. Reeve studied Deacon as he spoke, searching for clues to his sudden almost buoyant attitude. He'd never met a man harder to read. But in his gut, he knew Deacon was hiding something behind his smooth assurances and bland smile. Something bad, if not dangerous.

"So," he drawled out. "If not from the bank, where did you find this sudden fortune?"

He looked Reeve right in the eye and said without a flicker of expression, the biggest, boldest lie Reeve had ever heard. "From overseas investments Father made before the war. I'd forgotten them until the solicitor came out to the Manor this morning."

Reeve glanced at Patrice. He saw her mouth purse slightly, but she said nothing. She must have felt the same jangle of suspicions that rattled through him, only this time, she let them go unspoken. Her acceptance of a blatant falsehood alarmed him more than the lie itself.

Noting the focus of Reeve's stare, Deacon turned to his sister with a pleasant and totally out-of-character smile. Like watching the sun rise in the middle of the night.

"Patrice, I want you and Mother to come into town with me tomorrow. We need to order papering and window things. I'll turn that over to you. And I want you both to buy yourselves new dresses, shoes, whatever you need. I don't want to take you home looking like poor relations."

Hannah's concern deepened. "But Deacon, we can't afford—"

He still smiled, but his gaze held a definite rebuke. "Hush now, Mother. I can afford anything you want. Don't worry your head over it."

"If you say so, dear," came her meekly murmured reply.

But Reeve noticed that the uneasiness never truly left her. She knew something was not quite right about their sudden riches, too. However, she'd been trained since birth never to reveal her doubts, especially not in public. And not when her son wore the same forbidding mask her husband had adopted when he absolutely would not tolerate any questions.

The rest of the meal went quickly, with Deacon speaking casually of the repairs to Sinclair Manor and no one daring to challenge him on how. Reeve pointedly ignored the squire's urgent stares, knowing this new twist in things disturbed him. Patrice back under Deacon's thumb at the Sinclair home did not bode well for romance and the continuation of his name. And he wanted to know what Reeve meant to do about it.

Reeve didn't know what to tell him. He didn't know the answer himself.

The meal over, Patrice excused herself, looking weary and a bit wan. Solicitously, Deacon pulled back her chair and personally escorted her to the base of the stairs, careful not to touch her even accidentally. She'd used something to cover the mark of his heavy-handedness, but that didn't relieve his guilt, knowing it was there and he, the cause. His sister's malleability made him edgy. She was far from docile by nature, and he'd expected her to clash with him over his announcement at the table. Proper time and place never deterred her from loudly voicing her views, but something had.

She began to climb the stairs, halting at his hesitant call of her name. She turned slowly, her features a lovely blank. At her elevated position, they were almost eye to eye. He longed to reach out then but, more afraid than he'd ever been of anything in his life that she would flinch away, he left his arms hanging heavily at his sides.

Finally, she spoke, her voice barely above a whisper.

"I hope you've forgiven my behavior last night. I don't know what came over me. I didn't mean to doubt you, Deacon. I'm so sorry if I—"

His fingertips settled on her lips to stop the rest of her quavering confession, then did a light sketch across her injured cheek. When she didn't withdraw, he brought her to him to press a kiss upon her forehead.

"Sleep well," he murmured, as she drew away.

And he stood, watching as she ascended the stairs, the want to confide all battling with a grim sense of justification.

"What are you up to, Deacon?"

He didn't favor Reeve with a look, but a defensive tension quickly overtook him. "I don't answer to you, Garrett."

"But you best be answering to your family, 'cause I know you don't have a conscience. And no investment return, either."

"I'm taking care of my family." His gaze followed the trailing edge of his sister's skirt as it disappeared with a graceful shimmer into the upper hall.

"Where'd the money come from?"

Deacon pivoted. Their stares collided. Neither faltered.

"We take care of our own, Garrett. You forgot that when you turned on everything you once knew."

"I didn't turn away from what was right. And I didn't lie to my family or myself." If he'd hoped for a reaction, he didn't get one. "I won't let you use Patrice in whatever scheme you're tied up in."

"You won't *let* me? Patrice is none of your concern, and if you think I'd ever let that change as long as I'm breathing, you're dead wrong."

Reeve leaned in closer, involving his larger mass with the intended threat. His tone lowered, loaded with menace. "You won't be breathing long if you ever put a mark on her again."

That got a wince of response, so perhaps he had a conscience after all. But it wasn't strong enough to overset his possessive male pride. Casting off his remoteness, Deacon bristled, letting the matter become very personal.

"Stay away from me and my family, Garrett. It could prove very bad for your health. You're on borrowed time already."

With that sinister warning laid out plainly, he stalked away, gait stiff, straight, as rigid as his ideals. But something had bent and possibly broken in Deacon Sinclair. Reeve had to find out what it was. Before Patrice or her mother got hurt.

A shiny carriage arrived in the morning to take the Sinclairs into town. Deacon's casual acceptance of it warned the ladies to say nothing. Their provider was full of surprises and not forthcoming with any answers.

Patrice tried to tell herself it didn't matter as the well-sprung conveyance bounced down a road left rutted by two passing armies. It wasn't her place to question her brother. He'd said he would take care of things and, apparently, made good on his word.

In the past, she'd never thought to demand an accounting from their father when he purchased equipment, nor did she ask where he'd gotten the money for it. Deacon said it was from investments.

Perhaps it was.

She wanted very badly to believe him.

Reeve didn't. She tried not to put any undue weight on that fact. Reeve didn't like her brother, so why would he trust him? There had always been a conflict and rivalry between them.

She studied Deacon from her side of the carriage, looking for . . . what, she wasn't sure. Guilt, maybe. No trace of any wrongdoing tugged at his handsome features. He looked sinless as a saint even when he caught her scrutiny and returned it unblinkingly. He was no saint. She glanced away first, uneasiness roiling.

Where had he gotten the money?

Confrontation wouldn't lend answers. He'd take it as another sign of her lack of faith, and she'd promised herself she would not undercut his confidence again. Whatever miracle had lifted him from bottled despair to this renewed air of authority, she should accept it gratefully. She *would* accept it regardless of its source. She owed him that loyalty.

A loyalty sorely shaken when she and her mother came out of the millinery shop later to find him in somber conversation with Tyler Fairfax.

Uneasiness burst into full-blown anxiety. Whatever brought the two unlikely compatriots to put their heads together boded ill for all concerned. She knew what her brother thought of Tyler. He wouldn't nod to him in passing unless Patrice made him. In his estimation, Tyler ranked with something to be scraped off the bottom of his boots. And she knew Tyler and what dangerous business he was involved in. Putting the two together chilled her like an early frost.

Tyler lit up with Fourth of July brilliance when he saw her. Her brother's reaction was considerably more subdued.

"Heya, darlin'." Tyler snatched up her hand. His mouth scorched a hot, wet trail across her knuckles, while green eyes engaged hers in a dance that was more than just friendly. An insinuating passion smoldered there. It startled her. When he kept her hand a beat too long, she pulled it away with an accompanying frown. Unaffected, he turned his charm upon her mother. "Why, Miz Sinclair, you are lookin' lovely this mornin'." He paid gallant homage over her hand as well. Wickedly gorgeous, he exuded the sultry invitation of still-warm rumpled sheets. His open-throated shirt looked as though he'd buttoned it up hastily on his way out of someone's bedroom window. Deacon's glare could have cleaved him in two.

"So," Patrice began on a falsely cheery note, "what have you gentleman been discussing with such interest?"

Tyler sidled up next to her, his arm winding about her waist with an easy familiarity. She could almost hear her brother's teeth gnashing. "Well, darlin', I'm sorry to say, nothin' as pleasant as askin' when I can come acourtin' you in earnest." His wide smile and mischievous eyes turned toward Deacon. "We was just finishing up our talk about the acres your brother plans to turn over to rye production for my daddy's distillery."

"Really?" Patrice pinned Deacon with a look. "I

had no idea we were thinking of putting in a variety of crops."

"Progress, Miz Patrice. Gotta move with the times."

Knowing her brother was as deeply entrenched in past traditions as the foundations of their home, that explanation fell far short of believable. But she could hardly call him and her brother liars. Not on the middle of Pride's boardwalk.

"Why I surely wish I had more time to chat with you ladies, but I promised Deke, here, that I'd advise him on the best kinda seed to sow."

Too nonplussed by the idea of Deacon taking Tyler's advice on whether it was day or night, let alone soliciting his suggestions about what mix to plant, Patrice barely protested when Tyler ducked close to fondly buss her ear. Again, fury pulsed from her brother in palpable waves. Odd behavior in a new business associate.

After the two men crossed the street, heading toward the feed and grain, Hannah remarked, "He's quite the forward young man, isn't he?"

"Tyler Fairfax? He hasn't the slightest notion about propriety. Both he and Starla are that way. It must come from losing their mother when so young."

"A handsome boy. I'd say he's every bit as pretty-featured as his sister, except for a certain . . . I don't quite know what it is."

Patrice knew. There was an edge to Tyler Fairfax, a razor sharp, right-for-the-throat edge drawn like the flash of his lethal blade when he was crossed. Both he and Starla hoarded secrets they wouldn't share with another living soul, a darkness Tyler drowned in liquor, Starla hid behind her dazzling coquette's smile. That bond of silence between them created a protective closeness no one could penetrate. If there was decency in Tyler, his love for Starla anchored it there. And in her absence, dangerous currents went unchecked, making him, in Patrice's mind, quite unpredictable.

"Funny," Hannah continued as they began to stroll down the walk, "he doesn't seem at all like someone your brother would have as a friend."

Deacon had no friends Patrice knew of, not even as a child. His off-putting nature prevented that kind of connection with another human being. Though she agreed Tyler was an odd choice even for an impersonal partnership, she was unwilling to distress her mother with any unfounded worries.

And how could she prove them without going straight to Deacon, the source?

"Well, howdy, Miz Sinclair. What a nice surprise to see you in town."

Mother and daughter paused to let Sadie Dermont and her niece catch up to them. Sadie was a big, rawboned woman with a loud voice and uncouth manner. She and her consumptive husband, a third cousin, ran Pride's boardinghouse, where the quality of the cooking offset the offensiveness of its hostess. They had no children of their own, so her brother's lazy brood of boys showed up on occasion to earn drinking money, and their sister, Delyce, a fresh daisy abloom in chokeweed, served as maid and tended tables before returning to her own home to perform the same services. Hannah smiled and offered a polite greeting because she was too well bred to snub another living soul. Patrice said a friendly hello to Delyce. She pitied the girl for her wretched circumstance, yet admired her ability to endure and remain somehow untouched by her family's vulgarity.

Sadie wasn't known for her tact. If a rumor spread through Pride, one could bet it started at her loose lips. She leaned in, her attitude one of conspiritorial privilege.

"I bet the two of you will be so thankful to be back in your own home. Why I don't think I could have closed my eyes at night whilst under the same roof as a murderer."

Patrice was about to ask if she suffered from insomnia when her nephews visited, but Hannah's serene intervention caught her up in time.

"Why, Mrs. Dermont, I'm afraid I don't know what you mean."

"That Yankee vermin," she hissed in a booming aside that was overheard by everyone within two blocks.

"Mr. Garrett?" Hannah managed to look both mildly shocked and gently disapproving. "Why he's been the perfect host. He's even helped my son with the rebuilding of the Manor."

Sadie's meaty brow furrowed, her small mind confused by this news. "But I heard tell he was responsible for executing poor little Miss Sinclair's fiancé . . . his own flesh and blood." A nasty gleam brightened her bovine gaze as she waited to learn some juicy tidbit of scandal. She was doomed to disappointment.

"What happened to Jonah Glendower was indeed a tragedy, but I don't believe Mr. Garrett is personally to blame for every atrocity committed by the Union Army. I cannot imagine anyone so silly as to believe that as the truth."

Sadie flushed a ruddy hue, smart enough to recognize the delicately phrased barb. Her tone roughened. "I heard he gave the order hisself."

Hannah sighed, unwilling to be pulled in by Sadie's baiting. "War was a truly awful experience for us all, and I for one, will be thankful when all the ugliness is allowed to settle. Don't you agree, Mrs. Dermont?"

Flattered by the elegant woman's warm inclusion, Sadie smiled and nodded until her ridiculously over-decorated bonnet threatened to come undone. She beamed at Patrice. "At least you've some happy news to celebrate."

Patrice regarded the smug harridan in bewilderment.

"You don't have to worry that I'll spoil the announcement," Sadie gushed, pleased to share a secret with the Sinclairs.

"Announcement?"

"You and Tyler Fairfax. There are some who've frowned about it being so quick after your fiancé went into the ground—"

"Tyler Fairfax? Where on earth did you hear that?"

Delyce spoke up. "From my brothers, Miss Patrice." And big soft eyes went round, asking if it was untrue.

Patrice struggled for a moment, forcing even breaths to stave off her outrage. Finally, in a remarkably level tone, she said, "That information is quite premature. Nothing's been discussed with my brother yet. I do hope you've been discreet."

Sadie's florid cheeks darkened, and Patrice groaned to herself. *Dear God, everyone knows.* She was going to strangle Tyler until those pretty green eyes popped right out of his head. The bad feeling she already had got worse.

"What shall I tell folks to ward off the gossip?"

"Tell them that Starla Fairfax is special to me and that as he is her brother, I think of Tyler as an old and dear friend. You should tell them fie upon their ungenerous spirits. Though Jonah and I weren't wed, I mourn him as a widow. I haven't even begun to have thoughts of romance yet."

That should shut up Tyler and his cronies.

She held to her dignity as they continued along the walk, leaving Sadie Dermont to stew on the news—or the lack of it. The Dermonts would see Tyler got the message. But was there more to it than reckless boasting? Would her brother barter her off without consulting her first? Was that the reason behind all their whispering? She couldn't believe it of him.

But then a week ago, she wouldn't have believed she'd ever cringe at the slightest upward movement of his hand.

Self-consciously, she touched her cheek, where carefully applied powder hid the rapidly fading imprint of his slap. She hadn't backed down because she was now afraid of him. Deacon would never harm her. *But he had*, whispered a wary voice. Alcohol brought on that fit of violence, came an anxious excuse, not the desire to hurt and intimidate her.

But it had, hadn't it?

One blow, intentional or not, quelled her spirit and put a quick end to her rebellion. The tender kiss to her brow was to earn her forgiveness. Or was it to placate her? *No man has the right*. She'd refused to heed Reeve's words then, but now they made an unpleasant echo in her mind.

Because even if she didn't want to admit it, Patrice was afraid of the man her brother had become.

Chapter 16

⟨⟨**A** penny."

Patrice turned away from the gallery rail to see Reeve's impressive silhouette framed against the doorway. She expressed no alarm at him coming upon her in her softly draped nightclothes. False modesty wasn't something she subscribed to. Still, he didn't come any closer, as she asked, "What?"

"For your thoughts."

She gave a wry laugh and looked back out into the night. "You'd be cheating yourself tonight."

"Oh come now, it can't be all that bad," he cajoled with a gentle teasing.

The words just came, pushed out by a spirit full of anguish and uncertainty. "Deacon slapped me, Reeve." Her chin notched upward. "He's never put a hand on me before, but if he does it again, I'd like very much for you to beat the hell out of him."

A thoughtful pause, then a firm, "It would be my pleasure."

There was more. He could feel it. He could see it in the tense set of her shoulders as they hunched forward to keep the world at bay. He heard it in the forced calm of her voice. Alone and vulnerable, she huddled inside her silky robe, arms hugging tight to wrap the isolation in and ward the fear away. The need to add the strength of his embrace to that insulating circle almost overruled caution. He saw opening and opportunity in her unhappy stance. Their time together was growing short.

He'd heard disturbing news from Dodge. Even an outsider was privy to gossip if he eavesdropped carefully. The Sinclairs' tax debt had been paid almost in full, and not by Deacon Sinclair. Dodge hadn't caught the particulars. He'd added one further rumor, one Reeve found ridiculous at first, and then damned threatening.

Patrice and Tyler Fairfax.

Patrice laughed it off the night of their party. Because it wasn't true or because she didn't want it known? He had to know, now, before he took further risks with his heart.

"I'm a good listener. That's what you used to tell me."

She didn't respond right away. He could almost hear her thoughts churning, weighing the benefits, the dangers.

"We can walk, if you like. Just walk. You don't have to say anything if you don't want to." A casual offer, no pressure, no strings, no reason to stir objection or suspicion of his motives. He waited, mentally urging, *Take it, Patrice. Don't be afraid.*

She looked back out over the deep evening shadows, where the scent of honeysuckle perfumed the air and silvery moonlight shone blue and rich upon the far pastures.

"It's a nice night," she commented without committing.

"It is."

She started for the gallery steps, not looking back to see if he followed, unconcerned that she was hardly dressed for an excursion with a man in shirt-sleeves. He didn't crowd her, but rather let her precede him down the outside stairs and out across the springy side yard. She moved like a flickering moonbeam in her pale ivory robe, drifting in and out of the latticework darkness cast down from the live oaks above. She didn't speak, so he didn't either, content to follow, to wait, to give her plenty of room until the right moment arose.

They'd come to one of the upper meadows, where nothing obscured the beauty of the heavens and the peaceful sense of solitude. He hadn't expected her to walk so far, but maybe what weighed upon her mind needed more than a short stroll to sift and sort. Maybe it took that long for her mood to lose its restless edge and the inhibiting presence of family. Then she stopped, without facing him, and abruptly began talking.

"You were right ... about a lot things." She paused, expecting a reply. When it didn't come, she continued, her own need to release her troubles goading her rather than his prompting. "I'm scared, Reeve. I've never been so scared of anything before."

He couldn't help the gruff texture in his voice. "Because of Deacon?"

"No. Yes ... no." She shook her head. To clear

her thoughts or to convince herself. Then her answer. "I'm not afraid of him." A lie. "For him. For our family." A pause to gather her courage. "Reeve, where do you think he got the money?"

He had some pretty good ideas but wasn't ready to push them on her yet. Instead, he asked, "Where do you think?"

"Not from the bank. I . . . I asked him to go there, to talk to your friend."

"Did you?" That surprised him. She hadn't seemed that open-minded about their guest at dinner.

"Deacon—he got very angry because I suggested it."

That was when he struck her, the bastard. Quietly, he asked, "So if not the bank, who else has money to lend?" And at what price? That was what really had her worried.

She hugged herself again, chafing her palms over upper arms as if cold. "I think he got it from Tyler Fairfax."

So did Reeve, yet still he asked, "Does Tyler have that kind of money to lend?"

"He's got lots of it. His father's distillery never shut down during the war. Apparently, alcohol was one of the fuels that powered our brave armies." Bitterness tinged her voice as it lowered with conjecture. "I think they were engaged in illegal trade with the North, too."

"It wasn't illegal, Patrice. Kentucky as a whole supported the Union."

"Immoral here in Pride County, then. They were making profit off our enemies."

"Why would Tyler give credit to your brother?"

"For the free use of some of our best acres to

grow the rye his father needs to make bourbon."
She hesitated as if there was more she wanted to
say but chose not to. Or was afraid to.

For her. Was Patrice part of the price Tyler named
for his generosity? She didn't say, and he couldn't
ask. Not yet. She hadn't lowered her guard enough
to let him get close. It was time to nudge her in that
direction.

She flinched beneath the weight of his hands on
her shoulders, out of surprise, not resistance.
Slowly, firmly, he began massaging the corded tendons running from taut shoulders to her neck. "You
look tired."

"I am. I haven't been able to sleep, worrying over
what we're going to do."

She gave her head a luxurious roll. Lose tendrils
of her hair caressed the backs of his hands. Reeve
struggled to maintain the impersonal pressure and
unhurried rhythm. He eased up closer behind her,
not touching but near enough to convey the heat
and strength of his presence. He felt a shudder of
awareness ripple through her on a level that was
sensory not cognizant as the tension began to melt
away in warm rivers.

"I don't trust Tyler," she told him. "I know him
too well to think he's just being neighborly. He's
involved in some unsavory doings with the Dermont boys and others like them. I don't have proof
of it. It's more like a feeling. Reeve, how could Deacon be so foolish as to entrust our property, our
future to men like that?"

The last thing he intended was to make apologies
for Deacon Sinclair's stubborn stupidity, but that's
exactly what he heard himself doing. Anything to
ease the torment he heard in her words. "He's

scared, too, 'Trice. He's seeing his whole way of life ending, and he's trying his best to hold on to it. A desperate man makes bad decisions to protect those he loves."

"I don't know that he does," she confessed in a tight little voice. "Love me, I mean. He's so much like our father. It's the land, the name, the status they love."

Reeve nodded to himself. Like his father, like generations of Southern men to whom possession and pride were all and family fell into those categories right next to breeding stock and immortality. It wasn't personal. It was business, tradition like crops and politics and slaves—something to hold and control for the power it gave them.

Patrice's strength suddenly left her. She sank down upon the lengthy grasses, lying back with her arms stretched out above her head, her legs curved to one side in a graceful bend. Her body relaxed with the deep expression of a single sigh.

God, she was beautiful. Reeve wondered if she had any idea how stunned he was by his own desire. By the way her robe pulled taut over her untethered breasts, the way they jutted high and full against the strain of sumptuous fabric. How the slight lift of one knee caused the overlap of her robe to slide open so only her thin nightrail covered the gentle rounding of hip and thigh. The way she looked with such yearning toward the evening sky and scattering of distant stars, wistfulness softening her features, moonlight gleamed pearlescent upon the sweet curve of her cheek and sleek line of her bared throat—by the time he remembered to breathe, his chest was clogged tight and aching with want. He released it in a gust as shaky as his will.

Afraid she'd catch him gawking down at her like a lovesick pup, Reeve sat himself beside her, then lay back to pillow his head atop laced hands. Easier to keep them out of trouble that way. While Patrice lounged next to him as languorous and mellow as warmed custard, he was strung taut as a rope around the neck of a wild horse. Only one thing could fulfill him, and he was as scared of frightening her with the forceful demands of his body as he was of her rejection. It was hell to be so close and not touch. Torture to hear her soft breathing and not swallow it up with an urgent kiss. The self-control it took just to lie there shook like a fever chill to the bone. She made that airy sighing sound again, and he nearly groaned aloud with the struggle it took not to roll himself on top of her.

He could feel her studying him. He didn't dare glance her way, certain she'd see the cauldron of need roiling red-hot all the way to his soul.

"Reeve?"

"Hmmm?"

"You are a good listener. I'd forgotten how easy it's always been to tell you anything because you don't push your own opinions and you never judge. I've missed our talks."

He went completely still, muscles tensed. He jumped at the light touch of her fingertips beneath his chin, refusing to look at her until she caught his face in the vee of her hand and angled his head toward her. Then he opened his eyes, wary, ready to leap away at the first sign of weakening.

And then she struck his will a shattering blow by saying softly, soberly, "I've missed you."

"Have you?"

He was afraid she'd take that as a challenge, but

hostility never surfaced. Instead, she edged closer to rest her head upon his arm. He froze, not daring to pull away because he could guess how long it had taken her to reach this juncture, to speak with such openness, such trust.

"We parted badly when you went off to war, and I was so afraid I'd never have the chance to tell you how sorry I was about that."

" 'Trice—"

She shook her head in a silent plea for him not to stop her. "I didn't know how to treat you when you came home. I was so relieved and, at the same time, so damned mad. It was easier to stay mad than to say I was sorry."

"You don't have anything to apologize for."

She rolled onto her back, but not before he glimpsed the depth of anguish in her eyes. He knew then she was ready to speak about the subject they'd kept silent between them. It was Jonah. But she didn't tell him more. Instead, her lips curved with a poignant smile.

"Remember how the three of us used to sneak out here to watch the stars?"

"I remember." He shifted slightly, twisting his arm around so that she rested within its easy loop. An instinctive gesture though not the wisest. It brought him up onto his side so he looked down upon his every dream. "And the two of us."

I'll love you until the day I die, Reeve Garrett. She'd said that to him here, on such a night as this one.

Her smile grew even more melancholy. "And my birthday when you made me cry because you wouldn't come inside and have cake with everyone else."

He remembered the scald of those eight-year-

old's tears and how pride prevented him from telling her that her father had forbidden him to follow
the other children into the Manor. He'd understood
even at that young age even though she hadn't;
one's servants were allowed to romp in the yard,
but were not guests to be invited within the home.
He hadn't told her the truth then because he wanted
to protect himself. He didn't tell her now because
he wanted to protect her.

"How could you have missed me with all those
other boys trying to steal kisses?" He tried to light-
ened her mood with teasing but her features remained solemn.

"You were the only one I let kiss me, Reeve. Why
didn't you come inside?" The emotion behind that
question went far deeper than an eight-year-old's
disappointment. Her eyes darkened. "I was afraid
it was because you didn't like me."

Finally, he was able to say, "I was afraid I'd like
you too much."

She gazed up at him, stars shining in her eyes.
"What about our kisses?"

"What about them?"

"Were you afraid you'd like them too much,
too?" she clarified in a whisper.

How could he taunt her when such naked vul-
nerability glistened in her eyes?

"Too much not to want more of them."

Her lips parted as his callused fingers skimmed
her cheek. He breathed in her soft gasp of anticipation as his mouth lowered, closing over hers. Ah,
the sweetness he found there. He was drunk with
her taste, her nearness. Intoxicated by the willing
way she invited him inside with the timid touch of
her tongue to his. Her fingernails rasped against his

stubbled jaw as she reached for the back of his head. Drawing him closer, half over her in her eagerness, drawing on his mouth as if his each breath provided the sustenance of life.

Patrice closed her mind to thought and concentrated just on feeling. Too much thinking, too much rationalizing, kept her from reaching for this particular paradise the moment he'd come home. Worrying that he'd reject her. Fear over what people would say. Wondering if her motives were ones of true passion or a rebellious response to her father's restricting rule. She matched Reeve kiss for kiss, swept away by glorious expectations fully met, giving herself over to the desperate arousal always rumbling between them. The raspy sound of his rough palms snagging over the silk of her gown was enough to incite an anxious trembling, a fear that if he stopped now, she would go out of her mind with want. He didn't stop, and she moaned against his mouth as he captured her breast beneath the spread of his hand.

He wasn't gentle, but that was all right. Patrice didn't want gentle, she wanted the thrill of his impatience, his urgency, the raw, unfettered proof of his desire for her. He kissed her hard, bruising her lips beneath the slanting pressure of his own, his tongue plunging deep to conquer. Harsh stubble abraded her skin with a wildly erotic prickling as his mouth scrubbed down the taut arch of her throat toward the tender mound he'd been shaping with the strong rhythmic flex of his fingers. First, she felt the moist heat of his ragged breaths scorching through the bodice of her gown. Her nipples beaded with unbearable sensation. Then his mouth fastened upon one turgid peak, sending hot tremors streaking through her. It was too much, too intense. Her head rolled wildly side to side, the clean scent of crushed grasses filling her nose. Her legs shifted restlessly, encouraging him to settle hard and heavy between them. He rocked into her, prodding her thigh with the exciting and alarmingly large evidence of his need.

He took her mouth again, groaning her name in a hoarse, thick voice she would never have recognized. The sound provoked an even greater urgency. Her palms pushed over his tense shoulders, rubbing hard, pressing him into her so that her breasts flattened beneath the solid wall of his chest, pinning her, dominating her with his weight. As she yanked at the back of his shirt to free it from his trouser band, his hand slid down between them, his caress insistent, seeking, tunneling within the wrap of her silk gown between the juncture of her thighs until he discovered the heat and startling dampness the thin fabric couldn't hide, pressing into it until she gasped and strained against him. Helplessly, she cried out his name.

The sound of her voice was the shock it took to awake her to the reality of what he was doing. Abruptly, she pushed away from him, dropping him over onto his back. Stunned by her own willingness to surrender up more than kisses, Patrice closed her eyes, her breath laboring against the tide of runaway passions.

"I'm sorry, 'Trice. It didn't mean for it to be more than talking."

"Don't be sorry. It's my fault, too." She took a shaky breath and confessed. "I wanted it to be more than talking."

He was silent, not knowing how to respond so she continued.

"It's just that my heart and mind are so confused."

"Because of me?" A brief pause, then a husky, "Or someone else?"

She looked at him them, admiring his strong profile, the hard set of his jaw, the rapid way his chest rocked with agitated breathing. "It's not because I don't want you . . . you're the only man I've ever wanted. You know that."

He glanced at her warily. "Is it Jonah?"

"Not everything has to do with what was between you and Jonah." She smiled sadly. "It's me, Reeve. I can't give you the only thing that's left for me to give. It wouldn't be fair to my family . . . or me. I've lost everything else."

"So," he stated in an expressionless conclusion, "you're going to let your family hold you for the highest bidder."

She came up over him, her eyes ablaze with fierce sincerity.

"No. It's my choice. And I'll make it when I'm sure, when I'm thinking with my head instead of my—my—Oh, Reeve, I can't think at all when I'm alone with you."

He caught her beautiful, bewildered face between hands that were far from steady, pulling her down, claiming her lips with a kiss that went quickly from savage to aching sweet. He kissed her chin, the tip of her nose, her forehead, then he pushed her off of him. "Does that help you decide?"

The fire in her eyes told him with graphic clarity what she'd wanted. But she held to her resolve even as her palms pushed over the front of his shirt, charting the firm terrain of his chest and shoulders. "Don't confuse me, Reeve. I need time to sort through things. I—I need you to be my friend."

Reeve smiled slightly as he pulled the gaping front of her robe together and retied her belt. "I've always been that. And more." The throaty quality of his vow increased her frustration.

"I want to be more, Patrice."

"Not now."

"When?"

"Give me time. Why start something we may not be able to finish?" She pushed up off of him, wobbling to her feet, staring down in an almost panicked dismay at him in his untucked and all too inviting sprawl.

"Oh, we'll finish. I promise you." He gripped her wrist and tugged her down on top of him, rolling her beneath him to still her struggles. She gave up the fight as soon as he began to lower his head. Her lips parted to welcome the press of his, and the curl of her arms about his neck held him there longer than she'd planned. Long enough to be dangerous. He sat back, breathing hard.

"You don't kiss like you want me for just a friend."

Reeve's smiled faded. "You have more to give than just the Sinclair name. What makes you think I hold any value there? It's not the name I want."

Her cheeks reddened, growing hot as she explained, "I wasn't talking about the Sinclair name. I was talking about my virtue."

His eyes narrowed into glittering slits. "What else is there to hold on to, Patrice, that Jonah hasn't already taken?"

"Jonah? Where did you get such an idea?" Her

features tightened with hurt and annoyance as she surged to her feet, brushing the grass from her robe. "Jonah never so much as opened his mouth when he kissed me. He wanted to wait until we were wed out of respect for me and my family. He valued both my name and my virtue, Reeve Garrett. You apparently place little regard on either thing."

Reeve was too surprised to try to stop her angry retreat back to the house. He lay there under the stars, slowly piecing together a truth that stunned him. He'd gotten the idea from Jonah, who'd told him flat out before he rode off in Union blue that he and Patrice were already lovers.

Reeve couldn't believe it, even as understanding finally dawned. Aware of the attraction between his brother and Patrice, Jonah said the one thing that would keep him forever at a distance. A lie that sent him off to war with no hope of anything to return to. With the certainty that Patrice could never be his.

If he'd known that Patrice had given no more than her pledge to his brother, he would have fought their union to his very last breath, instead of letting Jonah have the woman he loved without a single protest.

He'd been tricked into a premature surrender.

Now he was ready to do all-out battle for the love of Patrice Sinclair.

Even bolstered by elation and a pint of whiskey, Tyler Fairfax hesitated before entering his family's home. He knew the instant he opened the door that smell would come rolling out; sour mash, thick and strong enough to intoxicate just by inhaling. That stink permeated his every childhood memory, now compounded by the old, stale odors of musty rooms too long without light or cleaning and the lingering decay of death. Taking a deep breath, he clenched his stomach muscles and stepped inside. The place was closed up like a tomb, and in a way, that's what it was. Inside its dim, deteriorating walls, his father was dying by slow degrees.

"Daddy, where you at?"

He called out from habit. He'd learned early on that his daddy didn't like unexpected intrusions. Especially when too often it meant surprising Cole Fairfax in the midst of diddling one of the terrified chambermaids. Those kinds of surprises were followed by a swift session in hell, not something he cared to invite if he could avoid it.

So even though he knew his invalid father was holed up in the men's parlor room, which had been converted to his bedroom, he made the obligatory call before opening the double doors.

The space within reeked of disease and incontinence. Tyler couldn't enter it sober without needing to retch. Since he was rarely sober these days, it wasn't quite so hard to take. He forced a smile and walked into the heavy shadows.

"Heya, Daddy. How you feelin' tonight?"

Coleman Fairfax had once been a huge man, thick with muscles born of carrying liquor casks since he was old enough to run away from home. What was left of that strong body huddled shriveled and trembling beneath a pile of nasty-smelling quilts. The powerful features that had once been cut with bold strokes to fashion a harsh handsomeness had sunk into cadaverous hollows. But there was no change in the old man's eyes. They still blazed with fury and discontent, and Tyler approached with caution.

"How do you think I feel?" growled the rusty voice. "I'm dying. You just ask 'cause you like hearing it."

Tyler ignored the petulant complaint and began speaking with enthusiasm as he circled slightly behind the thronelike wing chair. His father didn't like looking at his face, so he'd learned to stay carefully out of his field of vision.

"Got some good news, Daddy. Know how you been wantin' to step up production? Well, I jus' got us some of the best bottomland you could wish for. Oughta bring in rye to the tune of—"

"Damned fool! You go spending all my money on some worthless plot of dirt?"

"Nossir, Daddy. It's prime land, already cultivated. Got it from the Sinclairs."

"Then it's more than I can afford."

"I didn't cost you nothin', Daddy."

"Liar. Little sneakin' liar. Jus' like your mama. Can't abide a liar. Get over here where's I can see you."

Tyler froze where he was. "I ain't lying. Made me a deal with Avery's boy, Deacon. Ain't costin' us nothing'. Alls we got to do is bring in the crops and cook up the profits."

Cole shifted uncomfortably in his chair, the sound of his breathing growing rattly in his agitation. "I don't like you back there breathin' down my neck. Get out here wheres I can keep an eye on you and see if you're tellin' me the truth."

Tyler edged around the side of the chair, cautious but sure he was out of reach. Until the sudden swoosh of his father's cane came at him. He had no time to duck away from the fierce blow. It caught

him square in the face. He went spinning to the
floor, taking a table with him.

"You spilled my supper. Who's gonna clean that
up?"

Blackness and the taste of bile swamped over Tyler as he stayed down. The puddle of chicken broth
darkened with the blood gushing from his nose. After a long minute, he blinked away the swirling pin
dots and levered up to his knees. Quick as a snake,
the crook of the cane snagged the back of his neck,
dragging him up almost into his father's bony
knees.

"Where's your sister?"

Sickness threatened to overcome him. He
clamped his jaw tight, swaying into the dark, bitter
waves.

"Where did you hide her, you sneakin' little bastard?"

Tyler managed a breath and the sudden cold
courage to look the old man right in the eye.
"Where you'll never find her."

Cole's features screwed up with a fearsome fury.
"I want her back here. I want her home."

Tyler twisted back, escaping. Hatred seethed
from him along with a vicious sense of satisfaction.
"She's never comin' back. She's safe. Safe from
you."

The old man's gaze went rheumy with distress.
Tyler might have felt sorry for him if there'd been
a scrap of affection in the bastard's dark heart. He
knew there wasn't.

"I'm dying, boy. I want to see her."

"Well, she don't want to see you." He staggered
up to his feet, using his shirtsleeve to swipe away
the blood pouring over his mouth and chin. "It's

jus' you and me, old man, until you die. When's that gonna be? I ain't gonna wait forever."

Sullen eyes glared at him. "If you're in such a hurry, why don't you end it for me?"

Tyler grinned wide, his green eyes, his mother's eyes, glittering with cold animosity. "Oh no. You deserve to die slow. I wouldn't think to deny either of us the pleasure."

Grabbing the bottle of bourbon off the floor next to the chair, Tyler reeled out of the room, away from his father's gurgling shouts of, "Come back here, boy! We ain't through talkin'! Get back here you worthless, lying son of a whore!"

He closed the doors on the rest of the tirade. After wiping the top of the bottle off, he took a long steady pull, swallowing down enough to numb the dull ache of his father's words.

He made it as far as the stairway. Lying back upon the steps, he took another deep drink and waited from the shaking to leave him.

"Die, why don't you? Why can't you just die?"

His eyes drifted shut, and the remaining whiskey from the bottle made a tiny river down the steps.

Chapter 17

A sound like thunder shook the foundation of the Glade. Surging hoofbeats woke memories of dangerous renegade units crisscrossing the county during the war years. Self-preserving instinct brought everyone within the dwelling out to the front porch, each of them armed and ready to face any enemy.

Reeve was already down at the rebuilt paddocks welcoming the arrivals in with whistles and the wide wave of his arm; a dozen of the most beautiful horses imaginable milling about the enclosure as Reeve swung the gate closed.

Unable to check her excitement, Patrice clasped her morning robe about her and ran barefooted down to the whitewashed rails where Reeve leaned. The Glade and sleek horseflesh was synonymous in her mind and seeing those empty paddocks was a heartbreaking reminder that life would never be the same again. Having them filled with tossing manes and churning hooves brought a lightness of hope to heart and soul. With childlike joy, she stepped up onto the bottom rail, hanging over it to catch the dusty breeze stirred up by the circling animals.

"They're wonderful!"

She looked at Reeve then, exchanging a moment of shared pleasure until the darkening of his eyes reminded her of the more intimate enjoyment they'd experienced hours earlier. Her cheeks warmed with an answering mix of longing and frustration.

She'd slept poorly after leaving him out on those mashed-down grasses. She'd tossed in her restlessness, chafing with need. The irritability that came with morning light fled as she detailed the smoky heat of his gaze, as a small smile teased about desirable lips, provoking remembrances of how thoroughly he'd kissed her.

The spark between them was too evident for daylight hours and the approaching company. She turned back to watch the horses, aware of an accelerated pulse driven by the same agitation that moved the animals in reckless patterns. She gripped the top rail to fend off the urge to touch him, to connect once more and experience the powerful movement of man and muscle, so like the heaving flanks of the thoroughbreds weaving in and out as they settled into their new surroundings.

"Look at those lines." The squire's tone was ripe with appreciation. "Beautiful." He faced Reeve in animation and confusion. "How—where—?"

Reeve didn't answer right away. He walked over to the waiting drovers who'd wrangled the animals from the train. A bill of sale was exchanged, then the dirty riders nodded at the offer of hot coffee up at the house. While Hannah saw to them with her innate graciousness, Byron repeated the question, this time with a stronger emphasis.

"Reeve, where did these animals come from?"

"Pennsylvania."

From the North. That said too much yet still not enough. His father began to frown, initial excitement dimming. Reeve went back to the rail, noting wryly that Deacon was now situated in his spot next to Patrice. He settled in a less preferable space on Sinclair's right to watch the horses move, the sight stirring up feelings of pride and accomplishment he knew were about to be crippled.

"Reeve, what are these animals doing here?"

He pointed to a leggy chestnut instead of answering. "Look at her. Look at that balance, the symmetry. Any foal of hers by Zeus would be worth the cost of the lot of them."

But Byron wasn't looking at the mare. He was glaring at Reeve with suspicion and massing outrage.

"Answer me. Where did you get these horses, and how did you pay for them?"

"A fellow I served with was from Valley Forge. We got to talking, and he was telling me about his surplus of blooded mares. I took a chance and had him send these down to me. Here are their papers. The lineage is solid. See for yourself."

Byron dismissed the registrations. "By what right did you bring them here? Without asking me?"

Reeve's expression closed down tight, revealing none of his emotions. "Sir, I—"

"What made you think I'd take charity from one

of your damned Yankee friends for inferior horseflesh?"

"There's not a thing wrong with those mares. And it wasn't charity."

"How did you pay for them then? With pilfered Southern goods? With silverware taken from loyal neighbors' homes over their dead bodies?"

Reeve's features were as stony as a cliff face. He spoke slowly, without inflection. "I paid for them in gold. Glendower gold. From accounts set up in the North by Dodge's bank before we lost it all in useless Confederate paper."

Byron went scarlet with fury. "You had no right! You stole money that wasn't yours! Without my permission!"

"I didn't steal it. And I didn't tell you about it because I wanted it to be a surprise." He made an angry gesture toward the paddock and hissed, "Surprise," before stalking toward the house. He'd nearly reached the front steps with his fierce strides before the squire caught up to him. The older man grabbed his elbow and jerked him about.

"How could you think I'd ever agree to this? I will not accept those weak-hocked Northern hobby ponies!"

"Look around. See any Kentucky purebreds wandering loose? They've all been broken, shot, or eaten. We've no choice but to take some risks in expanding the line if we want to survive. And there won't be a single weakness in those mares that a few months cropping our bluegrass won't cure."

"You've overstepped yourself, Reeve. Jonah would never have made such a decision on his own—"

Reeve's patience snapped. He yanked his arm

free, snarling, "You didn't give control of the Glade to Jonah, did you? You never would have as long as you were alive to pull the strings. You gave it to me. You told me to build it up again, and by God, I will. Now, if you'll excuse me, Squire, I've got men to pay."

He went inside, leaving his father to fume. Not seeing the old man sway, clutching his chest as he grabbed the porch rail for balance.

"Reeve?"

He glanced up over Zeus's saddle at the sound of Patrice's voice. For a moment, the sight of her snatched his breath. Her face was pink from the exertion of running down from the house. Luxurious copper tresses peeped from beneath the sassy tilt of her silly little hat. The fitted shape of her tobacco brown riding jacket accentuated perfect breasts and trim waist before flaring over the full swirl of her skirt. A thoroughbred. No mistaking those strong, classic lines.

"I'd like to ride along with you if you're going into town."

He thought of the two of them alone, of the dangers on the road—not from possible ambush but from the likely collapse of his own restraint. *I've never wanted anyone but you.* The words whispered through his mind in silky provocation.

"I don't think your brother would approve of me as your escort." He bent down to finishing with the cinch.

"Well, Deacon has already left for the Manor, and Mama said she had no objections."

He looked at her again, noting her pleased pout.

Such kissable lips . . . "Did you tell her you'd be rid ing with me?"

She refused to be daunted by his cynicism. "Yes, I did. Whether you believe it or not, my mama is quite fond of you. She always has been."

Reeve ducked his head, not wanting her to see the surprise and unexpected delight in his expression. "Your mama's a grand lady. She knows I'd never let any harm come to you." His tone growled, censuring his own erotic thoughts.

"Is there a horse I can ride? I've been dying to get back in the saddle again."

Her breathlessness sounded too husky to stem from the thrill of riding horseback. Reeve didn't dare speculate farther.

He cut a flashy bay mare from the corral and slapped a saddle on while Patrice stroked its velvet nose and murmured soft acquainting words. The tender caressing tones pulled a strange anxiousness through him even as it calmed the high-strung animal. The animal in him prowled in painful arousal.

Not waiting for a boost, Patrice vaulted lithely into the saddle to settle in a graceful sideseat, gathering up the reins in gloved hands. With a nudge of her heel, she sent the bay cantering down the drive. Reeve had no fear for her. She was an excellent horsewoman, always had been. In no time, he thundered after her in a chase lasting only as long as it took them to be out of view from the Glade. Then Patrice skillfully drew in her mount and Reeve fell into a companionable pace beside her.

Patrice patted the satiny neck. "She's got a beautiful gait, Reeve, as strong and sure as any of our Kentucky-bred."

Then she surprised him completely. "That was a

brilliant idea, converting the Glade's assets into Union gold."

Though he wished he could take the credit to bask in her praise, he couldn't. "It was Jonah's."

"But how did he get together with your friend, Dodge?"

"I wrote him about Dodge and his banking firm in Michigan. He saw to the transfers." Reeve felt Patrice's gaze.

"I didn't know you and Jonah corresponded."

"When we could."

"I wonder why he didn't tell me."

Her musing made Reeve wonder why, himself. Lately, he'd discovered a whole new side of his half brother in contrast to all he'd believed about him. A human side. A weak side, vulnerable to emotions like jealousy and spite. He thought of Jonah's letters, full of glowing, gushing details concerning his and Patrice's happiness. To make him feel closer to things at home or to emphasize the separation? He wondered, and it soured his mood.

Then Patrice made it worse by asking in a fragile voice, "Did Jonah write about me?"

"Not much. Just that you were planning the wedding and he was hoping I could get leave to stand up beside him."

"And would you have?"

An emotional snag in her question made him turn to catch the intensity of her expression. "Would I what?"

"Give your blessing to my marriage to another man?"

"Not to another man, to Jonah. Then, I would have."

That obviously wasn't what she wanted to hear.

She went back to staring straight ahead, her chin angled high, her hands clenched on the reins. He brooded over her snub, growing more aggravated by the minute.

"Had you expected me to do something different?" he asked at last, a demand rather than a question.

She canted a fierce glance his way. "It doesn't matter now, does it?"

"Doesn't it? It must, or you wouldn't be in such a squawk."

"A squawk?" Her glare was double-barrel direct. "You're a fool and a coward, Reeve Garrett, and I shouldn't have expected so much from you."

Her haughty manner and refusal to look at him wore hard for the next few minutes, until he could take no more of it.

"What did you expect me to do, Patrice? Protest? Offer you somethin' better? Like what? Your daddy wouldn't even let me walk in the front door! Were you plannin' to give up your fancy parties and frilly clothes to sew the lace on other ladies' dresses with my mama every night until your eyes couldn't focus anymore? Were you willin' to have folks in town stare through you like you didn't exist? Were you ready to suffer your family's scorn and never be welcomed in your home again? Were you, Patrice? 'Cause that's the best I could have offered you! Are you still mad 'cause I wanted you to have somethin' better than that? Someone better than me?"

Her ice-cold stare slashed through him. "It would have been my choice, at least. My choice. But you didn't have the courage or the trust to ask what I wanted." She kicked the mare into a brisk gait, permitting no further discussion.

Reeve looked after her, agitated and angry. Would she have chosen him? Unlikely.

With Pride up ahead, Reeve lagged back, letting Patrice ride in alone. He assumed she wouldn't want to be seen with him. Was it a lack of trust in her that had him making that decision alone? Or was it the fear of hearing her ask him to hang back?

Coward.

He gritted his teeth and nudged Zeus to a quicker pace. He caught up to her on the edge of the sprawling town. She didn't spare him a look, but every citizen they passed looked plenty. And those looks were far from pleasant. Patrice paid them no mind. Because she was embarrassed to? Or because they truly didn't matter to her? Discovering that would solve many things.

"Will you be ready to go about noon."

She shot him a cool glance. "That's fine."

Reeve reined in and watched her continue straight through town. Only one thing waited on the other end. The Fairfax home and distillery. She was going to see Tyler.

Though she considered herself Starla Fairfax's best friend, Patrice could count the number of times on one hand that she'd been invited to her home. Though a constant visitor at the Manor, Starla was a reluctant hostess. Patrice figured it was because of her father, Cole, and his reputation for a vile temper and an overindulgence in his own product. Avery Sinclair never said a good word about him as a Southerner or a gentleman. It was said the best thing his exotically lovely Creole wife had ever done was to run far and hide well to escape him.

But Lorena left behind her two children, breaking

Starla's heart. Patrice wondered what kind of woman would think of her own freedom over the welfare of her son and daughter.

After that, the Fairfax home, Fair Play, closed its doors to the outside world. Fearing the ridicule of his peers, Cole Fairfax was rarely seen. Tyler and Starla grew up running wild in the grimly shadowed house with only the affection of their mother's maid, Matilda to give them any direction. Whispers of what went on at Fair Play were hushed in Patrice's presence, but even as a girl, she'd recognized the scars of tragedy upon the hearts and souls of brother and sister. She'd opened her arms wide to both of them in friendship and sympathy.

Fair Play stood, a square of rose-colored brick buried beneath the gnarled branches of a half dozen century-old live oaks. Stark and desolate in the winter, it sat shaded in heavy secrets once foliage appeared to shut out the light. Patrice shivered when approaching its deep-pilastered porch and blank sheen of tightly curtained windows.

Matilda answered her fourth knock, peering out warily from behind the door.

"Is Mr. Fairfax at home?"

"Mista Cole or Mista Tyler?"

"Tyler."

"He be here Missy Sinclair, but I doan know if he's seeing visitors right yet."

Anger at Tyler's dealings with Deacon overruled her manners. Patrice put a palm on the door and pushed hard enough to make the elderly black woman take a few quick steps back. "He'll see me," she announced with a stiff confidence.

The stench inside the house knocked her back a step. Patrice grabbed for her linen square, placing it over her mouth and nose as a defuser. Obviously, the place hadn't been aired since Starla's sudden departure early in the war.

Through the muffle of her handkerchief, Patrice murmured, "Would you tell Tyler that I'm—"

Her sentence fractured. The handkerchief dropped away from her mouth, the odor forgotten, as she gasped in dismay.

Tyler Fairfax lay sprawled, unconscious, on the main stairs, his face a mass of bruising and bloodstains. Dried crimson streaked the front of his untucked shirt. One arm dangled limply between the stair rails into empty space, and the other trailed down the hardwood steps, hand open, palm up as if reaching for hers. She cried out in horror at the sight of a huge dark stain on the floorboards, thinking it was more blood, but then saw the bottle one riser below his slack fingers and guessed the rest.

She turned on Matilda in a low fury. "How could you leave him there like that?"

The wrinkled features took on a weary dignity. "Dat's the way he wants it, Missy Sinclair. He done tole us to leave him where he falls, and dat's what we do." Her dark eyes flashed with a momentary challenge, then she stared down at the floor again in a pose of meekness.

"Get me some water and clean cloths. Hurry!" As the old woman went to do as bid, Patrice sank down on the stairs beside the insensible man, shaking her head in tender exasperation. "Oh, Tyler, why do you do this to yourself?"

When Matilda returned, Patrice dredged the cloth through cool water and began gently to wash the gore off his face so she could see the true extent of the damage. It was bad, but not as terrible as she'd first assumed. His nose was smashed from what must have been a terrific blow. The black-and-purple crescents smudged beneath his eyes were from bruising, not actual injury. As she sponged the chill dampness down his neck, he muttered softly and started to come around. His head lolled loosely.

"Star? Starla darlin', don't be fussin'." He pushed at her hands in an uncoordinated effort.

"Shh. Lie still."

His eyes snapped open, then immediately squinted tight against the needlelike assault of daylight. "Patrice?" He shoved at her hands again and tried to avert his face. "You shouldn't be here. I don't want you here."

She stilled his head, easing it back with the gentle coaxing of her palm. Anguish and upset was plain in his reddened eyes and stark expression.

"Go home, 'Trice. Please—don't—"

"It's all right," she soothed, settling the remoistened cloth across his brow. "Rest a minute and get your bearings."

His eyes closed and he took several increasingly deep breaths. When tension eased enough to leave him in a nearly liquid state upon the stairs, she risked a question.

"Who did this, Tyler?"

A smile crooked his lips. "Coulda been anybody, darlin'."

"But it wasn't. Who hit you?"

He wasn't going to tell her. Instead, still maintaining the weak smile, he asked, "What're you doin' here, Patrice? That reverend brother of yours ain't gonna like the notion of you tending this poor ole drunken sinner inside o' his lair."

"I'll tell him you were no threat to my virtue."

"Damned shame," he muttered. "So if not to seduce me, why are you here?"

"It's about Deacon."

Tyler groaned and rubbed his scratchy cheek against her palm in a blatant bid for more of her affection. She didn't begrudge it, lightly brushing aside the dark straggles of his hair and stroking his discolorations with the pad of her thumb. When it looked as though he was content to remain in her care indefinitely, she prompted, "About Deacon?"

He sighed. "Now?" With a glance up for confirmation, he groaned and called, "Tilly, darlin', would you show Miz Sinclair out onto the terrace and serve her up some of your fortifying lemonade whiles I get myself more presentable?"

"Yessir, Mista Tyler. Missy Sinclair, if you'd c'mon with me?"

As Patrice stood, Tyler flopped over onto his belly and levered his knees up under him. His movements were sloppy, his balance none too certain. When she placed a concerned hand on his shoulder, she felt him start with unwarranted alarm, which he quickly tried to grin away.

"I'm fine, darlin'." But the way he was swaying on hands and knees didn't reinforce that claim. He reached up a flailing hand to catch hold of the banister to drag himself upright.

"Mista Tyler, you should ought to check in on your daddy."

Tyler glanced down at the old woman, his expression going flat and still. "Is he dead?"

Matilda was taken aback. "Nossir."

"That's all I want to know." Then he smiled at Patrice, waving her away as if she hadn't just witnessed a shocking scene. "Go on with Tilly. I'll join you direct."

Frowning slightly, a doubtful Patrice allowed herself to be led outside to gulp up the revitalizing fresh air.

As promised, Tyler returned fit for company in fawn-colored trousers, tucked shirt, and a brown silk-brocaded waistcoat, managing to look both proper and negligent at the same time. His usually swarthy face was clean-shaven and pale, accentuating the dark circles beneath his still-bloodshot eyes. All the smiling charm was there, with none of the animation behind it. To Patrice, he looked worndown and strangely somber, even though his first act was to bend close to nuzzle her cheek.

"I'm sorry to keep you waitin' on me. Now what was it you wanted to talk about?" He sat opposite her at a small wrought-iron table and possessed himself of both her hands, placing kisses on the backs of both, then continuing to hold them.

"I want to know why you're lending my brother money?"

He blinked at her directness but lost none of his outward amiability. "Did he tell you that?"

"No."

"Then why would you think it's true? I'm not a bank, darlin', and you know the good reverend has no use for me."

"Tyler, you're weaving a tight web around my family, whether you'll admit to it or not, and I don't like it."

His tone went deep and silkily persuasive. "I would never hurt you, Patrice." But it still wasn't an answer.

"I can't think of what we might have done to

make you wish to ruin us, but I feel it. Tell me why, Tyler. Is it something I've done? I thought we were friends."

"We are, darlin', an' I can't tell you how much your friendship has meant to me." His expression steeped in tense sincerity. "I have always loved you, Patrice."

Then before she could react with surprise or dismay, he flashed his brilliant grin and went on as if he'd never made such an abrupt confession.

"Where are my manners? Is that drink cold enough for you, darlin'? Can I have Tilly bring you anything else?"

"N-no. This is fine." His admission stunned her. She didn't know what to say to him, if she should say anything. Tyler saved her from floundering with a squeeze of her hands and a smooth explanation.

"Deke and I made an agreement for the land, that's all. We needed the space, and he needed to take care of his family. Nothin' suspicious or worrisome in that, now, is there? Don't you trust your brother to act in his family's best interest?"

What she didn't trust was the way Tyler was taking advantage of her brother's desperation. She didn't trust his assurances or his deceptive smile. He was lying about something, trying to distract her, but was it about his feelings for her or his motives for the loan? Tyler Fairfax was a complex piece of work.

There was nothing to learn from her inscrutable host. Patrice stood, bringing Tyler up with slightly unsteady gallantry.

"I'd better be going."

"Afraid folks'll talk?"

She scowled. "They already are, but I'm sure that's not your doing."

He grinned at her searing sarcasm. "Darlin', I wouldn't spread such a rumor, though I might wish it were true."

"When's Starla coming home? This place could use her."

The light in Tyler's eyes went out like the snuffing of a candle. Even his dazzling smile couldn't put life into the dull misery in his tone. "I don't rightly know. She's havin' such fun in Louisville, she hasn't had time to miss us."

He was lying.

"I thought you said she was in Chattanooga. Tyler, what's wrong? You can tell me. Is it Starla? Is she all right?"

It wasn't anything obvious, nothing she could see or name, but suddenly she sensed a deep, dreadful fear in him that made her want to scream and shake the truth out of him.

Then the glassiness of his expression disappeared, replaced by his natural gregariousness. "*Ah non, chère,*" he crooned, slipping into his mother's Deep South patois, drawling the way he did when he was particularly moved by something. "Starla's fine. She's flirting with all them officers and steppin' out every night to some *fais do do.* Don't mind me. I jus' miss her." He grinned. "She's the only one who could ever make me mind my manners."

Patrice relaxed. "Tell her I miss her, too."

He nodded. Then came the uncharacteristic shift to sobriety once again. "Patrice, Deacon is a big boy, and he don't need you meddling in his affairs. You listen to him, and you do what he tells you. Don't get yourself caught up in no trouble."

"What trouble?" Her demand shook with apprehension.

Instead of answering, he drew her up in a loose embrace. His lips moved soft and warm against her temple, then he murmured in a husky aside, "Don't be too quick to think the worst of me. And don't ever be afraid to come to me."

But because he'd felt the need to give her that assurance, Patrice was very, very afraid.

Chapter 18

Tangled up in her thoughts, Patrice hurried down the boardwalk only to run face first into a solid masculine wall. Stunned by the impact, she stumbled back and was righted by a pair of strong hands gripping her upper arms.

"Why, Miss Sinclair. Fancy running into you."

She regarded Reeve's obnoxious Northern friend with an indignant glower. "Mr. Dodge, please be so kind as to watch where you are going!"

His jaw unhinged, then a smile cut its way through his whiskers. "Why, ma'am, I am not opposed to letting pretty women walk all over me. In fact, I throw myself at their feet regularly and let them use me as they will. But ma'am, I don't take abuse where none is due."

While she huffed and tried to think of how to save herself from making an apology, the brash banker saved her the trouble. He released her arms and brushed away the creases he'd made in her sleeves.

"I regret standing in the path of your righteousness. Next time, just let me know you're coming, and I'll throw myself prostrate so as not to give you such a jolt."

She laughed, at his raw charm and her own unprovoked rudeness. "I'm sorry, Mr. Dodge. I didn't watch where I was going."

"I enjoyed doing the watching for you, ma'am."

She responded to his broad grin with a relaxed smile. Then gave a gasp to find herself hauled up in his bearlike embrace. He smelled earthy, all manly smells—cigar, leather, coffee, and wool. The brotherly hug was over before she could protest, then he laughed at her expression of dismay.

"I didn't mean to shock the petticoats off you. It's just that I haven't seen a halfway friendly look since I got here and was dying for a glimpse of someone who wasn't measuring me for a noose or a coffin. I hope I didn't offend you. Fifteen and a half, if you're wondering. That's my neck size if you're looking to buy rope."

Surprisingly, she found herself warming to the abrasive Michigander.

"I was just about to go have my tenth cup of coffee over at the boardinghouse. Only place that'll take my money. I know it's a lot to ask, but I'd be forever grateful if you'd come sit down with me. You don't have to talk or anything. Just sit there and let me pretend I'm not alone for a little while. I'm so starved for company I could spit."

"Please don't spit, Mr. Dodge." Her gentle chiding was followed by the lift of her elbow. "I could use some coffee."

Surprised, then grinning profusely, he tucked her arm through his with judicious care and towed her toward Sadie's.

Every head in the dining room turned when they entered. Dodge hitched her arm in closer to his side. " 'Into the valley of death,' " he muttered. Then his smile broke wide as Delyce Dermont approached them. " 'Morning, ma'am. You're looking as bright and shiny as a freshly blued barrel this morning."

Delyce froze at the gruff compliment and, after darting a furtive look around, allowed a blush to creep up into her wan cheeks. "Good morning, Mr. Dodge, Miz Patrice." If she felt any particular curiosity about the two of them together, she didn't make it known. "Breakfast or just coffee this morning?"

Dodge glanced at his willing companion. "Breakfast, a big one. Miss Sinclair?"

"Just coffee, Delyce. Thank you."

Delyce led them through the bristle of hostile glares to a table tucked back in an obscure corner. After he'd seated Patrice, Dodge dropped into his chair and sent those angry stares scattering with the direct fix of his own.

"Funny how I always seem to get this same table. I wonder why that is?"

Patrice chuckled. "Could be you're bad for business, Mr. Dodge."

"Or very good for gossip." He drew out a thick cigar, trimmed it, and had a match to its end before thinking of his dining partner. "You mind, ma'am?" he asked around the Havana clenched between his teeth.

"Go ahead, Mr. Dodge. It won't be the worst thing I've inhaled this morning." Not bothering to explain her remark, Patrice settled back to observe her companion. A cloud of blue smoke unfurled to conceal his features, then dissipated, baring shrewd eyes for her study. Hamilton Dodge might be unpolished, but there was no doubting the intelligence in his gaze as he likewise studied her.

"Are you from a small town, Mr. Dodge? You seem familiar with their politics."

His lips bowed up around the fat cigar. "Medium-sized and growing, but lots of small-town minds. They're the same all over, North or South." He continued to stare at her, gaze friendly, curious, and penetrating. Nothing mysterious about a man who laid his cards out faceup. She liked that. She liked him, despite his politics. Or perhaps because he wasn't ashamed of them.

"Do you have family up North, Mr. Dodge?"

"Oh hell, yes. Six older sisters, mother, father, uncles, aunts, twenty-four cousins, passel of nieces and nephews. We could populate our own territory." The warmth in his expression made her think of the engulfing hug.

"You must miss them."

"Like a pair of thick, dry socks, ma'am." He concentrated on his cigar for a long moment, expression going wistful.

"Why did you come down here?"

He made it sound simple. "Reeve asked me." He sent a smoke ring spiraling toward the tin ceiling and gave her a steady look. "When a man takes a bullet for you, you don't ask why."

Breakfast arrived just then, platters of it, along with a pot of steaming coffee. Conversation and questions were interrupted while Dodge devoured the huge quantity of food like someone who'd gone without long enough to appreciate its value. Patrice sipped the strong dark brew and wondered over the loyalty of a man who'd uproot from home and family because of a debt to a friend. And she was a little envious. Imagining the alienation and homesickness made her marvel at him all the more.

After the last drip of gravy was sopped up in biscuit, Dodge tipped back in his chair to enjoy the rest of his cigar over coffee. He smiled at Patrice.

"Go ahead and ask."

"About what?"

"Whatever's making your eyes cross like that."

Patrice leaned forward onto her elbows and pitched her voice low. "I understand you handled the conversion of the Glendower estate into gold."

Dodge puffed leisurely, then said, "Ma'am, you want to know my deepest, darkest secrets, I'll spill them at your feet. You want to know if I sleep naked or what I fantasize about, I'd tell you that, too. But when you ask me to break a business confidence that doesn't concern you, you'd have to rip out my gizzard and I still wouldn't divulge a single decimal point."

Blunt. Truthful. Honorable. Yes, she liked him very much.

"So, Mr. Dodge, do you sleep naked?"

The casual way she broached the question took him off guard, then he threw back his head and let out a whooping laugh. "Goddamn, you're something. If it weren't for Reeve having prior claim, I'd surrender up my bachelor state in a second. And no, I don't, but you might be able to persuade me."

Patrice fell silent, prickling over his statement. "Reeve Garrett has no claim on me."

He grinned at her brittle announcement. "If you say so, ma'am."

Ignoring his smugness and the way it both alarmed and agitated her, Patrice changed the subject. "If you can't talk about the money situations of others, are you at liberty to share information concerning mine?"

"What do you want to know?"

His willingness to be forthcoming surprised and scared her a little. How much did she really want to know? She gathered up her gumption. "I know we're mortgaged to the bank. How deeply?"

"Ma'am, you might say the bank owns everything right down to your lacy garters."

She shuddered to hear it spoken at last. Seeing her pallor, Dodge slid a large hand over hers, not pressing but just letting it rest there for a moment.

"Miss Sinclair, I see banking as a way to build up a community not to tear it apart. If I was in the ruination business, I'd be in politics."

She managed a wan smile. "Then you'd help us with a loan?"

"I'd do my best. I'm just waiting for someone to ask. The people in this town are too busy looking for my pitchfork and horns to consider that I might be here to help them. Are you asking for extended credit?"

"My brother borrowed a great deal of money from another source." She couldn't believe she was confiding all to a total stranger, but the relief of having someone she could trust brought the words out in a flood. "I don't know the terms. I don't know the amount. Are we in trouble, Mr. Dodge?"

She looked up at him, desperate for reassurance. His hesitation shot down that hope.

"How much do you owe on back taxes?"

"Some have been paid off. I don't know how much is left."

He snubbed out the stump of his cigar and stood, amicability replaced by a crisp professionalism. "Why don't we go on down to the bank and I'll see what kind of paperwork I've got on file."

Patrice went weak with gratitude. He wasn't promising miracles, but he wasn't sawing off their last branch either. All traces of guilt about sneaking the information behind Deacon's back were gone. She couldn't help if she wasn't prepared. And Deacon wasn't telling her anything.

On their way out of the dining room, they passed behind Sadie Dermont. She hovered over one of the tables, too busy with her rumormongering to notice them.

"The poor squire thought they'd lost it all. Heard his bastard boy stole the family's money and hid it in a bank up North under his own name. And that Yankee banker he brought down here helped him do it. They're in cahoots, I tell you."

Dodge paused long enough to say loudly, "Thank you for another fine meal, Mrs. Dermont. You make me feel like I was in my mother's kitchen."

Sadie whirled, her homely features stark with dismay, then flushing a deeper crimson of embarrassment. But not apology.

Dodge tipped his flat-crowned hat to his hostess and fixed her with a leveling stare before shepherding Patrice out into the clear morning light. "Shall we take that walk, Miss Sinclair?"

"It's Patrice."

"I know." He cupped her elbow with a proper

deference and said, "I was just waiting for the liberty of using it."

All the boards had been pried free from the bank's windows. The close-set bars were as solid as ever, but much of the glass was reduced to jagged shards. Dodge stopped at the door and Patrice gasped, looking away quickly.

"Wonder if it's edible?" Dodge murmured as he took down the ratty carcass of a small furred animal left nailed to the door. Beneath it, the words *Go Home* were spelled out in uneven strokes. He sniffed at the mutilated creature and reared back. "Guess not." He gave it an unconcerned toss into the street. "Thought someone might be leaving me supper." He touched the still-wet lettering. "Think they'll give me a discount on paint over at the mercantile? This is the fourth time this week I've had to touch up." He didn't share what the other messages imparted. Patrice shivered. She could guess.

"Aren't you afraid?" she asked as he herded her inside.

"I was afraid of cannon fire. I was terrified of rolling over a dead man for fear of knowing him. Certain sounds at night were enough to make me ruin my long johns. But I'm not afraid of ignorance, ma'am. It just makes me mad as hell."

He didn't look angry or in the least disturbed as he waved her into a leather chair across from his big desk. A bunch of his loose papers were pinned under a glass paperweight shaped like a windmill. Patrice blinked back a rush of unexpected tears. She'd given it to Jonah, laughing that he'd been tilting at them all his life. He'd always kept it in a prominent place of honor to show how much it had meant to him, both the gift and the fact that she'd given it to him. A week later, she'd accepted his proposal. She jumped slightly at the feel of Dodge's palm against the small of her back.

"Patrice, if there's anything here that you want, you just go ahead and take it."

She took a breath and smile determinedly. "Thank you, Mr. Dodge, but I have everything I need to keep my memories alive."

He nodded without further comment, then said, "You can drop that Mister." He settled into Jonah's big chair looking right at home. That should have disturbed her, but it didn't. She sensed Jonah would have liked him sitting there. Dodge unlocked a bottom drawer and shuffled through some files. He drew out a heavy one marked Sinclair at one corner in Jonah's precise hand. Dodge flipped through the contents with unreadable interest before regarding her.

"It's not good."

"How 'not good'?"

"I just might own your firstborn, too."

She put a trembling hand to her lips, fighting the quiver of helplessness. Dodge said nothing, giving her time to deal with the news and find her own strength. Which she did.

"What can we save and how?"

"What do you have to keep?"

Everything. Every handful of dirt, every blade of grass was precious to her. But she was practical. "The house. Enough land to grow a self-sufficient crop."

He pursed his lips thoughtfully. "It'll be tight."

"But not impossible."

His crooked smile bolstered her sagging spirits. "But not impossible. First, I think you ought to—"

He broke off as his gaze went beyond her. Patrice twisted in her seat to see Reeve at the doorway. "C'mon in," Dodge called. "Patrice was just filling me in on all the county's eligible females."

An easy-to-read lie that stated a private conference had been in progress and don't ask about what. Reeve didn't.

"Patrice, are you about ready to go?"

Patrice nodded and stood. Impulsively, she extended her hand to Dodge. He got to his feet and clasped her small fingers within the curl of his larger ones, not bringing her hand up for a kiss but rather pressing it firmly.

"I'm glad we got the chance to get to know each other better, Mr.—Dodge."

"Yes, ma'am. I am, too. And if you get to wondering about any of my other sleeping habits, you just ask." He winked, then grinned at Reeve's stiff expression. "We can finish our talk next time you're in town, Patrice. My guess is you'd rather not have me at the house."

"It's not that you wouldn't be welcome—" she began.

"That'd be a first. We'll keep things between us until you decide what you want to do."

Patrice exhaled in relief. "Thank you."

Then his mood grew somber as he looked at his friend. "Reeve, there's some reckless talk being bandied around town. Watch your back. I'd hate to comfort this little lady over your loss, but I'm confident that I could fill your shoes in time."

"You can't know how relieved that makes me feel," Reeve drawled, with just a touch of suspicion to narrow his gaze.

* * *

That crease lingered between his brows as they started back toward the Glade. Patrice wondered if he was worrying over his friend's insinuations of danger or about the cheeky Northerner's wink at her. She hoped he was fretting over both. The thought of Reeve's jealousy, no matter how unfounded, pleased her almost to the point of forgiving their earlier conversation. She was restless with the silence and eager to get him talking.

"How did you save Dodge's life?"

Dodge. Not Mr. Dodge anymore. Reeve's frown deepened as he muttered to himself, "Might not have been such a good idea, after all." But to her, he said with a matter-of-fact shrug, "He was an officer who didn't know how to keep his head down. I saw a glint in the trees. Snipers took down a lot of our best men. Anyway, 'fore I could warn him, I saw the muzzle flash. I only had time to knock him out of the way."

She watched his features, seeing the intensity absent in his voice. "You were hit instead."

"Just a crease." His indifference said it was much more. "It would have taken off Dodge's head if I'd done nothing. Hell of an introduction."

"You took a bullet for someone you didn't even know?"

Again the shrug. "Didn't have time to philosophize over it. He was a good officer, and you want to keep those kinds of men around. Dodge came to sit with me every day until I recovered. Told me about his family, their furniture business, about the bank he'd built after some crooked investor swindled most of his folk's money. He was one of the few who never had a word to say about my accent or my allegiance. Meant a lot to me then. Still does.

He's a man who let's you know right where he stands, and if it's beside you, you're damned lucky."

Patrice hadn't considered how difficult it might have been for Reeve with his drawling intonations in a Union brigade. Probably the same kind of isolation she'd sensed in Dodge in the midst of Pride with his biting Northern syllables. She understood having no one to trust or talk to.

"I think he'll be good for Pride, if they'll let him."

Reeve gave her a measuring look, weighing the unprejudicial tone of her words against the known sentiments of her family. "He's a good man. He's going to have to win them over one at a time." The same way he was going to. Dodge had the advantage of deep-seated patience.

"So what are your plans for the Glade, Reeve?"

He could hardly say they had to do with her and marriage, but that's what they were. The reason he'd bought the horses, why he'd agreed to the squire's terms. For her. Each a step toward proving himself. But now wasn't the time to be telling her that. Instead, he stuck with the safer topic of the new stock.

And as he discussed them in an animated tone, she thought of Jonah, who'd displayed the same enthusiasm for business. She couldn't imagine the livestock flourishing under Jonah's indifferent care. He'd have turned the farm into a gentleman's farm, or worse, sold it off. Had the squire realized that? Is that why he'd never given Jonah the reins to let him run the Glade the way he did Reeve? Reeve and Byron were of the soil, like Deacon and her father. It would have been a tragedy to turn over the lush acres to a man who couldn't appreciate their worth and beauty. But Reeve would. He'd give his last ounce of sweat and drop of blood for the Glade.

She found that one of his most admirable qualities.

A time would come when Reeve Garrett would be seen only for the man he was, not by the quality of his birthright. Tolerance had to be learned, it wasn't instinctive. It was knowing Reeve that gave her the courage to ignore convention and sit down with Hamilton Dodge. Maybe it was time to let Reeve see for himself how her mind was expanding.

And maybe then, she could find the bravery to tell him the truth about her part in Jonah's death.

Chapter 19

B yron Glendower's summons to his study came the moment Reeve entered the house. There was no invitation to have a seat, no small talk, just a fierce over-the-desktop glare and a demand of, "What the hell do you think you're doing?"

"You want to narrow that down some?" His casual drawl brought a darker flush to his father's already-florid face. Slitted eyes watched as Reeve assumed one of the chairs and settled in with a negligent ease.

"Would you like me to number them?" he snapped.

Reeve shrugged and waited for the tirade to continue.

"First you bring that Yankee carpetbagger down here to strip all of us of our pride and properties? Everyone in Pride knows it was your doing."

"Then they'll have me to thank when Dodge gets

them square with their debts and looking forward again."

"They're not going to thank you. They're looking for an excuse to tar and feather you. And you're handing it to them, boy. No . . . you're sticking it down their throats."

"They don't need an excuse, Squire. They pinned every one of their sorrows and grudges on me the minute I rode back into this county. I'm just doing what you suggested."

"I told you to win them over, not stampede over them!"

"I won't go crawling. I won't beg forgiveness for something I didn't do." Though his relaxed posture didn't change, a foundation of pure steel supported his words. "I can't make them want to get on with their lives. I can't force them to accept me. I didn't ask Dodge here to win public popularity. I asked him to take over where Jonah left off to save their stubborn hides. The same reason Jonah moved the Glade's money up north."

"It was treason."

"It was survival."

Silence thick as slave brick slapped up a wall between them—Byron unable to bend, Reeve unwilling to beg, too much alike to compromise. How could they have ever thought they'd find a common ground even when both were standing on it? Finally, Byron spoke the words burdening his heart.

"I let them call you traitor. I did nothing to stop it because I could see they were right. But I wanted to believe you were still loyal to this family."

Reeve's jaw tensed, the muscles flexing, working on the anger, the frustration, the fear that had been so much a part of him since the day he'd ridden north. What good would it do to pour out his soul, to cite his reasons atop tomes of logic? Byron Glendower wasn't interested in politics or practicality. It wasn't about North or South, pride or proper surnames. It was about why Reeve Garrett took arms against his own blood.

"What I did, I did for this family, for this community." And to him, further explanation was inconsequential.

Byron Glendower studied him for a long somber minute, powerful emotions struggling for domination. But in the end, his belief wasn't strong enough. "No matter what was behind it, the fact is, you stood against us instead of with us. That's what they'll remember. That you were their enemy"

"Their own traditions were their enemy. Ask Jonah . . ."

Their father's features went cold as the stone over Jonah's grave. "I can't because Jonah died for what we believed in."

"No." Reeve stood, a pillar of furious denial. "He died for what *you* believed in. And I will never forgive him for that. Or you for insisting upon it!"

Byron surged up as well. "Why? Because he was more of a man than you were?"

"Because he failed himself by not being the man he could have been. By not doing what he knew was right."

He turned toward the doorway, chafing in his frustration, only to confront a pale and anguished Patrice Sinclair. He strode past her without a word, the condemning ring of his words strangling her hope of finding happiness with him.

Byron dropped into his chair, the fervor of his convictions deserting him, just as his only remaining son deserted him . . . again. The pain of it pressed upon his heart in a crushing fist.

"Why did I ever think it could work between us?" he mourned aloud, not fully aware of Patrice's presence in the room. "All I ever wanted was for that boy to love me. What else could I have done? What more did he want from me?"

"A little love in return?"

He looked up through a glaze of regret and remorse to focus upon the lovely features bending near his. He shook his head, not understanding. "I did. I gave him a home. I gave him a chance to better himself."

"But did you ever give him anything of yourself?"

He was too swamped with agony to see the wisdom in her words. Instead, he struck out blindly, in wounded anger. "Everything I did was for him. Don't you understand? It was all for him. Not Jonah. For Reeve. It was all for Reeve. And he wouldn't take it, damn him! Why wouldn't he take it?

Patrice knelt down, taking one of the blue-veined hands in hers. The coldness of that suddenly fragile hand shocked her. It felt so . . . old! Her own heart twisted with grief, filling her words with passion.

"You wanted to give him things, Squire. But what you would never give him was respect for who he was, who he is. You made it impossible to accept your love without surrendering himself."

Byron shook his head again, dazed by denial, confusion.

"Don't you see," Patrice continued to plead. "You did the very same thing with Jonah. You made your love conditional upon his bending to what you wanted him to be. I know . . . because I'm guilty of doing the same thing." Her breath hitched in an tight sob. "We both used Jonah and his love to get what we wanted. What we wanted was Reeve, not him." Byron angled away, refusing to acknowledge her with his gaze but unable to shut out the horrible truth of her words.

"You don't think he knew that? We killed Jonah. Not the North, not the war, not Reeve. We did it; you and I. With our own selfishness."

"I loved Jonah," Byron cried in torment. "He was my son."

"So did I. But did either of us tell him? Or did we make him believe we could only love him if he was more like Reeve? Reeve was the only one who loved him for the goodness of who he was. And he's right to hate us now for what we've done." Tears streamed down her face as shame washed over her in a bitter tide. Too late to make amends to the dead, too late to make repairs with the living. She drowned in that sorrow, head buried in her arms, weeping upon the lap of her would-be father-in-law. But even as his gnarled hand stroked her hair, Byron fought for a way to offset his share of the blame.

"He has no right to punish me. Reeve was the one who refused to be honest about what he wanted. He pretended to scorn what I had, what I built, but he wanted it." His breathing grew labored as the hidden cache of bitter feelings worked their way out like a long-festering splinter. The price of their release ravaged him, rending heart and mind, pressure building instead of finding a safe avenue.

"He's lied to me," he went on in an aching mumble. "He's going to destroy it all to spite me. Doesn't he understand? Doesn't he know I did everything I could? I loved his mother. If I'd been other than who I was, I would have married her in a minute and conceived him proudly. It wasn't because of who she was, it was me, the obligations I already had to this place, this county, to my wife. Still I would have given them up for her, for the pride of calling him my son. But then Jonah was born. What else could I do?"

Patrice had no answer to that lament. She understood their world too well and the strictures that went with it. He couldn't have had Abigail Garrett any more than Patrice could have had Reeve. Love wasn't enough to brave the separations between them, the vast ocean parting their social classes, the expectations of their peers, the fears and prejudices of a lifetime and the burden of future generations. They couldn't break those unspoken tenets any more than her own brother could have surrendered his station for the love of a mulatto slave. It wasn't done. It wasn't condoned. More than just difficult, it was dangerous. Even if one were willing to risk the sacrifice, how could they wish such hardship on the other and still claim to love them.

That was what Reeve had tried to tell her, and she hadn't wanted to listen.

Byron continued in a failing voice, each syllable ripped from him at great physical and mental cost. He bent forward, gripping his shirtfront, twisting it in his knotted fingers as if trying to wrench his heart free from its agonized containment.

"I offered him everything, Patrice. Everything he wanted. The Glade, my name and all that went with it. All I asked from him was that he give me what Jonah promised to give me. A son, an heir, through you, Patrice. With the Sinclair line and the Glendower name, he could have had it all!''

Patrice's mind went numb. She was a condition of his inheritance. A payment. Jonah hadn't hesitated, because he loved her. But Reeve had never said those words to her.

Hurt and disappointment spread like a sickness, burning her trust, her hopes to ash in a fever-hot flash. Her head whirled as hundreds of images bombarded her anguished mind. Hungry kisses, fiery explorations, the taut, unbearable suspense and yearning afterward. Betrayal cut deeper than any truth he might have told her, severing her will to go on as surely as if he'd cut the vital flow to her heart.

Through the roar in her head, through the mists of foggy pain, a sound intruded. A wet gurgling sound coming from Byron Glendower. Stark reality jerked her out of her cocoon of injury.

The squire sprawled across his desktop. A sharp spasming of his arms knocked his papers, his prizes, to scatter upon the floor. He choked, clawing not at his throat but at his chest. Only when she saw his contorted features purpling did she recognize what was happening.

His heart.

"Oh, my God!" She surged forward, hands fluttering about his hunched body, uncertain of where to grasp, not knowing what to do. She leaned him back in his chair and tore loose his neckcloth and shirt collar, but those small things gave no relief. His rigid arm swung wildly, smashing the glass he'd been drinking from against the hardwood molding. From somewhere inside her, Patrice seized upon the necessary calm.

"Try to breathe, Squire. Try to relax. Let me go get . . ." Reeve was the only choice. As she stood, Byron's hand caught her forearm. His grip was surprisingly strong.

"Tell . . . Reeve . . . tell him . . ."

Tears skewed her vision. "I'll get him. Save your strength."

But he continued to pull her down toward him, to hear those hoarse whispered words as if he knew they would be his last.

"Tell Reeve . . . I asked his mother . . . She said no. Tell him . . . I forgive him for Jonah. That I lo—"

The rest was lost as his back bowed, arching him out of the chair as if some great fist was plucking at him, pulling him, then let him go. He fell back silently, his eyes still open, fixed upon hers for that final promise.

From the doorway, her mother cried out, the sound of it shrill, threading away to nothing as Patrice sank down onto her knees. Cold, dead fingers yet clung to her, demanding her vow. She couldn't speak, not a word, even as Reeve pushed her aside.

"Daddy? Daddy?"

She remembered thinking how odd to hear Reeve call him that.

He felt for a pulse, hand shaking. Feeling, waiting. Waiting. Finally closing pale lids over lifeless eyes.

Then the squire's fingers loosened, releasing her to an endless swoon into darkness.

Byron Glendower lay in state in the parlor. Hundreds came from throughout the county to pay respects and to cast suppositions about the new master of the Glade.

Had he killed his father, just as he'd killed his brother?

Reeve was a solid, somber presence not to be ignored. Dressed in dark attire, carefully groomed and shaven, he greeted each guest by name, offering a hand few chose to take and direct eye contact most shied from. He didn't look like a gloating schemer or a grieving son, but none could fault his manners.

They took exception to him and the fact that he would no longer be content in the shadows.

He was now the owner of Glendower Glade. Their economic, if not their social, peer. And it stuck in their craws like the crosswise fit of his Union saber.

Quietly, Hannah Sinclair saw to the food and the arrangements for the burial when she would rather have attended her still-too-dazed and silent daughter. Tyler Fairfax assumed that duty with surprising decorum despite his startling appearance, both eyes as blackened as a roving racoon's. He kept to Patrice's side, her limp hand pressed between his, smile constrained, fending off those who would engage her in conversation; a gentleman for once instead of a rogue. Sober.

Deacon commandeered a far corner for himself, keeping a brooding eye on Reeve and a more covert one upon his sister. He remained tight-lipped about the rumor that the squire's death followed several violent arguments with Reeve, one immediately prior to his death.

It didn't help matters when Hamilton Dodge arrived to take a very public stand at Reeve's side.

"You all right?"

Reeve nodded as if he wasn't the first to think to ask that. It was nice someone had.

"Helluva surprise."

Again, the noncommittal nod. A beat later, Reeve said, "Thanks for coming."

"Thought I should stop by. Do you want me to stay or go?"

"Whatever you want." But Reeve's stare caught his. The look didn't reveal much, Reeve was too good at packing things down tight and keeping a lid over them. But the flash of gratitude was obvious.

"I don't want to make things more uncomfortable for you . . . you know."

Reeve did know. And he was damned resentful that his good friend, his only friend in the room, should feel unwelcome in his home. His tone was gruff. "Get something to eat. Mingle."

Dodge grinned, able to find amusement in the hostile scrutiny. "A wolf among sheep. Divide and conquer, eh? They can't glare at both of us at the same time."

A faint smile from Reeve. "Before you go, we'll toss down a brandy. Or two."

Dodge was agreeable. Then he caught sight of Patrice and Tyler. "What's that about?"

Reeve followed his direction. An expressionless glaze crept over the brief flicker of something dark and dangerous. "Nothing."

"Right."

Dodge's problem was that he saw too damned much.

"Think I'll go say my hellos to Miss Sinclair."

For Patrice the past twenty-four hours had passed in a blur. A protective numbness blanketed the savage shocks she'd received; Reeve using her to meet the terms of his inheritance, Byron's death. Because she couldn't absorb it all, she pushed it away until strong enough to deal with it. Though she wasn't watching Reeve, the image of him burned against her mind. The memory of his touch, his scent, the texture of his body pressing down over hers played havoc on an innocence she'd been ready to shed for him, with him. Twined between those scorching recollections was the insidious serpent of Byron Glendower's claim. Relentlessly, that truth coiled tighter, choking her as she sat demure and silent in a room filled with friends who had no idea that just a short time ago, she'd been rutting with the man they abhorred.

Tyler provided an unexpected source of comfort. He'd sat close as an attack dog on a short leash, warding off unwanted company and, at the same time, not pressing his own upon her. All his self-serving ways he'd abandoned to support her in her unspoken need. She vowed to thank him later; for right now, she hadn't the strength.

Her wounded gaze focused upon a hand out stretched patiently before her. She looked up to meet the warmth in Dodge's eyes.

"Hello again, ma'am."

The instant Tyler felt her imminent withdrawal, his clasp tightened about hers, keeping it in his possession while he seized Dodge's hand himself and stood.

"I don't believe we've been introduced. I'm Tyler Fairfax. My daddy owns the distillery in town. We're old, dear friends of the family. You must be our new money changer. Welcome to Pride, Lieutenant Dodge."

There was no welcome in a the challenging grip or in the fix of cold green eyes, but Dodge smiled wide in unassuming pleasure. "It's 'Mister' now. The war's over. I've heard of you, Mr. Fairfax. Reeve tells me you are a helluva good friend."

Tyler blinked, but nothing else in his insincere facade wavered. "Did he? It's right nice to hear he regards me so highly. Might I hope we'll become friends as well, Mr. Dodge?"

"Man can't have too many friends." He withdrew his hand and smiled at Patrice. "I was wondering if we might finish our talk, Miss Sinclair. Unless you think this isn't the proper time."

Patrice felt the tension in a Tyler's grip. Gently, she rubbed her fingertips over his knuckles. The effect was immediate and tranquilizing.

"Tyler, would you be so wonderfully kind as to excuse us for a moment? Mr. Dodge and I need to have a private word. Business." She smiled up at him, and his will melted down into his shoes. "But don't go too far away, you hear?"

Recovering from his surprise, Tyler lifted her hand to his lips for a feather-light touch. His stare was intense, devout. With just a hint of suspicion. His voice was a purring caress. "You take your time, darlin'. I'll just go make some talk with Reeve." His stare skewered Dodge's. "Mr. Dodge, I'll have to come pay a visit on you. Soon."

Dodge said nothing until Tyler wound his way through the crowd. Then he exhaled. "That's Reeve's friend?"

"Once, he was."

"Touchy fellow." Dodge angled, looking over his shoulder at the broad back of his coat. "See anything?" At Patrice's puzzled frown, he grinned wryly. "Just thought he might have left his card stuck there on the point of his dagger."

Patrice didn't smile. "It's not anything to joke about, Dodge. Don't make the mistake of underestimating Tyler Fairfax. And don't forget that he's my friend. I wouldn't want him hurt."

Without asking, Dodge assumed Tyler's seat but not the same liberties. At least not with his touch. Instead, he shared his observations to the prickly woman beside him. "You look like you're held together with a fraying baling strap."

Patrice chuckled at his aggravating charm. "You have a subtle poetry about you, Dodge."

He still smiled but a deeper concern steeped in his eyes. "Had a rough day of it?"

"You might say that."

She didn't say half enough, but the redness around her eyes and the pinched quality of her expression said quite a bit more. Especially when Dodge nodded toward Reeve.

"You wouldn't know to look at him, but he's having a hard time of it, too."

Patrice's gaze went to flint. "I gave him my condolences."

"He could use a lot more from you, Patrice."

Her stare snapped to his, angry, alarmed. "And what does that mean? We were going to discuss business, Mr. Dodge."

He lost none of his warm appeal but she sensed a sudden toughness about him. "It is business to me, ma'am. I take my friends very seriously. I don't like to see them hurting, either."

"I'm sorry, Mr. Dodge, but you are mistaken if you thought I could do anything about that."

He stood, smile knowing. "I don't think so, Patrice."

The familiarity made her bristle, then he completely disarmed her with his soft offer of, "If you ever need someone to talk to, I'll be there for you."

She didn't know how to respond. Dodge was Reeve's friend. Would his confidentiality extend from accounts to acquaintances? She wanted to believe it would. She trusted Hamilton Dodge more than anyone else in the room, more than her own brother. But she let him walk away without revealing a hint of that hope.

With his father's friends and neighbors milling about inside under the gracious care of Hannah Sinclair, Reeve was left to his own devices. He made no effort to intrude upon the mourning of those who'd come, knowing it wouldn't be well received. They hadn't come because he'd asked them, and most of them would probably never set foot through the front door again now that Byron was gone. The situation demanded civility, and so far all were behaving, even Deacon and the rowdy Dermonts. But tomorrow, after Byron Sinclair was in the ground, things would change dramatically. Reeve didn't kid himself about that for a minute.

He cast a glance to where Dodge and Patrice were talking and happened to intercept her withering glare. He'd given up trying to predict the hot and cold of her moods, and now was not the occasion to demand an accounting from her. Having Byron die in a her presence, almost in her arms, had shaken her. Death was never easy to accept but having to be in attendance was an awful thing, especially for one as sheltered as Patrice. In a respect for her distress and her reputation, he stayed away.

"Reeve, take some air with me."

Bemused, Reeve followed Tyler out onto the

empty porch. The warm breeze erased the close smells of smoke, perfumes, and death lingering inside. Reeve pulled the clean air in appreciatively, then waited to learn what was on Tyler's mind.

Tyler walked to the edge of the cement porch. He stared down the green sweep of lawn to the whitewashed gazebo. Reeve wondered if he was remembering the stormy summer days he, Reeve, and Jonah sat within its shelter attaching flies to their fishing lines. Or the cold fall evenings he'd slept there under one of Reeve's blankets, too drunk to go home. Or too scared. He must have recalled some of it, for in a sedate voice, Tyler began, "You and me, we been friends a long time, Reeve."

Curious as to where this was going, Reeve agreed.

"I didn't have too many friends. You an' me, we kinda stuck together 'cause nobody else'd have us. But I always liked you, Reeve. I still do. I got nothin' against you or what you did. That's why I want you to know this is nothin' personal."

He turned. There was no fond recollection in his stare. His expression was deadened, his eyes chips of opaque glass.

"You've got to leave here before someone dies."

Chapter 20

"**A**re you saying it's gonna be you or me?" Tyler shook his head, his stare never flickering. "That ain't what I'm sayin'. Hell, I don't want to hurt you. I got no choice in this."

"Yes, you do. Walk away, Ty. You can keep it from happening."

"You give me too much credit. I can't stop things from being the way they are."

"Or you don't want to. Isn't this what you've always wanted, to be a big fish in a small pond? Having folks looking up to you? You're confusing respect with fear. Your daddy do that to your face?"

The sudden shift of topic caught Tyler off guard. For an instant, his reactions were genuine. He flinched back, stare going dull as unpolished jade. Nervously, he wet his lips but couldn't bring the words up to deny it. Instead, his voice hollow as a dry well, he said, "I got careless."

"You know what I'm talking about." Reeve could see he did. No one knew his circumstances better. "The pond stinks, Tyler. Get out before it sucks you under."

Maybe it was too late for the truth to reach Tyler Fairfax. Perhaps Reeve was counting on touching something in his old friend that no longer existed. He'd had enough things in his life trying to push him over the edge. If Reeve could just manage to restore that delicate balance.

"Tyler, if you go through with what they're planning, you'll be just as bad as he is."

Turmoil darkened his eyes and worked the lean angles of his face. Then the disturbance settled like ripples disappearing on deep waters. Reeve knew he'd lost his chance.

Tyler walked the edge of the porch in his rolling amble, speaking casually while avoiding Reeve's eyes. "I can only give you this one warnin'. Things will get worse if you stay. They won't ever forget Jonah or which side you chose to fight on. Not as long as Patrice wears that engagement ring and you're sitting here in this house atop the corpses of your brother and father."

Reeve's insides chilled at the picture his friend painted but didn't interrupt the deadly quiet of his words.

"Your protection is gone, Reeve. You don't have the squire to hide behind. When he's put in the ground, they'll come for you. You know that."

"I do."

Tyler confronted him with a brief flare of intensity. "Then get the hell out. Go far, far away. You don't like them any more than they like you. Sell this place and get out. Start over. I would if I was you."

"But you're not."

Tyler studied the set lines of his friend's face, the determination in his eyes, and, resigned, he momentarily hung his head. Then he crossed to Reeve and encircled him with a lightning embrace. It took Reeve a startled second to respond. Then they held tight to one another, enfolding the times they'd shared, good and bad, with a fierce, almost-angry desperation. And then Tyler stepped back to surrender the friendship they would never know again.

Features mobile and expressive, Tyler hesitated. Reeve thought he had something to say, but, in the end, he turned without comment or regret and walked away.

Through a misty gaze, Reeve watched him go. He considered calling to him or going after him but did neither. Instead, he returned to the house and to the brandy he'd promised Dodge.

And later, when the house was quiet, he mourned the loss of Tyler Fairfax as if he was burying him tomorrow, too.

A misty drizzle darkened the morning gloom settling over the fresh earth of Byron Glendower's grave. Several dozen had braved the weather to hear the preacher's intonations, words echoing those spoken not so long ago over Jonah Glendower's plot. Words Patrice was so heartsick of hearing.

As soon as the short service was over, the mourners filed quickly to their carriages, not stopping to pay respects to the lone figure remaining with the gravediggers in the Glendower cemetery. Reeve stood motionless, head slightly bowed, rain plastering his hair against his brow, not at his father's open grave but next to Jonah's, his hand resting atop the cold stone. He didn't respond to the press of Dodge's hand on his shoulder, so his friend followed the others, leaving him to whatever grief moved behind the immobile planes of his face. When the banker walked past Patrice, water runneling off the brim of his low-crowned hat when he nodded, his words hung like the chill fog, bringing a shiver.

He needs more than that from you, Patrice.

What more could she give? What more could she afford to risk? She knew the squire's ancient lawyer waited inside in Byron's study to apprise Reeve of his father's will. Was there a clause in there with her name attached? Inheritance of the Glade conditional upon his marriage to Patrice Sinclair? A twinge of pain stabbed through her heart as she allowed Deacon to lead her and their mother across the spongy ground to the shelter of the porch. There, Hannah, her eyes swollen from the weight of burying too many loved ones, went directly inside to change out of her sodden shawl. Patrice made to follow when she saw her brother walk back out into the gloom. She paused to watch him, as he strode, unbent despite the worsening downpour, to meet with someone beneath the negligible cover of one of the Glade's live oaks. Puzzlement grew to alarm when she saw that the man was Tyler.

Their meeting was brief. Tyler did most of the talking, his gestures becoming more emphatic as Deacon shook his head. Patrice wished she could hear their words. Finally, Tyler jabbed a forefinger against the center of Deacon's chest to punctuate his message then left her brother standing there for a long minute, apparently to mull over whatever Tyler deemed so important. Patrice grew chilled, wondering over the reason for their intense discussion. She had scarcely enough time to duck out of sight as Deacon turned toward the house once more. Caution warned not to let him see her spying upon his business.

She'd just mounted the stairs when Deacon called to her. Arranging her features carefully, she looked to him, trying not to be obvious in her scrutiny of his mood. There was nothing to discover from the void of his expression.

"Patrice, tell Mother we leave as soon as the rain lets up."

"Where are we going?"

"Home. Get your things together, all of them. We won't be coming back here again."

Surprised, though she shouldn't have been, Patrice blurted, "But Deacon—"

"Don't argue, Patrice. Do what I tell you."

It wasn't the command. It was the faint plea in his tone that made her comply, fearing whatever had him so unsettled.

"We'll be ready."

He didn't say anything. The slight drop of his shoulders spoke eloquently of his relief.

Three hours later, their trunks were piled in the back of the shiny new carriage. Patrice took one quick look back at the house that should have been hers to call home. They hadn't seen Reeve before their departure. Hannah protested it was rude not to thank him for his graciousness. Deacon replied that he'd taken care of the niceties. Patrice wondered. As sorry as she was not to have a final word, a final glimpse of the new master of Glendower Glade, she was relieved as well. It made not looking back once the carriage began to roll that much easier to bear.

Though she never allowed the knowledge to surface fully, Patrice knew deep in heart and mind that they were leaving the Glade on a run so as not to be caught up in whatever retribution the citizens of Pride planned for Reeve Garrett.

Patrice hadn't been inside the Manor since workers bought by Tyler's bribe took over the refinishing. After climbing the rebuilt steps to the entryway, Deacon held the door open to usher them in with poorly concealed anxiousness.

"Don't expect too much," he told them. "It could never be the way it once was. There's still more to do."

Hannah stopped and drew an awed breath. "Oh, Deacon. Deacon, it's lovely." She whirled to hug her son, weeping softly into his shirtfront. Over the top of her head, Deacon watched for Patrice's reaction.

Polished wood floors reflected in their mirrorlike sheen the wonders Deacon managed. Fresh paper lined walls edged in gleaming natural woodwork. The reupholstered rolled-arm sofa was restored to its place against the stairs, inviting a guest's repose. Cleaned and reframed portraits of past Sinclairs looked down upon them in approval as a breeze from the open door stirred the prisms of overhead chandeliers into a tinkling dance. Patrice's eyes welled up as she took it all in.

"Is it home?"

Deacon's quiet question broke her reverie. She turned to him with a teary smile and watched his reserve collapse at her emotion-filled, "Yes."

When he freed one arm and opened it wide, she was quick to join her mother within the tight circle of family.

"I couldn't bear to give you any less," he whispered against the tops of their heads. "Having you back here is worth everything. Welcome home."

Worth everything.

Patrice squeezed her eyes shut, burrowing her face into her brother's shoulder. She wouldn't think about it. It didn't matter now that it was done. All Deacon had done, was done for them, for their father's dream and their future prosperity. She couldn't condemn him for that, for seeing to duty above personal honor. And for the first time, as she felt him relax upon a satisfied sigh, she realized how awful it must have been for him to make the sacrifices to restore their world.

Or the illusion of it.

With an arm curved about each of them, Deacon gave mother and sister a tour of their refurbished home. Hannah couldn't stop crying, and Patrice was close to tears herself. It was a magnificent restoration on the surface, and she enjoyed the feelings of security and tradition surrounding them, at least for this moment of her brother's triumph. She couldn't deny him that. She loved him too much.

After a fine meal, Deacon consulted with Jericho behind the closed doors of his father's study, while Patrice saw her mother off to bed. When she came back downstairs afloat on memories of the past, she found her brother in the parlor seated on the same sofa where he'd nearly lost his life to blood poisoning. The sofa was recovered, as was her brother. He stared pensively into the fire, long legs stretched out toward its heat, one arm draped along the carved trim of the sofa's back. His other hand cradled a nearly empty snifter.

"I've never seen Mama so happy."

He looked up, expression quiet, strangely vulnerable as he asked. "And you? Are you happy, Patrice?"

She settled on the cushions beside him, nudging under his extended arm and tucking her slippered feet up beneath her. His breathing seemed to stop when she pillowed her cheek on his chest.

"It makes me happy to see you like this."

He took in her evasive answer, then set his drink aside. His fingertips touched tentatively to the side of her face.

"I've done this for us all, Patrice. To keep our father's legacy alive. To give Mother back her memories. To see you have everything you deserve and more."

"And what do you get, Deacon?"

He was silent for a long moment, apparently surprised by the question and unable to grab at an easy reply. He phrased his reasonings precisely but passionlessly.

"All my life, I watched our father put heart and soul into the preservation of our name. That's the one thing he instilled in me, over and over, that I was a Sinclair and that this was my destiny. Everything he did was to groom me to assume his place as head of this family, to take control the way he would have. I understood why he had to be harsh, sometimes cruel. It was to make me stronger, ready for this day."

To make him over into the man their father had been. Patrice understood, too. And suddenly that frightened her. Avery Sinclair had been a man of his times, content within the microcosm of Pride County where change never came and pride rested on the laurels of past glory. Unlike his son, Patrice had to wonder if her father would have survived the upheaval to their world. And that made Deacon the better, stronger man. Did he know that? Did he know the perfection he'd struggled to attain all his life had already been far surpassed?

"You're not Father, Deacon."

He took it wrong. His fingers tightened upon the cap of her shoulder, the embrace no longer inclusive but rather constraining. "But I will carry on with the things that mattered to him. I promised him that when he rode off to war. I vowed I'd see our family stayed together and that nothing we'd do would disgrace the name Sinclair. I watched you break our father's heart with your rebellions and your disregard, but you were a child then. Grow up, Patrice. Grow up and take responsibility for your part in this family."

She cringed under his words, twisting inside for a way to escape them, finding none. He spoke the truth. She'd seen the pain, the disappointment in Avery Sinclair's eyes whenever she fell short of the standards he set. Knowing that many times, she'd failed on purpose just to provoke him, brought her no pleasure now. He'd died to preserve their unchanging quality of life. The only time she'd ever given him a moment of unblemished pride was the day she'd accepted Jonah's offer of marriage. How good it felt to bask in the glow of his regard, a reward well worth the sacrifice. That's what Deacon meant. She recognized all her brother set aside of himself to be subordinate to their father's ideals. But was it right and good for him to bow before the pressures of the past, or was he being cheated, were they all being cheated by the oppression of that rule?

Then Deacon extinguished any further argument with an abrupt shift in tactics. Whether cunningly calculated or straight from the heart, it didn't matter; his words had the desired effect.

"You were right about one thing, Patrice. I can't do it alone. The choices I've had to make—" He drew a deep stabilizing breath before he could go on. "I had no idea they'd be so . . . difficult. Just knowing you and Mother were here to support me made all the difference. Father never said so, but I'm sure he felt the same way. We do what we have to do to protect the ones we love. When we can't do that . . . something just dies inside."

Patrice straightened slowly. A catch in her brother's voice snagged her heart as well. He stared into the fire, expression taut, almost unreadable. Almost. Perhaps because of her own divided loyalties, she was extrasensitive to the same torments in another. His wistful anguish telegraphed loud and clear.

"Deacon?"

He glanced at her, gaze wary, veiled yet still vulnerable. She touched his jaw to keep him from turning away.

"What happened while you were away? Was there someone?"

The sadness in his faint smile devastated her.

"It doesn't matter now. It's too late to look back."

His air of resignation stemmed the questions

forming on her lips. *What happened? Who was she? Where is she now*? And most importantly, *Did you love her?* Instead, she whispered, "Oh, Deacon, I'm so sorry," and enveloped him in the wrap of her arms. He leaned against her, just for a moment, resting his head on her shoulder just long enough for her to know the depth of his heartache. She wanted to weep for his lost love because she knew he never would. And that was so sad to her.

He rubbed his face against the collar of her gown as if to dry his eyes, then he pulled back, but not completely out of the comforting loop of her embrace. The naked emotion displayed on each long angle of his face crippled her with despair, making her yearn to do anything, anything at all, to relieve his pain.

"You're all I have," he told her in a fractured voice. "You, Mother, the Manor. I'll never have anything else that means as much to me. Don't break my heart, Patrice. I don't think I could stand it."

Then he put a defensive distance between them, both physically and emotionally, by standing, leaving her alone all weak and weepy with arms crossed tight beneath her breasts to hug in the hurt the way she wished she could hold him. She rocked herself trying to ease the ache of blame for all her selfishness long after she heard his footstep muffled by the upper-hall runner.

Don't break my heart.

What could shatter it worse than her feelings for Reeve Garrett?

Drawing her knees tightly to her chest, she pressed her face into them, lacing her fingers over her head to keep out the steady barrage of shame.

Don't break my heart.

Oh, Deacon, you don't know what you're asking.

Or, perhaps he did.

Perhaps he knew exactly.

She sat back, wiping at her eyes, struggling with the gulping sobs. Could her brother be so coldly clever? No. No. Stuffing her fist against her mouth, she stifled a wail of denial. But she couldn't be sure, and the uncertainty was worse than knowing the whole truth.

Worn-down and weary from the constant battle of will and want, Patrice closed her eyes. It couldn't go on, this relentless strife between head and heart. Too many things lay unresolved for her to even consider rest.

And that left only one alternative. Answers. She had to know. She had to put the endless turmoil at rest. Was it love or loyalty that would control her future?

The only answer was in Reeve.

Chapter 21

⏤⏤◜◝◞◟⏤⏤

Reeve did the necessary chores by rote, keeping busy so he didn't have to think. He curried, fed, and stabled the horses after first cleaning and replacing straw. He lugged fresh water for the troughs, slipping and sliding in the muddy drive as the heavy buckets pendulumed in his arms. He shoveled stones into the deepest ruts of the entry road and stamped the filler flat. Finally, exhausted, filthy, and aching, he trudged up to the house, only to pause on the front steps and look up.

What a huge difference between belonging to a house and owning a house. The Glade was his, yet he felt no shift of pride or pleasure within him. Just because some old lawyer said it was, didn't make it so. Words and paper didn't make the feelings settle any easier inside him.

He felt the shabbiness of his attire. He hadn't changed out of the severe black suit he'd worn at his father's grave. He'd taken off the coat and vest, pushed up the sleeves, and gone to work. The fancy shoes were dulled by dirt and manure-straw mix. The sharply creased trousers sported a tear on one knee from a nail off the feed bin. Mud smudged up and down the thighs where he'd wiped his palms. His shirt had long since lost its whiteness and starch under the stress of body heat and perspiration. He and the fancy clothes didn't go together any more than his living in the big house alone.

For a moment, uncertainty got ahold of him, swelling big and hurtful within his chest. What was he, Reeve Garrett, bastard son of a seamstress, doing on the threshold of this new world? He had none of Jonah's extensive training in deportment and things prim and proper. He knew the land, the soil, the four-legged beasts who grazed on its bounty.

The twilight hour was still, laced with the wet-earth scent of the earlier rain. All was quiet. Waiting. Waiting for him to make a move.

He took the steps slowly, stride growing more confident with each one he climbed. He crossed the porch at a brisk pace and went in the front door, pausing only to lever out of his shoes. Not because he had to, but because he didn't want to clean up after them later. Standing in the cavernous front foyer, he took in the grandeur and dominating wealth and refused to back down to its mocking intimidation.

Mine.

The notion surprised, then surrounded him with an empowering sense of control. His. All of it. Every room. Every rug. Every board and brick.

And every inch of its emptiness. All his, and here

he was wondering why having it had been so important to him when getting it left his spirits so deflated.

The heavy curtains were still closed in the study to yield an air of privacy. Reeve left them that way, preferring the darkness for the way it catered to his mood. Here, he'd had his last argument with the squire. Had he known there would never be an opportunity to speak to him again, would he have said anything different? His fingertips traced across the top of the desk. The only thing upon it now was his copy of his father's last will and testament. He'd resented the man who'd fathered him, and admired him, too. A hard combination to justify, at least so soon after his passing. A time would come when he'd wish that last moment back, knowing exactly what he'd have said, and he would probably despair the rest of his life over missing that chance. But not tonight.

Tonight, he remained slightly disoriented by the idea of loss. In truth, he felt Patrice's absence more keenly than Byron's. The house was too quiet, as if it held its breath in expectation. Waiting for what, he wondered. He found himself listening for the sound of movement, but the air was still. He cocked his head, thinking he'd heard voices, but it was just the wind stirring the bushes outside. Suddenly, the huge space grew too small, too confining.

And then the sound of smashing glass brought him running back into the hall.

A rock rested on hardwood in a litter of window shards. Reeve bent, relieving it of the scrap of white paper tied about it. The message was succinct.

Murderer! Tomorrow is judgment day!

Nice of them to let him know when they were coming.

Bottle of bourbon in one hand and rifle braced across his knees, just in case they got the date wrong, he sat on the front porch, listening to the night sounds.

The echo of hoofbeats reached him through the rustle of the trees and the stirring of the horses. He took his time, setting the bottle on the step below him, thumbing back the hammer of his Spencer repeater. Then he waited to receive his first guests.

Totally unprepared for who'd come calling.

Night raiders bent on burning down his house wouldn't arrive in the Sinclair's fancy carriage.

"Were you expecting company?"

His whole body went tight at the sound of Patrice's sharp-edged observation as the carriage pulled up at the end of the walk. He let out a hint of a smile. "Not really. But I don't want to appear a bad host by not being ready." His gaze hungered over the sight of her; the arrogant way she sat in the carriage, the flippant tone meant to conceal her nervousness, the rapid flutter of her jacket lapels that had nothing to do with exertion. Then he asked.

"Why you here, Patrice? Forget something?"

She met his gaze, and neither could look away. "Yes," was all she told him.

Patrice waited until Reeve eased off the porch and sauntered to the carriage. He put up both hands and she leaned into them, her pulse jumping at the sudden strength of them clasping her rib cage. Her senses spun giddily as he swung her down, keeping her suspended that last inch above solid ground for just a moment too long. Just long enough for their stares to fence in token resistance before surrendering up a mutual truce. He set her down and stepped back.

Without looking at him, Reeve said, "Thanks for seeing her safely over here, Jericho. I'll make sure she gets home."

Jericho hesitated, caught between the roles of obedient servant and protective man. "Mista Reeve, I don't know—"

"It's all right, Jericho," Patrice cut in to calm him. "I won't be long."

"I'll be waitin' up for you, Miss Patrice," he murmured, then added more prickly, "to sees you gets home proper."

"Thank you, Jericho."

Even before he angled the carriage around to take his leave, he'd been dismissed from both their minds.

Smiling, Patrice touched Reeve's once-crisp shirt. "This will never come clean again."

"Hope I never have another occasion to wear it."

She glanced down uncomfortably, wondering if she'd made a terrible mistake. Not caring because of the way her heart was thundering with forbidden excitement.

"Can I get you something?" The obligations of host sounded forced on his lips, but she couldn't take her gaze off them as she watched him speak.

"What's that you've got there?" She nodded toward the steps.

"Some of the Fairfax bourbon."

"That'll be fine." At the upward leap of his brows, she smirked. "I've had it before."

"Tyler trying to relax your resolve?"

She smothered the smile provoked by Reeve's

sarcasm. "Actually, Starla. We were trying to feel wicked and worldly."

"Did you?"

"Until we woke up the next morning." She sat down on the top steps with a swirl of her skirt to one side so he had room to join her. He didn't, not at first, preferring to stand over her in a somewhat wary pose. She hefted the bottle daintily and drank from it. One swallow. Two. She sucked a quick breath, then handed it to him. He took it, ignoring the challenging lift of her smile. He took a drink, then cut right to it.

"What did you forget, Patrice?"

She didn't reply at once. Instead, she hugged to her knees and gazed out into the darkness. "I forgot to tell you how sorry I was. It was such a shock. I cared for him, too. He was almost . . . almost a father to me."

For a moment, they were silent, sharing the thick sense of sorrow. Then she spoke again, her tone less steady, less sure.

"I wasn't able to speak to you after the service, but I wanted to know that you were all right, to tell you—to tell you I'm sorry." She ended lamely, words confusing the real issues.

"You didn't have to ride all the way over here in the middle of the night to tell me that." His tone chided, goading for the real reason as he dropped down to the step beside her.

"Yes, I did." Patrice fidgeted, fingering the fabric of her skirt, wishing she had the courage to ask for the bottle back. "I—I wanted to talk to you about some things the squire said to me before—before he died." She had his full attention. She could feel the scorch of his questing stare.

"What things?"

She caught herself before the words formed. If she asked about the terms of the will, and he answered the way she expected him to, nothing would be the same between them again. Yet, she would have to ask, she had to know, but not just now, not right at this very minute as emotions twisted and churned inside her, feelings she'd denied, then tried to repress, ever since she'd first seen him standing at his mother's grave.

"Can we go inside? I'm getting a little chilled."

Reeve quirked a doubtful smile, but he didn't challenge her. He took her elbow to assist her, and together they went into the big empty house. Patrice was surprised she couldn't hear the banging of her anxiousness echoing all around them. Suddenly, she felt rushed by the urgency of her feelings, by the confusion in her mind. She'd needed more time. Shyly, she brushed his soiled sleeve.

"I'll wait if you'd like to clean up a bit."

Reeve stepped back and sniffed unobtrusively. His expression puckered. All his earlier work outside left him a little less than presentable to a lady. The delay would give him a chance to plan out the words to begin his campaign upon the heart of Patrice Sinclair. She'd made the first step by coming to his door. It was his intention to see she didn't regret it. "Be back in a minute. Make yourself at home."

He'd left a change of casual things in the back washing porch. Reeve hurried there, stripping off his offensive shirt as he went. Why was she really here? He heard serious business in her tone of voice and read pure promise in her sultry eyes. He tossed off the trousers and shimmied out of his sweat-soured long johns once he'd reached the small enclosure where the floorboards slanted away from the house to channel off rain and water. Grabbing up a cloth and sudsing it up well, he scrubbed himself down until the only thing he could smell was soap and his discarded garments. He kicked them into a corner.

Why had she come back, alone? For talk? Or touching?

Toweling dry, he cast about for a set of long underwear. Seeing none, he shook out a pair of freshly laundered denims and stepped into them. The waistband was just skimming over his bare buttocks when he heard a slight gasp behind him. After buttoning himself together, he turned, expecting to have sent her running.

She was still there. Her eyes glittered, sapphire-bright, as her gaze rose from bared toes to bare belly, to his chest and finally to his face. He was still dripping wet, the towel hanging forgotten off one shoulder.

"I'll do that."

Boldly, she took the towel and stepped behind him, blotting the beads from his back. Then the loosely woven fabric began to move up and down, side to side, charting the broad terrain of his back and shoulders in slow strokes. It was all he could do to stand still for it. The towel moved down one brawny arm as her palm slid down the other. A shudder rode through him, settling heavy and low.

Patrice eased around until they stood toe-to-toe. She didn't look up into his eyes but instead focused on the vee his collarbone made in front, where she could see his sudden, jerky swallowing. She pushed the towel across his chest, fascinated by the moisture glistening in the bronze hair curled upon it. Her breathing labored apace with his. Then, the towel dropped to cover his bare feet.

Her hands continued their gliding exploration over taut muscle and tight midriff. Her fingertips trembled when they reached the band of his britches, then moved on brazenly over the jut of his hipbones, down the bulge of his thighs, circling around and up to flatten upon the firm contour of his rump.

She shivered hard as his palms rubbed up the sleeves of her jacket, capping her shoulders briefly before sliding up to encase the slender column of her throat. He lifted her chin with his thumbs, her gaze resisting for a moment, then rising as well.

He was lost the instant he looked into the pooling blue of her eyes. He bent.

Patrice stretched up for his kiss, moaning softly at the reacquainting pressure, opening quickly to let heat and wetness wash away the last of her reluctance. Her questions, her sense of injury could wait. This could not. Not another second.

They stood as almost a minute passed by, mouths locked, bodies pressed close, hearts thrusting in fervor and trepidation of what might or might not follow. Finally, Reeve twisted away. His hands shook where they supported her upturned face. His breathing was all out of control. For a long moment, they stood, joined only where her fragile jaw filled his palms.

"Reeve—"

His fingertips brushed over her lips, quieting her as he said, "Thank you for coming. Maybe we'd better finish this conversation later." When it wasn't so dark, when he wasn't half-dressed.

When he wasn't feeling so unsettled inside, he needed something to hold on to. "I want to do this right."

"Do what?" she breathed, light-headed from his touch, lost to his intensity.

"Court you."

Her heart skipped a beat, then hurried on frantically.

"I should talk to Deacon first—"

"No," she interrupted. She knew how Deacon would react. Her eyes squeezed shut as his tormented words replayed in her mind, calling upon her loyalty, her responsibility; those things that meant all to him and suddenly, not nearly as much to her as the promise of love. How could she pledge her soul to her brother at the forfeiture of her heart. Her heart was here, with this man, as it always had been. That truth was now crystal-clear. Deacon and his demands of duty were not her future. Reeve was. She took a breath and finished with a firm, "Talk to me first."

He swallowed, then he said, hoarsely, "I'd better finish getting dressed."

She angled to one side, dipping slightly, coming up with his clean shirt in her hand. Tossing it out into the night. "Talk, first."

His eyes were hot and lit by mysterious lights of gold and green. But the innate gentleness in his touch, in his voice mesmerized her. "I don't want to make any mistake."

Is that how he saw himself, as Byron Glendower's mistake? The revelation shot through her mind, but the rest of his reply obliterated conscious thought.

"I never wanted anyone else . . . but you."

While she stood, still and breathless with shock, he expanded his reasonings.

"Every time I saw you wet your lips at some prancing fool, I wanted you. Every time you walked by me and pretended not to notice, I wanted to take you right down to the ground and make it impossible for you to ignore me. Even when you stood there on my brother's arm, tellin' me you were marrying him, I wanted to make you mine. There wasn't a night that went by for four whole years that I didn't dream of you, of what it what it would be like to touch you."

She trembled as his fingertips skimmed down her throat.

"Of what it would be like to hold you in my arms."

He hooked the collar of her jacket peeling it back, letting it slide down her arms to lie forgotten on the floor.

"Of what it would be like to taste the mouth I'd watched smile and pout and scowl at me all these years."

He fell silent for a moment, kissing her slowly, languishing over every soft and willing detail. When he straightened, she leaned toward him, breathing in quick, gulping breaths.

"I wanted to take you out of your fine, fancy clothes." He started down the buttons of her white batiste blouse, baring skin as he bared emotions long covered by propriety. "To strip you down to the woman underneath."

Her taffeta skirt pooled at her ankles followed by the practical muslin-and-lace petticoat, leaving her feeling naked and vulnerable in her corset cover and pantalettes. But never did she think to cover herself or protest the way his hot stare assessed her with one fluidly molten glance. She trembled wildly in the thrall of unknown sensations.

"And?" she prompted.

A smile of raw sensuality shaped his mouth.

"And I wanted to hear you say my name, saying you wanted me just as much."

Her resistance evaporated. She swayed against him, pressing her lips to the damp wall of his chest, tasting the salty warmth with greedy abandon.

"I want you, Reeve. I've always wanted you. That's why I came here tonight . . . for you, for this."

Her confession absolved him of doubt.

"Do you want to go upstairs with me?"

She damned them both with her husky reply.

"Yes."

One powerful arm curved about her waist, lifting her out of the circle of discarded clothing, hugging her against him until her head was forced back and her mouth quickly taken beneath his own. In a moment of floating ecstasy, he carried her down the hall, up the curve of the stairs, into his room, straight to his unmade bed. He leveled her across the tangle of sheets, mattress giving under his weight atop her own, as he kissed her hard and openmouthed until nothing existed except those wet, intensely unique textures.

This was what she'd been holding herself for. Not as a proper gift for an unknown stranger her parents might have picked for her, not for a financial ally chosen for her brother's benefit, but this man, for reasons of love, not propriety. As a gift to convey that love in a way no other could.

He broke away, reaching down to ruck off her drawers, big hands trembling clumsily over the laces to her corset. And through it all, he kissed her, hurriedly, hungrily, along her torso, between the scented valley of her breasts, over the full swells and tender peaks, never lingering in one place even as she arched up in offering, crying out his name.

His legs thrashed, freeing themselves from the hug of denim. And then there was nothing between his hard, toned body and the sleek satin of her skin.

He moved against her, creating an agonizing friction.

"I'm gonna explode if I don't take you now," he mumbled frantically into her kisses.

"Then take me now," she breathed back.

A unison gasp of shock and surprise marked their first joining. Quick, hard thrusts followed, rough with excitement, deep from urgency too long denied. Soon, too soon, he cried out, passions spilling upon that hoarse shout of wonder.

Crushed beneath him, Patrice lay tense, stunned by the invasive hurt, by the pressure of him within her. She shook all over, alarmed by the unexpected pain, intrigued by a brief streak of expanding pleasure that ended with his completion, uncertain of what to do now that all was *fait accompli*.

Mumbling something that sounded like, "Worth the wait," Reeve stirred, easing up on his forearms so she could breathe. Too shy with him and with her own emotions, Patrice couldn't meet his gaze.

"That was . . . nice."

When he laughed at her inarticulate description, Patrice glared upward only to melt down to hot butter beneath the intensity of his gaze. His expression held awe and dazed delight and a tenderness that relieved her tremulous fears.

Then he shook the walls of heaven with his quiet claim.

"That was the lightning. Now I'll bring on the storm."

Chapter 22

 ❧❧❧

For the next few unhurried hours, they explored the luxury and limits of passion, satisfying curiosities, sating fantasies, tasting, touching, exploring until Patrice slept fiercely in the aftermath of her own discoveries.

"Patrice."

She moaned, the sound soft and sensual, new. Her head turned to expose the curve of her throat for his nuzzling kisses. Her hand reached languidly to ruffle through his mussed hair, finger-combing it into some semblance of order. After a moment, he spoke again.

"Patrice, you have to go."

She made a negating noise and rolled to fit against him, no longer bashful or innocent in her welcome of her body's response to his emphatic differences.

" 'Trice, you can't stay here."

"Want to," she murmured, nipping at his shoulder, tonguing the hollow of his collarbone until he groaned and clutched her closer. They nudged and rubbed up against one another, thighs shifting, hands gliding, pressing until, with a lengthy moan, Reeve admitted to himself that there was nothing more he could do about it, at least on this night. He gave her one bruising kiss and rolled away.

"C'mon, Patrice. Let's find your clothes. I've gotta take you home."

She burrowed into his covers, all soft, honey-sweet sensuality to purr, "I'm at home right here."

Feeling the irresistible pull of her yearning gaze, Reeve threw himself away from it before he was lost once more. The shock of cold floorboards beneath bare feet cooled lusty passions to a calmer sensibility. He snatched up his denims and shimmied into them. When they were buttoned, he dared look back. A mistake. Patrice, now on her back with knees bent up at alluring angles, stretched creamy arms over her head for the expulsion of a leisurely, luscious yawn. Heat roared through his veins, thundering into his well-satisfied sex with a rejuvenating energy the rest of him couldn't quite match. Having learned full well the extent of her power over him, Patrice smiled like a sultry temptress and reached out her hand.

"Come back to bed, Reeve," she crooned in a smoky caress. Her gaze grew heavy lidded.

A feverish chill shook him as he looked upon the substance of his every wish fulfilled—Patrice Sinclair sprawled naked in his bed and still warm from his possession.

And as out of his reach as ever.

Intimacy changed nothing. It made everything

worse. Now he knew full well what he was missing. Because passion hadn't been prefaced with words of love or commitment.

She hadn't said it was more than that, and he hadn't asked. She said she wanted him. Want implied a lot of things. A desire of his body, a need for his restorative wealth now that he was Byron Glendower's heir. He wanted more than that.

He stuffed his fingers between hers, twisting, fisting them together to haul her out of his sheets. Patrice floundered in surprise and put her feet on the floor to anchor herself from being dragged over the edge.

"Reeve, what's wrong?" There was no cocky self-satisfaction in her voice now. He heard an edge of panic, and it fueled his own.

"Get dressed."

The brusque command brought a sparkling brightness to her eyes as she asked, "What did I do to make you so angry?"

"I'm not angry," he lied through the clench of his teeth. He was angry, but at himself, not her. "I just have to get you home before your brother finds out where you've been."

He'd dreamed of winning her love without complications, so he would know beyond a doubt that she wanted just him, Reeve Garrett, accepted at face value. He'd lost his chance at that coveted, precious gift, and he could never get it back. He would never know if she'd shown up at the front steps of the Glade because she loved him or because she wanted to make love with him. Very different, very important meanings to a man of his background.

But Patrice didn't understand his reasonings. Wrapped up in his sheets and her own indignation, she said, "Is this where you thank me for the good time and sneak me out the back door?"

"No," he grumbled irritably. "This is where I take you home and sneak you in yours."

Her pout settled into a more matured frown as consequence settled, scattering any lingering thoughts of intimacy. His curt statement was a correct summation of their situation. She'd come to him in the night, on the sly, they'd stolen a few hours of secret pleasure, but now it was time to get back to the reality of their lives. And she was as cross about that as he was.

"Go saddle your horse. I'll be out in a minute." She stood, dragging the sheet behind her like the train of a royal robe. Brought up short when he placed his foot upon it. He gave her a faint smile.

"That looks good on you."

A return smile flirted across her lips. "Thank you. Save it for me."

Because there was a hint of somberness to her teasing, he frowned. "I plan to."

She searched his face, needing to find reassurance after taking such a huge step away from the strictures of her upbringing. She found it in the sudden mellowing of his gaze.

The ride back to the Manor was a time of reflection, but not regret. How could she regret something so spectacular? But memories alone couldn't fend off the uncertainty she took home with her.

He wanted to court her. That meant marriage. The flutter of expectation within her breast was stilled by grim circumstance. Deacon would never allow it. The town would never condone it. It formed a delicate balance; what she owed them weighed against what she owed herself and Reeve. She hugged to the broad security of his back, wanting to believe there was enough strength there to shore up her own wavering doubts. The fragile state of her emotions provided a weak defense against her insecurities.

Don't break my heart.

How she wished she could close out her brother's urgent plea. How she wished she could face him boldly with what resided within her own. She loved Reeve Garrett, and he wanted her.

Wanted wasn't the same as loved. Was the other true as well?

She tried to think clearly over the anxious beat of confusion. If not for love, then why else would Reeve pursue her? All she had was the Sinclair name, no fortune to go with it. If he was intent on claiming her in marriage to win his inheritance, he wouldn't be so concerned about Deacon catching them together. In fact, he'd relish the idea. If it was the result of unbridled passion, why would he show such concern for her now? Guilt? It had to be more. But what? What meant the most to Reeve?

The Glade. Jonah.

This was Reeve's day of triumph. He'd taken the Glade from the father who'd denied him dignity. He'd taken the fiancée of the man who'd threatened to take his future.

Had their night together been a culmination of desire or an act of revenge and pride?

Reeve reined in the lathered stallion as they approached Sinclair Manor. Damp earth muffled the sound of loping hoofbeats. Her spirit writhed in turmoil by the time he brought her to the door of her darkened home.

"Do you want me to go inside with you?"

His question startled her. Was he thinking to protect her or make a claim upon her? One thought warmed, the other agitated. "No. That won't be necessary. Everyone's asleep."

He twisted in the saddle, giving her a long, inscrutable look that dared her to act ashamed. Her chin tilted up of its own accord, winning his slight smile.

"Well, I've talked to you first and you seem to have no objections to my courtship." Patrice blushed at his confidence then stiffened at his next words. "When do I talk to your brother?"

He saw the fear jump into her gaze, that flash of expression more honest than her hestitant reply.

"Please don't rush things with Deacon. Let him have time—"

"To what?" His tone was soft yet steely. "Have a change of heart? Patrice, you're dreaming if you think he'll ever come around."

She drew a panicked breath, knowing he was right. "Then give me time."

"To do what, Patrice?" Seeing her distress, he eased back on his intensity. "Do you have second thoughts about me?"

"No."

He considered her answer, his reaction to it hidden. "How much time?"

"I—I don't know, Reeve."

His guarded look grew, his voice thinned. "Have whatever time you need. But Patrice, I will not sneak around behind your family's backs. To do so as children is one thing. It left a bad taste then. Until you give me leave to declare my intentions, it's best we not see each other alone again."

"I agree," she said, not because it was what she wanted but because she could see it was the wisest course.

He reached around to assist her dismount, his arm brushing her breasts. Their startled looks collided with jolting awareness.

"Reeve—"

He palmed the back of her head, anchoring her for the hard ravishment of her lips by his. His kiss was different from the others they'd shared. This one hurt as much as it pleasured with its frustrated slanting pressure. Then abruptly it sweetened to a soft feathering of tenderness, telling of his reluctance to let her go with so much unresolved between them. She was gasping and disoriented by the time he let her breathe. Then he lowered her to the steps and, without a word, left her there on unsteady legs, with uncertain heart.

Unaware that her brother witnessed everything from the dark vantage of the parlor window.

It took every ounce of her will to get up the next morning, to leave the fantasy of dreams and go down to breakfast as if nothing had happened. She'd washed vigorously, nearly peeling off skin to make sure Reeve's scent didn't linger. Weary and sore, it was torture just to walk upright, but she managed. If she could survive Deacon's probing look, she could get through anything.

He already sat at the table buttering a biscuit. The knife paused in mid-stroke. Slowly, his gaze lifted, touching on hers, flickering back down before any identifiable emotion registered. He continued slathering on jam, the pressure he applied breaking the biscuit into crumbles within his palm. He let it fall to his plate and wiped his hands off on his napkin.

She settled shakily into her chair across from him and reached for the coffee just as he did. They exchanged a quick look, and Deacon picked up the pot, filling her cup, then his. She could feel the tension in what he wasn't saying.

Hannah swept in bestowing a bright smile on both of them. "I never sleep so well as when under my own roof," she declared after kissing Patrice's brow and allowing Deacon to seat her.

"In your own bed," Deacon agreed without betraying more.

He knew.

Patrice went cold inside as she sipped the scalding coffee. It took both hands to steady the cup. She waited for him to say more, but his silence was worse.

"I'm going into town this morning to pick up our new dresses from alteration. Patrice, can you be ready in an hour?" Then Hannah's cool hand pressed to her forehead. "You look a bit peaked. Perhaps you should stay home and rest."

Rest? At home, alone, with a brother who knew she'd been in a man's bed?

"I'm tired is all. I'm sure I'll feel more myself after breakfast." She supplied a wan smile and risked a glance across the table.

Perhaps he didn't know where she'd been or who with. Maybe he'd seen her tiptoeing to her room all breathless and blowzy. If he knew it was Reeve, wouldn't he be on his way to kill him even now instead of calmly eating his grits?

She watched him, growing more agitated by the moment, trying to read something telling into his measured movements.

Finally, Hannah pushed back from the table with a dainty dab at her lips. "I must be getting ready. Unless you'd rather I stayed home, dear?"

Patrice glanced up guiltily to murmur, "No, Mama. There's no need for that."

"If she needs anything, I can take care of it."

Deacon's cool offer stirred a prickle of gooseflesh.

"Really, Mama, I'm fine. Just let me finish here." Patrice studied her plain coffee cup, lingering over it, praying Deacon would leave the room without calling her on her betrayal of his trust. *Don't break my heart.* It was one thing to discard that wish when in a lover's arms and quite another to do so within the home he'd struggled to rebuild to keep his family safe.

Deacon sipped at his brew. She fought not to cringe beneath the bore of his stare. Perspiration trickled under her collar, and her breaths grew shallow, fast, as she waited for his next move with all the dread of a small animal in a snare, unable to escape and almost looking forward to the killing blow to relieve the suspense. She jumped when his chair scraped back. Tremors rose up in tiny eddies as she tracked his progress around the table by the sound of his footfalls.

In the next moments, he had the power to destroy her life.

He stopped directly behind her. Carefully, she set down her cup, gripping her hands in her lap so he wouldn't see them shake with tension.

Her heart gave a leap as his knuckles grazed her cheek.

"You do feel a little warm. I hope it's nothing serious."

She closed her eyes, hysteria swelling, threatening

to take hold. If he knew, why didn't he say so? Why did he keep her twisting in dread, trembling in fear of his condemnation? For the sake of torture? To grind in the fact of his absolute control over her future? To make certain she understood how in error she was to defy him? Confession pressed at her tightly sealed lips, pushed by the need to apologize, anything to earn a reprieve from the calculated stalking perfected while he played the deadly game of espionage.

"I'm sure I'll be fine, Deacon. Thank you for your concern."

"I thought I made it clear last night how important you are to me. I hope you were listening. I hope you heard more than just the words." His dramatic pause left her close to weeping. "Patrice, is there anything you need to tell me?"

She twisted in her chair, lifting her guileless gaze to his. "No, Deacon. Nothing."

For the longest moment, he just looked down upon her, seeing right through her deception, right to the lying core of her soul. A flicker of emotion touched his features, so briefly she almost missed it. On anyone else's face, she'd have thought it compassion, but she didn't think her brother knew what it was to feel another's pain.

"Are you sure, Patrice?"

What else could she do?

She smiled up at him, said, "Very sure, thank you."

His expression remained unchanged from its cool detachment. The words, *I'm sorry, forgive me,* were so close to escaping, as was the need to feel the tight security of his arms as she poured out all her woes. She hesitated.

Then he told her quietly, "You can trust me, Patrice. I understand more than you know."

Because it was herself and her own faltering emotions she couldn't trust, she let his offer pass in silence.

His hand dropped to her shoulder, resting there without pressure. But to Patrice, the weight of it was spirit-crushing.

"Patrice, you said it yourself. I'm not our father."

With that curious claim, he left her. No accusations. No demands. Just that opening for her to turn to him. And the veiled promise that he might not judge as harshly as he had been judged.

She sat at her family's table for a long while, shivering and uncertain, trying to decide where to turn with her troubles. She loved her brother fiercely, but she knew where he stood concerning Reeve. He'd made that very clear. There would be no calling Deacon back once he was set on the path of family honor. She couldn't be sure if he would force her to wed the man who'd taken her prized purity, or if he'd choose simply to kill him. She could lose either way.

She'd lost so much already to the whim of war and her own capricious nature. She'd had the promise of security torn out from under her twice; with the death of her father, with the sacrifice of Jonah. Deacon was smart and loyal and coldly cunning. He would always see to their protection—always. But Reeve, with his quixotic moods and unspoken agendas, could she afford to risk her heart, her future, on him? He'd given no guarantees. She blushed to remember the way she'd wailed his name in the throes of pleasure. But wouldn't she find the same pinnacles of delight with any man she might marry?

She considered Tyler Fairfax, replacing Reeve's bed with his. The sharp green fire of his eyes instead Reeve's deep secretive depths, the grace of his sinewy form rather than abruptness of Reeve's hard contours. She tried to imagine Tyler's mouth, his hands, his body meshing with hers, driving her to the point of abandon and beyond.

She gasped and jumped out of her chair, greatly disturbed and cold all over. No, not the same. Not with anyone else. She rubbed her palms over her arms to restore their warmth, the intensity of her reaction upsetting her.

There was a knock at their front door. Wearily, she went to answer it, then paused in the foyer when she saw Deacon already there, opening the door to the last person she expected to see on their doorstep.

Reeve Garrett.

She watched the stiffness spread through her brother's stance like ice across a shallow pond.

"Garrett. Is this a social call?"

Reeve's gaze touched upon Patrice's pallid features but didn't linger. "No."

"Then what kind of business brings you here this time of the morning?" Challenge bristled in his tone even as hospitality demanded the door stay open.

"My father's." He bent to pick up a huge box and strode inside with it, heading straight for the dining room, passing Patrice without comment. Patrice and Deacon followed, both of them wary of him and each other.

Reeve had the box on the table and the lid off. Patrice gasped as he unwrapped the first piece of elegant stemware.

"The Squire wanted Patrice to have these. Speci-

fied it in his will. I'm afraid the set is short one of
the glasses." He glanced at Patrice, then went on in
the same brisk clip. "Anyway, here it all is. Do
whatever you want with it."

Patrice came close to peek into the box. A poignant pleasure constricted her words as she placed
her hands lovingly on the contents. "Thank you,
Reeve."

She looked up at him, gratitude glimmering in
her eyes. His narrowed into unreadable slits as he
took a step back, increasing the distance between
them.

"No need to thank me."

His tone had the same effect as a hard shove. Her
emotions staggered, taken aback. Was he afraid she
meant to cry defilement while Deacon stood right
behind her? Did he expect her to come undone because the attraction between them pressed in like
the sweltering summer heat, making her light-
headed and oddly breathless?

He should have known better.

"Thank you for the extra burden on your time for
delivering them, is what I meant."

His mouth formed a thin pale line, scarcely moving as he said, "No trouble at all."

Finding no excuse to prolong his visit, Reeve nodded to her, then to Deacon with the same crisp formality. He'd reached the door when Hannah
hurried down the stairs, a ship under full sail in her
billowy flounces.

"Why, Mr. Garrett! I didn't know you'd come to
visit." A quick glance chastised her children as she
extended her hand.

Reeve took it up gallantly. " 'Morning, ma'am. It

wasn't a visit. Jus' tying up some loose ends from the squire's estate."

Hannah's gaze went soft with sympathy. "Poor dear. How hard this must be for you to handle. I truly wanted to express my condolences yesterday, but what with the weather and the shock and all . . . I hope you understood?"

"Yes, ma'am." He smiled, flustered by her kind attentions.

"Deacon said he spoke to you on the behalf of our family, but I did want to add my own sentiments."

Reeve's gaze slid to Deacon's impenetrable facade.

Patrice chilled. Deacon never said anything. Her brother hurried his family out of the Glade without a word of regret, without a syllable of thanks. The thought of such an intentional insult would devastate their mother. And Reeve knew it.

But he turned back to Hannah with his most humble smile. "Yes, ma'am. Your son was very gracious, and I thank you for your sincerity. I took much comfort in it."

There wasn't a touch of cynicism in his words, no reason for Hannah to suspect he told anything but the truth.

"I've got to go now, ma'am. Thank you again for presiding over things at the Glade like you did. I won't forget your kindness." He kissed her soft hand to prove he meant it. And his slashing stare at Deacon said he wouldn't be forgetting anything else, either. "Deacon. Miz Patrice."

Reeve let his smile uncramp once he stepped out onto the porch. Patrice answered things for him quite nicely with her stony silence.

He'd spent restless hours anxiously conceiving a way to see her before he went out of his mind. He remembered the glassware, the way her look had gone all dewy and dreamy over it and he'd seized upon that convenient explanation for his visit. He'd promised to give her time and didn't mean to pressure her. Yet he feared time would push a distance between them that he'd never breach again. He thought she might need reassurance and a show of support. And he had to know where he stood.

The minute he'd stepped over the threshold of Sinclair Manor, he'd known the truth of it. Patrice cowered behind her prim and proper manners, afraid to say boo to their feelings for one another. As if ashamed. As if she was sorry. As if she'd rather die than have her starchy brother know she'd been with a man of no consequence, a man like Reeve Garrett.

Feeling the fool for letting himself believe in her again, he stabbed back his heels, and Zeus lunged forward, carrying him swiftly off Sinclair property.

Chapter 23

Too cowardly to endure another moment of pretense in her brother's company, Patrice retreated to her room, only to have her sanctuary disturbed by her mother's gentle presence. Hannah settled on the bed beside her and after taking up her daughter's hand, asked, "What's wrong, dear? And don't tell me you're ill, unless it's a sickness of heart."

The opportunity was too important to let slip away.

"Mama, were you and Daddy in love when you married?"

Hannah gave her a startled glance, then quickly recovered. "We hardly knew one another, dear. Of course, I knew who he was, everyone knew the Virginia Sinclairs. We'd danced a quadrille or two at summer parties, but we'd never shared any conversation or unchaperoned time together. Those times forbade such intimacies between young people. Our fathers considered us a good match, and arrangements were made. That's how things were done then."

"So you married a stranger?"

Hannah laughed softly. "Heavens, I knew all about your father. He was ambitious, protective, honorable, hardworking. All the men were—at least those worth knowing. They had values and would not compromise them. So you see, I knew exactly what I was getting. I only hope your father was not disappointed."

"In you? Oh, Mother, how could you think so?"

"My family had tolerant views. He and my father often argued. Avery didn't like his opinions challenged, especially in public. I made the mistake, shortly after we wed, of expressing myself on the slavery issue at the governor's tea."

"What did Father do?"

"Nothing, dear. He didn't speak to me for weeks and pretended not to hear me or even acknowledge my presence in the room. Looking back, it all seems so silly, but then, I was young and terrified of being sent home to my father in disgrace."

"So what did you do?"

"I apologized, of course. Profusely. And I promised never to unman him in public again."

Patrice's mood sank pensively. "How awful for you, to have views and be forbidden to express them."

"Oh, no. My views were heard, loudly and often. In you, my dear. You spoke up for everything I kept quietly to myself. You were my champion, and imagine your father's shock when he could not control you. You frightened him to death."

"Me?"

"Of course. Men are their most blustery and belligerent when they have to justify what they've done. They dislike being made to feel guilty or not in control. A woman who questions or demands reasons threatens them. A husband depends upon his wife for unwavering support, even when both know he's wrong."

"But that's living a lie!"

"A small illusion perhaps but nothing so terrible. What is it you want in a husband? For him to provide and protect his family. For him to go out each day to face whatever hardships await him so you feel secure. What would you give in return?"

"Children?"

"Delightful, yes, but an added worry upon the shoulders of a man who is now both husband and father. Peace is what a man wants from his wife, a place to feel safe from worldly pressures. When in his home, a man wants understanding, not strife. Respect is the only reward he needs from his family."

"What about love? Did you love Father?"

"Not with youthful passion, no. Passion makes demands and is often cruel to those who cannot control it. Admiration, respect, trust, those are things that bond a man and woman for a lifetime. I loved your father for his stability. I loved his determination, his pride, even when he was his most bullheaded. I loved the fact that there was nothing on this earth he would not do if I asked it of him. I bore his children, kept his household, and made him feel comfortable in confiding his worries and woes to me. I understood the importance of my role and was content to keep it, and he loved me for that."

Patrice stayed silent. These weren't the words she'd expected to hear. She'd wanted marriage to be romance and indulgence, not practical complacency. Her confusion must have shown, for her mother put an arm about her shoulders for a bolstering squeeze.

"It's not a prison, Patrice. It's glorious freedom . . . if it's with the right man. If I hadn't thought your father was that man, I never would have married him."

"How do you know? I mean, I was pledged to Jonah, and I never felt—I never knew—"

"If he was the right one? He'd have made you a fine husband, which is why we agreed to the match. He could have been the right man, if you hadn't found that man already."

Patrice sat completely still, not daring to betray herself with the slightest movement. Her mother went on unconcerned.

"I always liked your Mr. Garrett. A good choice, even if he was not your father's choice."

Patrice twisted on the coverlet to stare at her in dismay. "If you knew I was in love with Reeve, why did you allow me to say I'd marry Jonah?"

"Loving and living with are two different things, Patrice. You may have loved him then, but you didn't have the strength to live the life he would have demanded of you. You were too young, too full of your own needs for a complicated man like Reeve Garrett. Jonah was wiser, more willing to forgive your inexperience than his brother would have been. It was not an easy decision to make, but it was made with your best interest in mind, just as the one we made for Deacon years before. Your father and I thought Jonah would be the stabilizing influence you needed, neither harsh nor wild. I'm sure you would have made him a good wife, Patrice, had things not turned out as they did."

If Jonah hadn't died. If she hadn't been forced to grow up so fast. If Reeve's return hadn't quickened those old desires.

"Do you think I'd make a good wife for Reeve?"

"That depends?"

"On Reeve?"

"On what you're willing to give up to have him."

What was she willing to give up to have Reeve Garrett? If she truly loved him, why was there no easy answer?

Hannah touched her chin, guiding it toward her. "It's more than Mr. Garrett, isn't it? What else has you so concerned? Is it your brother? Don't look so surprised. You see, I know your father never had any overseas investments."

"Oh, Mama. I'm so worried about Deacon. He's in terrible trouble, I know it. He's so—"

"Like your father." Hannah sighed. "Perhaps you should pay another visit to your banker friend and see what he can do."

Patrice gaped at her. How could she have been so wrong about the woman who raised her? Hannah Sinclair was anything but unaware. For the first time, Patrice could see her gentle, guiding touch upon the family, unobtrusive but always there.

"Go into town, my dear. See Mr. Dodge. Have your brother take you. Use the time on the road to talk to him, not lecture at him. He loves you, Patrice. He'll listen."

* * *

Deacon didn't question his mother's request that he take Patrice into town to do her errands. The ride was uneventful and silent, both brother and sister preoccupied by troubles tied up with the other. Deacon dropped Patrice off in front of the dressmaker's but didn't remain to actually see her go inside, relieving her of having to tell him a lie.

Patrice felt a strained undercurrent ripple through the citizens of Pride as she hurried down the walk. Tension created a palpable static, like the crackling before a lightning storm. Those she encountered hushed their whispering to stare at her oddly, then turned from her attempts at a greeting. It reminded her of their treatment of Reeve at the Glendower gala. But why would they shun her? What reason would they have, unless . . . Unless they somehow knew about her and Reeve.

Cold panic settled in her stomach, hurrying her steps toward the bank. She didn't try to hide her destination. Deacon would learn of it soon enough.

"Why g'morning, ma'am." Dodge came to his feet, cigar clenched between his teeth as he smiled and pulled out her chair. Patrice sank into it, desperate to appear nonchalant beneath his too-observant gaze.

"Mr. Dodge, how are you?"

"Well, I haven't had any sacrifices left on my steps lately, so I suppose I'm doing all right. Unless the good people of Pride are planning something on a grander scale."

Patrice swallowed hard. "Why would you think that?"

Dodge pinned her with a direct gaze. "Something's got them all stirred up today. Fairfax and his unpleasant friends have been circulating some kind of ugly talk. My guess is there'll be a run on sheets at the mercantile."

Gathering her courage, she asked, "What kind of talk?"

"No one exactly confided in me, but it has to do with some goings-on out at the Glade last night. You know anything about that, Patrice?"

She cringed in her seat, rattled, anxious. "Why would I?" She glanced away, sure he could read lewd acts all over her expression. Which he apparently could.

"So if you're not here to taunt me with the fact that I'm the only one in this whole damn county with no love life, I'd guess you're here on business."

Used to his shocking bluntness, she didn't bother with blushes. "Help me, Dodge. I-I don't know what to do. If I can't find some way to buy our debt back from Tyler, I-I'm afraid of what might happen. This is my fault." Tears sprang to her eyes and to her embarrassment, she couldn't keep the dampness from falling in a scalding stream. "If I hadn't pushed my brother so hard—If I'd only stopped thinking of myself long enough to understand what he was struggling with—"

Dodge's handkerchief was in her hand. She blotted her eyes as he crouched down beside her chair, all burly sympathy.

"It's not your fault."

"It is!"

"No." He sound so certain, so convincing, she gave a miserable sniff and blinked forlornly. He smiled and opened one arm wide. "I'm told I have a good, solid shoulder."

Without hesitation, she leaned upon it, relying upon its broad strength while searching for control.

His arm made an uncompromising loop about her, the gesture sheltering, comfortable in its warmth and unpressuring weight. He gave her the time she needed to pull her ragged seams together, not speaking, just there with sturdy, dependable support. Finally, she straightened to met his gaze, finding it calm, encouraging.

"What can I do, Dodge?"

"Your brother's going to have to do it. I can go to him, or he can come to me."

"You can go to hell." Deacon's cold tones intruded like a harsh slap. "Get up, Patrice, before I forget you're my sister."

Dodge's hand settled upon her shoulder, holding her down as he slowly stood to face the seething Southerner. "Nothing's going on to get riled up over, Mr. Sinclair. It's just business."

Deacon's eyes slitted. "Funny business. I'm not laughing."

"Deacon—"

"Shut up!" he hissed down at her. She shrank back. The fearful movement didn't escape either man. Deacon froze over. Dodge became dangerously soft-spoken.

"Mr. Sinclair, your sister came to ask for my help. She's done nothing wrong. She's concerned about you."

"What kind of help, Yank? Help to bury us all the faster?"

"She asked me to help save your ass before it gets chewed off by your so-called friends."

"And why would you want to help me?"

"It's my job, Mr. Sinclair. I don't have to like you to save your neck, and you don't have to like me to be smart enough to stick out your hand so I can keep you from losing everything you've worked so hard for."

"I don't need help from the likes of you," Deacon snarled. He snatched Patrice's arm, dragging her out of the chair. She had the presence of mind to throw up her hand to stop Dodge's fierce stride forward.

"No, Dodge, it's all right! It's all right."

"Are you sure?" He glanced up into Deacon's frigid mask of hostility, his own glittering in narrowed eyes.

"Yes."

Not fully convinced, he put his hand over Patrice's, feeling the tremors racing through her. He pitched his voice low and steady. "I owe Reeve my life. If you need help, you send someone to get me."

"She won't," Deacon vowed. "You stay away from us. You're the problem, not the solution."

"And you're a fool for believing that, Sinclair, but you've a right to your opinion. But God help you if you think those rights extend to raising a hand to that little girl."

Deacon ignored the threat, pulling Patrice out of the bank, scattering the curious who lingered outside on the walk. He stalked to their carriage and practically threw her up onto the seat. A crack of the whip sent the horse lunging forward, leaving a dust devil in their wake to choke the citizens of Pride.

A mile, then two, passed in tense silence. Patrice sat stiffly, angry, frightened, upset. She glanced at her brother, seeing no promise in the jutting angles cut into his face.

"Deacon—"

"Do you have any idea what you've done?" His

accusation slashed sharper than the whip. "How could you go begging to that man? Don't you have an ounce of shame?"

"Shame?" she railed at him. "Don't talk to me of shame after the way you humiliated me in front of my friend, in front of half the town!"

"This isn't about hurt feelings, Patrice. It's about keeping you safe from your own foolishness."

He sounded so genuinely anxious, Patrice backed down her own arguments to look at him more closely. He was more than just furious. He was afraid.

And as he drew back on the reins, she knew why.

A dozen hooded riders swarmed around their carriage, forcing it to stop in a shadowed nave of trees. Deacon thrust Patrice behind him but had no time to reach for his sidearm as a rifle barrel pressed to his temple.

"Heya, Reverend. You an' me need to have us a talk." Tyler circled around the carriage, the only one of his band brave enough to show his face. Or careless enough. He tipped his hat to Patrice, smiling wide. "Hey there, darlin'."

"What do you want, Fairfax? Get on with it, then get your thugs out of my way."

Deacon's gruffness wasn't appreciated. The man holding him at gunpoint swung viciously, catching the side of his face with the stock of his rifle, toppling him from his superior pose to the dusty road on hands and knees. Gritty laughter sounded beneath the muffling hoods. One of the riders slipped onto the seat to restrain a furious Patrice.

"Well, then let's get right to it." Tyler swung off his horse to hunker down beside the dazed aristocrat. "Me an' the boys here are gettin' kinda wor-

ried about you. Seems you can't control your little
sister. She's been stirrin' up talk with the company
she's keeping. Looks bad, her being so disloyal to
you . . . an' to us. A lesson's gotta be learned here.''

Deacon swayed up onto his knees to snarl, ''Don't
you touch her, you son of a—''

The back of Tyler's hand silenced the rest of the
epithet. ''Now, Deke, you know I'd never put a
mean hand on Patrice. I'm blamin' you for lettin'
her stray.'' He stood and moved away, purposefully
not looking up at Patrice.

As soon as Deacon gained his feet, the riders
wove around him, kicking at him, knocking him
with their horses, trying to force him off-balance
again. It didn't take Deacon long to tire of it. He
grabbed the closest man, jerking him out of the saddle, flinging him to the ground to drive his heel into
the man's windpipe. While the fellow wheezed and
purpled, he snatched his pistol free, intent on using
it until the hooded figure holding Patrice called out,
''I wouldn't, Sinclair.''

Deacon looked up to see the man's arm curled
about his sister's neck. A tight squeeze had her
clawing ineffectually at the woolen sleeve and convinced him to let the gun drop. Immediately, he
was felled by a savage kick in the side.

''Be careful a him, boys,'' Tyler drawled. ''The
reverend here's a dangerous man. A real killer.
How many unarmed folks you shot down in cold
blood, Deke? An' you sneer down at us after all you
done?'' Tyler crossed to where Deacon sat in the
dirt, nursing his ribs. He squatted down fearlessly
so that they were nose to nose.

''I got me a surprising offer the other day from
someone who wants to buy the Manor real bad. Of-

fered top dollar. What's a-matter, Rev? Got nothin' to say about that?''

Clamping down hard on his shock and panic, Deacon gritted out, "What do you want, Fairfax? You wouldn't be here if you didn't have something in mind.''

"Well, that's true 'nough. I been askin' myself what do I want with that big ol' place? There's only one thing in it that has any value to me, and it surely ain't you.''

"Cut to it, damn you.''

"Well, I got no use for the house an' I don't need the money. Guess that leaves your pretty little sister.''

In one swift move, Deacon had him by the throat, hands constricting, jerking Tyler off-balance. And just as fast, the tip of Tyler's blade nicked in below Deacon's ear.

"Let me go, or I'll cut you a new smile.'' The green glaze in his eyes sliced as sharply as his knife. It took a minute for the compression to ease and Deacon's hands to open. Tyler rocked back to rub at the bruises each finger left. "That was stupid.''

"You son of a bitch. You won't make Patrice your mistress.''

Tyler actually looked surprised. His voice lowered for their hearing alone. "Mistress? I don't want her for a mistress. I want her for my wife. You may not believe me, but I'd take good care of her. 'Sides,'' he added with a viper's smile, "no one else is likely to offer for her now that she's whoring with Reeve Garrett.'' When Deacon didn't recoil with the proper horror, Tyler frowned, perplexed. Then he laughed out loud. "You already knew that? I can't figure you out, Sinclair. If it was my sister sneaking behind my back like that, making me a laughing-stock in front of my friends, I'd have killed them both."

"We're not the same kind of men, Fairfax. I walk upright."

"Have your little joke, Rev. It don't change nothin'. You know what I want. I want your blessing on my upcoming nuptials, and in exchange, I'll make Patrice a nice wedding present—the mortgage to the Manor signed over to you."

"Go to hell."

Tyler's sly grin never faltered. "Oh, you don't have to give me your answer right away. Think about it while you're sleeping under your roof tonight. You got until tomorrow. In the meantime, my friends want a little show of your support to our cause, a token for their hard work on your behalf."

Deacon waited for the price of his pride to be named, tense, sick inside at what he couldn't evade.

"We'd like your company tonight when we visit your neighbor." He glanced at Deacon through eyes void of feeling. "We got a little housewarming planned for Mista Garrett."

"No!" Patrice surged forward, struggling against her captor's hold. When her elbow found a tender spot, the man growled a harsh oath and hit her, hard. Senses going black, she scarcely felt him throw her off the seat to the ground. Through dazed eyes, she saw Tyler spring up onto the carriage seat like a panther. The blade in his hand flashed, slicing through the mask where the man's ear would be. The fellow howled, clasping at the spot where red rapidly soaked through white.

"Nobody touches her. Didn't I make that clear, *cooyon*?" Then as quick as it blew up, Tyler's temper mellowed. "Don't go makin' me do such things," he murmured as his arm draped about the man's shoulders as if all was forgiven. Then loudly, he called, "What you say, Deke? Ready to earn that money?"

Deacon scrambled around the horses on all fours to crouch protectively over Patrice. She clung to him, consciousness ebbing. The last thing she heard was Tyler's confident laugh.

"I think he'll be ready, boys."

The carriage rocked to a halt in front of the Manor's porch. Patrice came around in woozy degrees as Deacon lifted her down from the seat. His jarring steps woke her the rest of the way as he elbowed into the front parlor. He laid her upon the couch, then strode to the mantel to reach for his scabbard. The blade sang free, glittering like her brother's intense stare.

"Deacon, no . . ." She levered up into a sitting position, ignoring the pounding ache in her jaw to grab his coat as he tried to sweep past her. "No!"

"They're going to pay," he muttered ferociously. The darkening marks on his brow and cheek lent a savagery to his claim. Patrice hung on, refusing to let him go.

"We're all going to pay, Deacon. Can't you see that? We're all going to pay for your vanity and pride."

He stopped then, frozen in place by her angry outcry.

"Is this how you planned to keep your promises?" she shouted into his impassive face. "By gambling on the nonexistent charity of men like those? By ignoring honest men like Dodge who could re-

ally do some good—just because of their accent? By
selling me off to Tyler Fairfax to buy back your
honor? Damn you, Deacon! Damn you to hell! You
are exactly like our father! You don't care about
anything but the precious Sinclair name!"

He recoiled, revulsion flickering through his
slated stare.

She wrenched the saber from his hand to fling it
across the room. "Don't bother tossing away your
life to preserve something you can no longer claim."

"Children!" Hannah bustled into the room,
shocked by what she'd overheard. "What's going
on here?"

Patrice turned to her with eyes flashing. "Deacon
can tell you, Mother. Make him tell you everything.
I'm going for air."

As she stormed out, Hannah looked to her son,
repressing her alarm at his battered face. "Deacon,
what have you done?"

His breath escaped in a shaky rush, and with it,
went the last of his pride. "Oh, Mama," he mumbled softly, "I've made a terrible mistake."

Deacon, how could you? Her heart cried out in anguish as Patrice raced to the barn. Jericho met her
in the doorway.

"They mean to put a torch to the Glade, Jericho.
Tonight."

Shock quickly gave way to grim purpose. "He'll
have to be warned." Then his eyes narrowed.
"What you plannin', Missy?"

"I'm riding over to the Glade—"

"Not alone, you ain't. Not wid dem hooded cowards out there riding the night."

"All right. All right. Tell my mother . . . tell her I

forgot something in town and that you're driving me there. I hope to be back home before they suspect otherwise."

Jericho nodded, smiling crookedly at her sudden flare for deception. He was back in less than ten minutes, but to Patrice it seemed like hours. She kept imagining Deacon intercepting him with questions he couldn't answer. But then the carriage pulled up, and she went weak with relief.

"Did Deacon ask you anything?"

"I didn't see him, ma'am."

Wherever her brother was, she prayed she wouldn't see him at the Glade taking up the torch under one of Tyler's hoods. She scrambled up onto the front seat beside Jericho, stuffing her skirts in around her with a sharp command of, "Go."

Shadows of twilight stretched out across the pale walls of Glendower Glade by the time the carriage careened to a stop at the front walk. Patrice scanned the glazed windows, seeing no sign of smoke, no red gleam of fire.

They were in time.

She fought with her hoop and petticoat, making a graceless exit from the conveyance. Once aground, she told Jericho, "I want you to go into town."

"But—"

"I'll be fine here. I want you to go to the banker, Lieutenant Dodge. Tell him to come quick. He'll understand. Go on now. Don't spare the horse. I don't know how much time we have."

"You tell Mista Reeve what you got to, then you hie yourself home, you hear?"

Patrice smiled tightly at the paternal rumble of

his tone. "I will. You go on now. Lieutenant Dodge, at the bank."

"Yessum."

As the carriage spun away, Patrice hurried up the front walkway, only to come to an abrupt stop at the sight of Reeve Garrett framed in the front door. Her mind blanked, flustered by his sudden presence, unprepared for what to tell him.

He wasn't interested in hearing her say anything.

"Call him back, Patrice," Reeve ordered flatly. "I don't want you here."

Chapter 24

Patrice didn't let his harsh tone discourage her. She came closer, up onto the steps, across the porch. "Reeve, I have to talk to you. This is important."

"Not now. Go home, Patrice. I'm in no mood for games."

"This is no game!"

But he'd stepped back from the door and swung it closed, leaving her to argue with its impersonal wood panels. More afraid than angry, she pulled it open and went inside to hurry after Reeve's retreating figure.

"Reeve!"

He didn't pause in his walk to his father's study. He didn't bother to close that door to her, going, instead to pour himself a hefty drink of Fairfax Bourbon. He swallowed, then without turning, said, "All right, Patrice. Speak your mind."

His words wounded on the periphery but her mission was too urgent to allow the luxury of pain. "Tyler and his hood-wearing friends are planning to visit you tonight."

Reeve took another drink. "I'll be sure to set enough places at the table."

"It's not a social call. They're planning to burn you out!"

He was frustratingly indifferent to her news. "You've been a good neighbor. Now, I suggest you go home before someone finds out you've been here."

"Then you'll leave. Right?"

"Got no place else I have to be."

Stunned and terrified by his casual acceptance, she cried, "So you just plan on staying here and letting them burn the house down over your head?"

He looked at her then, face quiet, eyes icy calm. "I don't plan to let them do anything."

She understood in one gut-twisting instant. He meant to stand his ground against whatever the odds. Impossible odds. "They'll kill you." Her tone flattened with horrible certainty.

Reeve smiled, thin and humorlessly. "They'll try." Then his features went rock-hard. "You've warned me. Now go."

If he expected her to turn tail and run for safety, he was sorely mistaken. Patrice squared her shoulders, her jaw adopting a mulish angle. "I'm not going anywhere."

She meant it. Reeve saw it in the set of her expression, in the cool conviction of her gaze. And it scared him to death. He responded to that fear with a slashing anger.

"Yes, you are. I don't want you here, Patrice. I

don't need another of your meaningless sacrifices to weigh me down."

He saw her flinch and knew his cruel words pierced her heart. He couldn't care. Patrice had to leave, and he'd do anything necessary to see her safely away from the Glade.

"Don't use me as a excuse to strike back at your father and your brother. I won't be the reason you pick for throwing caution to the winds just to prove how independent you are."

She paled. Her confidence wavered. "I'm not—"

"Yes, you are. Don't you think I had enough of a brain to figure out you were using me to flaunt your disregard for their rules? Did you think I didn't know you were always chasing after me jus' to get them good and riled and ready to bend to your demands? You didn't want your freedom. You just wanted to be pampered and fussed over. You wouldn't have run off with me. You wouldn't have had the courage to turn your back on proper tradition. All that teasing. All that talk. But when it came right down to it, you folded and grabbed on to Jonah, jus' like I knew you would. You didn't love him. You jus' wanted the things he could give you, the things you were used to having."

Somehow, during the intentionally provoking speech, Reeve forgot its purpose was to scare her off. He took a deep breath before his shaky emotions got the best of him, then pitched his voice low and cold to make her angry enough to walk away.

"Did you tell your folks you couldn't marry Jonah because I was the one you were in love with? No. You were afraid you'd lose their support. You were afraid of disappointing them and the Sinclair name. Think that'll change now that I've got this place? The folks in town say I killed Jonah to get it. They're probably busy trying to find some way to fix the squire's death on me, too, so I could get him out of the way. They'll say I seduced you so I could steal your family's respectability along with your honor."

Voice fragile, she spoke her greatest fear. "Did you?"

Reeve fell silent for a long moment then, his tone deadened, he asked, "Is that what you think?"

She stared at him, eyes huge, luminous with gathering tears. She didn't answer.

Reeve tossed back the rest of his whiskey before saying, "Go home, Patrice. Game's over. Nobody wins."

Demoralized, Patrice fled. Her confusion carried her as far as the front hall. There, she grasped the staircase's newel post to keep from collapsing under the pressure of hurt and shock and uncertainty. Heartbeats thundered in her ears yet still couldn't quiet his awful words. Or an even worse truth.

He was right.

She sank down upon the bottom step, legs strengthless, energy drained by an avalanche of misery. For all her bold statements, for all her brazen acts of defiance, never had she gone so far as to threaten her safe return into the family fold. That's what her mother had tried to tell her.

Though she'd always known well the state of her heart, she'd been afraid to act upon it. Though she'd prided herself on her tolerance toward all manner of men, her words were empty. She backed away from practicing what she preached so vehemently. Many times, she'd rocked tradition with her outspoken views, but never, ever had she broken from it. She'd gone along with her marriage plans to Jonah, hoping, praying Reeve would intercede, relieving her of the burden of breaking her family's hearts.

Rocking in short thrusts, Patrice tried to still her trembling before it engulfed the rest of her. Through a blur, she studied the ring she still wore, a symbol of her insincerity.

She might not wear a hood, but with her own silence, she was condoning all that they did. And that cold knowledge shook her to the soul.

Reeve reached to refill his glass, then thought better of it. Whiskey wouldn't drown his regrets. It would take fire to purify them, a service his friend Tyler would most likely provide before the night was over. He crossed to the squire's fancy gun case and pulled out a couple of sleek Henry rifles. He stuffed the chambers with a crisp well-trained efficiency that required no conscious thought.

What he'd said to Patrice was unforgivable. And untrue. He didn't blame her for not having the superhuman courage to go against her family, her friends, her beliefs to have an uncertain future with him. He'd hurt her and could only pray he'd have the chance to apologize, but outside shadows stretched across the lawn, deepening, blending together, thickening relentlessly. Those shadows reaching the house within a few short hours weren't going to be charitable enough to let him tie up his loose ends. Better she hate him as a heartless bastard than to let her risk her life here beside him.

Tucking both rifles under one arm, he picked up several cartridge boxes and turned toward the hall. Stopping in absolute, mind-blanking surprise.

"I'm not leaving, Reeve."

How could she manage to look so drawn and delicate and at the same time braced by a foundation of steel? He was too stunned to react at first. So Patrice continued.

"You were right, Reeve. About everything. I've always expected you to have enough courage to change things for the both of us, so I wouldn't have to take the risks, and I see now, how unfair I've been, how cowardly. I didn't want to believe it. I wanted to make it anyone's fault but my own. But it wasn't. It was my doing. I chose Jonah because it was what was expected of me. Then I would have spent the rest of my life wanting you, wishing I'd had the strength to tell you so before you rode off to war. I'm sorry, Reeve. I'm sorry that I hurt you."

He took a quick step toward her, intentions halted by the sudden brace of her palms.

"Don't. Not until you hear everything."

"Patrice, you don't have to—"

"Yes, I do. Then if you never want to see me again after tonight, I'll understand, and I'll stay away."

Reeve hesitated, alarmed by the intensity of her grief and her determination to confess sins, real or imagined.

"When everyone in Pride said you were responsible for Jonah, I never spoke up to say different, even though I knew you would never do anything to harm him, that you would have given your own life first. I never said anything to them or to the squire or even to you because I was so ashamed of what I'd done."

"What you'd done? But 'Trice, you had nothing to do with what happened to Jonah." He stopped just short of telling her the rest. His hesitation gave her the opportunity to grab a quick breath and spill all.

"I killed Jonah."

"Patrice—"

"No! I did! I'm responsible. You said you were angry with Jonah for not standing behind his beliefs. I made him go against them by taking up a cause he didn't support, and it killed him."

She had to look away, unable to endure the awareness of her treachery when it began to dawn in his perplexed gaze. He would loathe her. When he learned all of it, he would curse her for her shallow sentiments and her vindictive spirit. And she would be deserving of it.

"It was just after we learned of my father's death," she began in a leaden voice. She spoke flatly, expressionless, so as not to evoke any sympathy for her situation. She wouldn't let him feel sorry for her. "The news was such a shock. I knew men were dying on both sides, but I never considered Deacon or my own father—" Her words fractured for a slight moment, then continued more strongly.

"All I could feel was this huge hole of loss in my heart and a terror that Deacon would never come home, either. There was Jonah, safe at home, risking nothing, always bragging about you and your noble honor, and how he wished he could be as brave. I wanted to hurt him because you had hurt me by leaving, and fate had hurt me. I-I told him that you were a traitor to our love for you. I told him that if he was to be deserving of the same kind of love I'd felt for you, he'd be man enough to avenge my father's death and to earn his own father's respect. I told him I could not care for a man who didn't defend his family's pride, that I would despise him if he did nothing. He died to prove that he was worthy of my love. I pushed him to it. I killed him, Reeve. I did, because I was too selfish to love him for the man he was, and he loved me enough to try to be the man he thought I wanted him to be."

The purge of secrecy wrought relief as well as shame. She hung her head, choking on her sobs, letting them crowd up in her throat until it ached from the effort at containment. She had no right to cry for Jonah now. Or for the result of her own foolish mistakes. The sudden settling of Reeve's hands upon her upper arms made her start, the contact unexpected. As was the warm brush of his cheek against her damp one.

"Patrice, it wasn't you. It wasn't me. It was Jonah."

Too overwhelmed by the heat of his nearness and the tenderness in his tone, Patrice's objections never formed.

"Jonah made his own choices. That's what he was trying to tell me the morning he—that morning. No one pushed him into it. He didn't make that choice out of envy or to prove anything to you. He didn't have to stand up in front of that firing squad. He could have saved himself by naming others, but he made the sacrifice himself. He died a hero, Patrice. His choice. His way of taking a stand for what meant the most to him."

Reeve left it at that. He saw no need to involve Deacon. Not to protect him, as Jonah sought to, but to spare Patrice from any further disillusionment. Let her continue to regard her brother as a paragon. It would do less harm than the truth.

Patrice revolved slowly within the lax circle of his arms. She looked weepy and haggard and still was the most beautiful thing he'd ever seen. Her wrists slid over his shoulders so small hands dangled against his back. Thoughts of Jonah deserted him. Now, there was only Patrice. And she demanded the truth.

"I wanted you to win that kiss from me on the day Jonah broke his leg. Why didn't you?"

Her question dragged up issues long stored away but never truly forgotten. "Much as I wanted that kiss, I wanted to disgrace Jonah more. Instead, I ended up almost ruining his life. He stood up for me, knowing that I'd done what I'd done on purpose. He still protected me. I made a promise to myself that day that I would do everything I could to be worthy of that gesture. Jonah was the first one ever to think of me as an equal. I'll never forget that or forget him."

Her thumbs rubbed soothingly behind his ears. "You made him stronger that day by becoming his friend, his big brother. He was so proud of that fact." She glanced down to frame carefully her next question. "Is that promise the reason you stepped back and let Jonah ask me to marry him?"

"Partly. And partly 'cause I knew he'd be better for you than I would have been."

"How can you be so sure of that, Reeve Garrett?" Her gaze probed his.

"I was waiting for you to correct me."

Darkness crept closer, edging up to the porch, reaching for the steps, bringing danger with it. It put an edge of intensity into the time they had left them. A fierce refusal to let the moment go with so much unrealized. Patrice's hands spread along the jut of his collarbone, her thumbs resting on his top shirt button.

"How long before they get here?"

"I don't know. After dark."

"And that's about a half hour from now?"

He nodded, distracted by the way the vee of her thumbs popped open first one button then the next. Her stare was unwavering and so was her voice.

"I love you, Reeve. Let me show you how much."

An entire lifetime of heartache fell away at that simple claim. His hand fit to the curve of her waist, pressing slightly to guide her toward the stairs.

His room held all the familiarity of a patient lover awaiting her return. She entered without reluctance, without hurry, led by a full range of emotion, not just the fickle passion her mother warned about. There was no virginal excitement, no urgent suspense, just a building intensity, a sense of certainty. She released the tapes connecting her hoops to her waistband. They collapsed in concentric circles growing ever outward like the expanding magnitude of her love for Reeve Garrett. She stepped from the hoops into his arms as if that progression was the most natural in the world.

His kisses rained down upon her uplifted face, dotting her cheeks, her chin, her nose, her brow, adoring each before finally settling firm and fast upon her mouth. Slanting, lingering over soft textures, shaping them to his own contours. His arms encircled her, drawing her against him, flattening her breasts to his hard torso, tucking her hips into the cradle of his thighs. Reveling in her receptive form. Making them as close to one entity as they could be through the boundaries of their attire.

They stepped apart only long enough to strip that barrier away.

The mattress chimed beneath their combined weight, Reeve easing back, Patrice riding him down until she was leveled above him. They kissed again, a long exploration involving tongues and increasingly hurried breaths. Her hands began a slow sweeping study of his heated skin, traveling over rugged swells and valleys, mapping each change in texture from sleek biceps to tight abdomen, rippling over it the way water flowed along a river bottom. Caressing the jut of his hipbones, the coarse bulk of his thighs, testing the fullness of his groin with the gentle rocking of her belly. Sighing, as his hands spread wide on her rib cage pressing her down, moving her in suggestive circles. Arching as his palms rubbed down her back to cup the curve of her bottom, kneading with the heels of his hands.

She gasped into his mouth as his touch grew intimate, then insistent, their kiss wetly devouring as he coaxed the rivers of her body to overflow their banks in a sudden flood. In the shivery aftermath, she opened her eyes languorously to find his gaze fixed upon hers. The knowledge that he'd watched her passions crest upon the plays of her expression sharpened her pleasure. And made her want to return it.

She kissed him softly, lapping, nipping gently at his lips until his eyelids lowered to a sultry half-mast.

"Now you." Desire rasped in her throaty whisper. "I want to watch you."

He inhaled as the potency of that suggestion struck, and struck hard. He'd been buffing the curve of her hips with his palms. Now his hands stilled and held tight, all the while, meeting the tender temptation of her gaze in his own fiercely focused way. He raised her up, shifting slightly so she was positioned above him, then lowered her, filling her in gradual increments until he was hot and snug inside. His breath escaped, a harsh hiss.

Patrice caught his hands, and with fingers entwined, pressed the backs of them to the mattress beside his shoulders, leaning against them for the leverage to begin small lifts. She watched the angles of his face sharpen as tension thinned his lips and darkened his eyes. Quickening breaths flaring his nostrils. His fingers curled and clenched convulsively causing the bunched muscles in his arms to dance beneath the taut glossy bronze of his skin. Like sitting astride a powerful thoroughbred, Patrice rode out the tremors, controlling them with pressure from her knees, urging a faster pace with her rhythmic rocking.

His eyes rolled wildly, glazing, focus gone as they squeezed shut. His mouth opened to emit a ragged, guttural sound that wracked her body with answering need. Raw sensation poured through her in shuddering waves. In her concentration on him, her own response took her unaware, making it all the more shattering.

With a quick surge, Reeve reversed their positions, coming up over her, driving into her, fast, hard, deep, deeper until clutched by the same ferocious rush of urgency that had him spasming thickly inside her.

Then, it was a relief to hold to one another, to languish in spent luxury, nuzzling, kissing softly, touching with total freedom. Finally, Reeve lifted Patrice's hand, pressing a kiss upon its palm, curling her fingers to caress each knuckle. Until he reached the fourth one to find it as naked for him as the rest of her. Jonah's ring was gone.

The tide of exquisite emotion nearly took him under.

But instead, he touched his lips to that strip of pale skin, then said, "They'll be here soon."

And without another word, he rose and began to dress.

Chapter 25

‿‿◠◯◯◠‿‿

Reeve stood at the front door, peering out into the fast-settling darkness. One loaded weapon rested against the jamb beside him, the other he wore in a sling across his back. Boxes of shells were stacked ankle high at his feet. Just in case, he'd wedged a pistol into the waistband of his denims, a handful of rounds weighting the pocket of his Union jacket. Might as well give them a target worth aiming at, he'd decided when slipping it on.

A rustle from behind him made him turn. The sight of Patrice descending his stairs, her ladylike elegance a dusky contrast to the signs of their recent lovemaking, made his chest seize up. She paused when she saw him, her chin going up a notch, not in a gesture of arrogance but of proud confidence, instead.

A terrible fear threaded between the pangs of fierce possession and anxious longing.

338

"I'll saddle up one of the mares. You shouldn't run into any trouble if you go cross-country and stay off the main roads."

She continued her descent and swept across the foyer, her mood disturbingly calm. "I don't plan to run at all. I thought I made that clear to you."

He didn't want to fight with her. But he didn't want her to die with him, either.

"You have to leave." His tone carried enough terse authority to make any raw recruit pale and scramble to obey. Patrice never flinched. Instead, she hefted one of the rifles to expertly check the chamber.

"Careful with that."

She gave him a jaundiced look. "I know what I'm doing. Mede taught me." She hoisted the long gun to her shoulder, testing the sights, then nodding in satisfaction. "What direction do you think they'll come from?"

Short of physically moving her, Reeve realized he stood little chance of convincing her to go. As aggravating as that was, he couldn't help the welling sense of pride.

"Straight on is my guess."

"Do you think a few shots will scare them off?"

His flat, "No," ended any optimism.

Patrice took a breath and studied the lay of the land. "If we catch them in a cross fire, it should—"

Reeve gripped the rifle barrel, shoving it toward the floor. "Patrice, we're not talking a pigeon shoot here. You'll be firing on friends, on folks you know."

Her expression grew maddeningly impassive. "They'll be shooting at us."

"Not at us. At me." He emphasized that, hoping she'd listen. But her determination never wavered.

"What's the difference?"

Whether nonchalance or sheer bravado, Reeve suffered a stab of searing panic, knowing she wasn't going to leave. She planned to make a stand beside him, whatever the risk or consequence.

She picked a damn fine time to declare her independence.

And suddenly he had a very personal interest in this confrontation.

He pointed to one of the front windows. "Crouch there and stay out of sight. Don't want to risk a bullet putting a hole in anything I'm fond of."

She smiled. "You do the same."

His mouth twitched. God, she was infuriating. And gorgeous. And too dang gutsy for her own good or his peace of mind. He gestured into the night. "They'll come head-on. When they see we're serious, they'll try to break off and flank us. Aim at the outside. Hem 'em in so they're grouped where we can see 'em. The two of us can't protect the whole house."

"Dodge is on his way."

He stared at her. "What?"

"I sent Jericho to get him."

Reeve bit out a low oath. The last thing he wanted was his friend caught up in a cross fire.

"He wanted to help," Patrice said, feeling the need to justify her decision. "He's scared for you— with good reason. We're not going to let you take on the world alone."

"I'm not worried about the world . . . jus' a couple of damned fools determined to get themselves shot for nothin'."

"Not for nothing, Reeve," she corrected quietly.

He thought for minute. Chances were, by the time Dodge reached the Glade, it would be over. Jericho wouldn't have time to race a fancy carriage to town to issue the call for assistance. Dodge would be safely out of it. And that left Patrice. The heavy press of fear settled back in his chest.

" 'Trice, if something happens to me—"

"Nothing will!"

"If something happens, and I can't protect you, you throw out your gun and yell for Tyler. He's a sonuvabitch, but I trust him not to let them hurt you."

Patrice gripped her jaw tight, not answering one way or another.

"Dammit, you do it! Promise me. Patrice, you promise me, or I'll truss you up like a Sunday turkey and leave you out in the drive for them to take care of."

Her lips pursed. Her eyes flashed. But she nodded. "All right." Her mood lifted. "Maybe Tyler won't let them shoot at all if he knows I'm in here."

This time, Reeve got mulish. "I won't hide behind your skirts."

Her grin dazzled. "But you don't mind getting under them so much, do you?"

He cursed, then his arms wrapped convulsively about her waist to yank her up to him. He kissed her hard, snapping her head back, bringing her hands up to clasp his head. Not to push him away, but to tangle in his hair, making fists at his temple. His mouth softened to a tender seeking, then he pulled back, to lean his forehead against hers. His eyes shut, his breathing labored. Turmoil ravaged his voice.

"I don't want you here, Patrice."

Her reply was strangely hushed.

"I don't think that choice is mine to make anymore."

He lifted up, following her somber gaze out into the night, where approaching torches bobbed like fireflies. He ducked back instinctively, though there was no backlighting inside the house to give him away. To Patrice, his order was crisp, meant to be followed without hesitation.

"Get over there and stay down."

Wordlessly, Patrice obeyed. She knelt by the open window, rifle ready, as she watched the night riders form a semicircle in the drive. Firelight cast an eerie illumination over the faceless men, making them shimmer like ghosts ... or demons. She wasn't able to identify any of them by their borrowed horses, but she was sure Tyler Fairfax was among them. Was Deacon? But neither of them called out. She recognized the booming voice as Ray Dermont's, Delyce's eldest brother.

"Reeve Garrett, show yerself!"

She caught movement from the corner of her eye and turned to see Reeve step out into the frame of the doorway.

"Reeve, no!" But he ignored her hissed warning.

" 'Evening, gentlemen." Even though he appeared unarmed, his bold stance set his visitors back in wary surprise. Being cowards themselves, they hadn't expected such a direct challenge. "If you all would care to leave your hoods at the door, I'd invite you in for some of Tyler's daddy's fine bourbon."

"This ain't no social call, Garrett," Dermont snarled.

"Too bad." Reeve brought his rifle up into plain view. "Then state your business and get off my property."

"Your property?" That was Poteet, the next eldest Dermont, as truculent as his older brother. "You stole this land by killing two good men. We got no tolerance for that sort of thing."

"If you believe that, go fetch the law."

"We're the law in Pride." Tyler's slurring drawl was unmistakable. He sat his horse, not out in front as leader, but on the periphery, behind the rest. "Put down your arms and we won't have to get ugly."

"Men like you all were born mean and ugly. I don't recognize the kind of law that sneaks out at night and hides under sheets. I know who each and every one of you is. You and your folks have been guests in this house and friends to my father and brother. You may not like that I'm living here now, and that don't much matter to me. But nobody's tellin' me I have to leave. Any of you think you're man enough, come up here and move me."

Horses milled about as the raiders murmured amongst themselves. Patrice prayed they would just ride out now that their identities were exposed and Reeve made it clear he meant to put up a fight. He wasn't some simple farmer who kept an old muzzle-loader for hunting squirrel. He was a military man, armed, dangerous, and trained in his own defense. She hoped the realization that not all of them were going to ride away alive would deter them from this madness. But stirred up by liquor and hate, they were single-minded in their purpose.

"You got to the count a five to get on outta there, Yank, before we light it up." Then Ray Dermont spilled his venomous character. "I hope you don't. I been wantin' to put a bullet in you for a long time, you arrogant bastard."

Reeve didn't acknowledge the slur. Instead, he directed his attention to one man. "Tyler, Patrice is in here with me."

One of the riders reined in abruptly, going still.

"I want your word that if she comes out, you'll see to her safety."

"No," Patrice cried out. He didn't look at her.

The riders circled, their rumbling growing louder.

"I say if the bitch is in there with the likes a him, let her roast," came one angry voice. Others took up the cry. A sudden upward blast from Tyler's rifle silenced them all.

"This ain't up to any a you." Tyler pulled off the feared mask of anonymity so he could face his friend, letting Reeve see his earnest. "I give you my oath, Reeve. Send her out now, and I promise I'll see she gets home."

Patrice saw Reeve's shoulders slump with relief, then he turned to her, his expression carefully veiled. "You've got to go, 'Trice. I'm carrying too many sacrificed souls already. I won't add yours."

Tears sprang bright and glittery into her angry eyes. She rose slowly, and she could tell he was hoping for a sign of her agreeability. He would be disappointed.

She whirled toward the open window and shouted, "I'm staying right here, Tyler Fairfax. You be sure and tell your sister that you helped burn a house down on top of her best friend. Then you and those yellow-cur, hood-wearing bullies can go straight to hell." She fired off a shot, placing it right between the forefeet of his mount. The animal reared back, nearly unseating its rider. She couldn't hear the oath he spoke but was fairly certain it was a close echo to the one Reeve spat out. She ducked back from sight and returned Reeve's fierce glare with her own. "I'm staying, I told you."

He didn't smile. "So you did."

She jerked her gun up. "They're coming!"

Reeve faded back into the shadows of the house just as one of the mob separated to charge up the front walk, his torch swinging in wild loops. Reeve took his time, sighting and squeezing off one round. It caught the rider high in the shoulder, sending him rolling off the back of his horse. The torch fell from his hand to spark harmlessly on the ground. The frightened animal clattered up onto the porch, bugling in panic as it circled and finally found its way back down to gallop, riderless, across the lawn. The distraction gave the other raiders time to fan out, some dismounting to take cover and aim, others still intent upon setting the house ablaze.

Tyler restored his hood, blending in with the others. As she crouched down, resting her barrel on the sill, Patrice searched the shadowed group anxiously. She didn't know which of the night riders was him. How could she shoot Starla's brother, who was so much a part of her happy memories? She remembered the green-eyed boy who'd taught her to swim by starlight while she wore only her combination drawers. The sly, smiling youngster who'd taken her deferentially into his arms to show her the steps of the scandalous waltz. Resting her brow against the cool wood-grain stock, she fought down a moment of shivery sickness. What if her own brother was out there? Reeve was right. It was no game. People she knew and loved might die in the next minutes.

She never stopped to consider her own danger.

" 'Trice, on your left!"

Reeve's sharp cry snapped her to attention. She swiveled automatically to track one of the masked men galloping out of Reeve's line of sight in an attempt to circle around back. She pulled the trigger, smacked breathless by the gun's recoil as wood splintered on the sill next to her. She didn't see the rider fall, but the horse cantered away with an empty saddle.

She'd shot someone.

She had no time for that numbing fact to settle. A barrage of bullets peppered the front of a house spared from the scarring of war. The assault felt as personal as the attack upon Sinclair Manor. Hundreds of Pride County's best had gone to fight a neighboring enemy over the same feelings starching up inside her. Pride and property. Enough to tear a country apart. Enough to prompt her well-timed shots at men she'd known all her life.

Ray Dermont had been with the infantry—at least until his rumored desertion. At his precise direction, the chaotic siege took on a military tone. While several of the men laid down a fierce covering fire, the rest began swift flanking maneuvers. In the confusion of darkness and the distorting glare of torchlight, there was no keeping track of all of them. Patrice did as Reeve told her, disregarding the shooters stationed in front to concentrate her shots on the shadows veering off to the sides. She closed her ears to the sound of a wailing shriek. While her mind hung on to a steely calm, her body reacted of its own accord, seized by a fitful trembling that wouldn't be stilled. Her breath came in hoarse sobs, tearing up from the fright and horror packed down in her soul. She risked a fleeting glance at Reeve, needing to see that he was all right.

He was positioned by the bullet-chewed door-frame, wielding his weapon with an emotionless efficiency. He might well have been picking off rats in a grain crib so little showed in his expression. He was a man possessed by the need to protect what was his; his home, his birthright, his woman. A dangerous, disciplined warrior born of bloodshed and sorrow. And for the first time, she truly understood the pain he'd carried for four years while forced to confront his own kind on the battlefield.

A flicker of movement by the inside stairs distracted her. Pressing her back to the wall, she jerked up her rifle, aiming it dead center on the figure rising up like a copperhead from the coil to launch a deadly strike at Reeve's unprotected back. She pulled the trigger. Nothing. Again. Only an impotent click as the chamber jammed. Paralyzed, knowing she couldn't stop the fatal round from firing, she screamed out Reeve's name. The sound was swallowed by the roar of gunfire.

And amazingly, the assailant fell back upon the stairs, his unused pistol bouncing down the steps.

Reeve whirled, ready to face this new danger when he caught of whiff of good cigar over the acrid bite of gunpowder.

"Starting the party without me?"

A glowing circle announced Hamilton Dodge as he stepped into the foyer.

"Dodge this isn't your fight."

The lieutenant-cum-banker stared at his friend in affront. "That's a hell of a thing to say to me." He bent to relieve the dead man of his sidearms, tucking them into his trouser band. "Followed this fellow in the back. Suppose you wanted me to just let him ventilate you. Excuse me all to hell for interfering."

"Dodge."

"What?"

"Thanks."

Dodge's grin broke wide. "Seem to recall you stopping a similar bullet for me. Just glad not to have to step in front of it. 'Evening, ma'am."

While Reeve sent several shots whining toward shadowy targets, Dodge knelt beside Patrice and took the rifle from her. After a little tinkering, he ejected the fouled casing to clear the chamber. "There you go, pretty girl. Always have a backup piece, just in case. These things are about as dependable as Confederate currency." Then he looked surprised to be on the receiving end of her quick hug and her whisper of, "Not as dependable as you are, Mr. Dodge."

"How'd you get here so fast? Jericho fly to town in that buggy?" Reeve scanned the darkness for sign of movement.

"Met him on the way here and sent him packing for the Sinclairs. He doesn't need this kind of trouble."

Patrice leaned back, perplexed. "So who—?"

"That little gal from Sadie's. Guess she heard her brothers talking and didn't like what she heard."

Amazed and grateful for meek Delyce Dermont's sudden flash of courage, Patrice scooted over, letting Dodge share her window.

An ominous quiet had the defenders of the house growing restless. Patrice gave up hope that the sheeted vigilantes would give up and slink home. Their names were known. Several were wounded or dead. The time to back down was past. They were up to something else, something new and potentially deadly.

Patrice cried out, seeing the first bright tongues of fire. "They've set fire to the stables! Reeve, the horses!"

The raw fury in his face told he knew the consequences of prize breeding mares bolted into box stalls with combustible feed and straw and the suffocating roil of smoke. Then came the sounds, the awful animal squeals of terror and pain.

Through the daze of her fear, Patrice had a moment of clear insight. Reeve meant to rush out, risking his life for the salvation of the Glade. She couldn't let him do it.

Dropping her rifle, she surged up from the floor, tearing out the door before either man thought to stop her. The glare of torchlight illuminated the loose whip of her bright hair and flutter of her gown. They couldn't mistake her for Reeve or Dodge or perceive her empty hands as a threat. Counting on that, knowing Tyler would never allow any harm to come to her, Patrice gambled all in a frantic race toward the flaming barn. She heard Reeve shouting after her but trained all her energy on the open stable door. A horrible red flare shone from inside. Stumbling in the twist of her heavy unhooped skirts, she almost fell. That's when she felt a stinging slap to the side of her face, the shock of it making her stagger. Hearing Zeus's maddened whinnies, she struggled onward, dragging her hem and petticoat up off the ground so they wouldn't slow her.

"The sons of bitches are shooting at her," Reeve cried out in dismay. The picture of his own mother's death defending those stables shot through his mind. He stuffed rounds into his rifle's hot chamber, readying to go to her aid, bringing hellfire with him. Dodge pushed by him, shouting, "I'll get her. Cover me."

"Dodge, wait!" Frantically, he crammed in the shells as he watched his friend duck and weave through what was left of the ornamental shrubbery, knowing the bastards would be waiting, watching for such a brazen move.

Patrice reached the stables, disappearing inside the blaze, out of the line of fire but darting headlong into a new danger.

Dodge was almost there, running hard, sending off a scattering of shots from pistols in both hands.

Reeve never knew who was responsible for the single bullet that plowed into Hamilton Dodge's back, knocking him forward and off his feet. The guns went flying from his hands as he fell unchecked, skidding face first in the dirt to a motionless stop.

The sight took Reeve square in the chest with the force of a DuPont load. He stumbled back, wobbling on boneless legs until the solid support of the wall braced behind him. He leaned into the heated barrel of his Spencer, eyes squeezing out the horror as a name formed soundlessly on his lips. *Dodge . . . No!*

Crouching low, Ray Dermont ran to where the fallen man lay, ruthlessly kicking him over onto his back. Dodge's head lolled loosely as Dermont's shotgun barrel pressed against his throat.

"He's still breathin', Garrett! Step out or he's finished!"

Reeve hesitated. He'd seen the bullet rip into Dodge's lower back. But if there was a chance, even a thread of one . . .

He threw his rifle out the open door and strode onto the porch, hands lifted, as the hooded devils swarmed him.

Patrice heard nothing but the roar of flames consuming roof timbers and the agonizing scream of the horses. Her eyes teared into an immediate blur and breath clogged up in her lungs from searing smoke. She plunged ahead, feeling for the first in a row of stalls. Shoving open the panel, she charged on, coughing, gasping, throwing open the bolts and swinging the gates wide. Many of the animals were too terrified to flee, forcing her into the stall with the mass of churning muscle and hooves to wave and slap the mares in the right direction. One of the crazed beasts swung about in the small space, catching her a glancing blow to the chest with its powerful hindquarters. Winded, she felt herself going down in a swoon, sure she would be pulped beneath the stomping feet. Then, miraculously, the mare bolted out of the stall, galloping after the others to freedom. She found her balance clinging to a rail as hot ash filtered down on her face and scorched through her lungs. That left only Zeus.

A tremendous rush of sound exploded from the rear of the flaming building as the hay went up with the velocity of a steam train. Patrice fell to her knees, blackness swirling over her senses. From some distant spot in the roar of confusion, she heard Zeus's trumpeting call. Reeve's pride and joy.

Trapped in its stall while the fires of hell caved in all around.

Crawling, scrambling, she managed to find the main aisleway. She heard wood splintering, not from above but from straight ahead, as the stallion's hooves shattered through the slats of its stall door. She felt the huge animal bump past her and flailed out with her hands, grasping, twisting them in a hank of mane. One of the red-hot ceiling joists came crashing down, landing on the hem of her dress, threatening her precarious hold.

"Zeus, go!" The words croaked up through her charred throat, enough to send the big horse surging forward, dragging her, her skirt in flames, out into the cool evening. The last thing she remembered was a streak of heat boiling up the back of her calves before darkness swallowed her.

Chapter 26

❧ ⟨◦⟩ ⟨◦⟩ ❧

The chill of water sluicing over her face and trickling into her mouth, brought Patrice up with a sputtering cough.

"Easy, darlin'. Jus' lie back now. You'll be all right."

Recognizing the thick drawl, she tried to drag her eyelids open, but they were too burned by smoke to focus. The dredging of a wet cloth across them granted some relief. She could make out Tyler's smiling face, but the concern in his dark jade gaze confused her. So did the fact that it was evening and she was on the ground, propped up against his knees. He continued to bathe her face and neck with gentle strokes, never looking away from her even as some commotion played out behind them.

"Ty-ler?" His name clawed up through the pain in her throat, wrenching out another spasm of coughing. He caught her uplifted hand in his to press a firm kiss upon it.

"It's all right, darlin'. Don't fret. I'm here."

Patrice looked at his hand, puzzled by the blistering redness of his palm and forearm. Burns? "What—?"

"Your dress was on fire, darlin'."

And he'd smothered the flames with his hands.

Awareness sucked the fragile breath from her. She struggled to sit up within the protective curl of Tyler's arms, panic stealing her air and almost her consciousness.

"Reeve—"

She fought, climbed, scratched her way practically over the top of Tyler to gain her feet then, was dependent upon him to keep her there as her system suffered another jolting shock.

Reeve on his knees, face in the dirt, as his wrists were lashed behind him. Dodge sprawled a short distance away, his head averted, a pool of crimson seeping out from under him.

"Oh, Dodge." She tried to gulp back a knot of emotion too big to force down. Faintness lapped up over her senses in soothing waves, as welcome as Tyler's unwavering support. The desire to succumb to both engulfed her she buried her face in handfuls of Tyler's shirt. His hand covered her hair, holding her fast against him.

Reeve grunted as his arms were jerked up high behind his back. He let himself be manhandled, not resisting the burn of the ropes, the thud of boots against his ribs. Nothing could have beaten him down more than the thought of Dodge dying for him, except the sight of Patrice clinging to Tyler in tears.

When he'd seen Zeus drag her out of the blazing
stables just seconds before its collapse, it was reward enough for any sacrifice to come. A large section of her skirt had been consumed by fire. The
stench of fabric, hers and flesh, Tyler's, hung sickly
sweet in the air upon choking threads of smoke and
charred wood. A gash along her cheekbone oozed
only slightly now. She was grimy and weary but
alive. Thanks to Tyler, his friend and foe. She would
be safe. Nothing else mattered. He had no curiosity
over his own fate.

"String him up."

Ray Dermont's vicious growl woke Patrice from
her misery. She pushed against the pressure of Tyler's hand to see what was happening. They were
going to hang Reeve from the proud entrance to
Glendower Glade.

Seeing the glaze of understanding on her face,
Reeve looked to Tyler. "Get her out of here." His
harsh demand won a small nod as Reeve was
hauled up to his feet and shoved toward the porch,
where the youngest Dermont tested the noose to
make sure it would hold his weight. It wasn't a long
drop off the cement edge, not enough to ensure a
clean snap instead of a slow strangle. Reeve walked,
clinging to the memory of Jonah's courage.

"Reeve!"

He winced at her raspy cry. Why didn't Tyler get
her away?

Tyler tried, but her fright was quickly replaced
by fury.

"Let me go!" She struck at him, slapping his face,
pounding on his chest, battering him with her
curses and desperate tears. He wouldn't relent.

"Don't, darlin'. You can't stop it now. Neither can I."

"Liar! Coward! Let go! I'll hate you forever for this!"

He believed her. She could see the pain of it in his eyes. But it was nothing compared to the agony in her heart.

On the ground, away from the wash of torchlight, fingers twitched in the dirt, hand rolling, pushing toward a discarded revolver. Brushing the smooth grip. Stretching with every last bit of energy.

"Forget it, Yank."

A heavy boot trod down on Dodge's palm, ending his effort.

Watching them angle Reeve under the swaying rope, Patrice clutched at the arm Tyler braced across her chest, her fingers biting deep, her body trembling. Hysteria threatened. Desperate, wailing pleas for mercy clamped behind her quivering jaw. She sought Reeve's gaze, locking on to it for strength, for the will to survive even if he wouldn't.

The panic fell away. The need for sobs and begging faded. How Reeve would hate that for a last tribute. What could she give him to carry to eternity?

Her voice rang out strong and clear and unashamed.

"I love you, Reeve Garrett. I would have been proud to be your wife."

Just before Ray Dermont pulled his hood down over Reeve's head, Patrice caught a glimpse of his small smile. Then he was masked to shield the murderers from his condemning glare. The rope dropped into place and was fitted tight about his neck.

"Don't look," Tyler mumbled, trying to force her gaze away.

She glared at him. "You look. You take a good look at what you've done."

She let him press her face into his shoulder as she tensed, listening for the snap of the rope going taut. Tyler ducked his head next to hers, soft words whispering under his breath.

"I'm sorry, Reeve. Forgive me."

Never! Never, she promised, clinging to him with eyes tightly closed to all but the image of Reeve's brief smile.

"Cut him loose," came a cold command, "or you'll be dead before he is."

Patrice's head flew up. Her cry quavered with weak relief.

"Deacon!"

Her brother sat his horse with the deadly end of his rifle fixed on Ray Dermont. Next to him was Jericho Smith, mounted on the wheezing pony, just as well armed and dangerous. Not overwhelming odds, but enough to take cowards aback. Killing Reeve Garrett and his Yankee friend was one matter. Taking shots at Deacon Sinclair was another. And none of them doubted his willingness to shoot them dead with the slightest provocation.

Seeing everything going to hell, Tyler stepped back from Patrice, keeping his crisped hands empty. Instead of going to Deacon, Patrice ran toward the porch.

"What the hell do you think you're doing, Sinclair?" Dermont growled as Patrice shoved by him to reach Reeve.

"Putting an end to this insanity. The blood on my

hands will never come clean. No more. Do you understand? No more."

Patrice slipped the knot loose and tossed the noose away. She yanked off the hood and had her mouth fixed upon Reeve's for a long fierce second before turning her attention to the binding on his wrists. The instant he was free, he was off the porch, racing toward Dodge.

"But you're letting a murderer go loose," Dermont railed, gesturing at Reeve. "He killed Jonah Glendower, his own brother! And he murdered his father! We jus' gonna let him get away with those things?" He reached for his pistol, but Deacon's icy stare froze him in place.

"Byron Glendower told my mother that he had a bad heart. The doctor had been treating him for it since before the war. And as for Jonah—" Deacon broke off, his gaze flickering to Patrice, then back. "Garrett didn't kill him. I'm responsible."

Patrice drew up, posture rigid, grimy features pale as she stared at her brother in tragic disbelief. Deacon didn't pause.

"Jonah was shot by firing squad because he wouldn't give me up to them. He knew I was the one spying on Federal troops. When they got too close to finding out, he confessed to it so I wouldn't be arrested. I let him die for me because the information I was carrying had to get through to Richmond. His blood is on my hands, not Reeve's. Mine."

Stock-still, Patrice met his gaze for a moment longer, then she turned away to follow Reeve.

Deacon gestured to the vigilantes with his rifle barrel. "Now get the hell out of here. Go haunt some other house."

"You're gonna regret this, Sinclair," Dermont promised as he bent to snatch up his mask and retrieve the rope that had failed to accomplish its purpose.

"I already do."

While the night riders gathered their wounded and dead, making fierce promises of retribution toward both men on horseback, Reeve knelt beside his fallen friend. He took up the hand marked with a dirty bootprint, curling it in his own.

"Dammit, Dodge, you said you wouldn't take a bullet for me."

"Not for you."

The faint whisper surprised both him and Patrice as she knelt behind him. Dodge's eyes fluttered open, touching vaguely on Reeve then holding on Patrice.

"For her," he murmured, following the claim with a wink. A sob caught in Patrice's throat. His breathing suddenly quickened into shallow gasps. Fingers clenched about Reeve's as his head tossed side to side restlessly until Reeve placed his other hand on Dodge's sweat-dappled brow to still the movement.

"Dodge? Dodge! Don't you dare die on me. Don't you dare. Get a doctor!" Reeve looked up, expression stark, desperate.

"I heard tell that Doc Anderson was up and around again," Jericho offered. "I'll go fetch him, Mista Reeve."

Reeve nodded. "Take Zeus."

Jericho blinked, startled by the command, by the degree of trust. "Yessir."

Dodge crushed Reeve's hand, drawing him down closer. "No. No doctor."

"You're going to make it, Dodge. I swear to God."

"No." His gaze held his friend's in a moment of intense lucidity. "Reeve, I can't feel my legs."

Reeve took in his meaning on a sharp inhalation, then after a slight pause, yelled up at Jericho, "Go on!"

While his attention was diverted, Dodge slipped his hand free and came up on one shoulder, lunging for the pistol he'd dropped earlier. He had it halfway to his head before Patrice's cry alerted Reeve. He snatched the piece away. Dodge fell back with an anguished moan, his forearm braced over his eyes.

"Don't do this, Reeve. You owe me a life. Mine's not worth living. Not like this."

Reeve was too stricken to respond, so Patrice bent down to take the lieutenant's damp face between her palms. She spoke gently, firmly, allowing none of her own fear to escape.

"Dodge, listen to me. You listen to me. We're going to need you to stay with us. Pride needs you. Reeve's going to need you at our wedding. My friend Starla will be there. You'll want to meet her, Dodge. She's gorgeous and single and always on the look out for a handsome fellow like yourself."

He edged his arm up so he could see her. His face was taut, fever-flushed with pain. "She mind the smell of a good cigar?"

"Knowing Starla, she'll probably smoke one with you."

He swallowed hard then muttered, "You gonna leave me out here lying on the ground all night?" He blinked, the movement slowing, growing more and more gradual until his eyes finally stayed shut.

Reeve rocked back on his heels, staring at the men who'd tried to kill his friend and the woman he loved as well as hang him. Two of the group draped facedown over their saddles. He knew them, though not well. Others nursed wounds and animosity barely restrained by Deacon's gun. Finally, he looked at Tyler. The other man didn't evade his stare but met it with an emotionless blank. No apology, no trace of what went on inside his head or heart. Reeve's gaze lowered to the injured hands, studying them for a long moment before saying, "When the doctor's finished here, I'll send him to check on those burns." His stare was steady, unblinking.

Tyler understood. What once existed between them was no more. His gaze flickered to Patrice, who had her arms about Reeve's broad shoulders in a fiercely protective circle. He gingerly caught up the reins to his rented horse, swinging up to follow the rest of the sullen riders back into the night.

When they were gone, Deacon sheathed his rifle.

"Help me carry him inside, Deke."

Deacon eyed Reeve for a long second, then dismounted. Between the two men, they managed to move Dodge to the unyielding sofa in Byron Glendower's study. There, Deacon touched his sister's shoulder, not missing the way she flinched from him.

"Patrice, let me take you home. You need to let Mama put something on those burns."

She didn't acknowledge him but instead spoke quietly to Reeve. "Will you be all right here?"

He nodded, busy making Dodge comfortable.

"I'll be back . . . soon."

Reeve made no sign of having heard her.

* * *

Patrice underestimated the extent of her own injuries. Once the shock wore off, her body surrendered to its weaknesses. Her head pounded from the bullet crease on her cheek and temple. She'd have a scar. The knock to her ribs left them bruised but not broken. The backs of her legs were painfully scorched by the flames. Under the numbing balm of laudanum, she drifted.

Her ragged thoughts were consumed by Reeve, by Dodge, by fleeting images of Tyler Fairfax as the charming young man he'd once been waltzing her about the blue grass. By her brother. *I'm responsible.* Her mind ached. Her heart felt both full and painfully empty.

Deacon hovered close by. She didn't see him but heard his low tones in the hall outside her door. Her feelings for him fluctuated, sometimes fierce with outrage that he'd let her believe the worst of Reeve when his own actions held the blame, sometimes softening with sentiment when she considered his confession which must, even now, be circulating through the gossips of Pride. He'd tarnished her view with his own candid words, knowing he might well lose her love. He was a despicable deceiver, a selfless hero to the Southern Cause. Too many things for her weary spirit to sort through as her body healed.

The doctor returned the third day to redress her burns, check her lungs, and pronounce her progress satisfactory. She half listened. What about Dodge? The doctor grew grim.

"He has a bullet lodged next to the spine. Because of its position, an operation to remove it would have a 99 percent chance of killing him. I don't have

the facilities or the knowledge to guess the extent
of damage. If he recovers, he'll probably have no
feeling from the waist down.''

The news buffeted her, leaving a bereft heaviness
in its wake. ''You're just going to leave the bullet?''

''Shouldn't hurt, 'less infection sets in. Or it
shifts.''

''Then?''

His failure to answer told the worst. Dodge
would die. As the doctor packed up his bags, his
observation was as cruel as it was compassionate.
''Maybe that would be best.''

But Patrice was appalled.

Deacon lingered in the doorway as the doctor exited. His hands stuffed deep into his pockets as he
levered his weight from one foot to the other as if
unable to strike a comfortable balance within himself. He glanced at Patrice, his gaze flickering
quickly away.

''You look better.'' A flat summation that didn't
request her reply. She didn't give one. He fidgeted
a bit longer, his awkwardness touching upon tender
sympathies and, at the same time, wringing a savage sense that it was well deserved. Humility didn't
look good on him. Finally, Deacon straightened,
freeing his hands so they hung fisted at his sides as
his features gelled into familiar impassivity.

''It was my duty, Patrice.'' No apology.

''You don't need to explain war to me, Deacon.''

''The things I did were dangerous. My life was
always right there on the edge. I couldn't afford to
let sentiment get in the way of judgment and still
do the job.''

''That's not war, Deacon. That's you.''

If her observation struck a nerve, he didn't show

it. "I don't expect you to understand, Patrice."

"I may not like it, but I've always understood you."

His eyes closing briefly, he drew a deep inhalation and let it out slowly. "I don't. I don't understand. I liked it, Patrice. I liked what I was doing, and that scares the hell out of me." Then he looked at her, the mask back in place. "I thought I'd drive you over to the Glade if you're up to it."

A peace offering. A way to make amends. By accepting it, she'd absolve him. She let the invitation dangle, letting him squirm a moment longer in his own guilt. In the end, she wasn't feeling particularly charitable, and that surprised her.

"I'm capable of driving myself."

Her cool response hurt him. Pain winced through his eyes along with the dread that nothing would ever be the same between them again. It wouldn't. She would never again be so naively trusting or look to him and expect perfection. She would see her brother, with all his faults, fears, and hidden feelings.

"But I would like the company," she concluded quietly.

Reeve shifted in the leather wing chair he'd been living out of for the past few days. He uncrossed his long legs so he could bend to press the back of his hand to Dodge's brow. Still no trace of the feared fever. That was good, he told himself. The contact woke Dodge to a now-familiar listlessness.

" 'Morning."

No response. Reeve suppressed his frustration to continue the conversation. It was important that his

friend feel among the living even though he wasn't
interested in participating.

"Got a wire from your folks. They want to come
see you."

That sparked a reaction. His gaze flashed to
Reeve's. "No! I don't want them to come." He
blinked several times, then went on staring at the
ceiling, his voice going flat again. "They can't afford
the ticket or the time. I don't want to burden them."
His eyes closed after saying that last but not before
Reeve saw the awful crowding of fear and anger.

"Doc said you could start sitting up, a little at a
time."

"That's something to look forward to."

If there'd been bitterness, sarcasm, or even a hint
of hope in that statement, Reeve wouldn't have
been so alarmed. The toneless disinterest made him
wonder if Dodge still considered suicide. And if he
had the right to stop him a second time. He'd came
to Pride because Reeve asked him—for no other
reason than that. He'd ridden out to the Glade to
take up a fight not his own, forfeiting his future.
That was the kind of friend he was. What kind of
friend allowed another to make those sacrifices? Agitated, anguished, Reeve pushed out of his chair
and paced to the window, aware that Dodge followed the movement.

"I've been thinking, Reeve," he began quietly.
"I'm thinking I want to go home."

Reeve pinched his eyes shut against the sting of
helplessness. "All right. If that's what you want."

Silence fell, growing more awkward and uncomfortable by the minute. Until a breezy voice intruded.

"I declare it smells of musty men and old liquor

in here. Reeve, throw open the window so I can breathe."

Patrice swept in, a breath of fresh air, herself. Dodge smiled. He couldn't help it. She looked great, she smelled delicious when nudging in to perch on the edge of the cushions. She smiled at him, her expression warm with fondness. No pity. No guilt. No sorrow. He soaked it up thirstily.

"I'd kiss you, but you're a regular porcupine." Her knuckles buffed the stubble on his chin.

"Hold that thought. You can shave me."

Reeve snorted. "I offered, and you wouldn't let me."

"Well, she's a helluva lot better-looking than you are."

She kissed him anyway, her lips touching softly to his temple, her scent swirling his senses, purposefully making him acutely aware of how much of him was still very much alive. She sat back, her smile teasing and tender, coaxing him back to his old brash self as her fingers rumpled through his hair.

"We'll get you one of those chairs with wheels on it, and you'll be chasing skirts in no time."

His vision wobbled for a moment, then cleared. "You're a helluva woman, Patrice Sinclair. If that damned fool Kentuckian isn't man enough to hang on to you, just you let me know."

"It would serve you right if I did, Mr. Dodge. I'd enjoy clipping your wings."

He chuckled. "Then I'd be totally at your mercy." He canted a look at a glowering Reeve and winked at her. "Somehow, I don't think we have to worry about that happening."

Patrice glanced at Reeve, the cadence of her

pulsebeats suddenly accelerating. His return gaze told her next to nothing, reminding her of all that had yet to be said between them. Soon.

Dodge tipped his head back, noticing for the first time that Patrice wasn't alone. "Mr. Sinclair. Come to say I told you so?"

Deacon ignored him. "When are you going to be back to work?"

"Are customers lining up outside the bank to help me pack?"

"I'll be waiting so you can help save my ass." Direct and to the point.

Patrice's stare shot up to her brother, amazed. Admiring.

Interest quickened in Hamilton Dodge. He levered himself up, pushing with his arms, gritting into the pain. Instead of helping, Patrice propped a pillow behind him. "What kind of help were you looking for?" Wheels turned behind intelligent eyes.

Noting that Reeve had stepped out onto the front porch, Patrice stood and let her brother command Pride's banker's attention. Hers was elsewhere.

On securing her own future.

Chapter 27

~~~~~

Reeve stood at the edge of the porch, toes off the edge, gaze fixed on the still-smoldering ruins of the stables. The mares had long since been corralled in one of the remaining paddocks with a strutting Zeus prowling the other side of the rail, tail arched, nostrils flared, anxious to get to the business of rebuilding the Glade's stock. Reeve watched the animal's restless movements, his gaze distant, unreadable. Patrice was hesitant to approach him.

She'd told him more than once that she loved him. She'd proved it in his bed and at his side. She had spoken of marriage, twice. He had yet to comment on any of those things. She wanted to push him for his feelings, but didn't dare, not completely sure what she'd hear. So she stuck to safer topics.

"Will he be all right?"

Reeve turned slightly. "Who? Dodge?" He nodded. "He's tough. He can do anything he puts his mind to." His gaze darkened. "Thank you."

"For what?"

"For what you did inside. For bringing him back."

"Oh, that wasn't me. That was Deacon talking business. Mention dollars and cents and the man lights up like a Roman candle. He'll be good for Pride. I know it."

"And you're good for me."

Patrice didn't move. Slowly, he extended his hand. Only then did she go closer, folding her fingers through his. He lifted her hand, pressing it over his heart, expression mysterious, aloof. She wasn't sure how to break through.

"You knew about Deacon, didn't you?"

He nodded slightly. "Jonah never said right out, but I guessed it."

"Why didn't you tell me? Why did you let me blame you?"

"I know how much your brother means to you."

"But do you have any idea what *you* mean to me?"

His mouth lifted slightly. "I'm beginning to."

She let it go for the moment, choosing instead to look out over the lush, rolling acres of the Glade. "It's all yours now. Everything you've ever wanted." She slid a look up at him. "All without strings?"

"You know the squire. He had to tie a few."

She stiffened in spite of herself. "Such as?"

"He wanted my children to take on the name Glendower."

"Children?"

"That was one of the conditions."

"And what about a wife?"

"Usually helps in having children." He grew guarded. "How much did he tell you?"

Patrice's past bravery failed her. She couldn't meet his eyes. "He said I was a condition of your inheritance. That to get the rest, you had to take me."

Reeve mumbled a soft oath. He released her hand and left the porch, striding purposefully across the lawn, away from her and the grand house. Anxiously, Patrice hurried after him, matching his pace. Neither said anything until they'd reached the far stargazing field. He slowed, finally coming to a solitary oak that stood like an old, grizzled caretaker proudly surveying his surroundings. Reeve sank down, back against the tree, and began plucking at the grasses. Patrice remained standing, uncertain, uneasy, almost feeling unwelcomed. Until he looked up at her.

"The Glendower name, the heirs to carry it, those were what the squire insisted upon. *You* were my condition, Patrice. I told him I wouldn't settle for anyone else."

Her heart leapt. But still, she was cautious. "Why?" She needed to hear him say it, just once.

"Because I have loved you all my life, and I've never wanted anyone else to share my future with me."

She closed her eyes, overcome by the words, by the wonder of hearing them spoken at last. Her legs weakened, refusing to support her. She sank down in the grass beside him, trembling inside and out. "Why—why didn't you ever say so?"

It was his turn to evade her questioning stare. "Thought you'd think it was because I wanted the name Sinclair and all that went with it."

Her sudden chuckle startled him. He shot her an aggrieved look, only to be taken by the relief in her lovely features.

"The name Sinclair?" She laughed again, then sighed, opening the bag she'd carried with her since coming to the Glade. "Here's all that comes with me, Reeve."

As he watched bemused, she drew out two exquisite glasses, a pair of candlesticks, and a length of embroidered cloth. She spread them out carefully for his appraisal.

"This is all there is, all I have left of who I am. It's not much to settle for."

The intensity of his gaze engulfed her. "Looks like an awful lot to me. More than I can offer."

"I don't want the Glade, Reeve. I don't want the name Glendower or the properties or the gold. I want you, just you, for the man you are, the man I love. That's worth more to me than everything in Dodge's bank vault, than the opinions of anyone in Pride."

His arm went about her shoulders, drawing her to him so that she leaned upon his chest, her head resting back against his shoulder. His mouth moved in a light sweep across her hair.

"So there's no reason I shouldn't ask you to marry me?"

She closed her eyes again, willing time to stop so she could savor this moment forever. "None at all."

"Deacon? Your mother?"

"Deacon will be agreeable to anything I want. Mother picked you long ago. I fear she's been dreadfully disappointed in me for taking so long to grow up."

"Jonah?"

She refused to let the name separate them any longer. "Jonah is dead, and I shall always miss him. But Reeve, you and I are alive and in love, and no ghost or ghosts are going to stand between us." She rolled to look him in the eye. "There's something more I need to tell you. About your father's last words." She touched her love's face, soothing away the creases furrowing his brow. "He asked that you forgive him. And he wanted you to know that he had asked your mother, and she was the one who refused him. Probably for the same silly reason that you refused to tell me how you felt before you rode off to enlist. Pride. I know enough about pride to know it's no substitute for love. I love you, Reeve. Ask me now."

His hand fanned wide across her damp cheek. "Marry me, Patrice."

"I will."

He hugged her in tight. A tremendous weight let go within him, a tether to the past. "Thank you, Jonah."

Patrice lifted up slightly. "What did you say?"

Reeve smiled. "I said I love you, Patrice."

And she was happy to believe him at last.

Dear Reader,

Here at Avon Books, we're thrilled over Stephanie Laurens, author of this month's Treasure, DEVIL'S BRIDE. Stephanie, a bright new voice in historical romance, has written a sensuous, witty love story with an unforgettable hero. When an intrepid governess is caught in a compromising position with a dashing duke he proposes marriage. But is this a match made in heaven?

The MacKenzies are back! Fans of Ana Leigh's MacKenzies series, will be happy to know this unforgettable Colorado family is back. And if you haven't yet discovered the MacKenzies, what are you waiting for? This month, don't miss THE MACKENZIES: DAVID . . . and get to know the rollicking MacKenzie cousins.

Fans of dark and dangerous heroes won't be able to resist Cassian Carysfort, Lord Bevington, hero of Margaret Evans Porter's THE PROPOSAL. Cassian has decided that Sophie Pinnock will become his mistress, but she is not easily persuaded in this sensuous love story set in 18th-century England.

For lovers of contemporary romance we present Curtiss Ann Matlock's IF WISHES WERE HORSES. Curtiss Ann's special ability to create emotional, heartwarming love stories between strong, steadfast heroes and down-home, delightful heroines is unsurpassed. Discover why best-selling author Susan Elizabeth Phillips has said, "Her books are wise and wonderful."

Happy reading!

Lucia Macro

Lucia Macro
Senior Editor

Avon Romances—
the best in exceptional authors and unforgettable novels!

Avon Romantic Treasures

Unforgettable, enthralling love stories,
sparkling with passion and adventure
from Romance's bestselling authors

EVERYTHING AND THE MOON *by Julia Quinn*
78933-7/$5.99 US/$7.99 Can

BEAST *by Judith Ivory*
78644-3/$5.99 US/$7.99 Can

HIS FORBIDDEN TOUCH *by Shelley Thacker*
78120-4/$5.99 US/$7.99 Can

LYON'S GIFT *by Tanya Anne Crosby*
78571-4/$5.99 US/$7.99 Can

FLY WITH THE EAGLE *by Kathleen Harrington*
77836-X/$5.99 US/$7.99 Can

FALLING IN LOVE AGAIN *by Cathy Maxwell*
78718-0/$5.99 US/$7.99 Can

THE COURTSHIP OF
CADE KOLBY *by Lori Copeland*
79156-0/$5.99 US/$7.99 Can

TO LOVE A STRANGER *by Connie Mason*
79340-7/$5.99 US/$7.99 Can

Discover Contemporary Romances
at Their Sizzling Hot Best
from Avon Books

TILL THE END OF TIME *by Patti Berg*
78339-8/$5.99 US/$7.99 Can

FLY WITH THE EAGLE *by Kathleen Harrington*
77836-X/$5.99 US/$7.99 Can

WHEN NICK RETURNS *by Dee Holmes*
79161-7/$5.99 US/$7.99 Can

HEAVEN LOVES A HERO *by Nikki Holiday*
78798-9/$5.99 US/$7.99 Can

ANNIE'S HERO *by Maggie Shayne*
78747-4/$5.99 US/$7.99 Can

TWICE UPON A TIME *by Emilie Richards*
78364-9/$5.99 US/$7.99 Can

WHEN LIGHTNING STRIKES TWICE *by Barbara Boswell*
72744-7/$5.99 US/$7.99 Can